The Taste of Veronica

Veronica's Life, Volume 2

Stephanie Bull

Published by Tau Press Ltd, 2019.

The Taste of Veronica by Stephanie Bull.

Copyright © 2019 Tau Press Ltd. All rights reserved.

ISBN e-book: 978-1-913199-09-8

ISBN paperback: 978-1-913199-10-4

ISBN hardback: 978-1-913199-11-1

Published by Tau Press Ltd.

Edited by Zoë Markham (markhamcorrect.com).

Cover by Jane Dixon-Smith (jdsmith-design.com).

For the White Rabbit

i

"How often do Mr Laughton and Mrs Jenkins—" Veronica searched for the right word "—meet?" She and Polly were idling along a path in the main gardens. There was no one within earshot and she enjoyed talking about sex in the open air. It felt both daring and safe.

Polly was less confident of their privacy and replied in a quieter voice. "At least once a week."

"Always in his office?"

"Always. He can lock the door and no one disturbs their private meetings."

"And everybody knows?"

"Everybody."

"Doesn't that make it difficult for Mrs Jenkins with the other staff?"

"Everyone's scared of her anyway; nobody is going to make any trouble."

Veronica looked down at the gravel of the path, all neatly raked, cleared of any encroaching weeds and edged in tiles. She paused to admire a particularly bright display of blooms in the flower beds. She could hear the birds above and feel the brightness of the sun warming her clothes, but looking up was such a strain on her back she seldom bothered even trying.

She was glad to get out of the house though because it still swarmed with workmen. The initial violence of destruction—taking down walls and making holes—had given way to building work. New walls, new doors, even a new stairwell, as well as the laying of lines to carry the electricity, and the new plumbing. The list went on and on. A fellow by the name of McCloud was the project manager, in charge of ensuring all the changes were in place before her wedding in three weeks.

Veronica did not see how the work could possibly be achieved in that time, but it was not her problem: her husband-to-be, the Honourable Edwin Jameson, had ordered it, and his family was footing the bill.

Since her eighteenth birthday in June, everything about her life had been disrupted, though not all of it was bad. She smiled at the pleasant memories of her nights with Polly, the unusual lessons with Mr Plumley, and her little adventures with Seth the under-gardener.

The only fly in the ointment had been the unexpected announcement of her forthcoming nuptials—which had come as a shock to everyone in the household, not least Veronica. However, there had been some positive consequences.

Veronica pursed her lips. "No one's scared of me though, are they?"

Polly said nothing.

"And when I'm the lady of the house, and we're doing the same thing, what will they think?"

"I don't know."

Veronica reached out and took Polly's hand. Her maid did not resist.

Polly was now officially appointed as lady's maid to the future Mrs Edwin Jameson. Sadly, there was no title to go along with the marriage. Edwin was the sixth son of Lord Jameson, the Viscount Launceston, but there were limits to how far aristocratic titles could stretch. He might be an *honourable* but he wasn't a lord. But even without a title she would still be the wife of an aristocrat, however minor. And that was more than she had ever imagined she would be—a hunchback, hidden from the world for her entire life up to that point, with no prospect of it ever being different.

Yet her stars had changed after all.

They reached an arbour set back from the path, pleasantly shaded from direct sunlight, and completely hidden from the house. Veronica drew her maid within its sheltered bosom. They sat, legs touching, hands still entwined.

Gently, Veronica cupped Polly's cheek and drew their lips together. The kiss began chaste, a simple touch of the lips, but Veronica breathed in her maid's scent, closed her eyes, and pressed harder. Their lips parted and the mistress's tongue darted into her lover's mouth. Her passion was returned in full measure. It was Polly who had taught Veronica how to kiss, the pair hiding in a cupboard, Veronica's teacher, Mr Plumley, just the other side of the door.

Veronica sucked on Polly's tongue as it penetrated her, then pushed back to receive the same treatment in return. Polly's hand disengaged from Veronica's, but, moments later, landed on her breast and pressed it. Veronica moaned into her lover's mouth. Her breasts were so sensitive she could reach paroxysm simply from having them manipulated.

"All a robber would have to do, Nika," Polly had commented without a scrap of jealously, "is mistreat your bosom and you would fall over before him and hand over all your gifts."

Veronica could not deny it, but those sensitive breasts had started her on the journey to carnal pleasure and, for that, she would forever be grateful. Before her awakening, she had considered herself nothing more than a monster, happy to live as a spinster for the rest of her life in this house.

"I love your taste," said Veronica, pulling away slightly, but clamping Polly's hand in place with her own.

Polly shrugged and squeezed hard. "You always say that, Nika."

"Harder, my love."

"I can't, you're wearing too many clothes."

"I'll take them off."

Polly laughed. "You won't."

Veronica put her hand to the ties at the front of her bodice. "Are you challenging me?"

"Of course not, don't you dare." Polly scanned the garden just in case someone was watching.

Veronica smiled and dropped her hand, then gave Polly another quick kiss.

"How's your friend? Ursula?" said Veronica.

Polly let her hand drop. She sighed. "Not happy—"

"But you can't let her hold you back."

"Let me finish, Nika."

"Sorry."

"Not happy, but she understands. She won't stand in my way. Our way."

Veronica sighed and turned on the bench so she was facing directly out towards the garden. Sometimes the pressure from her back weighed more heavily than others. Now was one of those times and there was nothing she could do about it. It matched her mood, or had caused it. Sometimes it was difficult to tell the two apart.

"What am I doing, Polly?"

"Mistress?"

"I don't know what I'm doing."

There was silence from Polly for a few moments. "This isn't self-pity, is it? Because I thought we agreed you wouldn't do that any more."

"That's easy for you to say."

"Do you need a spanking?"

"You wouldn't dare."

"Perhaps not in public, but when we get back to the room…"

"It's not self-pity, no. Not exactly." Veronica sighed. "There's just so much going on. I have to take over the housekeeping, and I don't have any idea how. And that means I'll have to talk to Mrs Jenkins every day, and she hates me."

Polly took her hand again and gave it a squeeze.

"And I'm getting married." She knew there was a kind of desperation in her voice, but she couldn't hide it.

"I'll be there."

Veronica felt the cool of Polly's hand clasping hers. Looking down, she saw the delicate fingers, pale skin, and tracery of blood vessels. It was the most real thing she knew, the only constant.

"What would cheer you up?" said Polly.

Veronica smiled and slipped her own hand down the inside of her bodice. As her fingers brushed her nipple, she shuddered.

"Stop it, someone will see. We can't do that here."

Veronica reluctantly removed her hand. "You know it reduces the pain in my back."

There was a crunching of gravel on the path, the heavy footsteps of a man. Veronica sat back on the bench while Polly moved away a short distance.

"Miss Clifford-Hughes?" said a dark pair of trousers and shoes, plus a legal satchel. Veronica could not raise her head high enough to see who it was, but she recognised the voice—and the briefcase

"Mr Slack." She stood, which gave her a better view, though she still had to strain to look into his face. "How are you today?" His suit was a good fit and, she noted for the first time, he was quite broad-shouldered.

"I am well, madam, though the day is very warm."

"It's tiring," agreed Veronica. "But better than rain in July."

"Quite so. Let us hope it's the same for your joyful day."

"Yes, let us hope."

There was an awkward pause.

"I take it this is not a social visit?" Highly unlikely, since the Slacks were lawyers and secretaries in the employ of Edwin and his family.

"No, indeed. Your future husband has given me a list of tasks to carry out, and some to pass on."

"Pass on, Mr Slack?"

"Oh, not to you, Miss Clifford-Hughes," he said, "but I do have some items to communicate with you."

"Perhaps we should adjourn to the house? We can be in the shade and have some lemonade while you deliver your communications."

"As you wish," he said and immediately offered his arm.

Veronica was not used to such solicitation, but knew how she was supposed to act and put her arm on his. They crunched slowly back up the path, with Polly bringing up the rear. Veronica giggled at the sudden thought of Polly doing interesting things to her rear as they walked.

"Something amusing, Miss Clifford-Hughes?"

"A passing thought. It is of no consequence."

He did not pursue the matter, which was just as well.

She imagined what Mr Lawrence Slack might think if he knew the kind of thoughts she was prone to. Ladies of the modern era were not expected to be as restrained as their Victorian forebears, but she doubted she was expected to be quite *that* unrestrained.

She had another thought. "Do you know my parents, sir?"

He paused for a very long time.

"I do not know them."

"But you know *of* them."

"Of course, Miss Clifford-Hughes, they are your parents."

Veronica saw Seth coming through a gate on the other side of the garden, pushing his wheelbarrow ahead of him as usual. She seldom saw him without it—she managed to suppress another giggle as she imagined him bringing it up to the bedroom.

"I think you're avoiding the question, Mr Slack."

"You put me in a difficult position," he said. "Since my father's office was responsible for drafting the agreement between your father and Viscount

Launceston over your betrothal, we are privy to a certain amount of private information that I am honour-bound to remain silent on."

This long sentence had brought them to the stone steps that led up from the garden proper to the patio. A portion of it was in shade.

"Would you prefer we sit out here?" he asked.

"Inside, sir, you will sit on a sofa and I will take a hard-backed chair, that way I will be able to look at you properly."

"Oh."

Veronica smiled to herself; it seemed she was being too forward for his delicate sensibilities, which was perfect since she enjoyed unbalancing his reserve.

Polly opened the door for them and they went through into the pleasant coolness of the ballroom. Heavy tarpaulins protected the parquet floor from workmen's boots, while the furniture was covered in sheets. Polly drew back a portion of cloth from a sofa, then found a chair for Veronica. She sat back gratefully, which allowed her view to encompass Mr Lawrence Slack. His face was as pleasant as the rest of him, with his brown hair and blue eyes.

"This is the safest place," said Veronica.

"Safest?"

"At present time, we have workmen the way most houses have mice."

"And..." he said hesitantly, "they make much larger holes in the skirting board?"

Veronica laughed. Polly raised an eyebrow and smiled.

"Why, Mr Slack, you are more than a legal automaton."

"I certainly hope so, Miss Clifford-Hughes."

"Call me Veronica."

"I couldn't possibly," he said, "it would be unprofessional."

"I insist," she said. "And I shall call you Lawrence."

"Please, I would rather you didn't."

Veronica sighed. "Would you like some of the lemonade I mentioned?"

"Thank you, I believe that would be agreeable."

"Could you arrange it, Polly? And for me too."

"Of course, miss." She gave a little curtsy and went out through the far door, her feet making no sound on the tarpaulins.

"Your personal maid?"

Veronica nodded. "She has been doing the job for years, it was time she received the proper recognition."

"And commensurate wages?"

"That too."

Another awkward silence. Veronica crossed her legs and, in the process, pulled up her skirts to expose her ankle. She saw his eyes flick down to the bare skin. *Not an automaton at all.*

"You said you had some communications?"

He opened his briefcase and pulled out a folder. The case was replaced neatly on the floor, and from the folder came a number of sheets. He studied the topmost.

"Mr Jameson wanted first to bestow his good wishes on you."

"Is that written there?"

"It is."

"I see."

"And then he wished to invite you on a short holiday after the wedding."

Veronica's mind whirred like a clockwork that had lost its ratchet. "A honeymoon?"

"It doesn't say that."

"A holiday after a wedding, Mr Slack. That's a honeymoon."

"I suppose it is." He seemed surprisingly awkward.

Veronica laughed out loud again. "Really, Lawrence, you're just being obtuse now. Surely you went on a honeymoon with your wife?"

"I am sure we would have done, Miss Clifford-Hughes, if I had a wife."

"You're not married?"

He frowned as if he could not quite understand how the conversation was suddenly about him.

"I am not."

"You should do something about that."

He was so nonplussed he opened his mouth to say something and then shut it without emitting a single sound. He finally gathered his thoughts. "If I may continue?"

"Of course, but where will the honeymoon be?"

"I have a sheet on it to give you—" He looked through the papers in his hand, found one, and read it. "Switzerland, a town called Ascona."

"Switzerland?" she said in absolute astonishment.

Just at that moment, Polly entered with a tray. She heard the word and frowned.

"Honeymoon in Switzerland, Polly!"

"Yes, miss."

Veronica calmed herself, switched legs, and pulled her skirts even higher, halfway up her calf. Lawrence Slack focused his attention on the papers in front of him.

Polly handed her the glass of cold lemonade, then found a small table for Mr Slack so he did not have to juggle the drink with all the papers. He gave her a quick smile in acknowledgement.

He seemed to take quite a long time looking at the papers in front of him.

"Is that everything to be communicated to me?"

"Not, um, quite."

He held a single sheet between thumb and finger.

"Yes?"

"Well, um, Mr Jameson wished to make your, um, sleeping arrangements clear."

"I'm sorry?"

"Yes, this is quite ... um, I do apologise for your embarrassment."

Veronica smiled. "I believe it is you who are embarrassed, Lawrence."

"I would rather you didn't—"

"Say my name."

"Miss Clifford-Hughes."

She arched her brow.

"Miss, um, Veronica."

"Veronica."

"Veronica."

She shifted her position and quite deliberately pulled her skirts almost to her knees.

"I really—"

"Yes?"

"You shouldn't, um, V-Veronica."

"What, Lawrence?"

He waved his hand in the general direction of her legs.

"Don't you like my legs?"

She uncrossed them and placed her feet apart with her skirts still around her knees, knowing there was now a dark place of mystery between her legs. She looked at him. His eyes were focused between her knees. She could imagine the thoughts his mind would be conjuring.

"Now," she said. "What does my future husband wish to communicate about our nights together?"

There was a long pause as he gathered his wits. "Sleeping arrangements."

"Yes, Lawrence."

"As you know, your parents' bedroom is quite opulent. While Mr Jameson feels it should remain as is, he has decided he will not be using that bedroom."

Veronica frowned. "But he had a door put between that room and the one next door."

"Yes. I understand, however, he has given it more consideration. Being a vegetarian and an adherent of the Diefenbach principles, he will sleep in a small room on the ground floor where he has easy access to nature."

"Easy access to nature?"

"Yes."

"And I am to sleep with him in this small room on the ground floor with its easy access to nature?"

"No."

"No?"

"Mr Jameson appreciates that it would be difficult for you."

Any remaining wisps of lust and enjoyment in teasing Mr Slack evaporated, to be replaced by a burning anger.

"He said that?"

"Wrote it."

"Did he?"

"Yes."

"I see. He doesn't want me in his bed because I'm a hunchback."

"I don't think that's his meaning."

"He thinks because I'm abnormal I can't live his lifestyle, and chooses to condescend."

"He's being thoughtful."

"He could have asked me!"

"Please, Miss Clifford-Hughes, I am only the messenger."

"My name is Veronica," she hissed, then caught herself. She forced her anger back inside. "Where do I sleep?"

He consulted the paper. "Wherever you like."

"My parents' room?"

"If you wish."

"Lawrence, do you know whether my future husband intends to consummate our marriage?"

The gentleman went very pale.

"It's not mentioned." He fiddled with the papers in front of him.

Her eyes narrowed as if she might explode with anger again.

"But there is, as you say, the honeymoon," he said in desperation. "Also, of course, if he failed to do so you would be fully within your rights to have the marriage annulled."

"I see," she said and sat back in the chair, letting her skirts drop to the floor—despite his earlier protestations, he looked disappointed. "Lawrence, I have some demands of my own."

"Demands?"

She pasted a smile on her face. "Requests."

She waited while he found his pen and some fresh paper. He moved the lemonade and used the table. "Please go ahead."

"In consideration of my physical deformity, which I assure you is painful all of the time and, some days, like today, worse than others."

"I'm sorry."

"Thank you. In regard to that, it has been suggested—" *Thank you, Seth,* "—that a Faraday device under my bed would make my nights considerably less difficult."

"I believe that is a sound thought."

"Yes, well, I want one."

"I have made a note. Is there anything else?"

"Oh yes. I have an interest in extra-planetary botany." Mr Slack looked blank. "I'm interested in plants from Mars and Venus." He smiled and noted that. "I want a hot-house and a cold-house, so I can nurture these plants."

He scribbled.

"And a photographic dark room."

"You like photography too?"

"Yes." Even if it was images of Mr Plumley licking her feet, and shots of either herself or Polly naked on the bed. They had yet to determine how to get a picture of them both together. They had a couple of cans of exposed film, but had not been able to proceed any further.

He noted it down.

"Anything else?"

"Nothing more that I can think of at the moment."

He put down his pen.

"I have another set of notes," he said and waggled a very thick sheaf at her. "As you know, Mr Jameson is a vegetarian, and these are his initial notes on diet for the staff. They include recipes for your cook."

The excitement and anger of the previous minutes froze in her heart. This was her nightmare. Not only was she expected to take control of the household when she had absolutely no idea how—despite Mr Plumley forcing her to study Mrs Beeton's sixty-years-out-of-date book—but she was also expected to somehow persuade Cook to prepare vegetarian food, and the staff to eat it.

They would all leave, Polly had told her. It was one thing to leave a house under a cloud and without references, but when that house had tried to enforce vegetarianism on the staff, it would be no crime to leave whatsoever.

She was doomed.

ii

The younger Mr Slack was apparently as good as his word. Veronica was at breakfast in the ballroom—most of the house still being off-limits—when the Honourable Edwin Jameson was announced by the butler, Emlyn Jones.

Veronica looked at her plate of kedgeree, poached eggs, and bacon. She stuffed her mouth with the bacon and washed it down with tea. Fish and eggs were, Mr Plumley suggested, less abhorrent to vegetarians, who were concerned about the effect of red meat on the body's condition.

The bacon was delicious.

She swallowed the remnants as her future husband entered, Lawrence Slack in tow and Polly rushing in behind. It wouldn't do for her not to be in attendance. She walked past the two men, stopped for a moment to deliver a curtsy to the young lordling, and continued across the room to Veronica. In the process, she gave her mistress a wink and pursed her lips as if it was a kiss.

Veronica was unable to respond since her face was visible to their visitors. Polly took up her position at Veronica's side, slightly back.

"I have interrupted your breakfast," said Edwin, then apparently as an afterthought. "Veronica."

"You have, Edwin," she said. "But that is not a problem."

"Is that kedgeree? Egg?"

"It is. I do hope it does not offend your fine sensibilities."

He waved his hand dismissively. "Fish have no blood to addle the mind, and chickens are not murdered for their eggs. It is a proper management of nature. Please continue to eat."

"Can I offer you tea?"

"Tomato juice, if it can be provided. I prefer not to drink stimulants."

Veronica had no idea whether tomato juice could be found. "Polly, if you wouldn't mind ringing for Mr Jones?"

"Yes, miss, of course." She selected a cord on the wall and pulled.

Although she would have liked to have continued eating, it was clearly going to be up to Veronica to get the conversation going. It was unlikely she was going to get any more breakfast.

"To what do I owe the pleasure of this visit, Edwin?"

"Ah, yes. Mr Slack has provided me with your list of requests..."

She was expecting him to continue, but his attention seemed to have wandered and he was staring through the French windows into the garden. It was strain enough on her neck maintaining her head in a position so she could speak to him directly. It was impossible to add a turn to see what he was looking at. She took the opportunity to take a mouthful of rice and fish—there was a nice tang of Worcester sauce in there too.

"Oh, it's a new bath," said Edwin.

There were panicked shouts and then a crash.

"They've dropped it," said her husband-to-be. "Make a note, Slack. If it's damaged, subtract the value from the contractor's bill."

"Yes, sir."

Veronica ate more kedgeree.

"Where were we?" said Edwin.

Veronica was still chewing a mouthful of rice, but exchanged glances with Mr Slack who seemed to understand her predicament and responded.

"Miss Veronica's list of requests, sir."

There was a pause as the butler arrived and the order for tomato juice was made. Veronica ate more kedgeree.

"Yes. We have them, Veronica."

Veronica swallowed enough to speak. "Thank you." She swallowed again. "And can they be fulfilled?"

"We can most certainly provide a therapeutic Faraday device for your condition. An excellent proposal, I must say."

"Thank you." If only you knew it was an under-gardener who suggested it...

"Of course, it would have been impossible without the electricity supply I am having installed."

"Yes, Edwin. You are very kind."

"I have re-examined the floorplans of the estate, and I believe we may be able to convert one of the rooms in the outhouses as a dark room for photography. I did not know you had an interest."

"I'm sure there are many things we will learn about one another once we are married," she said, and caught a curious look in his face that she was unable to decipher.

"Do you have any pictures?"

"I'm only a beginner." She wondered what his reaction would be if he knew what images they had already captured on film. Mr Jones returned with a small glass on a silver platter.

"Your tomato juice, sir."

The Honourable Edwin took his drink and sipped it, before placing it on the table beside his seat. The butler withdrew. The young lordling looked at his secretary.

"Exotic greenhouses, sir."

"Oh yes." This time he looked in pain. "I'm afraid your final request is impossible."

"Why?"

Edwin looked nonplussed at her abrupt response. "What?"

"Why is it impossible?"

"The Vegetarian Society finds itself at an impasse in regard to the categorisation of the species of life found on the other planets."

"But they are plants, are they not?"

"They are, as I say, difficult to classify. Their natures are so very far removed from those of this world. In particular, many of the plants of Venus could be classified as animals; some of them move with considerable rapidity. Most are predatory in one way or another. I understand this is due to the extreme nature of their environment."

Veronica paused; she had not realised that. When the idea had been suggested, it was simply a way to occupy her time and hopefully disguise some of the fun she wanted to have with her gardener and maid. Looking after predatory plants was not something she wanted. She needed to lose this argument; thankfully it was already going that way.

"Are you sure you cannot compromise your principles even a little?"

"I am sorry, my dear. Until a judgement is arrived at and handed down, there is nothing I can do in this matter," he said. "My hands are tied." He lifted them up as if to illustrate.

"That's a shame," she said. "However, as your wife, in principle if not yet in name, I must bow to your wisdom."

Polly spluttered and coughed. Veronica even got the impression that Mr Slack was suppressing a smile.

"Very good, Veronica. Yes, quite the right attitude. I am honoured by your devotion to your duty, even though it is not yet upon you."

She bowed her head as if to acknowledge him, but mostly to ease the strain on her neck.

It was Edwin who continued their discussion. "Have you looked through the notes I have provided in regard to the dietary arrangements for the staff?"

Her heart froze again; she had managed to forget the issue. "I have only glanced at them as yet." *From a distance.*

"It would be well to apprise the housekeeper and the cook as soon as possible," he said. "I imagine they will have to take steps to alter the deliveries."

"You're right, of course."

The shouting from the workmen outside the window grew in volume. Apparently they were attempting to get the bath through an upstairs window but it didn't want to fit.

"I understand, Edwin, you plan for us to honeymoon in Switzerland?"

"Honeymoon? Oh, I see, yes, that is correct. We will have two weeks in the mountains," he said. "It will be quite invigorating."

"I have never been to Switzerland—" she hesitated "—I have never been anywhere except London. And then only the once."

Polly gave a little cough. "If I may ask something?"

His lordship gave a slight nod.

"My mistress, as she said, has not been to places. She doesn't have the proper clothes."

Edwin waved his hand again. "Spend what you need."

"And can we know what sort of place we'll be staying? Will there be walking in mountains? Or balls to attend?"

"I will provide Mr Slack with an itinerary, and he will advise you."

"Thank you, Edwin," said Veronica. "I must apologise for being so ill-prepared."

"Think nothing of it."

There was a long silence.

Edwin stood. And everyone else did the same. "I am going to inspect the work with Mr McCloud, and apprise him of the changes."

"Shall I accompany you?" said Veronica.

"That won't be necessary. I believe you have a considerable amount to do."

He turned away and, with Mr Slack in tow, left the room.

Veronica sat down. Edwin was right, she had things she had to do, and they would be her complete ruination.

iii

Veronica spent the rest of the morning on the patio outside the ballroom, staring into the garden but barely seeing it. It was almost as if she were on some unearthly plane, and the name of that place was hell.

She could not ignore the diktats of her husband-to-be, but to carry them through would bring the house to a standstill and lead to the resignation of all the staff. The argument went round and round in circles in her mind.

Did Edwin have no idea what he was doing?

"How many staff in the whole world would be vegetarian?" she said into the air.

"Well, I ain't," said Polly. "And I won't give up beef nor pork nor lamb for no one."

"That's a double negative," said Veronica quietly, then turned to look at the maid who was sitting nearby. "Would you leave me if you were forced to?"

Polly pursed her lips and shook her head. Then glanced behind Veronica's head.

"Shall I serve luncheon, Miss Clifford-Hughes?"

Veronica jumped; she hadn't even heard him enter, but she did not need to worry about him overhearing her words. He knew about the relationship with her maid, and didn't seem to mind.

"Yes please, Mr Jones, though I don't have much appetite today." In the distance there was a crash and a lot of raised voices. "I'll be glad when this is over."

"It is rather trying, miss," he said. "Shall I lay a place for Polly as well?"

Veronica smiled. "It's better than eating alone—or being watched by someone who isn't—but I don't think Mrs Jenkins would approve."

"Indeed she would not, miss; the staff should know their place."

"But you suggested it."

"I did. I cannot imagine what came over me. Still, what's said is said. I will lay the table for two."

"Thank you."

"My pleasure, miss."

She couldn't look him in the eye because he was so tremendously tall. But they had an understanding, a fellow feeling, both freaks in their own way.

———⬥———

IT WAS NOT LONG BEFORE the table was laid and mistress and maid sat facing one another. Lunch consisted of buttered bread, cold meats and fruit. Veronica had not lied about her lack of appetite, but Polly made up for it, making sandwiches and scoffing them down.

Veronica just watched. Polly's blonde hair was tied up, of course, which exposed the pale skin of her neck. The muscles moved as she chewed and swallowed. Gently, Veronica lifted her foot and placed it touching Polly's. There was a flicker of acknowledgement in her eyes, but no other sign. It was difficult to manage, but Veronica raised her leg so that she ran her soft shoe leather up the inside of Polly's calf. Not only was it awkward, but she was resisted by the weight of dress material she had to lift at the same time.

Polly looked up and smiled. "I appreciate the thought, Nika, but I don't think we're going to get very far like that."

"Nothing's going right today."

"Your hair looks nice."

"You dressed it."

"Your dress suits you."

"I am a hunchback, Polly, no dress suits me."

"You seem intent on making nothing of anything positive, Nika. What do you want?"

Veronica leaned forward with both her palms flat on the table. "What do I want? I want to break something. I want to smash all the glass in the French windows. I want to throw a rock and shatter a mirror. I wish I had never seen the Honourable Edwin Jameson. I want to go back to the way we were."

Polly reached across the table and took her hand. "I know, and I would happily return to being a housemaid, but it seems that is not to be."

Veronica was breathing heavily. "I want your mouth between my legs. I want to feel your tongue on me and in me. I want your finger in my behind."

Polly harrumphed. "Well, I like it, and so do you. You just won't admit it." She felt light-headed. "I want Seth to take me so I'm no longer a virgin. I want Mr Plumley worshipping my sweaty toes." She stopped suddenly, let her head down to rest on the tablecloth, and burst into tears. "And I don't want any of *this*." She waved her hand in the air.

Someone cleared their throat from across the room.

Polly jumped to her feet, knocking over her chair which landed with a muffled thump on the tarpaulins.

"Mr Slack."

"It seems I am forever interrupting your meals."

"My mistress is indisposed," said Polly.

"Shall I come back later?"

Veronica sniffed. "Summer cold." Her voice was broken and the words barely distinct.

"I can just come back later."

"Stay."

Polly brought her head down closer to Veronica's. "You look a sight. Let him go and I'll clean you up."

"I'm a cripple. I always look a sight. He stays." She pulled herself into a more upright position and turned towards the young solicitor. He was still on the other side of the room. She did not know whether he had heard, but she didn't care.

"Come and sit down, Mr Slack. Have some luncheon if you wish."

"I couldn't possibly—"

"Sit!"

He came over almost at a run, and sat.

"What do you think of me, Lawrence?"

"I think you have been crying, Miss Clifford-Hughes."

"Veronica."

"Veronica."

"And why do you think that is?"

"I couldn't possibly say—"

"Why?!"

"I understand women are very gentle and sensitive creatures."

Veronica closed her eyes. They were stinging with the tears. Why would tears, which came from the eyes, make them sting? It made little sense.

"That's what you think, is it? Women are weak."

"That's not exactly—"

"It's what all men think."

Polly was still standing. "Mistress, perhaps you should withdraw to your room for a rest."

"Stop." Veronica put her hand out, palm towards her maid as if she were controlling traffic.

"I am quite out of sorts, Lawrence, so I am being rude and unpleasant and I doubt that you deserve even half of it. So, for that which is not your due, I apologise." She took a deep breath. "However, your master—my future husband—puts me in an impossible position."

"He does?"

"You do not see it? No, of course you don't. I pity any woman that marries a man."

He frowned. "Who else would a woman marry?"

She eyed him carefully and then glanced at Polly, who wore a look of terror, in case Veronica was about to divulge their relationship.

"That is hardly the important thing. Is the Honourable Edwin's intention in forcing the entire estate to vegetarianism absolute?"

"I believe it is."

"Would you do it?"

"Me?"

"You."

He said nothing.

"Let us consider for a moment, Lawrence: what if Edwin said that in order to continue as his solicitor you and your entire family would have to become vegetarians?"

"He would not ask that."

She slammed her palm on the table, making him jump. "That is exactly what he has done. He is a tyrant and a despot. He has usurped this land and made it law that all within it must dispense with red meat immediately."

He held his tongue but she could see his mind was now working.

"What happens to despots, Lawrence? All through history, what becomes of them?"

"They are overthrown by their subjects."

"Quite so, but in this case there will be no revolution. They will just leave."

She let him stew in that, and discovered that she had an appetite after all. She started to assemble a sandwich, but Polly stepped in and finished the task. The first mouthful of cold ham and cucumber between the slices of fresh bread and lashings of butter was quite refreshing.

"I see your problem," said Mr Slack the younger.

"Finally."

Veronica glanced at Polly, who was still glaring at her, but she no longer cared.

"I am bound by duty to my husband to do as he orders, but that will cause almost the entire staff to leave. Edwin wants the impossible, and I am forced to attempt it."

There was a short pause.

"You could lie," said the solicitor.

"I must promise to love, honour, and obey my husband."

"And do you love him?"

Veronica hesitated and looked at Polly. "How can I? I do not know him."

"So you'll be lying before God anyway."

Veronica opened her mouth but no sound came out.

"Oh, don't worry about it. People tell untruths in church, in court, they lie as they take their oath to speak the truth. They may be caught in the lie, but I have never seen a single one of them struck down by the Almighty. You'll be safe."

She was still dumbfounded. Her anger had evaporated and been replaced by nothing but a void.

He smiled. He had a nice smile; she thought it looked honest, but perhaps it wasn't. "You did not come here to give me advice," she said.

"No, that's correct. In fact, I merely wished to make an appointment with you to go over the itinerary of the honeymoon so your staff—" he nodded at Polly, "—would know what you needed to pack for the journey."

"I have little to do," she said. "I am at your disposal."

"How would next Wednesday be?"

"I have lessons."

He smiled. "Lessons?"

"I receive tuition every day of the week, and Saturday mornings."

"What manner of tuition, if I may enquire?"

"Science, the humanities, history, languages, literature, philosophy, and, more recently, household management."

"Perhaps you could take half a day on Wednesday?"

Veronica blinked. It had not occurred to her, but why could she not? What was it that Mr Plumley himself had said about cages made of shadows?

"Yes, that would be acceptable."

"Would you be able to come to our offices in the town?"

The thought of being visible to the townsfolk was not pleasant, but she nodded.

"Would half past two be convenient for you?"

She smiled. "I will have to check my appointment book, but yes, I think that will be satisfactory."

"Then, Miss Clifford-Hughes," he stood and gave a little bow, "I look forward to seeing you."

"Thank you, Mr Slack."

"I am delighted to be of service."

He left the room.

Somewhere a hammer pounded, but Veronica found she no longer cared.

iv

Sunday morning, July 24th, two days since Mr Slack's revelations. And fifteen to the wedding. Her rampant self-pity, tears, and rudeness to Mr Slack had been explained when her monthlies arrived the next day.

It seemed there were not a lot of arrangements to be made. It was only required that she turn up at the church at the appropriate time, go through the ceremony, and then return home with her new husband. There were to be no guests, no wedding breakfast, no speeches by groomsman or father of the bride.

She had not seen her parents for at least two years, and now the house had passed to the ownership of Edwin Jameson, or would on the completion of the wedding. The parties involved, excluding herself, were only interested in what limited value she had as a bride. Her parents had probably been surprised when it turned out she had any at all.

She lay on her side. She could not lie on her back unless supported by a dozen cushions, and even then her back would ache, but she did not mind lying on her side because her face was buried in Polly's hair. Her left arm stretched beneath her lover's neck, reaching round to cup her breast while her other wrapped around Polly's body with her hand resting on her belly. Veronica's breasts pressed against her maid's spine, with her legs bent up against Polly's rear end.

It was perfection. Although Polly was dribbling on her arm.

Veronica wished Polly was not asleep, but was loath to wake her.

She kissed her shoulder. No response.

Moving carefully, Veronica brought her free arm round to stroke Polly's bum. The strokes moved further south until the tips of Veronica's fingers were rubbing against Polly's secret lips. She could feel the soft fuzz of her hairs, and pressed harder as she moved her fingers back and forth. Polly took a deeper breath.

Veronica dipped her fingers between the lips and set about pressing rhythmically, pulling first one way and then the other. Polly made a noise somewhere between a sigh and a groan. In the middle of a yawn she muttered, "That's nice."

Keeping her fingers on the move, Veronica gently squeezed Polly's boob, then dragged her nails across the nipple, which elicited a further sigh. Polly wriggled, but Veronica held her in place and rubbed between her legs more vigorously. The girl gave a more serious groan, and one of her hands covered Veronica's on her breast. Polly reached down to her nubbin, while Veronica continued to manipulate her from behind.

As her maid's wriggles and moans became more frequent, Veronica adjusted her position a little lower and pressed her thumb into Polly's opening. That elicited a grunt and a sudden jerk in the girl's hips as she tried to push it deeper. With her thumb buried, Veronica was free to use the fingers of that hand to continue to stroke the lips, now duelling with Polly's fingers. She found an engorged muscle beneath the skin that responded very positively to her rubbing.

Polly was now in constant motion, thrusting her hips backwards, both her hands on her own tits, squeezing and pulling, while Veronica pushed hard in time with the girl's motion. Moments later, Polly froze, her body tight as a wire. Her legs quivered with energy as the muscles of her pussy spasmed hard three times, then twice more with less intensity, until the girl slumped back onto the bed.

Veronica continued to massage Polly between her legs, slow and gentle now, leaving her thumb still buried in the damp warmth. The maid's breathing slowed until she seemed as if she might have gone back to sleep. Veronica gently pulled her hand free, then slid her arm out from under her lover.

She rolled over and sat up on the edge of the bed. She dipped her hand between her own legs to feel the wetness and gently rub herself. Without even a conscious thought, her free hand played with her breast.

There was movement on the bed behind her.

"Would you like me to do that?" said Polly.

Two hands came down on Veronica's twisted shoulders. There was only one part of her body she was self-conscious about, and only Polly was allowed to touch. Then one of those hands threaded its way under Veronica's arm and touched the other breast. The sensation was delicious.

By force of will alone, Veronica pulled her own hands away from her body.

"We can't," she said. "No time, not to mention my condition."

Sunday morning meant Veronica's weekly trip to church, with Mrs Jenkins. The other staff had to go as well. It had always been the most unpleasant activity of the week, since the housekeeper disliked her, and the people of the village had it in their heads she was some sort of demon.

What they would think in two weeks when she walked up to the altar in a Vionnet dress, not wearing any shoes, Veronica had no idea. What would her husband think? She hadn't even seen the dress yet. Mademoiselle Vionnet was going to come down from London the day before the wedding for the final fitting and adjustments.

She was brought back to reality by a sudden squeeze of her right breast. She said, "Ow" to make a point, but in truth it re-ignited her lust. She would happily allow Polly to bring her to paroxysm with simply one hand on each.

Instead, she stood up. The pull on her tit was delightful, but she ignored it.

"No time!"

"You were away with the fairies. I was bringing you back," said Polly, slipping off the side of the bed and padding across the floor towards the washstand. Veronica admired her shape, and the way the sunlight moved across her as she stepped between light and shadow.

"Of course you were. You need to get dressed and lay my clothes out."

"It would move along quicker if you brushed my hair."

"Me?"

Polly turned smoothly in the sunlight and put one hand on her hip. "Yes, Nika, you need to help me."

Veronica opened her mouth to say something and then shut it without a sound.

"Good, because if you were going to say anything about mistress and servant, Mrs Jenkins would probably have to wait a good while before you were fit to be seen in public."

Veronica nodded and Polly turned back to her own clothes. There were aspects to their relationship that were quite difficult. At first they had both been nervous and it was a matter of exploring themselves and each other, but things had changed; it wasn't that there weren't still things to discover, but they were confident with each other now. And in private they were equals, even if, to the outside world, they were still mistress and servant.

Their lives inside the four walls of the bedroom was the truth, their life beyond them the lie.

So Polly dressed and then Veronica brushed her hair. It was strange. It was not that Veronica couldn't do her own hair, but the twist in her back made it harder for her to reach everywhere. And Polly had been there to do it for her.

Even when Veronica's mother had lived in the house, she had never, as far as Veronica could remember, brushed her hair. That was what nannies were for.

But to do someone else's hair, even when she was not used to it, was peaceful and calming.

"Mrs Winstanley," said Veronica suddenly.

"Who's that?"

"That was the name of Nana."

"Who?"

"My nanny."

"Oh."

"I'd forgotten about her."

"Well, I hope you don't forget me that easily, Nika."

Veronica leaned forward and kissed the top of her lover's head. The hair blonde and glossy. "How could I forget a person I love as much as you?"

Polly stood and turned; pulling up her dress she placed a knee on the chair, then leaned forward and planted a kiss on Veronica's lips.

"Stop," said Veronica, "or you'll make me cry and I'll look terrible."

Polly had her hair up and pinned in no time, then set about dressing her mistress in the dowdy clothes she always wore to church.

The weather continued dry and that meant they would walk. Even more time in the quiet but angry company of Mrs Jenkins.

EQUIPPED WITH A BONNET and parasol, Veronica waited on the porch in the shade; there was work going on inside even though it was Sunday. The marble columns on either side looked impressive, but the facade was the only old part of the building, the rest had been rebuilt a dozen times, and were undergoing yet another remodelling for their new owner.

According to the agreement, as she understood it, the title to the property transferred to Edwin as soon as they married. She had been sold by her parents, for some *quid pro quo* she was not aware of. Though it occurred to her that Mr Slack (the younger) might be persuaded to tell her, if she could find the right approach.

The door behind her opened and closed.

Mrs Jenkins said nothing, she simply sailed by, expecting Veronica to follow. That was how it had been for all the years up to now, but that was not how it was going to continue. Once they were married, she and Edwin would go to church together, and they would sit at the front, not the back.

Although her taste of being at the front, when the banns were read, had not been that pleasant. When she was at the back, people didn't stare at her all the time.

A real stab of fear went through her as she imagined herself walking up the aisle in whatever Madame Paquin created for her. And without the foundational British undergarments that the French *couturier* despised. She might as well be naked. Then she cursed her perverse body for the warmth that grew between her thighs at the thought.

However, she had more important things to worry about.

The air was heavy with heat and the scent of the woods. Rich and still with a hint of moisture. Their feet made almost no sound on the well-worn path. Bare roots caught in the act of climbing from the soil. Beech and oak interspersed with groups of silvery ash. You could believe in tree spirits here.

And witches. Mrs Jenkins ploughed ahead seemingly heedless of the beauty and mysticism of the ancient woodland.

"Mrs Jenkins?" said Veronica, stretching out her stride to catch up with the woman.

"Miss." If the housekeeper was curious about what Veronica wanted to say, she managed to hide it completely.

"I need to talk with you on a very serious matter."

That brought her to a standstill.

"You need not fire me, miss. I will be handing in my notice as soon as you are wed."

"What? No!" Veronica's terror deepened.

"You can't stop me, miss."

Veronica took a deep breath and headed off again towards the church, and it was Mrs Jenkins who had to catch up.

They walked for a minute in silence, until Veronica managed to summon the courage to speak again.

"I do not wish you to resign, Mrs Jenkins. And I certainly don't want to fire you."

There was a distinct hesitation. "You don't?"

"No, but if you insist on resigning, I promise to give you good references."

"You do?"

Veronica sighed. "I know you don't like me, Mrs Jenkins, but I need your help."

"You want *my* help?"

"Not want, Mrs Jenkins. Far more than that. I need it. Something terrible is about to happen at the house."

"What do you mean by terrible?"

"My husband-to-be is a vegetarian."

There was a long pause, then, "I expect Cook can deal with that, and I'm sure you'll get used to it."

"No, you don't understand. He expects to feed everybody in the household the same way. Everybody."

The weather vane on the top of the church spire came into view above the trees.

"Everybody?"

"Yes. He gave me notes about it."

"They won't stand for it."

"I know!" Veronica found she was almost breathless, as if she had been running—or enjoying the heaven to be found between Polly's thighs. She pushed that image aside; she must remain steadfast. "This is why I need your help."

Mrs Jenkins shook her head. "This has nothing to do with me. I have said I will resign, and I will. This just makes it even more certain."

"And everyone else will leave too."

"I expect so."

And with that, she said nothing more.

V

They took their place at the back as usual. People stared and whispered. The church was hot and, as usual, Veronica sweated. Reverend Peacock had chosen forgiveness as the theme of his sermon, which made for an uplifting change. Perhaps he was trying to set the scene for her marriage, getting away from all the punishment that might be expected in hell.

It went on for a long time, but that was not unexpected. Two more hymns were sung, poorly accompanied on the organ, and finally they were set free.

As usual, she and Mrs Jenkins remained in their pew until everyone else had left.

Finally they stepped out into the sunshine once more.

"Only two weeks, Miss Clifford-Hughes," said the vicar. It was a strange turnaround, always in the past it would be Mrs Jenkins who passed the time of day with him. But Veronica would soon be the lady of the local area and, even if she had no title, the housekeeper became merely an employee. No longer the child's guardian.

Veronica smiled, even though she knew he probably couldn't see it in her down-turned face. "I am counting the days." *With mounting terror and horror.*

"I understand you are going away."

"My future husband has arranged for us to spend two weeks in Switzerland."

"Goodness me that is a long way. Well, they do have some lovely alpine plants, very hardy of course, you should collect some and bring them back for your own garden."

"Thank you for your advice. Perhaps you might like some for the church?"

"A kind thought. If you are able then it would be a very generous gesture."

Veronica hesitated. "May I ask a question, Vicar?"

There was a sharp intake of breath from Mrs Jenkins. She had been manoeuvred before by Veronica "asking questions"; she clearly expected the same sort of trouble.

"Of course, Miss Clifford-Hughes. It is my duty to assist all of my parishioners." He hesitated. "Do you think this will take long?"

"It may."

"Oh well, wrestling with eternal truths should not be attempted without tea and biscuits." He laughed. "Let us adjourn to the vicarage. My girl always prepares a drink after the morning sermon to ease my throat, and I know she has been baking. We can see what she has brought forth from the burning fires of her oven." He laughed once more at his own humour, then led the way to the vicarage—a large, brick-built house. They were greeted at the door by four cats. One sat indifferently off to one side in the shade, a second rolled in the dirt while the remaining two seemed intent on tripping them up.

"My wife did love her cats," said the vicar, and pushed on into an airy drawing room with large, wood-framed sofas covered with flower patterns—slightly worn. "Alice! We have visitors."

The maid looked about fourteen, with light brown hair and, because Veronica tended to notice these things nowadays, no bust to speak of. She must have known who Veronica was, and tried very hard not to stare until the spell was broken by the vicar.

"Ah, Alice, good girl. Tea for everyone, and biscuits, of course."

"Yes, Vicar." She curtsied and left.

They seated themselves, Veronica and Mrs Jenkins on one sofa, with Reverend Peacock in an armchair that did not match the rest. Much more worn, with a blanket thrown over the seat as well as the antimacassar at the back.

"Now, Miss Clifford-Hughes—goodness we must get as much use out of that name as possible, because you won't have it much longer—is this a question that can be discussed here, or is somewhere more private required?"

"I think this will be all right."

"Very good. Do you want to begin then?"

"Well, it's on the subject of deceit."

The vicar frowned. "Are you sure you don't want somewhere private?"

"No, really."

"Very well then, I apologise for my interruption."

"Can there be white lies?"

The vicar beamed. "Oh, that's an excellent theological question. Very good, Miss Clifford-Hughes, very good. My compliments to your tutor. Are you studying philosophy?"

"We have had a look at the American Pragmatists recently."

"And did they have an answer to this question?"

"Avoiding unnecessary harm seemed important." In truth, Veronica could not quite recall what they said about lying; she just remembered they were very keen on things that could be shown to work, as opposed to mere theories.

"Ah, good, yes, that's very *apropros*, don't you think?"

"I suppose, but I was wondering whether you had any thoughts about it?"

"Lots of them, that's why it's so much fun."

"Oh." They really didn't seem to be getting very far.

Tea arrived. Alice got out a small table which she placed in front of the two guests. She disappeared for a moment, and reappeared with a tray from which she laid out the cups and saucers, then left the teapot on a stand before heading back into the kitchen.

"By strict biblical verse, deceit is frowned on completely," said the vicar. "One only has to think of Mark 7. And there are plenty more, plenty more indeed. Being deceitful is unquestionably the devil's work."

"I see." Veronica thought about all the deceit involved in having Polly as her lover, and Seth, but then her lusts were no doubt inspired by the fallen one. She was doomed anyway, so would more lies make it any the worse?

Biscuits arrived.

"Do provide Miss Clifford-Hughes with a selection of your excellent produce," said Reverend Peacock.

Alice whirled around the room putting out small tables and placing plates with biscuits, pausing to pour each cup of tea and then add the milk. Finally, they were alone again.

"You seemed concerned at my response," said the vicar, dipping a Garibaldi biscuit into his tea. He certainly did not seem concerned as to how he was judged.

Veronica sipped her tea.

"I understand that deceit in general would be a bad thing, but white lies?"

"How white are they?" said Reverend Peacock. "Who is to judge their purity?"

"If you tell an untruth to protect someone from unpleasant consequences?"

"Such as?"

At this point the Reverend Albert Peacock was reminding her of her tutor, Mr Plumley. Which led her to wondering whether the vicar would like to lick her sweaty feet too. Or perhaps he had a different peccadillo, or curious preference, in his life? He and his wife had had no children, so perhaps he did not like carnal relations at all.

"What if carrying out a person's instructions would cause a terrible catastrophe, but the individual tasked with carrying out those instructions didn't do it, and kept said person in ignorance?"

"So, on the one hand, many people would be harmed, but on the other, only a lie is told. A white lie. Is that what you're saying?"

"Perhaps not harmed, but there would be a lot of trouble and upset, and the individual required to carry out the instructions would suffer. And, in fact, the person giving the orders might also suffer, but they can't see it."

The vicar nodded and sipped his tea. Veronica took the opportunity to do the same. There were several types of biscuit; the homemade ones were thin and round and very crisp, with just the right amount of honey to make them sweet. After that she chose a dark, oblong biscuit she had never seen before, a sandwich with a chocolaty cream centre; this one had come out of a packet, and it was delicious.

Reverend Peacock rested his cup on the saucer in his lap.

"A great deal of misery possibly to everyone concerned on the one hand, if the command is carried out, balanced against a little white lie."

"Yes, Vicar."

"What are the consequences if the lie is discovered?"

Veronica hadn't thought about that, her only concern had been justifying a lie to her husband-to-be. "Well, much of the misery would then happen anyway, I suppose, and the liar might suffer quite badly."

"Physically?"

Veronica wondered if Edwin would beat her if he discovered she had lied about something so important to him. It was at that point she realised that if she lied to Edwin, Mrs Jenkins would once again have power over her and the freedom she had been looking forward to could be stripped away in a moment.

In her mind's eye she could imagine the housekeeper going to Edwin and saying, *Your wife has lied to you.*

"Never mind," she said suddenly and surprisingly loudly. Both the vicar and Mrs Jenkins jumped. She put down her cup and saucer, brushed the crumbs from her dress, and carefully pushed herself to her feet. Reverend Peacock spilt his tea in his haste to stand when she did.

She turned and smiled at him. "Thank you, Vicar. Being able to talk it through with you has certainly helped, and I believe I understand the situation fully now."

"Oh, well, of course. That's good."

"We will not trespass on your time any more."

Mrs Jenkins had been slower getting to her feet, and was looking at the uneaten biscuits on her plate.

———◆———

A FEW MINUTES LATER they were under the leafy trees, heading back to the house.

"You think lying to your husband and letting Cook prepare meat for everyone else is going to work?"

"No."

"But what you said to the vicar..."

"Yes, that was why I started the discussion," she said, "but I realised it was not going to work. A white lie will only work if it's something small; this one would be found out, and then all the bad things would happen anyway, and it would be worse."

"I see."

"If you wish to tender your resignation you can, of course, but I would ask that you wait for three months. I am going to talk to my future husband."

And the younger Mr Slack. "Whatever the outcome, I promise to give you, and any other staff who feel the need to leave, good references."

Mrs Jenkins said nothing for a few moments. "That is very decent of you, Miss Clifford-Hughes."

Yes, thought Veronica, it really is. And far more than you deserve for the way you've treated me all these years. But if I did anything else, that would make me as bad as you.

Plans were forming in Veronica's head. She could not prevent Mrs Jenkins from leaving, but despite the woman's general unpleasantness, the house had always run smoothly. Was there any way she might provide a more convincing reason for the woman to stay? As one plan teetered with uncertainty, another solidified.

Veronica was less concerned about the steward, Mr Laughton. If he chose to leave, perhaps she could, with her husband's approval, promote the butler. But then she wasn't sure that would work; could a butler even become a steward? She would have to check Mrs Beeton's book, it might be in there.

———▶●◀———

"WE NEED TO GET SETH up to our room for a couple of hours," said Veronica as she wandered through the garden with Polly in the afternoon. The scent of the flowers was almost overpowering and the air was filled with the constant droning of bees. The green slopes of the Downs in the distance were hazy in the heat.

"Someone will see him, or miss him, if we try that."

The subject of their discussion was working on a flower bed a short distance away. His shirt was stuck to his back with sweat, but where his skin was revealed, on his arms beneath rolled-up sleeves, he just glowed.

"Yes, they would in the morning, but what if he came up this evening?"

Polly looked put out. "You want him to stay the night with us?"

"Yes, or just for the time we need."

"I know you said you wanted to fuck him."

"I've changed my mind about that," she said. "I don't think it would be fair to my husband."

"Well, I don't want Seth to fuck *me.*"

Veronica smiled. "I know. I have another idea completely. As soon as it's dark and the house has settled, he can come up."

"What about your monthlies?"

"Tomorrow night then."

The maid didn't look convinced. "I suppose you want me to go and tell him?"

"Yes. As you like to point out, I certainly can't."

Polly tutted and started to walk away, but Veronica spoke again. "And tell him to bring some carrots... in various sizes, and washed."

"Oh god."

vi

Veronica sat on the bed and looked at the clock. It was just past ten in the evening. The rest of Sunday had been uneventful, she and Polly had quiet night then Monday had crawled by. Though her lessons had filled much of it.

Finally the sun had gone down and now cool air drifted in through the open window. She had already changed into her nightdress and wore a light dressing gown over it, but Polly had refused to prepare for bed.

"Where is he?" muttered Veronica.

"He said he'd come up as soon as he thought it was safe."

"But he definitely said he would?"

"How many times, Nika? Yes, I told him, and, well, his thing got hard standing right there just at the thought of it. It would take Judgement Day to stop him, and perhaps not even that."

"The door's locked?"

"You saw me, and if you turn around you can see for yourself. Both bolts."

Despite Veronica declaring she would never use a candle again because she was waiting for the electric lights to be fitted, they had one burning near the dressing room providing just sufficient light to see by. The moon was not up yet and the sky was filled with brilliant stars. An owl screeched.

There was a scrape at the window as the ivy shifted.

"He's here," breathed Veronica.

"Oh good," muttered Polly without conviction. She went and sat in the armchair.

Veronica stared, transfixed, at the window and the shivering movements of the ivy leaves. The occasional quiet grunt drifted in with the breeze as Seth climbed. Veronica went round the other two windows and pulled the curtains. She jumped as four carrots flew in and thumped on the carpet. Veronica gathered them up. Little hair roots stuck out at all angles and they still had the leaves growing from the end. They would need some trimming. She dropped them in Polly's lap.

"Could you hide those?"

"Are we going to play Hunt the Carrot?"

Veronica's lips twitched into a smile. "I was thinking more Hide the Carrot."

"You ain't sticking any of those in me."

Both of Seth's hands were on the windowsill, and his head came into view.

"Of course not, they're for me," said Veronica, making shooing gestures at Polly before turning back to Seth, who had now got one leg over. Veronica went to the curtain and, as soon as he was inside, she pulled that closed too.

Now she felt safe.

Polly emerged from the dressing room brushing dirt from her hands. "Shoes off, Seth. And wash your hands properly."

Veronica thought she was being quite rude; she wanted to kiss Seth on the cheek to make up for it, but she couldn't get that high.

"I 'ad a bath."

"Good," said Polly, "but you've just climbed a wall carrying dirty carrots. Wash your hands."

"Yes, do that, Seth," said Veronica. "There's lots to do and we need you as clean as possible. And we do need to get some sleep tonight." She smiled. "At some point."

Polly almost marched over to where her lover stood, and then spoke quietly so their guest would not overhear. "You going to tell me what's going on, then?"

"Isn't it more fun to be surprised?"

"I know your surprises."

Veronica sighed. "I just want to teach him how to be a good lover."

Polly's eyes narrowed with suspicion. "Why? Don't you like him rough and uncarved?"

"Well yes, obviously, *I* do."

"You don't expect it to make a difference to me?"

"You don't think it would be good for him to be taught how to make you come?"

"That's not the point. I know you and you're not doing it for me—"

"Miss Veronica?" said Seth.

Polly turned on him. "Mistress Nika to you."

"Aye, Mistress Nika."

"Let me see your hands," said Polly.

He held them out like a child. She checked them and turned them over. "Clean your nails, use the little brush with the hard bristles."

Seth went back to the washstand.

Veronica was trying not to laugh. "Stop being so horrible to him."

"I'm sure you don't want dirty nails in your pussy."

"Perhaps not, but I thought you could be the model on which he practices," said Veronica.

"You can be a right cow sometimes, Nika," said Polly. "But I know more about this subject than you do, so if that's the game you want to play, you're going to be the specimen and I'll be the tutor."

"Me?"

"I ain't having him poking around my bits," she said. "Besides, Nika, this was your idea."

Veronica let her chin drop. "As you wish, Mistress Polly."

Polly hesitated, perhaps she had been expecting more of an argument. "Well, let's get you naked then."

Veronica stood there as Polly removed her dressing gown and nightdress. With her feet slightly apart, and her head stooped, Veronica waited. She had given in to Polly because the maid was right: Veronica always had ideas and it was Polly who usually had to live with them. Polly's body might be perfection, but she was the one embarrassed about it. Veronica had little shame and there was only one part of her that she preferred to hide.

Seth finally turned, drying his hands on the towel. Veronica had already felt those hands between her legs, but she realised just one of his fingers was equivalent to two of Polly's. The thought of where they might end up was already stoking her lust.

His hands went to his shirt buttons.

"No," said Polly. "You stay clothed." He looked forlorn. "For now." He perked up slightly and looked at Veronica.

"Seth," she said, "Polly is in charge. You and I must do anything she says. All right?"

"Aye, Mistress Nika."

"Just Nika now, we're the same, Polly is our mistress."

"Aye, Nika. Mistress Polly."

She couldn't really tell if he was laughing at them, but he seemed willing. And there was a bulge in his nethers that assured her he would obey.

Polly beckoned to Seth and he walked over until she stopped him about three feet away and spoke directly to Veronica.

"Listen, Nika, you must not speak. You stay silent though you may groan or sigh as needed."

Veronica nodded and suppressed the desire to say, 'Yes, Mistress Polly'.

"Seth, you're here to learn how to please a woman. You can only touch when and where you're told by me, but you can ask questions. Do you understand?"

"Yes, Mistress Polly."

Veronica watched as an almost cruel smile filled Polly's face. It was a little unsettling, but Veronica trusted her friend.

"All right, Seth, let's go through the body parts. I'll point, you tell me what I'm pointing at." Veronica was more than a little surprised when her own ruler was brandished in her face by Mistress Polly.

"Mouth," said Seth.

"Open wide, Nika."

Obediently she opened her mouth, and the end of the ruler went between her lips.

"Teeth? Tongue."

The ruler left her mouth and moved down her body.

"Boobies." Pause. "Tits?"

"No, the end."

"Teat."

"She's not a cow, Seth. Nipple."

"Nipple."

"Shut your mouth, Nika."

Veronica was grateful Polly had finally noticed, since her jaw was aching.

Polly scraped the edge of the wooden ruler down the side of Veronica's tit, making her shiver with pleasure. Then she slapped the nipple lightly with the flat part. Veronica groaned.

"Nika, here, has very sensitive tits, Seth. She can come just from having them touched." She gave the other nipple a slap. Veronica muffled a squeal; it had hurt, but her lust was burning hotter. "But, and this is important, Seth, Nika is unusual. Most women like having their breasts touched, but most are not like Nika."

Through the haze of desire, Veronica wanted to protest that Polly was only guessing, just because she wasn't that sensitive. But she held her tongue; she was already desperate. Polly must have known what this was going to do to her, and was surely getting her revenge for the "surprise".

"All right, Seth, let's move on."

"Belly. Belly button? Hair."

Polly tutted. "Turn around, Nika."

Veronica hesitated. If she turned, Seth would be looking directly at her deformed spine.

The ruler landed with a stinging slap on her thigh. "Turn to face the bed."

As she obeyed, Veronica told herself the tears in her eyes were because of the pain, and not the embarrassment.

"Legs further apart, and bend over, lean on the bed." Veronica did as she was told. "Nika, you can tell me if this position is too much of a strain."

"Thank you, mistress."

"Bum."

A small hand grabbed Veronica's left buttock and pulled it to the side, exposing Veronica's bum hole. There was a long pause. "Well?"

"I dursn't say it, Mistress Polly."

"Seth, you're staring at the naked body, specifically the bum, of your employer, Veronica Clifford-Hughes, and you won't say what I'm pointing at?" The end of the ruler touched Veronica's anus. She barely managed to suppress the urge to push against it.

"Bum hole."

"Good. Now, once again, Nika here likes having her bum hole touched. Don't you?"

"Yes, Mistress Polly."

"How much do you like it, Nika?"

"I like it a lot."

"'Specially when something gets pushed into it."

"Yes, Mistress Nika."

"Yes, you do. But, Seth, that's not true of all women, and it will hurt if you're rough. So you must be careful."

The ruler dragged lower. "What about this?"

"C-cunt."

"We prefer the term pussy."

"Pussy."

"But that's what we call the whole area, so this would be the pussy hole. Very good. Now, let's get down closer. I'll do all the touching for now, you keep your hands to yourself."

Veronica heard them moving, and moments later she could feel their breath on her skin. She realised she was panting and felt very hot, but her back was beginning to ache from the strain of the position. She was torn: she needed to move, but desperately wanted the examination to continue.

"Mistress Polly, may I adjust my position a little?"

"You may."

Veronica bent at the knees so they dug into the side of the bed and changed the way her weight was supported. She buried her face in the counterpane. It helped.

"Thank you, mistress."

She jumped when Polly's fingers touched her pussy.

"All right, Seth, we'll be looking at this in more detail in a minute, but I just wanted to show you this. See, Nika is very excited right now, and her body really wants more stimulation."

Polly pulled Veronica's pussy lips apart. "See, she's all wet. That's not piss." Veronica muffled her squeal with the bedspread as a small finger poked into her body and was then pulled out again. "All wet, but if you sniff it—" Veronica's eyes went wide as she heard Seth breathe in her smell, "—not piss. This is very important. This is like the oil in a machine, it lets things rub without hurting. You men are always too quick and you don't let a girl get wet before you start shoving things into her. Do you understand?"

"Aye, Mistress Polly."

"Well, go on, stick your finger in her and see how easy it is."

The rational part of Veronica's mind could not believe what she'd just heard. The lustful side welcomed it, just as it welcomed the tentative probing of Seth's huge finger. Then the delicious sensation of it moving into her, deeper and deeper. Rubbing the entrance so delightfully until she felt his knuckle touch her pussy lips. She could not hold back a long groan to go with it, tinged with desperation for more.

"That's where your prick goes, that's how it feels inside," said Polly, her voice deeper and almost a groan in itself. "See how much she loves that. See how much liquid she's making, she's desperate to be fucked. Now, slowly, pull it out."

Veronica whimpered as the finger retreated.

"Push it in again. Hard."

Veronica screeched into the bed. Her resolution not to have Seth fuck her was crumbling. She wanted him in her. Thrusting. Pounding. Lost in her imagination, it took her a moment to realise his finger was gone again.

The ruler stung her rump. "I said to get up, Nika!"

It was hard regaining her feet. And when she did so, her pussy juices slid down the inside of both thighs. She had not been told to turn around, so she didn't, but remained facing across the bed with her mind in broken pieces of lust and rationality.

"I think I want you in the armchair now, Nika."

Still dazed, Veronica turned towards the big seat. Polly was there ahead of her, while Seth stood still near the window. He looked as if his mind was in a similar broken state to hers.

Polly found a towel and placed it on the seat, then gathered cushions. She stuffed a few into the back of the armchair.

"Sit with your bum towards the front and a leg over each arm of the chair. Once you're in place we'll get these cushions placed to give you support."

Veronica did not question or protest, and within a minute or so she was there with her pussy fully open and exposed, leaning back as comfortably as was possible for her.

"Seth, come here and kneel down in front of Nika."

Now Veronica could see what they were doing, it added another level of intensity to what she was experiencing. It was almost as if she were detached from the world while the sensations of lust and desire were the only thing she felt. Polly had pulled up the hardback chair and sat to one side, but in easy reach of Veronica's nethers, while Seth knelt directly in front of her. She could feel his breath on her pussy. He was flushed, as was Polly, but the most unreal part of the experience was that they were both still fully clothed.

"All right, Seth, this is Nika's pussy and it's like most you'll ever see. You've got the pussy hole at the bottom there. Thicker lips on the outside—" the ruler scraped up one side and down the other, "—and then there are these inner flaps." The ruler repeated the route. "These can be all different sizes."

You don't know that, just say yours are different to mine, screamed Veronica in her head.

"This is the pee hole, but you don't need to pay much attention to that."

Veronica was sure Polly was panting but trying to hide it. Just like her.

"This part at the top is the most important, but why don't you use your finger to show me you've learnt the lesson so far."

She watched as Seth reached out and, pointing with his finger, touched it to her pussy hole. She convulsed with desire and he snapped back.

"You didn't hurt her, Seth. She's like a steam engine with too much pressure, she's ready to blow. But we don't want to set her off just yet. We want to build as much pressure as possible first, because then she'll explode."

Oh god.

"Touching her lightly for a short time will build that pressure; touching her hard will set her off. So just keep it light, and remember that when you're with another woman."

"Aye, Mistress Polly."

He reached out again and his finger touched her hole. Veronica jerked again, but this time he kept it there. "Pussy hole." Her eyes were fixated on his finger as he traced her outer lips. "Lips." Then tantalisingly up and down the thin folds of flesh. "Flaps." She groaned as his finger landed in the middle of her pussy—it was all very well for Polly to say it should be ignored, but there wasn't a single part of her that didn't respond to his stimulation.

"Pee hole."

"Good."

Veronica wasn't wrong, Polly was definitely breathing heavily. This was stimulating her too, much more than she was willing to show. Seth wouldn't notice, his entire attention was focused on Veronica's pussy.

Polly took the ruler and moved the end close. "This top part, the nubbin, see how it sticks out. That's because Veronica is filled with lust; normally it's smaller and that piece of skin—" the ruler touched her and Veronica grunted as sparks flew through her, "—would be over the top of it. But when it's like this, it's more sensitive than the entire rest of a woman's body put together."

Veronica's eyes were wide as she saw the ruler move, and it touched her ... every muscle in her body spasmed. She grunted; her hands gripped her knees, she wanted to grab Seth's head and grind his face into her pussy. *But I must not touch*.

"She wants you, Seth, but not because it's you; it could be me, or anybody. She's past caring who or what touches her."

Veronica dragged her eyes from Seth and saw the mirror of her own lust in Polly's face. She was as far gone, without being touched, as Veronica.

"How do you pleasure a woman, Seth?" said Polly, no longer able to hide the lust in her own voice. "With gentleness, and time, and little touches. You stoke her furnace one step at a time, until she is fit to explode.

"Touch Veronica's tits, Seth. Show me what you've learnt."

He was so much taller than her it was easy for him to reach up. His fingertips contacted her skin and it was like electricity. She squirmed trying to force him to touch harder, but he just dragged the rough tips across her flesh. Contacting a nipple then away again. Veronica grunted with every breath, punctuating it every now and again with muffled squeals as she held her mouth tightly closed.

Seth's nails were worn to a nub, but the skin of his hands was calloused and hard. He rubbed her tits a little harder.

"Sometimes, Seth, when it gets like this, pain is nice too—but remember, she could come from you touching her tits, and we don't want that yet. Dig your fingers in. Squeeze really hard. Just once, then let go. Do it. Hurt her!"

Both hands dug into her tits and the pain was excruciating. He had big hands and he worked with them every day. He was so much stronger than Polly. And then his hands were gone and she desperately wanted them back on her throbbing tits; she wanted the pain if she could get nothing else.

"Stroke her thighs, the inside. Rub up and down close to her pussy and back, but don't touch it. Until she settles again."

Tears dripped from Veronica's eyes. The pleasure so intense it hurt. Through the blur she saw him rubbing and felt the intense feelings slipping away.

She gasped as Seth's finger went into her and then pulled out again.
"Please, Mistress," she cried, "please…"

Polly did not chastise her for speaking out of turn, instead, "Seth, your tongue and your mouth can be your most powerful weapon. Lick her pussy, suck her nubbin. It's time."

He was so far gone in his own lust, he did not even hesitate. His head went down. A long lapping stroke from her hole all the way up to her nubbin. Veronica screamed. Then another mouth came down on hers. Polly was kissing her to muffle her cries.

A small hand caught her nipple in a pincer grip as Seth's mouth engulfed her swollen nethers.

The pain of her abused nipple and the intense waves of explosive pleasure from between her legs went through her like a cannonade. Her screams were swallowed by her lover as Veronica shook and convulsed with all the pent-up lust that erupted from her.

Everything went black.

⎯⎯◉⎯⎯

VERONICA SHIVERED WITH cold and opened her eyes. She was still sitting in the armchair with her legs wide and a breeze cooling her burning skin. The candle was still giving forth light and she could see two people on the bed.

Seth sat on its end with his face obscured by Polly's head. It took a moment to realise they were kissing. *Polly is kissing Seth?* Veronica smiled. Polly must have been so stimulated by what she had done to her mistress that it broke down her own defences.

Veronica's muscles and joints were stiff, and she had to help her legs off the arms of the chair. They had almost gone to sleep from being stuck in that position. The other two had not even noticed she was moving.

As Veronica's mind gained a better grip on reality, she realised that Seth's hand was hidden by the draping cloth of Polly's dress. She could see it undulating on her behind. The other hand was not in view, but it was not too hard to guess Polly's tits were getting a good massage.

Tentatively, Veronica pushed herself to her feet, keeping one hand on the chair. The shift in angle made her breasts move, and they ached. Even in the dim light she could see they were marked where Seth had crushed them. That memory did not please her so much; had Polly not considered how strong Seth was? Or the size of his hands?

The other memories, however, were very pleasant, and Veronica felt herself warming up just thinking about the way Seth's finger had felt inside her. It made her look forward to experimentation with the carrots.

Polly made a guttural sound as she mashed her face into Seth's. Veronica realised Seth's arm had moved and was no longer at Polly's bum. He was practising his lesson.

Veronica padded silently across the carpet, though she was not sure they would have noticed if she had been wearing cowbells. Carefully, she made a start on the buttons running down the back of Polly's dress. When she had undone a dozen and reached the maid's shoulder blades, she pulled the two sides apart and kissed the hot bare skin beneath. She gently bit Polly's neck, making the girl rear back.

Peeping over Polly's shoulder, Veronica could see she was right about Seth's other hand, squeezing Polly's tits through the layers of cloth. Polly was enjoying it, but it cannot have been very satisfying for Seth. She looked into his face and held his eyes for a moment—he was still mazed by the feelings aroused in him. He would need release too, but it was Polly's turn now.

Veronica went back to unbuttoning. It seemed to take an age, and was made more difficult because Polly was gyrating her hips on Seth's hand, and the rucked-up dress material was harder to deal with. Eventually she succeeded and pulled both sides wide apart, revealing Polly's pale skin and the white of her bloomers and camisole. Polly did not resist as Veronica pulled the sleeve first from one arm and, walking round, the other.

Finally she was able to drag the heavy dress from between the two and toss it to one side. She grabbed the hem of the camisole and pulled it up—but she couldn't raise her arms high enough. Polly whipped it from her head and went back to kissing Seth as if Veronica wasn't even there.

Polly had one leg up and over Seth's leg, spreading her thighs so he had easy access between her legs. Her opposite arm was now behind his head and holding his face to hers. Veronica closed in on her lover so her naked body pressed against her back. She slipped her right arm round and grabbed Polly's breast, taking over from Seth. She squeezed it gently and rolled the nipple in her hand. Polly groaned into Seth's mouth.

Veronica could have reached Polly's nubbin, but let Seth carry on there. Instead, she slipped her other hand under Polly's body and let her fingers stroke the girl's pussy. Polly's gyrations became more extreme, and the motion kept pulling Veronica's arm and shoulder which was not comfortable.

She pulled her hands back and gave the entwined bodies a hard shove. Seth toppled over backwards onto the bed, pulling Polly with him. Veronica stepped forward and slipped her hand back between Polly's legs; she slipped her thumb into the raging furnace of Polly's body—and was rewarded by another groan. Veronica could feel Seth's fingers rubbing Polly's nubbin lightly—the lesson had been learnt. The girl must be going as crazy as Veronica had.

That meant she would accept anything, and Veronica was not beyond a little petty revenge of her own. Keeping her left thumb moving in and out of Polly's pussy hole, Veronica wetted her other thumb and placed it in the groove of her lover's bum, resting gently on her anus.

Polly pushed back and the thumb pressed harder. The girl's breathing was fast and ragged, punctuated by grunts and moans. She was no longer kissing Seth; by now the only thing she cared about was her own body and the eruption of her lust.

"Hard, Seth!" said Veronica.

Polly was almost lifted into the air as he applied pressure to her nubbin. Polly squealed and rocked harder and harder against Veronica's thumbs. On the third stroke, the rear one popped inside Polly's bum. The girl had the momentary presence of mind to scream into Seth's armpit as she came.

Her body lost all its coordination as she tried to push and pull at the same time. Veronica felt the repeated spasms of her muscles in both holes, clenching and releasing. Polly clawed for breath as she panted. Veronica pushed her thumbs in hard again, and was rewarded by a second set of contractions. Polly pounded Seth's chest with her fist and whimpered into the counterpane. She came a third time, but more weakly, then collapsed onto Seth's chest.

Veronica extracted her thumb from Polly's pussy and then, very gently, pulled the other from her bum. Polly gave a disappointed grunt. Veronica resisted making a comment. Now was not the time.

Seth deserved his reward for being such a good student. Veronica wondered how many other men had spent an evening bringing two women to paroxysm without forcing himself on them.

She poked Polly's right buttock.

"What?"

"Seth's turn."

"You do it."

"I will, but you're going to help."

The response was a petulant grunt.

After giving Polly a sideways push so she rolled off Seth, Veronica applied herself to Seth's belt and managed to get it undone. Then she undid the buttons at the front and exposed his prick. It was in that partially excited state she had seen before. But the trousers were getting in the way. She was about to ask him to do it when she had an idea.

"Put your feet in the air," she said. It was a testament to his physical strength that he simply raised them up, without any seeming effort. He still had his socks on. Veronica pushed his legs so he rolled back and she was able to extract the trousers from under his bum, then pull them right off. She decided not to get involved with his socks. They could stay.

"Put your feet on the end of the bed, legs apart." This wouldn't have worked on her parents' bed, but now she had complete and easy access to his balls and prick. The angle was different to before, but she knew what she had to do. One hand cupped his ball sack and gently manipulated it, as she felt the egg-shaped lumps inside. His prick grew larger and harder in moments. She smiled and, with the other hand, began to stroke it up and down.

He had been trying to keep his head up to see what she was doing, but it was too much of a strain and he thumped flat. It seemed he didn't know what to do with his hands, but his left one searched around for Polly and found one of her breasts, which he kneaded gently. She made a gentle purring noise, then turned so her face was also towards his nether region. Veronica watched Seth's hand disappear between her legs.

Now Seth began to move his hips just the way Polly had done, as if he were driving his prick into the deep warmth of someone's pussy. She wasn't going to let him do that to her, and she was sure Polly wouldn't want it, so Veronica leaned forwards and took the glistening end of his prick in her mouth. It was awkward, and she knew she wouldn't be able to maintain it for long, but the way his prick expanded even more made her think she might not have to: he had had over an hour of unsatisfied stimulation.

His skin was soft and she used her tongue to stroke it, above and below. She tasted the clear liquid that he generated, which was salty but not unpleasant. She continued to massage his balls while moving her hand up and down. His prick twitched and he grunted.

Veronica opened her eyes and saw Polly leaning on Seth's stomach with her face mere inches from her own. She released Seth's cock and gave Polly a quick kiss. She had intended it to be quick, but Polly leaned in to it and let her mouth open. Veronica's tongue, which moments before had been probing Seth's prick, dived into Polly's mouth and the girl sucked her tongue as if it was a little cock.

They broke the kiss as Polly groaned with lust. Seth's fingers must be doing a good job on her, Veronica thought. At that moment, Polly gasped and her eyes widened then closed.

Veronica went back to Seth's cock and took the head into her mouth again. This time she started to suck, which elicited another loud noise from the back of Seth's throat.

Whether it was because she was sensitive to the problem of Seth being noisy, or simply that she wanted more stimulation of her own, Polly pushed herself up into a kneeling position—Veronica saw Seth's hand hard at work between her legs—threw one leg over his head, pulled the leg of her bloomers to one side and sat down on his face.

Veronica couldn't see Polly's face, but her hips were moving back and forth; at the same time, Seth's hip gyrations gathered speed. She left off playing with his ball sack and used both hands on the shaft as he pumped in and out of her mouth—she had to lift her head slightly to stop him hitting her throat.

The bed began a rhythmical squeak, but Veronica didn't care, her world focused on the dick in her mouth, and her hands pumping it in time to his own movements. Again, and again, harder and harder, faster and faster. She felt his muscles tense; he thrust hard once more and first her hands felt the spasms, then her mouth was invaded by his ejaculate. Again and again and again. He paused as if catching his breath—though Polly was still riding him hard. She took a moment to swallow. Then again and again and again. It was too much and it leaked out around his prick, though she swallowed as fast as she could. Again. He seemed to lose his strength and all the energy was gone from him.

He went limp, though his member remained solid in her firm grip. She managed to get everything down, and licked the glistening remains from his softening prick.

She was glad to see how it ended this time. Then Polly froze and whimpered as she suppressed her scream of pleasure at her fourth episode of paroxysm in such a short space of time. Then she slumped forward along Seth's body and gave Veronica a kiss.

"So that's what it tastes like," she said. "I suppose you could get used to it."

Veronica felt very stiff all of a sudden, and her legs were tired. She had been stooped over the whole time. She pushed herself back and watched as Polly lay her head down in Seth's crotch, her cheek nestled against his now soft prick.

"I hope you haven't suffocated him."

"I can feel him breathing on my thigh."

"Alive, Mistress Nika," he said.

She peered at the clock. "It's half past eleven. We need to sleep."

"I'll get out of thar hair, Mistress Nika."

"I haven't got you in my hair, this time," said Veronica. "I think I swallowed it all."

vii

Tuesday morning. Thirteen days to the wedding. Fourteen to their trip to Brighton Airfield and a flyer to Switzerland. Thirteen and a half to her wedding night. And this morning it seemed as if every muscle in her body was aching. Although she could not help but smile at how successfully her idea with Seth had turned out.

She was also very pleased at the way Polly had joined in. Although, perhaps that was not quite the correct choice of words. Polly had not 'joined in', she had taken control. Just thinking about it stirred up Veronica's lust, even though she was far too tired to do anything about it.

The girl in question was snoring gently on the other side of the bed, her blonde hair a tangled mess on the pillow. After Seth had managed to collect himself (and his clothes), he had left the way he had come in.

The timing had worked perfectly. She had been so obsessed with doing everything in the morning, just because that had been the way it had all started. All she had to do was broaden her ideas.

There had been plenty of broadening last night. When Polly had Seth push his finger into her, that had been so ... *exciting*. She let her hand descend between her legs and lightly ran her fingers through her hair. Her other hand went to her breast, which was when the lust went away. They really hurt.

Veronica slid from between the sheets and padded across to the mirror. There were four bruises on the top of each of her breasts where his fingers had dug in, and one below for the thumb. Her lover definitely had a vein of cruelty running through her, not much perhaps, but every now and then it would show itself.

She walked back to the other side of the bed.

"Look at my tits."

"They're lovely," came the sleepy voice from under the covers.

"No, I mean, look."

"What you talking about?"

"Sit up and look."

Yawning, Polly pushed her way up to lean against the pillows, stared blearily in the direction of Veronica's chest, and then rubbed her eyes. And stared again.

"Oh gawd."

"You did that."

"Seth did it."

"You told him to, and they really hurt."

Polly looked contrite and, with her hair sticking out as if she'd been dragged through a hedge backwards, innocent and sweet.

"He's a gardener, he works with his hands all day. He's very strong."

"Perhaps you should show him then, so he doesn't do it again."

"I can't do that, he'd be mortified and wouldn't trust himself to touch a woman again. I might tell him to be more careful, but I won't show him the damage."

"Can I kiss them better?" said Polly with a sly grin.

"It's Tuesday. Breakfast at nine, lessons from ten until four. While I'm doing that you can be collecting magazines, and send for catalogues from all the best shops, and the Army & Navy Stores. We need to select my trousseau, and new clothes for you, buy the luggage we'll be needing, travelling clothes, and also see whether there's a Bradshaw's Guide for Switzerland."

"Is that all?"

"No, later this evening we will need to have a knife so we can clean those carrots."

"Are you sure you want to do that?"

"We can practice our artistic skills; we know what a man's thing looks like, so we can fashion several sizes and I can see if I can accommodate them. I want to make sure that there is no problem on my wedding night."

Polly pulled a face.

"What?"

"I don't know."

"You think it won't work? My plan last night worked, and—" she leaned down and gave Polly a kiss, "—you were wonderful."

Polly looked embarrassed. "I'm not sure what came over me—and I ended up hurting you."

Veronica shook her head. "It was amazing, and so much fun. I'd love to do it again."

"You liked me treating you badly?"

"Well, I wouldn't want it all the time, but every now and then perhaps."

She fetched the sheet that Lawrence Slack had supplied with information about the trip. The flyer, which was a regular scheduled flight to Geneva, would depart Brighton at ten in the morning and arrive three hours later, then there was another flight to Locarno, and a shorter trip to *Monte Verità*.

"The mountain of truth?"

"What?" said Polly.

"We're going to a place called the Mountain of Truth."

"That doesn't sound good for us."

Veronica laughed. "Just a name. I wonder what's there."

——◆——

AFTER BREAKFAST, POLLY left and headed into Mayfield to collect as many magazines as she could find, and see if she could nab an Army & Navy catalogue.

It wasn't time for her lessons, but Veronica went to the library anyway and searched out the copy of Bacon's World Atlas, 1905. There was not much detail on the map of Switzerland and Northern Italy, but she located Geneva, then Locarno, but there was no evidence of a Mount Verità. Although there was a Mount Monescia just across the river from Ascona. The scale just wasn't good enough.

She changed pages to the map of Western Europe, which included the southern part of the British Isles. She put her finger on where Versyns Hall was located, traced a line to Brighton, and then across the English Channel and France, ending up in Geneva, then the rest of the journey.

It was unreal. She had never expected to even travel to London. In her entire life she had never gone beyond the local village of Seven Ashes until that point.

The clock on the mantle chimed ten.

She put away the atlas as Mr Plumley bustled into the room. Just as some workmen started up hammering upstairs somewhere. Her tutor seemed surprised to see her there, although she often preceded him, and stared around.

"Where is the maid?"

"Polly's gone into Mayfield to collect some things."

"Perhaps we should have someone else in to chaperone you."

"I won't tell if you don't, Mr Plumley."

She watched the effort involved in making the decision cross his face until finally he shut the door. She went and settled herself at the table they worked on, and he sat opposite her as usual. He pulled several folders from his briefcase along with his old and ink-stained pen-case.

"Are you not concerned I will try to take advantage of you, Miss Clifford-Hughes?"

"Of course not, sir. I know you are a gentleman."

He cleared his throat and looked down in embarrassment.

"Your preferences are always performed with respect, and you have never demanded more from me," she said. "That is why I consider you to be a gentleman, even if others might judge you otherwise."

"That is very generous, Miss Clifford-Hughes."

"How can it be otherwise?" she said. "Every day I am judged for my physical deformity by people who are oblivious to the pain I suffer because of it and the harm they do by taking that attitude. If I were to act in a similar manner it would make me as bad as they are."

"Your study of the American Pragmatists was not in vain."

She smiled though she knew he wouldn't see it. He still never looked at her face, only at her bare feet when they were available. "I think they have a valid viewpoint, and I find it more pleasant than being consigned to hell for being a monster."

"I do not argue religion, Miss Clifford-Hughes."

"Do you think we're both condemned, you for your peccadillo, and me for letting you indulge it?" *Never mind all the other things I've done.*

"Are you asking for my opinion on the matter? Is that not one for a member of the clergy?"

"I'd like to know how you balance it in your life, Mr Plumley; perhaps it will help in mine."

He made a sort of agreeable grunt and stared down at the desk in front of him. "It seems to me a person's choice of religious belief is that which provides them either with the greatest justification for their actions, or the most criticism. Depending on their nature."

"Isn't that very cynical? Do you not believe in anything then?"

He gave a shrug which was the most natural thing she had ever seen from him. It was so human, it was quite unlike him. "It is not that I don't believe there is something beyond," he said, "but I gave up the idea there was something to worship a long time ago."

"Except feet?"

"Quite so, as you say. Except feet."

"I—" She stopped. She wanted to talk about her relationship with Polly, as if she wanted him to tell her that everything was fine, and what she was doing was perfectly normal.

"Miss Clifford-Hughes?"

Somehow the words stuck in her breast, she could not even persuade them to reach as far as her throat.

"I wondered if you know anything of Mount Verità in Switzerland."

"The mountain of truth? A curious name, but no, I have not heard of it."

"Edwin is going to take me there for our honeymoon."

"You will get an opportunity to view the world from a great height then."

"Yes, we are taking a flyer from Brighton."

"Ah good, then perhaps we should examine the history of the Faraday device, and the influence it has had on society since its discovery ... when?"

"I'm sorry?"

"When was the Faraday device invented, Miss Clifford-Hughes?"

"1843."

"Very good."

⎯⎯◉⎯⎯

THE WHOLE OF VERSYNS Hall echoed with the banging of hammers and the shouts of workmen. It made concentration difficult, so when Polly knocked on the library door at half past twelve, Veronica was ready for the break. The effect of the antigravity machine on society was not as interesting a subject as Veronica might have hoped; even such noble endeavours as the relief of Lucknow by Faraday-lifted heavy artillery (and pulled by elephants) in 1857 failed to capture her imagination.

After all, they had moved far beyond big guns pulled by pachyderms. The Royal Navy now possessed huge flying machines mounting more artillery in one vessel than the entire East India Company could have provided.

Following Polly, carrying what looked to be a very heavy bag, came luncheon.

While they ate, Polly showed Veronica all the magazines she had managed to acquire, and the heaviest item, one thousand five hundred pages of the Army & Navy stores catalogue.

Then Mrs Jenkins strode in without knocking. "There's some men with a machine they claim should go in your parents' bedroom. Kindly explain?"

Veronica blinked. "Already?"

"What is it?"

"My Faraday device." Veronica recovered from her shock quickly and could not prevent the smile from spreading across her face.

"Don't be absurd. They put them in automobiles, trains, and aeroplanes."

"They've been used for the ballet," said Veronica, "and they have them in fairs on some of the rides. And they are used therapeutically."

"I beg your pardon?"

"It's for my back," said Veronica. "It means I can sleep easier at night."

It seemed Mrs Jenkins did not know what to say. So Veronica continued. "My future husband agreed that a therapeutic Faraday device would be ideal, and he has paid for it."

"I was not informed."

"No, I'm sorry. I did not expect it to arrive so fast."

"Well, since you seem to know all about it, Miss Clifford-Hughes, you can deal with it." And with that she stalked to the door and held it open. "You will find them at the delivery entrance." She left, almost, but not quite, slamming it.

"It's here," Veronica breathed, and all because Seth had suggested it. She looked at her tutor. "Would you assist me in supervising the installation of the device?"

"Of course, Miss Clifford-Hughes. I find that I am also very interested to see this machine." He tidied away his papers.

THE DELIVERY MEN, FIVE of them, were drinking mugs of tea in the kitchen; she could see them clearly as they descended the steps, but as she reached floor level, no longer able to raise her eyes high enough, the room went silent, and she knew they were all staring at her hump. She could hear the kitchen staff bustling about. The smell suggested they had some sort of roast for the evening meal. That in turn reminded her she needed to talk to Cook, and to her betrothed.

One thing at a time. Nobody said anything. Clearly, it was up to her.

"Who's in charge of the Faraday device delivery?"

A long pause. A chair scraped. "Pardon, miss, that'd be me. Brian Plessey, Plessey's Weight Reducing Applications. Is Edwin Jameson here? The house-keeper gave us short shrift, I have to say."

"The Honourable Edwin Jameson is my future husband, Mr Plessey, but this is my house, and the device is for me."

"Order says it's for installation in a bedroom?"

THEY SHOWED BRIAN PLESSEY the location of the master bedroom, and then the project supervisor, Mr McCloud, was fetched. He had a set of keys and knew the easiest way to get the necessary electricity from the cabling that had already been installed.

"We'll have to take up some floorboards around the bed," said Mr Plessey as they stood by the window. "To do that we'll shift the bed over there and move the carpet. Once it's done you won't even know it."

Polly fetched her mistress a chair, and Veronica sat while the men went about their business. She was impressed with their efficiency. They must have done it many times before.

The bed, even though it was quite large and had a cast-iron frame, was lifted and moved to block the entrance to the bathroom. She could hear the men making comments about the luxurious nature of the plumbing. She smiled; it was indeed very commodious, and she was looking forward to bathing with Polly, and perhaps Seth, possibly even her husband.

A very muscular fellow knelt down right in front of her to roll the carpet. She could smell his sweat and, through his shirt, could see his muscles working. She took a moment to imagine him without his clothes, using Seth's body as a model, and was pleased with the image she conjured.

Polly murmured in her ear. "You shouldn't stare at the help like that."

Veronica smiled.

The fellow rolled the carpet back.

"Will the machine sit on the bare boards, or on the carpet?" Veronica asked loudly, and was surprised at herself again. It hadn't been that long ago that she would have been terrified to be in the company of so many men, let alone speak to them.

The man rolling the carpet did not reply, but Mr Plessey spoke from somewhere near the door. "We just need to sort out the electrics, miss. Once that's done, we'll put the carpet back. The therapeutic Faraday has castors which lock off. It won't damage the floor, the locks prevent it moving, but with them off, it can be slid out for cleaning."

"I see."

"The next bit's a bit boring, miss, if you want to do something else?"

"I'll stay."

And she was glad she did, because it was only moments later that one of the men who moved in after the carpet was out of the way said, "That's handy, these floorboards are loose." She watched him pull up two short lengths and then, "What's this?"

He reached down into the gap and extracted a large card box, about four inches deep, a foot wide, and a little more than that in length. Although he'd lifted it with one hand, it drooped as if it was quite heavy.

"What you got, Charlie?"

He put it down and slipped off the lid. "Picture album. Very fancy cover."

Veronica stared at it. Her parents had placed a picture album in a secret place beneath the floorboards? It was not that she cared about them—they certainly didn't care about her—but she had so little knowledge of them that anything would be interesting.

"I'll take it," she said, trying to sound relaxed, and held out her hands.

"'Course, miss." He dropped the lid back over the top and it slid into place.

Polly went over and took it from him. She held it at arm's length and then sneezed. "It's really dusty," she said. "I'll take it to your room, miss, and wipe it down."

It was a good idea, but Veronica was loath to let it out of her sight. "Yes, all right, you might as well leave it in my room. I'll look at it later. Come straight back." She was desperate that Polly shouldn't look inside, but there was no way to say it easily without attracting attention. As it was, Polly gave her a funny look before leaving the room.

Mr McCloud sat on the edge of her parents' bed, poring over a book of plans. "The electrician took up the boards by the door to put in the cabling, so we need to get the wire from there to that hole." Mr Plessey stood beside him. "What way do the joists run?"

Charlie stuck his head down the hole. "To the door."

"That's a bit of luck, otherwise we'd have to take everything up."

Moments later the men were at the floorboards with tools for levering. It was almost as if they were killing the floor, as the nails screeched and wood groaned. Within a few minutes it looked as if an anarchist's bomb had taken the place apart.

One of Plessey's other men started working with the wires. He cut into them, then spliced in his own. Veronica had an idea of what was going on, because Mr Plumley had instructed her in the ways of electricity, and channelling it through wires.

"What's your power unit?" said Mr Plessey as he kept an eye on the work being done.

Mr McCloud looked distracted and just said, "Ferranti. One of the large domestic generators."

Mr Plessey nodded his approval. "Good choice."

The wiring was completed quickly and the floorboards nailed noisily back in place.

"Where would you like the control unit, miss?" said Mr Plessey. As he approached, she lost sight of his head until she could only see his waist to his feet. It was difficult to deal with people properly when you couldn't look at them.

"What is it like?"

"Well, it doesn't fit with the room's decor, I'm afraid. This unit is usually used in hospitals and such."

He crouched down so his face was within her eyeline, and placed a machine in her lap. The base was solid dark wood, with controls mounted on it. There was a large brass switch, and a dial with a rotating pointer controlled by a brass knob.

"The switch turns the field on and off, while the knob adjusts the level of gravity reduction."

She frowned. "I understood a Faraday grid could only be on and off," she said. "Some of the bigger vessels allow sections of grid to be disabled to reduce the overall effect."

The man looked surprised, and then grinned. "Well, you know your Faradays, miss, but this one's different. Latest designs from Tesla and Rutherford at Cambridge. They managed to make ones that are adjustable."

"What's the efficiency?" she said.

His grin widened. "Very good, miss, you certainly learnt your lessons. Maximum rating at sixty-seven percent."

"Not seventy-three? That's the best."

"The variable adjustment does have that drawback, miss, but what's six percent?"

"In my case, about half a stone, Mr Plessey, but I expect it will be fine. I won't miss it." The one on the tube train when she'd visited London had been full efficiency, she guessed, while the taxi had been almost pointless. She would be happy at sixty-seven percent. Losing two thirds of her weight would make a huge difference.

"Where would you recommend siting the control box, Mr Plessey?"

"On your husband's side of the bed."

"I am not yet married." *And he's not going to be sleeping with me.* It still made her angry.

"Oh well, whichever side you suggest then."

"Can it be moved?"

"We could make the wires long enough to stretch to both sides."

She smiled. "Well, since I cannot answer your question as yet, let's do that."

"A couple of things, miss. It's not recommended you stay in the field too much."

"How much is considered too much?"

"Not all the time."

"Is there a problem with it?" asked Veronica.

"Not the machine, no," said Mr Plessey, "but if a person doesn't exercise, their muscles become weak. Using a Faraday is like not exercising, so it's best to err on the side of caution."

"I'm only using it for sleeping." *And perhaps games with my lover.*

While they had been talking, Polly had returned, and the other men had been busy uncrating the machine parts in the hall outside. The device was brought through in pieces, but assembly went swiftly. Veronica could see it had been devised such that additional units could be added, or removed, both at the sides and the ends in order to match the size needed.

She presumed they had been given an estimate, but there was some measuring and adjustment. Each individual panel had its own cover to provide a smooth surface, and to protect the inner workings from dust and prying fingers. It was an excellent example of British design.

"This corner unit," said Mr Plessey, "that's the one that contains the cleverness. It drives all the other panels, so your control unit plugs in there. We connect the power thusly. And it's all ready to go."

At some point during the proceedings, Mr McCloud had left.

"Do you want to do the honours, miss?"

"What do you mean?"

"Sit on it."

She was struck by a strange wave of embarrassment; she could perform any lewd act, but she felt self-conscious about that simple act.

"I'm sorry, my back does not permit it."

"Fair enough."

He adjusted the knob so that it was at the lowest level, and flipped the switch. Nothing appeared to happen.

"Good," he said. "Charlie? Can you pop onto the platform then?"

The one called Charlie jumped up on the Faraday device and someone threw him a ball. He bounced it a couple of times and nodded to his boss.

Mr Plessey turned the dial slowly. Charlie kept bouncing the ball. He'd throw it down, let it fly up to head height, and then catch it as it fell.

At first nothing seemed to change, but as Mr Plessey increased the intensity, the ball flew higher on the bounce, and dropped more slowly, until it looked as if it were falling through molasses.

Then Charlie threw the ball gently towards the far wall. It flew from his hand in a high arc, moving impossibly slowly until it passed the edge of the device's effect, and then, once more under the full influence of gravity, it simply fell out of the air.

"That's working nicely," said Mr Plessey. Charlie waited until the power had been turned down and then off, before climbing from the grid. It took less than a minute for them to manhandle the bed back into position.

"And it's done," said Mr Plessey. One of his men came up with a clipboard and handed it to him. "Now if you can just sign the job off, miss, we'll tidy the stuff away and you can discover how much nicer your life will be with your very own Faraday grid."

He handed her the clipboard and she stared at it. There was a great deal of writing on it, the address and Edwin's name at the top, and a space for a signature at the bottom. She froze.

Mr Plumley shuffled over. "Just a moment, Miss Clifford-Hughes. Allow me."

He took it from her gently and she could hear him murmuring words. It took several minutes.

"That seems in order, Miss Clifford-Hughes. You can sign."

She wanted to scream that she was not in a position to sign, that she did not have the authority, that she would get into trouble—but instead she took his lovely fountain pen and wrote her name neatly in the space provided. She noticed there was a place for the date as well, so filled that in too.

Mr Plumley relieved her of the pen and clipboard, and handed the latter to Mr Plessey.

And then they were gone. Polly shut the door, and Veronica stood up.

Her very own Faraday device.

viii

The next couple of hours seemed interminable, and she found it very difficult to concentrate on the work Mr Plumley had prepared for her. More Latin so that she could read early translations of Greek philosophy. She wondered now if there really was any point in all this. They were trying to plough the same course in her studies, but her life had changed direction completely. They had done some work on housekeeping, and she had her Mrs Beeton book, but there was just too much in it.

As four o'clock approached, she decided it was something that needed confronting, and broke off from her conjugations and declensions.

"Why am I doing this?"

"W-what do you mean, Miss Clifford-Hughes?"

"I am about to become a married woman, and I'm conjugating words in a language nobody speaks, to read ancient translations of even earlier works that have no bearing on my future life."

"You do not f-feel this line of study is of v-value?"

"No, Mr Plumley, and with all due respect to your not inconsiderable knowledge, how will this help me with my future life?"

"A broad understanding of the world will assist you in your conversations when entertaining."

"I won't be entertaining."

"Your husband may require it."

She couldn't deny the truth of that. "Even so, I doubt the other wives will know any of this. I already know far more about science, philosophy, and art than anyone of my sex should."

A flicker of a frown went across his face, and Veronica was astounded. He became passionate about her feet when he had the opportunity, but she had never seen even the merest hint of emotion in the course of their studies. It wasn't until she had discovered his personal desire that he had even deigned to look at her.

"We do not live in the dark ages, Miss Clifford-Hughes. This is a new age of enlightenment. There are primitives in this world who would insist a woman is not the equal of man, that their minds cannot hold much in the way of facts. But you, Miss Clifford-Hughes, you if nothing else have proved that to be a lie."

She had never heard him utter anything so impassioned. Her breath was quite taken away. "Thank you, sir, but I am also a cripple. I will never be a beacon to light the world. However, I did not know you supported the suffrage movement."

He waved his hand dismissively. "I do not, though I may agree with their intentions. That, however, is not the point. You have not been in a position to deal with other women who are your equal; now is your opportunity."

"That may be so, though I doubt they will want to consort with one such as I, but it does not resolve my original concern: I do not think this line of study will be of any use to me."

He tensed. "Do you wish to dispense with my services? I would understand if you did. On the one hand you feel adult, and on the other, I understand you do not appreciate receiving my attentions the way I do giving them."

She paused. Did she want to stop the lessons? It was true that they occupied a great deal of time that might be used for other things. Such as bedding Polly and Seth. She gave her head a little shake. "No, sir, I do not, and please understand that while I might not enjoy your activities the way you do, Mistress Nika does like them in her own way." Having a man worshipping her feet was not unpleasant at all. "However, I think we must revise your syllabus and align my study with the activities I will be engaged in."

He nodded. "That seems an equitable approach. Perhaps if you would give me a list of subjects, I can prepare a course of study for each?"

"Photography, and the techniques for developing printed images from film. My future husband is installing a dark room, and we want to make sure our pictures come out well."

"That will be easy enough," he said. "And does have the benefit of having a practical side."

"I should brush up on my Italian for my honeymoon."

"The Swiss of the southern cantons do not speak a pure form of Italian," he said.

"Locarno is very close to the border with Italy. I think it will help."

"Of course, Miss Clifford-Hughes," he said. "Now that you are to be married and become a woman in your own right, I believe it is entirely proper that you should also take control of the course of your study. Unless you think your husband might object?"

Veronica sighed. "I think, Mr Plumley, that my future husband cares nothing for anything that does not directly impinge upon his life."

"Then I believe, Miss Clifford-Hughes, you have been blessed with a husband that many women would prefer."

———◦———

VERONICA AND POLLY retreated upstairs to her bedroom.

"Perhaps the situation resolves best for everyone, as Mr Plumley seems to think," Veronica said once they had the door closed and bolted. Going some way to blocking out the noise of the workmen. She looked at her bed with something resembling disgust. "I get my parents' bedroom, you can have the room attached. My husband sleeps in another room completely, which gives us all the time we need together."

Polly came up behind her, put her arms around Veronica's waist, then kissed her on the neck. Veronica was acutely aware that Polly's cheek rested against her hump.

"I think I'd like to move today," she said. "I don't want to sleep in here another night."

"Is that appropriate?"

"Honestly, Polly, I don't care." Then she broke down in tears. "I have been in pain for almost my entire life. And with a chance of respite, even for a short time, lying a short distance away, why should I wait?"

"You'll have to tell Mrs Jenkins."

"I know." She sniffed and wiped her eyes. "Start now, and get someone to help you. I will confront the beast in its lair."

———◦———

VERONICA GOT NO ANSWER at Mrs Jenkins' door. She could be any-where, but Veronica wondered if the housekeeper might be 'in conference' with Mr Laughton. It took her less than a minute to reach his door at the back of the building and have her suspicions confirmed by the regular grunt-ing and panting. She was tempted to try the door, but he would have locked it.

It occurred to her this might work to her advantage. If he behaved the same way as when she had spied on them, the steward would finish and de-part, leaving Mrs Jenkins lying across his desk in a state of *dishabille* and un-satisfied arousal.

She hid herself on a flight of stairs, for servants use, a short distance from his door, and listened to the sounds of sexual activity. Just as she had when she had been lifted by Seth to the window, she felt her own lust rising. The voluminous folds of her dress prevented easy access to her quim, so she made do with gently squeezing her breasts and dreaming it was Seth driving his prick between her legs. She was so far gone in her imagination, it took her a moment to recognise the sound of the door shutting and heavy male foot-steps moving away.

She took a deep breath and stepped down into the passage. She hurried along, as lightly as she could, and grabbed the door handle. This would be a very difficult moment, but she hoped Mrs Jenkins was still in a vulnerable position.

To Veronica's relief, she was still there, across the desk with her skirts pulled up over her back. Her pale rear-end completely exposed and, at the apex of her thin legs, the dark hair matted with sweat and Mr Laughton's seed. Veronica held down the lust that threatened to take control of her be-haviour—right at that moment she would happily bring Mrs Jenkins to her paroxysm.

But she must focus on what her own purposes.

The housekeeper did not move, but she spoke. "Did you forget some-thing?" Her voice seemed hurt and bitter, and why shouldn't it? The man left her unsatisfied every time he fucked her.

"I don't know why you let him do that to you."

Mrs Jenkins jumped and made to rise, but Veronica let the part of her that was Mistress Nika do the talking. "Stay where you are, Jenkins. Do not cover yourself. Do not get up."

The woman lay there, but her hand crept towards her skirts.

"I said leave it!"

The hand stopped moving. Veronica moved to a position directly behind Mrs Jenkins.

"Do you finish yourself off afterwards?"

"What?"

"Bring yourself off? Frig yourself."

"That's a sin!"

"But you'll fornicate out of wedlock?"

Mrs Jenkins suddenly seemed to be breathing harder and was making a strange noise. Veronica realised the woman was crying; it came from her throat and was more like an animal in pain.

Veronica reached over and pulled at the woman's skirts so they fell and covered her nakedness. "Get up." As Mrs Jenkins complied, Veronica fished out her own kerchief and handed it to her.

There were a couple of chairs by the window.

"Go and sit over there."

The alcoholic drinks were on the sideboard, but enclosed in a tantalus to prevent the servants from stealing a quick one when cleaning the room. There was a jug of water, however, so Veronica poured a glass and took it to Mrs Jenkins.

She was dabbing her eyes and seemed grateful for the drink.

"You shouldn't let him do that to you."

"What would you know?"

Veronica hesitated, and decided the complete truth would probably not be a good choice. "I know it's wrong for anyone to treat another like a plaything, merely for their own satisfaction."

"That's the world, little girl."

"You will refer to me as Miss Clifford-Hughes."

"Or what?"

"I'll dismiss you for fornicating with other members of staff, and without any references. You know how word travels."

Mrs Jenkins cleared her throat. "My apologies, Miss Clifford-Hughes."

"Thank you," she said. "Everyone knows what goes on between you and him. Even me. That's how I knew where to find you."

"I see."

"Honestly, Mrs Jenkins, I don't really care, although you could be a bit more discreet. If you want that man to fuck you—" the housekeeper flinched at the word but said nothing "—every other day, and leave you desperate each time, it has no bearing on me or my life, as long as the running of the household is not disturbed."

"I would never let it affect the house."

"Good. As I said before, if you want to resign in a few weeks that will be fine by me, and I will give you any references you need."

Mrs Jenkins took another sip of water. "Was that all you wanted, Miss Clifford-Hughes?"

"I wanted to inform you I am moving into my parents' bedroom today."

The housekeeper looked as if she was going to protest, but then simply said, "As you wish, miss."

———⟶●———

POLLY WAS PUTTING AWAY Veronica's clothes, but looked up as she came in.

"You're still alive."

Veronica turned the key in the door. Her encounter with Mrs Jenkins had been exhausting. "She was amenable to the idea."

"Really?"

"She's planning on leaving. I don't think she really cares."

"Leaving?"

"Don't tell the other staff, it may never happen."

Veronica sat on the bed. It was soft and not to her taste, but it was much bigger than her own, and it had its new addition.

"Are you going to try it?" said Polly.

"I'm scared."

Polly laughed. "What of?"

"That, after all this, it doesn't do what I hoped."

"It will."

"It might not."

"Not knowing won't help."

Veronica sighed. Polly finished putting items into one of the drawers, then came over.

"You get comfortable on the bed, I'll operate the machine."

"You know what to do?"

"I saw the man showing you. Doesn't take a clever-boots like you."

Veronica turned round and crawled across the soft surface until she could lay on her side with her head on a pillow facing Polly. "Ready."

Polly looked down at the brass controls, and Veronica got the impression she wasn't as confident as she had pretended, but then the maid reached out and clicked the big brass switch.

Before, the room had been full of people and there was noise from outside. Now, it was getting on for six, and the workmen had gone back to their little camp in the grounds. Where Veronica had assumed the machine was silent, she now heard a very low buzz.

"Feel anything?" said Polly.

"You need to turn the thing."

"I know, but I was just wondering."

"Nothing yet."

Polly took a deep breath and turned back to the controls. Her hand grabbed the knob and she turned it. The sound of it clicking seemed to echo round the room.

"Oh," said Veronica. She had experienced a Faraday device only twice, but she recognised it now. A feeling of lightness, a bit like floating in a bath.

"More?" said Polly.

"More."

The dial clicked again and the feeling of lightness increased—or was it that the heaviness decreased? Veronica had a vague sensation as if she was falling. "All the way!"

The clicking accelerated until it stopped completely.

Every ounce of tension was gone from Veronica's body. Her back still ached, but it was so much less intense.

Sitting on the edge of the bed, she wiped a tear from her eye.

ix

"If we keep the key in the lock, nobody else can open it," said Polly. "At least not without us noticing." The outside light was fading and her parents' bedroom—*her* bedroom—was dimly lit from the windows.

"What about your room?" said Veronica.

"Same, it has a lock."

After Veronica had stopped crying, Polly had cleaned her up and dressed her for dinner. They had gone down at seven, and were back in the bedroom at eight.

"We have electric light in here," said Veronica and walked over to the door. "Are you ready?"

If Polly nodded, Veronica couldn't make it out in the twilight. So she put her finger on the brass switch and pressed it down. It gave a click and the room was flooded in light.

Veronica almost cried again—no more candles—but her eyes were drawn to the box containing the photographic album, sitting on the dresser. Polly must have brought it when she was moving their things. It was time to see her parents again.

She went over, lifted the lid, and extracted the heavy book. The workman had been right, it was a very ornate cover carved from wood. The patterns were leaves and twigs with the occasional bud.

She hefted it over to the occasional table and drew up the chair.

"Do you want me to see?" said Polly.

"Of course, my love."

Polly smiled and gave Veronica a kiss on the cheek before sitting beside her. The bright bulb above the centre of the room illuminated everything clearly.

Veronica opened the book to the first sheet of images.

"Oh my," said Polly.

It was Veronica's mother lying on the very bed in this room. She was propped up by cushions and was completely naked. Her hips were angled towards the camera, and her left leg bent, so the hair between her legs, and the hidden lips, were quite visible too.

Veronica felt she was looking at herself. Even her mother's breasts were the same, full, with the wide dark area surrounding the nipples, but she had no hump, of course.

"You're just like her," Polly breathed.

"I'm nothing like her," said Veronica. She wanted to close the album now; she didn't want to see what her body might have looked like if she had not been crippled, but it was a compulsion. Her fingers moved to the edge of the page, and she turned it.

Four more photographs, all of her mother in different positions on the bed; only one of them failed to capture her nethers. One thing was certain: her mother was enjoying it. The smile on her face was not forced. The final picture on these pages had been taken from between her mother's widely spread legs, looking along her body.

"I suppose it's your father taking the pictures," said Polly, her voice tight, as if she was having trouble forming the words.

Veronica found she could only make an affirmative noise, almost as if she was clearing her throat and nothing more.

"I wonder where they got the pictures developed."

That was indeed a more interesting question. They had taken the film somewhere else and it had been turned into these images. Veronica did not know her parents well enough to know if that was something her father would do, but somehow she doubted it. Her father would have paid someone to make them.

Someone else had seen these pictures. Her mother was as shameless as Veronica. Perhaps Darwin was right and these were all inherited traits.

"Your pussy's like hers too."

"Could you please stop saying how much like my mother I am?"

"Oh, sorry."

Veronica gave Polly's hand a squeeze to show she wasn't angry. She took a deep breath and turned the next page.

"Oh!" said Polly.

The sequence on this page involved an object. Veronica could not make out exactly what it was, but she knew enough about Seth's prick to see this was an artificial one, although longer and thicker. In the first picture her mother was licking the end while looking into the camera, and so seeming to look at the viewer. At Veronica.

In the next three, her mother had pulled one knee up to her chest and had pushed the prick into her pussy hole. In each successive shot it was deeper, until at least half of it had disappeared by the final picture.

Veronica's body betrayed her, and the sight was stirring the lust that slumbered between her thighs. She wished it would stay quiet, but she could only imagine that phallus being pushed into her, and that could only result in pleasure. That was why she had got the carrots.

She felt the touch of Polly's lips against her cheek—cool against the fire in her flesh. Then the maid nuzzled Veronica's neck, kissing and biting while Veronica stared at her mother impaling herself on the fake prick.

"Please don't," said Veronica in barely a whisper. "I can't."

"You want to."

"Yes."

"Then do it."

"It's my mother."

"I know."

"It's not fair. She should not have that power over me."

Polly stopped and wrapped her arms around Veronica. "I'm sorry, all I can see is you."

Warding off any further comment, Veronica turned to the next page. Her mother naked on the bed again, but now on all fours with her bum in the air. That was the first picture; the next three showed a naked man half on the bed, reaching across and playing with her pussy, then with three fingers inserted into her. In the final picture his face was buried between her legs.

"That's not your father," said Polly.

"No."

Veronica turned the page quickly to reveal just what she expected. Her mother was in the same position, and the man, younger than her father with a longer nose, was fucking her.

Cuckoo in the nest. That's what Mrs Jenkins used to say about her.

Veronica stared at the man with his prick buried in her mother's body, probably spilling his seed into her. He might be Veronica's father, and if her mother had done it with him, perhaps she did it with others too. Perhaps her mother did not even know who Veronica's father was. Perhaps no one knew.

She turned the page.

The bed covers were twisted as if a lot of time had passed. The man she knew as her father lay naked on the bed, playing with her mother's tits while she used her mouth on him, and the other man was there, still fucking her from behind.

Veronica slammed the book shut. "Put it away, Polly. Hide it."

"Don't you want to see the rest?"

"No, Polly, it's just you who wants to see what else is in there to stoke your own desires," she said, her voice heavy with weariness. "I just want to go to bed."

Polly disappeared into the dressing room and emerged a short time later. "I put it on a high shelf under some hat boxes. You won't be able to see it."

And I won't be able to reach it because I can't stretch my arms high.

Polly helped her undress. Veronica kept looking around at the room: it was so strange to be sleeping here after all the years of being in the other room, and to know her mother fucked a man she did not know right here. Unnatural.

Once she was in her nightgown, Veronica slipped between the sheets, but sat up with her back supported by pillows. It wasn't cold, of course, and the windows were open, but she felt better if she was under a sheet.

Polly stripped quickly. She preferred to be naked. Veronica smiled as she watched her lover's body under the bright electric light—then she laughed at herself. She had sworn she wouldn't use candles once she had electric but the light was too bright. Candlelight was better because it made the shadows deeper and the curves more rounded. Perhaps if they could have another smaller electric light at a lower level, it might make the room more homely.

"What you looking at?" said Polly, a little coquettish smile on her face. She covered her tits with her arm and her nethers with her other hand, as if she was embarrassed.

"I'm looking at the most beautiful girl in the world," said Veronica, though her heart was still heavy.

Polly grinned and climbed into bed beside her.

"You have to put out the light," said Veronica, and looked pointedly at the switch by the door.

The room went completely dark when Polly threw the switch. There was the gentle pad of footsteps, then a slight metallic bang. "Ow."

"My future husband did not pay attention to the placement of the light switch," said Veronica, but her eyes were adjusting. The walls were ghostly grey, and Polly's pale skin made her a phantasm climbing into bed.

"We have a private marriage," said Polly. "You are my wife and I am yours."

"But which of us wears the trousers?"

"We share them."

Veronica shook her head and smiled even though she knew Polly could not see it.

"I'm going to switch on the Faraday now."

Polly grabbed her left breast.

"That's not helping."

Polly giggled and Veronica wished she was feeling as frivolous; today had been a good day until the picture album.

The control box was within reach on her side table. She made sure the knob was turned all the way to the left, and then reached a little further to switch it on. There was the hum again. She carefully adjusted the knob, hearing it click steadily.

Polly squealed and clutched her tighter as the reduction in weight became noticeable.

"Stop it, you're not a child, and that pinches."

Polly's grip loosened a little, and Veronica continued to increase the effect of the Faraday device. It was so strange, once more that feeling as if she was being supported in a bath of water. The bed springs pushed her up as her weight reduced. The strain on her back slipped away, although the ache only lessened.

Veronica let go of the control when she felt comfortable. Her hand was out beyond the field and, as she pulled it in, her skin felt as if it was being brushed by butterflies.

"How is it for you?" said Polly. Her voice shook a little, as if she was still very uncertain of the new sensation.

"My back still aches, though it's not so bad, but it's everything else. I did not even notice how much everything else hurt." Then she burst into tears again.

"What's wrong?"

Veronica tried to control herself enough to respond, but found it impossible. Her throat was choked with sobs and her eyes flooded, so what little light there was became nothing more than a grey blur.

And her nose was stuffed. Veronica sniffed loudly and swallowed a wedge of phlegm that became dislodged. Something was wrong. She pushed down on the bed to sit up, and launched herself in a low, slow, arc towards the end of the bed.

"Nika!"

Polly's hand caught her wrist and brought her flight to a halt. Veronica came down lightly on the counterpane. Everything was still a blur and she rubbed her fingers across her eyes, there was so much water there it was as if her tears had simply collected.

Of course they had. They had no weight so they just stayed put. And her phlegm piled up in her nose because there was not enough gravity to shift it. Swiftly, she pushed herself to the edge of the bed and off. She landed with the usual force of gravity on the carpet. Tears ran down her cheeks and she managed to clear her throat so she could breathe properly. All the aches across her body came back, this time she could feel each one of them.

"What happened, Nika?"

"Don't cry in a Faraday," said Veronica. She cleared her throat again and wiped her eyes with the sleeve of her nightdress.

"We don't have to use it."

"I'll be fine. I want to use it, it felt so good, so much better. I was just overcome by the relief and," she said, "it turns out crying when you're lying down in a Faraday is bad." She sniffed again. "Give me a moment."

Veronica took a deep breath and stared into the monochrome darkness of the room. Then glanced at the door to the dressing room. The day had been overwhelming in so many ways, but she was feeling better now. The shock of her parents' photographic album was waning, and she was almost tempted to continue going through it now. After all, they had electric light and could make the room as bright as day at any time of the night.

But the pictures could wait. Sleep, and her lover, would not. She gave her eyes and cheeks another wipe. Made sure that she was breathing easily, and turned back to the bed.

Moving through the edge of the field once more gave that tickling sensation, though she could not imagine what might cause it. She had to pull up her nightdress so she could crawl forward until every part of her, including her feet, were within the Faraday effect.

In the dim light, Polly waited, kneeling up with her delicate fair hair hanging around her shoulders, and her breasts delineated only by shadows. Veronica's tensions slipped away again as she closed on Polly, though her hump still prevented Veronica from raising her head, even if it did not hurt as much. Veronica reared up on her knees, then leaned forward with her hands on Polly's cool bare shoulders, and they kissed.

Veronica moved her hands down Polly's body until they could hook under the girl's behind. And with a feeling of strength she had never had, she lifted. Polly squealed and grabbed Veronica's head for balance as she went up.

One nipple brushed Veronica's cheek on the way up. Then Polly's knees got in the way, so Veronica tilted Polly backwards and she fell slowly. The bed was wide and Polly had been kneeling in the middle of it, so she remained inside the Faraday as she came down. But she fell so slowly and gently, Veronica had time to move her arms from outside Polly's thighs to between them. Once more lifting her lover's bum cheeks, Polly rotated until only her head struck the bed, leaving her quim directly in front of Veronica's face.

Starting from the rear and moving up, Veronica licked her, then clamped her mouth over Polly's nubbin, where she sucked and licked as her lover squirmed. Polly wrapped her legs round the back of Veronica's head, so her mistress no longer needed to hold her weight. Veronica reached along Polly's body and rubbed the girl's breasts, one in each hand.

Polly grunted and moved rhythmically. Veronica recognised her lover was about to come, and redoubled her efforts with her mouth. She grabbed Polly's nipples, leaned back as a counterbalance, and pulled her head from the bed. Polly tried, with limited success, to suppress her cries as she came and the muscles in her pussy hole contracted. Veronica sucked Polly's nubbin hard as the paroxysm took her.

Then she collapsed to the side, taking both of them down—but with the lassitude that only a Faraday effect could produce—until her head rested on Polly's thigh. She used her free hand to gently rub the area between the girl's pussy and bum. Polly moaned.

"More?" said Veronica.

"Please."

Veronica smiled, got her finger wet from Polly's pussy, and wiggled it up her bum before starting on her nubbin again.

Polly came a second time almost as quickly as the first. And complained when Veronica removed the finger from her bum, but moments later she was asleep and snoring softly.

Veronica harrumphed into Polly's nethers, but the girl did not even have the grace to hesitate in her snoring. So Veronica pushed Polly's upper thigh from her head and rolled out from between Polly's legs.

She sat up and moved to the top of the bed to lean against the cushions. In the reduced gravity it was all so easy. She pushed away the desire to cry again. That was not a good idea at all.

Instead, she thought about the photographic album. She needed to find a balance point; it was true it was her parents who had made them, with other people, but did it matter? They were not part of her life, and had effectively disowned her then sold her. She owed nothing to them, they might as well be strangers.

If her lust was ignited by seeing her mother pushing a phallus into herself, or being fucked, did it matter?

She got down beneath the sheet and pulled it up to her chin, squeezing her legs under Polly's. It felt so good with her body freed of the stresses and tensions her distorted spine caused, and then to be able to lift Polly the way she had—that was exciting.

Idly, she dragged her nails across her own breasts. Of course, there would be no Faraday device when they were in Switzerland, but that was only two weeks, and she had already borne the pain most of her life.

She did not notice when she fell asleep.

X

Twelve days to the wedding.

They had woken early as usual. Veronica had slept wonderfully well, better than she could ever remember, and her first sensation as she came awake was a growing warmth between her thighs as Polly repaid the debt of the previous evening. Veronica reached paroxysm squeezing her breasts as Polly plunged three fingers in and out of her body.

Then they cuddled for a little while in silence.

"You seem ... different," said Polly.

"Don't start that or I'll end up crying again." Veronica turned and reduced the strength of the Faraday and they sank into the bed springs. Then she glanced at the clock, only half past seven, there was plenty of time.

"Let's have a bath."

Polly complained, but rolled off the other side of the bed and padded into the bathroom. In the mirror by the window, Veronica admired her slim body as she walked away. Veronica sat up and, with a sigh, disengaged the Faraday device. All her weight returned. She stood and felt her spine move.

All the years she had lived with her deformity, it had become a constant and unfocused ache, but having been free of it for the hours of the night she could perceive it with a new clarity. It was no longer something that possessed her entire being; she could pinpoint it, feel it where it changed and twisted.

She was not sure she liked the sensation, but if she was going to keep using the Faraday then it would no doubt be something she must learn to live with.

———◦———

THE BATH WAS HOT, REFRESHING, and big enough for both of them. Polly took the end with the plug, although she suggested they could alternate. Veronica washed her, which was a new experience and a delight.

There was a little delay when she cleaned between the girl's legs, but they did not dally long.

Polly returned the favour and, as she was applying soap to Veronica's rear end commented, "I'll clean you out inside tomorrow as well, if you like."

"I might like that, but if we're going out perhaps you should be too."

"I can do myself."

"But it would be easier if I did it."

"I am concerned you might take liberties with my person, Nika."

"Do not be concerned, Polly," she said. "Rest assured I will definitely take liberties with your person." She smiled sweetly. "How many bulbs of water would you like?"

"We're only going to Maybury, so one will be quite sufficient."

"Perhaps I could practice now?" said Veronica.

"We should get to breakfast," said Polly, "then peruse the catalogue and magazines."

Veronica nodded. "And when Mr Plumley has gone, we'll look at the album."

Polly looked up from the water in surprise. "I thought you didn't want to."

"I didn't, don't, but I decided I need to."

"And you won't get upset if I get hot and want to touch you because of it?"

"No, you can get hot, and we can try the things we see if you like."

Polly looked dubious. "Well, I'm not sure I'll want to do *that*, but I know what you're like, Nika, you'll do anything."

Perhaps.

<hr>

WITHIN THE HOUR, THEY exited the new bedroom and made their way through the unfinished disaster that was now Veronica's home. Most of the restructuring work was complete, but workmen were still everywhere. They had torn down old wallpaper, and put up new. They were cleaning and painting surfaces—even the banister of the main staircase was being replaced, though Veronica was hard-pressed to think what had been wrong with the original. The air was filled with sawing, hammering, and shouts, and their noses assailed by caustic odours from the cleaning materials, paste, and the paint.

It was just as well they were not having a wedding breakfast or any sort of reception, because even if the work had been completed in time, the place would stink of decoration.

But for Veronica, it was all a marvel. Just one night with the Faraday seemed to have cleared her mind so much. It was as if she had been walking through the world with her eyes closed, and now they were open.

Breakfast was served in the ballroom as was now the custom, at least until the rest of the house was available. Veronica stared at the sausages, bacon, and eggs, sure that almost nothing here would be approved of by her future husband. It was an issue she was loath to deal with, but she had no choice. Edwin was being very foolish and she must see to it that he did not bring about the destruction of Versyns House.

The butler arrived a short time later with the post—another new feature, since she had never received post before her eighteenth birthday.

"Thank you, Mr Jones," she said. The highest up his body she could see was his waist. It was frustrating.

"An honour, Miss Clifford-Hughes."

She looked at the writing on the envelope; it was small and very precise.

"If I may, miss, you can see where it's been sent from, and the time, in the postmark."

"London?"

"The 'W' indicates London West."

"And sent yesterday evening at half past five. And it's a good quality paper."

"Indeed it is, miss." Emlyn Jones handed her the letter opener, shaped like a sword, and she sliced through the fold then extracted the letter. The butler relieved her of the envelope and opener. She unfolded the letter.

"Oh," she said, "it's from Mademoiselle Vionnet, and it's in French." She read silently for a few moments with her brows pulled into a frown of concentration. "She's coming down on Friday with two assistants and will stay all weekend to do fittings and adjustments." She knew her voice sounded desperate.

"Shall I inform Mrs Jenkins?"

"Yes, please, I'm not sure I could face it. Where can we put them that's not a complete disaster?"

"Do not concern yourself, miss, that is Mrs Jenkins' problem. Not yours."

"But she's sure to blame me."

"I will ensure that does not happen, miss."

Veronica sighed. "Thank you."

Once breakfast was complete, she and Polly uncovered another table and laid out the magazines, and the huge Army & Navy catalogue.

Veronica started at the beginning and browsed through pages of listings for various types of food, including five different grades of almonds at prices ranging from sixpence to half-a-crown a pound.

Turning to the back she got caught up with the advertising for teeth whitening powders, hair oil, perfumes, and a family-size chest of homeopathic cures. Candles. Tea. Soaps. Champagne. Italian wines. Pickles. Honey.

She slammed it shut. "There's too much. I don't even know where to start, and besides I can't buy clothes from a catalogue, they won't fit me properly." There was no response from Polly, whose attention was consumed by something in the magazine open in front of her. "What?"

Polly looked up and blinked, then pushed the magazine across. "Look."

More adverts for perfumes, face powders, collar starch ... *oh*: "Electro-massager for Feminine Health." There was a mechanism that seemed to involve an electric motor and a wire connection that could perhaps attach to the house electrics. "Battery option available." The motor had a rotor arm connected to a wheel, which in turn attached to the phallus-like attachment. She guessed the thing would move in and out; there was a knob and pointer not dissimilar to the one on the Faraday device, perhaps it had variable speed.

Veronica shook her head. "I think I prefer your fingers to that," she said with a smile to Polly. "And we'll see how we do with carrots."

"Cucumber might be better," said Polly.

"We'll ask Seth for a couple," said Veronica. "Anyway, that doesn't help my problem."

"I'm sure they have something."

Veronica checked the contents listing and found there was a section for clothes. She flipped to the thousandth page and then skimmed a few dozen more. "Everything for an officer and a gentleman. Nothing for ladies."

Polly peered at the page. "That's tailoring."

"It is Army & Navy. Why would they have anything for women?" She opened the catalogue at random pages. "Guns. Campaign tents. Furniture. Curtains." She found children's clothes and then "Found something!" a whole section on dresses for the outdoors and gowns for every occasion.

Something caught her eye but she'd already lost it. She searched back fifty pages. She stared. "They have bridal trousseaux."

"What's in it?"

"They have different ones at different prices."

They spent time looking through, but Veronica sighed. "Even the ones I like won't fit me properly."

"We'll order them, and I can make the adjustments. Better than getting all those people your parents used," said Polly. "And write back to Mademoiselle Vionnet, ask her opinion. If you do it now you can get a reply by tomorrow morning before you meet Mr Slack in the afternoon."

"I don't want to bother a *couturier* with mundane clothes like this."

"What's the worst that could happen?"

Veronica imagined a tirade of French insults. "She could ignore me."

"Exactly. Nothing at all."

"I'll do it later."

"Next post goes at twelve. Do it now."

Polly fetched the writing materials and Veronica composed a letter that she hoped was the right balance between a request and an understanding that Mademoiselle Vionnet had far more important things to do. Polly addressed the envelope and, once the ink was dry on Veronica's letter, she folded it and ran out to catch the post.

Veronica stared glumly out of the French windows to the garden where the sun's heat was making everything hazy.

"M-m-miss Clifford-Hughes?" Veronica jumped to her feet and turned towards the door where Mr Plumley stood. "You are n-not in the library."

Veronica glanced at the clock. Ten past ten.

"I do apologise, sir. I have been very busy this morning." She gestured at the table littered with magazines and the titanic Army & Navy catalogue. Her eyes lit on the still-open page with the aid to women's health. She looked up again to see Mr Plumley walking across the covered floor towards her—and there was a woman behind him who she did not recognise. She was, as far as Veronica was able to tell, in her mid-thirties with slightly curly black hair tied back very simply, with an olive complexion.

Her surprise meant that Mr Plumley and his ... associate? ... reached her before she had a chance to move away from the table or close the magazine with the device.

"This is Signora Martaci."

The woman was far enough away that Veronica could see she smiled and only glanced at the hump for a moment.

Then Signora Martaci moved closer and she held out her hand. "Sofia Martaci, Miss Clifford-Hughes, please call me Sofia."

"Veronica, Signora ... Sofia."

"I asked the signora to assist you with your Italian before you go to Switzerland."

"I ... thank you. You really don't need to trouble yourself, I'm sure I will manage."

Signora Martaci let fly with a long question in Italian. Veronica recognised a word or two in there, like *and* and *mountain*, she only knew it was a question because of the way it went up at the end.

"Miss Clifford-Hughes, my family live close to the border with Switzerland. I cannot help you speak their language precisely—they have so many—but if you work hard, and your tutor tells me that you do, I am sure we can make your stay easier."

Veronica didn't really know what to say, so she made do with, "Thank you."

———◆———

THE LESSON BEGAN ALMOST immediately, subject to acquiring a parasol, with Signora Martaci taking Veronica by the arm and guiding her out into the garden. They simply walked, with the older woman pointing out items, saying their names and having Veronica repeat.

They moved on rapidly to simple sentences. "I am testing you," said Sofia. "We will see where you are in your Italian, and then we will move on."

The sentences became harder; because Signora Martaci was Italian her accent was pure and that made the words harder to understand. She didn't say them the way Mr Plumley had when he was teaching.

"Are you tired, Veronica?" said Signora Martaci after a while.

"A little."

"Is there a bench in the shade?"

Veronica indicated the one that she and Polly often used, hidden from the main house, but with a good view of the garden. In a short time they sat.

"Does your back hurt you all of the time?"

"It aches," said Veronica. "But I'm used to it."

"And you are marrying?"

"To the Honourable Edwin Jameson, yes, in two weeks."

"Does he care for you?"

"It was arranged."

The older woman was quiet for a few moments, then: "There's a handsome fellow."

Veronica peered across the flower beds at Seth who had just entered. The gardeners were required to keep their shirts on, but his was open at the front and his sleeves rolled up.

"I suppose so."

"Do you not think so?"

Veronica felt a twinge inside. It was like the feeling she sometimes got watching the staff. The way they walked, so upright, so perfect. It was envy, she knew, and that was a sin. Another one to go along with all the others. At least she hadn't killed anyone—not yet—but the way the Signora spoke about Seth, even that seemed like a possibility. She wanted to say *He's mine, I have used my mouth on him and swallowed his seed.*

"Is your Edwin so fine?"

"Edwin is intellectual rather than physical."

Signora Martaci made a disparaging noise and flicked her fingers, as if she was brushing away a fly. Perhaps she was.

The lesson continued for another hour, until Polly called them in for luncheon which they took in the ballroom. Veronica was pleased to see that Polly had cleared away the magazines to one of the other tables, all closed and piled one atop the other.

"Your maid is accompanying you on your journey?" said Signora Martaci; it was barely a question.

"Yes."

"Then she must learn as well as she can in the time. If she must ask for you she must also be able to make herself understood."

"Lessons? Me?" said Polly abruptly with a belated "Miss."

Veronica couldn't disagree that it was a good idea, even though she knew Polly would hate it.

"Yes," she said. "I agree."

Polly didn't argue, but Veronica could tell from the look she was giving the floor that there would be sparks flying tonight.

Once they had finished eating, they went to the library. Mr Plumley sat in his usual place while Veronica and Polly sat on hard-backed chairs, and Signora Martaci continued the lesson.

xi

Veronica became more and more distracted as the afternoon wore on. When questioned, she claimed she was tired and went to recline on a divan sofa. This resulted in Signora Martaci concentrating on Polly for the last hour until four o'clock.

Even though she watched Mr Plumley carefully, he gave no sign he was concerned he would not be able to lick her feet on his assigned day. Did he consider her education to be more important? The fact he had spoken to Signora Martaci seemed to indicate that was the case, and she was not entirely sure how she felt about that—he was willing to forgo his own pleasure for her sake.

It was a kindness she had not expected.

Then they were gone and Polly came to sit at the end of the divan.

"I ain't happy, Nika."

Veronica closed her eyes; the heat and the activities of the day had tired her out despite having better sleep. "I know, but could we not argue just now."

"Who's arguing?"

Veronica sighed. "I think it's a good idea."

"Me too."

"You do?"

"I'm not stupid, Nika. I just didn't like being pushed into it, like it had nothing to do with me."

Veronica kept her eyes closed. "The people we are when we're alone together, they're not the same as those we have to be with other people."

"There's people—toffs, of course—who didn't want us commoners educated, thought we'd get above our station."

"Were they wrong?"

"You want me ignorant?"

"Of course not."

"I want more, Nika."

"I don't know how to give you more."

Polly didn't answer. Veronica opened her eyes to make sure she was all right. Well, she wasn't crying.

"Help me up, please."

Polly assisted in getting Veronica into a sitting position.

"If I can give you more, Polly, I will," she sighed, "but I don't think this is something we can rush."

She leaned forward with her hands covering her face, welcoming the darkness as she covered her eyes. The rest had not done her a great deal of good today.

"What's wrong?"

"Just tired, a lot on my mind." So many things to think about when only a month ago all I cared about were lessons and reading. I haven't read anything for pleasure in that time.

Polly crouched by her side with a hand on her knee. "I'm sorry, I'm supposed to help you, not add to your worries. You could go and lie down, I can have them send dinner up."

Veronica nodded and let Polly help her stand up.

"You go up, I'll tell the kitchen, and then I'll run you a bath."

————⬥————

VERONICA WOKE TO POLLY kissing her on the cheek. "Come on, sleepy head, the bath's ready."

It was all a little confusing, she barely even remembered reaching the bedroom and was now lying fully clothed on the bed with the Faraday on. Even as she noticed that, she heard the dial clicking and her weight increased.

Polly stripped her and helped her climb into the cool bath. "I didn't want to make it too hot, what with the weather."

Veronica just relaxed and let the water support her. She was almost dozing off again when Polly stepped in as well, making the water level rise alarmingly close to the lip.

"Better let some out."

A short time later, Polly lay down at the other end of the bath and placed her right foot at the apex of Veronica's legs.

She smiled tiredly. "I'm not really in the mood."

"I know."

They lay in the water for a while, then Polly found the soap and started washing Veronica from the feet upwards. She spent some time cleaning Veronica's nether regions and behind—which generated a pleasant warmth—but she did not linger and moved up across her body, but avoided the breasts.

"Turn over and kneel up, Nika."

Veronica did as she was told, although she felt such languor she did not really want to. The water poured off her as she pushed herself up then sat on her heels, head down, a hand on each side of the bath.

Polly's soapy hands roamed across her lower back, then up. Veronica frowned as if she were in pain as Polly rubbed the skin across her hump. It didn't hurt, but it reminded her of how deformed she really was. Then the hands moved round, sliding across her breasts, squeezing and manipulating them. A rush of lust boiled inside of Veronica, and even that was another sort of pain.

Then Polly's hands dropped away to be replaced by a cloth, wiping away the soap. The maid climbed out of the bath and pulled the plug. She lay a couple of towels on the tiled floor and helped Veronica out.

The drying focused only on hidden places where the water would not easily evaporate, and the warmth of the air did the rest. Polly found a dressing gown for each of them, then checked the time.

"Dinner will be here soon. I'll have to get dressed, but you can just get into bed."

⸻ ◉ ⸻

WHEN SHE WOKE, THE sun was pouring in through the window and the room seemed to glow with its light. The Faraday was on and she pushed herself into a sitting position with barely any strain.

On the table near the window was her evening meal, but the angle of the sun, and the clock, told her it was morning. Six o'clock, the time she had become accustomed to waking when she had revealed her body to Seth. Those days were like ancient history now.

Polly lay beside her with the bedclothes pushed back to reveal her pale and beautiful skin, as if she had been too warm in the night. She was like one of the house statues, pale and naked, but carved so perfectly even the individual hairs of her skin reflected the day.

Veronica smiled at her lover, then turned away and slipped over the edge of the bed, gaining weight as she moved out of the Faraday's effect. She landed on the carpet and stood as straight as she could. She had been so tired yesterday, but now, as her body adjusted to a new day, she realised she was famished, since she had not eaten since luncheon the previous day.

Last night's meal beckoned, as did the photographic album that sat next to the tray. Polly must have got it down since Veronica had said she was going to continue looking through it. Perhaps things had turned out for the best, she felt it would be easier to see the pictures without Polly looking over her shoulder and commenting.

Veronica found her copy of Mrs Beeton's Housekeeping book and used it to prop up the album, while she sat with yesterday's dinner directly in front of her. It was sausage and mash with peas. Thankfully the gravy was in a separate jug, because it had congealed.

The potatoes were always thoroughly mashed—she hated lumps—but eating it cold was not appetising either. But there were these lovely sausages, full of delicious pork—almost as good as bacon in the morning. She used her right hand to turn the pages while her left could get greasy with fat.

She moved through the first few pages quite quickly, deciding that she would appreciate the qualities of her mother's body, rather than condemning her for doing these things. *After all, I'm just as likely to do them, so perhaps I can learn how to do it better.* Almost as if her mother had left this album for her instruction rather than simply forgetting she had left it here, which was far more likely.

She reached the page where her mother was being taken by the man she did not know while using her mouth on Veronica's father. Veronica could imagine herself in that position. She had yet to discover what it was like to have a man pushing into her, but she liked the thought of it.

She slid a sausage into her mouth, pretending it was a man's prick, then bit off the end. She giggled to herself as she chewed and swallowed.

Next page.

This bedroom again, as usual. Veronica glanced across at Polly, who was still fast asleep. This set started with her mother and father; she was sitting on his face the way Polly had done with Seth, but leaning forwards and licking his prick.

That was just the first one. The next one was similar, but her mother appeared to have completely swallowed her father's member. Veronica put her head on one side as if that would give her a better view. She didn't think her father was any bigger than Seth in that department, probably smaller, but even so she was sure it would make her choke. She would have to experiment with the carrots—if they ever got time to carve them.

Then it was just her mother turned around and being penetrated as normal, except the camera angle was different. In this one, her father's legs were off the side of the bed, and so were her mother's as she squatted on him. The camera must have been positioned almost exactly where Veronica was now sitting. In the final picture of this set, the other man was back and standing beside the bed with his crotch tight up against her mother and father.

Veronica stared, trying to work out the angles. There seemed to be only two possibilities: either both men were in her mother's pussy hole (she knew what Polly had said, but she still couldn't imagine it stretching that much), or the man standing was penetrating her mother's bum.

That was an idea Veronica liked very much, though definitely after a good clean out. Which was the point she realised that the enema device Polly had previously used on her must have been used by her mother. It was a strange thought.

Remembering the sausage half-eaten in her hand, she consumed the rest of it then picked up the next one.

Next page.

Veronica's eyes widened in amazement. Her mother was not in these pictures, only her father and another man—a different one to before. She chastised herself; after all, if she and Polly could enjoy sexual pleasures together, though they were of the same sex, why not men too?

Her father was using his mouth on the other man's prick just like her mother had done to him. In the next image they were lying on the bed and doing the same to each other. This new man had a long and thin member, sizes were difficult to estimate, but certainly half as long again as her father's since she could see them in the same picture.

Then, if she had been in any doubt before as to the use of the rear for fucking, that was clearly what the man was doing to her father. The advantages of that approach were not lost on her because, with a woman, there was no chance of pregnancy, and Veronica knew it gave her pleasure. It must be the same for men.

The final picture was a little different. Her father was kneeling on the bed and the other man sitting on him—Veronica assumed he was being penetrated—and her father was holding the man's prick in one hand. And they were kissing. Veronica thought it looked odd, though again she had to be stern with herself, after all she loved kissing Polly.

But it meant there must be some tender feelings between her father and this man, didn't it? There had been no picture of her parents kissing each other, so far.

Even though she was trying to be dispassionate about the pictures, she could not help but find them stimulating. She pretended the next sausage was a phallus, she licked it—it was very tasty—and then sucked it into her mouth. She pumped it in and out for a while before slicing through it with her teeth. She must remember not to do that with the real thing.

Onwards.

The next image was similar to one on the previous page; it was her father with the man in the position where they could each pleasure the other, with her father on top. But it was the next one that rocked Veronica once more: her mother had returned, naked as usual—though her hair looked longer in this picture—but there were leather straps around her waist and reaching between her thighs. She was on the bed, behind her husband, and *fucking him* with a phallus held in place by the straps. The angle in this shot made it absolutely clear the weapon she was wielding penetrated him, even as his own prick was being sucked, and he reciprocated.

The next image was a man with his legs towards the camera. It might have been her father, but it was difficult to tell because there was a new, slightly older woman sitting on his face and sucking him. In the next one, her mother had joined them and was using the harness phallus to fuck the woman. The final one on this page had the older woman on the bed with her head hanging off the side, her mouth filled with Veronica's father's prick. Veronica's mother was between her legs, once more using the artificial phallus.

An arm came over Veronica's left shoulder while another wrapped round her chest. Lips gently kissed her hump, then her ear.

"You started without me—oh!" Polly's arms tensed. "That is..." Words failed her, it seemed.

Veronica had been surprised, but not shocked. There seemed to be no limit to the inventiveness of her parents in sexual pleasure. Nothing they would not do, perhaps. And she was their daughter, even if, perhaps, she was only her mother's daughter and he was not her father.

She thought perhaps she ought to be more upset, but she had so little to do with them that it was almost as if they were strangers, or acquaintances, at best.

"Your mum's fucking your dad," Polly said finally. "And that other woman."

"Yes, would you like to try that?"

"Get my revenge on him?"

Veronica smiled. "No, I meant on me, but if that would satisfy your revenge then perhaps."

"He looks like he's enjoying it. Perhaps I'd do it to him if it was twice as big," said Polly. "No, three times."

"Width or length?"

"Both."

It was almost a joke, but Veronica sensed that cruel streak coming to the fore once more. Yes, Polly would probably very happily hurt her father in retribution what he did. Who could blame her?

"You missed this." Veronica turned back a page.

"Gawd," said Polly. "They'll burn in hell for that."

"Meaning we will too."

"Nothing in the Bible about women lying together," said Polly. "Just men. And men ain't allowed by law neither, and there's no law says we can't do what we do."

Veronica shut the book. "Can I wear the yellow dress today? Or is there a law that says I can't"

"It's clean," said Polly. "Looking your best for young Mr Slack?"

"Of course, I want to look the best I can when I go out." *Even though nobody will see the dress, only the hump.* "Not too many petticoats either, it's going to be another hot one, I think."

"Bloomers?"

"Are they optional?"

"They can be."

"In that case, I'll go without," said Veronica. "I wonder how few clothes I could get away with wearing before anyone would notice."

"You could go stark naked if you like."

Veronica laughed. "I think that would be noticed."

"Mr Slack certainly noticed your ankles and legs. Are you trying to seduce him too?"

"He's not married."

"But you will be."

"I'm just curious."

Polly's arms unwound from Veronica's body, and she padded away to a chair over which she had draped her clothes.

"You need to move your clothes into next door, since I won't be using it," said Veronica. "It's perfect really. We have that adjoining door so no one will know where you spend your night."

"And I can listen to you and your husband making babies." She pulled up one calf-length stocking and then the other, snapping the garter in position over each one. "Or anybody else you fancy bringing to your bed."

Veronica admired the curve of Polly's posterior as she bent over. "I'd rather have you with me."

"Stop looking at me bum."

"You're not embarrassed, are you?"

Polly stood up, bloomers in hand. "A bit, yes."

"Sorry." Veronica brought her hand up to cover her eyes.

"But I'd rather you looked than not, Nika."

"I was going to peek anyway."

xii

Breakfast brought the post and, sure enough, there was a reply from Mademoiselle Vionnet. And not just a letter, it was a packet stuffed with clippings from magazines and catalogues. Each one had a price, size information, and address.

Veronica spread them out on a table. "There's so many…"

Polly eyed them carefully and set about rearranging them into groups. "See, she's got a range of suitable dresses, underthings, shoes, slippers, night clothes, cardigans, tops, jackets, and a couple of coats."

"But it's too much, I can't get all these, and you can't possibly make all the adjustments."

"Only the things that go around your shoulders need adjusting," said Polly. "I'm sure I can fit it in with the Italian lessons."

"But how are we to order them?"

"Give them to Mr Slack."

Veronica looked down at the advertisements for the underthings. "I expect some of those will get him very hot under his collar."

"They'll get him hot somewhere."

⸺◉⸺

MR PLUMLEY ARRIVED on schedule and was once more accompanied by Signora Martaci, who greeted her with a kiss on each cheek.

"That is how you greet friends or family, Veronica," she said. "But not someone you have just met. Follow their lead. That is a very pretty dress."

"Thank you."

"Today is only this morning?"

"Unfortunately, yes," said Veronica. "I have an appointment at half past two in Mayfield."

"Is it all afternoon?"

"I think no more than an hour."

The signora turned to Mr Plumley. "Would it be inappropriate for me to continue the lesson afterwards, in the town?"

Veronica went cold, and it was as if she was filled with a paralysis. "No!"

The signora turned back in concern, and Mr Plumley was frowning.

"Sorry," said Veronica trying to regain her composure. "But I can't."

"Can't, Veronica?" said Signora Martaci. Her frown now mimicked the tutor.

Veronica looked helplessly at Polly. She felt as if her energy was being drained, and she sat down heavily, almost missing the chair.

"I can't go out." Her voice was small and she wondered if they had even heard her. All she could see was the grain of the table wood.

A moment later she felt Polly's hand on her shoulder and her hip pressed against Veronica's arm.

"My mistress needs to rest. She is not used to the excitement the wedding is causing."

Veronica could feel the tears welling up, and when she closed her eyes the drops splashed on the tabletop. She reached up and placed her hand on Polly's.

"It's all right," she said, and cleared her throat as she sat up as straight as she could manage. Polly dangled a kerchief which Veronica took and wiped her eyes, then blew her nose as decorously as she could manage. "I can't go into the town. They will stare at me."

"B-but, m-Miss Clifford-Hughes, you went to London."

"And I dreaded every second, sir. And while it was true that all those people did not stop to point, there were still those who stared. Even the shop girls were rude. I am a monster. I expect nothing less."

"But there are fewer people in the town," said Sofia.

"They know who I am. They will stare. They will point." She took a deep breath. "Even in church sometimes things have been said."

It occurred to her, now she was becoming her own mistress, she need not attend church at all.

"But you are going into town, are you not?" said Sofia.

"The carriage will stop outside the solicitor. I will go in. When my business is concluded I will exit and climb into the carriage. I will not be exposed for long."

"And Switzerland?"

"Perhaps it will be as busy as London and, if it is not, I can keep to my rooms."

There was a silence.

"I do not think you should live your life controlled by what others think," said Signora Martaci.

Veronica felt herself flush with emotion; her cheeks were hot and she fought to control her voice. "Sofia, that is a pleasant platitude, but you do not look like me."

"No, Veronica, but I am a foreigner and, worse, a Catholic. I have lived here for many years, and I too am treated as a pariah."

"I'm sorry."

"You do not need to apologise for the shortcomings of your countrymen, Veronica, however, I will say that if you dance to their tune then they have won."

"They won a long time ago, Sofia."

Polly squeezed her shoulder and the older woman made a disgusted sound. "That is self-pity, Veronica. And nobody likes that."

Veronica frowned, and hoped it was hidden by the angle of her head. It was bad enough having Polly chastise her for self-pity, but to have someone she only met yesterday do the same was most galling.

The signora spoke again. "I invite you to tea at my home, Veronica, it is at the other end of the town from the solicitor's office. You cannot refuse. I will wait for you, at his office, from three o'clock in case you are finished early, and we will walk to my house and we will practise your Italian on the way."

— ◦ —

THE REST OF THE MORNING Sofia divided her teaching between Veronica and Polly. They did not stay in the library, but moved about the house practising sentences related to the things they saw.

They even went out the front door and proceeded around the estate. Sofia stood on Veronica's left so she could link their arms. Polly walked slightly behind on the other side. They reached the buildings that had been converted for the electricity generator. The machinery was already functioning, but there was still work being done on the roof and walls.

At the back of the main room were huge hoppers of coal. The machinery pumped and sighed with power as it turned the wheels and drove the pulleys. The gleaming furnace gave off tremendous heat. It was attended by two staff, one of whom was shirtless as he shovelled coal into the furnace's maw.

And Veronica could only stare. It was the first time she had ever seen a man with black skin. She had seen illustrations, and unflattering cartoons but, in the flesh, he was like an immortal. He was Hephaestus, the blacksmith of the gods. He even looked like one of the Greek statues. His sweat reflected the light of the sun, and the fires, until it seemed he was on fire himself.

Sofia said something in Italian which Veronica did not recognise at all.

"Non lo capisco."

"I said that he is a very handsome fellow."

"Is he?" said Veronica.

"Do not pretend, my dear."

Veronica was embarrassed at being so obvious. "He is very handsome."

"*Si*. Now say it in Italian."

"I do not think I will have the need to learn it."

"One cannot predict the future, Veronica."

And she went on to teach both Veronica and Polly a number of different ways of describing the attractiveness of men. If the man noticed their attention—and Veronica could not imagine how he could not—he gave no sign.

When they finally walked on, Veronica had Sofia teach them both how they might say the same things about a woman—claiming it was so they would be able to recognise if a man said it about them. But Veronica caught Polly's eye as she practised the sentences, and they shared a secret smile.

xiii

As they rode the open-topped carriage through the outskirts of the town, the people on the streets did glance in her direction, but Veronica was sure it was hard to see the shape of her back as she sat on the seat being bounced by the bumps in the road. They were passed by more than one motor vehicle and Veronica resolved to suggest to her future husband that it would be wise to get one, preferably with its own Faraday device.

"*Sei una bella ragazza*," said Veronica to Polly, and grinned.

Polly's face took on a fearful look; she pointed at the driver.

"Lui non parla Italiano."

Polly frowned as she tried to make out the words, then whispered, "He might."

"I think it highly unlikely, Polly."

They reached Market Street. Veronica assumed the signora's house must be around here somewhere. She stared at the shops that lined the wide-open area; there was a small market in progress too, and quite a lot of people. Veronica was revising her agreement to walk through the town. She could claim her back was aching too much.

But they passed along the road with almost no one taking any notice, and certainly no shouts of "Witch!" or "Monster!"

The carriage came to a halt at a very well-appointed Georgian building with a brass plaque on the wall declaring it to be 'Slack, Slack, and Mortimer, Solicitors'.

Polly had got down and was waiting to help her mistress. Veronica closed her eyes. The moment had arrived once more. She took a deep breath, found her walking stick, and stood up. She focused only on Polly to avoid any potential eye contact with a passerby.

The ground was uneven, which gave her another excuse to keep her eyes down, watching the placement of her stick as she moved across the flagstones. This was not the same as London. Here, the people knew who she was; they might even come to the wedding. There was nothing to stop them.

That was another horrifying thought. She still had no idea what sort of creation Mademoiselle Vionnet was creating for her—except she would be barefoot at the altar.

The wish that this had never happened coincided with her arrival at the door. Polly rang the bell as Veronica imagined the townsfolk staring at her.

A young chap in a neat suit opened the door and welcomed them in. She saw his eyes stray to her right shoulder. People always did that. *My face is here!*

"Miss Veronica Clifford-Hughes to see Mr Lawrence Slack," said Polly.

"This way, miss."

He led the way through the sombre—almost dreary—hallway to a door near the back. Veronica heard an odd clattering noise from a side room. The boy knocked twice then turned the handle and pushed the door back.

Sunlight filtered through a haze of dust, making it almost impossible to see the man behind the desk who rose to his feet and came out into the main part of the room.

"Miss Clifford-Hughes, do come in."

Veronica realised she was standing in the doorway. She had expected the boy or Polly to lead the way, but that was her prerogative now. She was the most senior.

But perhaps I am not my father's daughter. Perhaps I really am a cuckoo in the nest. She had no idea what that might mean, even if it was true. It was like a bad romance, the wrong way round. Usually people discovered their true ancestry as a solution to their problems, whereas here it might cause more problems. What if she were cast out?

"Please do come in and sit down."

She still hadn't moved. With an effort, she pushed forward, leaning heavily on her stick as its rubber tip caught on the ridges in the wooden floor. The air was thick with light and dust; it was like stepping into a fish tank and she felt she might drown.

The walls were covered in shelving stacked with document boxes. Lawrence Slack's desk was bare apart from the inkwell, pens, blotter, a small stack of folders to one side, and a telephonic device. She was astonished that he had one of his own. Did that mean that Slack, Slack, and Mortimer possessed more than one? A sign of real opulence, to be sure.

Mr Slack held an upright but well-padded chair for her and she settled into it. She wasn't sure whether it was the usual chair for his guests, but it was high enough off the ground that she could see his face when he sat. Polly had an unpadded chair off to the side.

"May I offer you refreshments? Tea, biscuits?"

"That would be kind, Mr Slack. I will have tea if I may, and biscuits would be pleasant. Do you have any of those new chocolate sandwich ones?"

He smiled. He did have a nice smile—he seemed much more relaxed in his own lair. She laughed at herself, a lair implied something predatory and Lawrence Slack did not seem to have anything predatory in his nature.

I am a hunter, though, and I want him the way I want others I meet. I am unnatural. Like my mother.

Lawrence called for the boy, gave his instructions, shut the door, then returned to his seat.

"Your itinerary," he said, lifting a sheet from the top of the folders and handing it over.

Veronica glanced at it. It had a set of precise departure and arrival times of the various flyers they would be using on the way out and coming back, but said little more than she already knew. She frowned.

"Are there no excursions once we are at Mount Verità?"

"I understand we will all be staying in the one location for the entire two weeks."

"We?"

"I will also be accompanying his lordship."

"Isn't that unusual?" she said. "I mean, on a honeymoon?"

"I understand he has business he needs to carry out while he is there and he requires my company's services. My father refuses to travel by flyer."

Veronica absorbed that information. "You are saying the honeymoon is a *business* trip?"

He had the decency to look mortified.

"Never mind, Lawrence," she said a little more kindly. "It will give us an opportunity to get to know one another better. How's your Italian?"

"I think you'll find they speak Swiss, Miss Clifford-Hughes."

She smiled. "I have asked you to call me Veronica."

"Veronica."

"You see, Lawrence, in Switzerland they have four major languages. Of those, one is like French, one is like German, and the one in the south is like Italian. I don't expect to learn the Swiss version, but I am brushing up my Italian with the help of Signora Martaci."

"Sofia Martaci?"

"You know her?"

If the light in the room were not so odd, she might have sworn he blushed. "It's a small town, miss, err, Veronica, and Mrs Martaci makes her presence felt."

"I'm sure she does."

Tea and biscuits arrived and they did indeed have some of the chocolate sandwich type. Veronica helped herself to three out of the four of them on the plate.

"What can you tell me about Mount Verità?" said Veronica. "I mean, will there be balls every evening? Will it be warm or cold there? Anything that can help me choose my wardrobe beyond what Mademoiselle Vionnet has suggested. And Polly's too, of course."

"I'll just wear me uniform, miss."

Veronica looked at her. "I don't want you to. You are closer to being a companion than a lady's maid and I want you dressed appropriately."

Lawrence pretended to be reading the paper in front of him during the interchange, as if he was not even there.

He cleared his throat and consulted the paper properly. "The health retreat is run by one Henry Oedenkoven."

"Health retreat?"

He peered at the paper. "I understand that the founder considers the sun's rays to be very health-giving. So, I would imagine there would be a good deal of being in the outside."

"Perhaps they have gardens."

"I expect so."

"Anything else?"

"It is, I believe, very popular with a number of famous people who attend it from all over the world."

"Oh dear."

"Is that a problem, mi—Veronica?"

She gave him a measured look. "Two months ago, Lawrence, I barely left the house. There were no visitors and my parents have been strangers to me since...well, for many years. I saw no one except the staff, and precious few of them. I did not converse with anyone except my tutor. I had no expectation of any change in my life and was prepared to spend the rest of it in spinsterhood, except for church on Sundays." She paused to let him absorb that information, and to let herself muse on how the first major change in her life had involved accidentally exposing her naked body to an under-gardener, but she did not think Lawrence was ready for that—if he ever would be. "And now, suddenly, I am traded into marriage, and honeymooning in Switzerland at a place frequented by those I have only ever read about in the newspapers. How do you think I might feel?"

He hesitated for a long moment. "I believe you are quite resilient."

"No longer the weak and sensitive female?" she said with considerable harshness.

This time he really was embarrassed. "My words were ill-considered. I am sorry."

"Which ones? Those you spoke before or the ones just now?"

He was wise enough not to respond.

"Well, Lawrence, there is a way you can make it up to me."

"Anything I can do to help, of course."

"Would it be inappropriate for you to be my solicitor?"

"Not at all, Veronica, and a wise move now that you are of age," he said. "In some respects, it would make matters simpler, though, as I mentioned previously, I cannot report on matters private to other clients."

We'll see, she thought, but she nodded. "I completely understand. Can we start now? Is there a contract or something?"

"We have a pro forma for managing a client's personal matters. We could start with that and if matters look to extend beyond its purview, we can rewrite it, tailored to your particular requirements."

"That will do."

He left the room.

"What are you doing, Nika?"

"Protecting myself."

It took him less than two minutes to return with the necessary documents.

"You should read them," he said.

"Will I understand them?"

He gave a half-smile. "Probably not. They are quite obscure."

"Then I will trust you."

He sorted out three sheets of paper. "You need to sign the bottom of each."

"This is actually easier," he said. "If you were to be signing with another partnership, you would require a letter from your parents, or from your husband once married."

"That's ridiculous."

"That's how it's done, particularly since you are yet to reach twenty-one. However, it is not required since we already represent both of those other parties. This is, in effect, simply an extension of their business. The difference is that you are specifically my client, whereas the other parties are clients of my father."

"Does that mean you can tell them what we discuss and the business we transact?"

"Of course."

"But you can't tell me about theirs."

"Naturally not."

Veronica sighed. "But you don't have to report everything to them?"

"We are not required to do that, no. Only if they asked specifically."

"And they don't even need to be told I have signed with you?"

"Engaged."

"I'm sorry?"

"You 'engage' a solicitor," he said. "No, that information does not need to be volunteered."

"And what about payment?"

"We will bill your husband for any services rendered, since he will be in control of your finances."

"But won't he see?"

"The bills are paid by us directly as his representatives."

She took a moment as she absorbed the fact they paid themselves from her Edwin's money without any oversight, and that Lawrence seemed quite unconcerned. But it was to her benefit, and meant she would not be found out.

"Thank you, that seems acceptable."

She approached the desk and the pen he offered. Their fingers touched. Carefully, she signed her name, just as she had done for the Faraday device, on each of the three sheets. She glanced for a moment at the wording of the text above it. The words were in English, but it was as if there was some dark magic that prevented them from being comprehensible. Lawrence let her signatures dry before giving them a final blotting.

"Is there anything else?" said Lawrence as he slipped her new contract into a folder and tied it with a red ribbon.

Veronica took a deep breath. The time had come to set in motion something that might result in her ending up not married at all and, while she was not keen on the idea, it had provided her with considerable freedom.

"There are a couple of things, Lawrence—" she glanced at Polly to be reassured by her presence, "—we discussed the issue of the vegetarianism. You said I should lie, but then I spoke to the vicar and I decided that lying was not a good idea."

"I see." He did not look happy, perhaps she shouldn't have mentioned Reverend Peacock. Too late.

"This is not a comment on you, Lawrence, and I didn't tell him what it was about. I was not happy about lying, and the things he said showed me that this particular lie could very easily be found out. In my life until now, Lawrence, I never had any cause to lie and had no secrets." *Now there are so many secrets I fear I will be crushed beneath their weight.*

"What are you going to do?"

"I need to talk to Edwin. He has to realise that if he insists on following this course of action, he will cause Versyns to fall apart."

Lawrence nodded. "I understand. I can arrange a meeting late next week."

"Wouldn't earlier be better?"

He smiled. "Not if you want the marriage to go ahead."

"What do you mean?"

"Simply that the less time you give him, the more pressure your future husband will be under, and the more likely he is to acquiesce."

It was Veronica's turn to smile. "So perhaps at the weekend?"

"The office is not open at the weekend."

"I could see him at the house—oh, more pressure because it's *official*. At the house he is in charge, but here we are equal. And you will be presiding."

"Well done, Veronica, you understand." He made a note in a small book, then looked up at her once more. "You said there were a couple of matters?"

Veronica glanced over to Polly. "Do you have the papers that Mademoiselle Vionnet sent?"

Polly stood up, found the envelope in her bag, and passed it to her mistress.

"I asked my *couturier* what I should take on the honeymoon, and she sent these. I need to buy them, Lawrence, and have them delivered by Friday, but you know I have no access to money." He was staring at the envelope with a look of concern. She smiled and emptied the contents onto his blotter. As luck would have it, the one uppermost was advertising silk bloomers. The illustration showed a woman's lower body and slender legs.

Lawrence cleared his throat.

Veronica placed her hand on it and slid it to one side, revealing the one beneath illustrating a modern corset with stocking suspenders—the drawing once more highlighting a partially clothed woman. "Oh, not this one," said Veronica. "I can't wear a corset because of my deformity. Just bloomers for me." She removed it from the pile and Polly retrieved it. In doing so it uncovered an advert for a modern brassiere. The model had breasts more Polly's size than Veronica's. "I'm looking forward to trying those on," she said and raised her free hand to press her breast. From the way he moved suddenly, she knew he had not missed her action. She squeezed again, enjoying the thrill and warmth.

"So—" Lawrence's voice was barely more than a croak. He cleared his throat again. "So, what, um, do you want me to do?"

"They all have notes on them, about sizes, colours, and such, so if you could order them and charge them to Edwin's account. And ask that they are delivered before the weekend."

"I see."

"It needs to be by Friday because Mademoiselle Vionnet is coming down from London, and will give Polly instructions on how to adjust them to fit me. Though the bloomers—" she slid that one back to the middle of the pile, "—won't need any adjustment, of course. Although perhaps they could be made with shorter legs. What do you think, Lawrence?"

"Shorter..."

"I think I would like to wear as little as possible."

He said nothing. The sun still shone through the window, lighting portions of the room brightly, and casting whole areas into shadow.

Veronica smiled. "Of course, I'm not wearing any bloomers at the moment," she said. She gripped her skirt and made it billow. "They can get so hot. Cool air is very pleasant up there."

She turned away and went to the window as if to look out, but placed herself in the deep shadow beside it.

As if she read her mistress's mind, Polly also stood and went to guard the door.

It seemed Lawrence finally broke the spell and looked up as if to speak. Not finding her directly in front of him, he scanned the room. He squinted against the sun's rays, but did not see her—he turned to see Polly standing by the door.

"Did..." The question trailed into silence. Veronica could almost see his thought processes as he doubted his own recollections. "Did your mistress leave?"

"Lawrence," said Veronica.

He turned to where the sound must have come from, and stared. "Ah, there you are..."

"Did you like my legs, Lawrence?"

His mouth opened as if he wanted to deny he had ever seen them, but he clearly remembered them.

"Well?" she said. "Did you like them?"

In the depths of the shadow he was trying so hard to penetrate, Veronica pulled at her yellow dress, lifting the hem to her knees. Leaning against the wall for balance and support she lifted her right leg and let it move into the sun. She ignored the ache in her neck at the strain.

Even to her own eyes it was almost as if her calf and foot were detached from the rest of her. Lawrence Slack stared at her exposed limb.

"Does my leg please you?"

The first word he tried to utter caught in the back of his throat. He cleared it. "It is pleasantly shaped, Veronica."

"Nika."

He peered into the dark. "What?"

"When we are having an intimate moment, Lawrence, you should call me Nika."

"Nika?"

"Say what you said again with the right name."

"Your leg is pleasantly shaped...Nika."

She allowed her foot to drop back into the shadow and, with considerable relief, she stood properly. Then, still holding up her dress, she stepped fully into the sun's light, knowing that he would see nothing but a silhouette. Perhaps he could imagine she was not deformed, but simply leaning forwards.

She glanced at the clock on the wall, surprised to see that her hour was almost completely consumed. She would have to hurry, and took a step forward into the room, remaining in the light.

"Bring me the chair to sit on, Lawrence."

He moved almost as if he were in a trance. His eyes still fixated on her bare legs. She turned herself so he placed the chair at right angles to the sun, and she sat. As she did so, she brought her dress as high as she could, exposing her thighs. He stood to her left where the sun must be full in his face, though she could see no more than the bulge in his trousers. She smiled.

"Touch my leg, Lawrence."

His left hand reached out, but stopped before it made contact—as if he did not know where to put it. Gently, she reached up, placed her hand over his, and brought it down on the bare skin of her knee. She thrilled to it and the lust bubbled within her. Even now her scent was spreading from the delta between her thighs.

She pulled his hand so his fingers slid up her thigh, then back. He did not need further instruction, and ran his hand gently back and forth. His fingers slid down between her thighs and he squeezed her flesh. Her breathing quickened.

Without prompting, he knelt at her side, so his hand could wander deeper into the darkness. And now his face was on a level with hers, she cupped his cheek—feeling the roughness of his skin—and pulled him in. He turned his face, and as he pressed his lips against hers, she let her mouth open and felt his probing tongue. He tasted of tea and biscuits.

As his left hand touched her pussy, his other hand managed to take hold of her breast. Veronica allowed herself a groan and his fingers slipped between the damp cleft and rubbed there gently.

He has done this before, how nice...

"We should go, Nika."

Polly's voice broke through her rising desire. Lawrence stopped rubbing her and his hand released her breast. She groaned in disappointment.

Then Lawrence kissed her again. Just a sweet, quick kiss. Like a thank you.

His hand withdrew from between her legs, but she caught it up and brought it to her nose, sniffing deeply.

"You smell of me."

"I'm glad," he said. He pulled away and stood straight, disappearing from her view save for the even larger bulge. She reached out and laid her fingers on it.

"I would like to experience this," she said. "Quite soon."

xiv

"That was frustrating," said Veronica to Polly as they stood in the entrance hall of Slack, Slack, and Mortimer. Her thighs were slick and she still felt hot. At that moment all she wanted to do was ravish Polly where she stood. Unfortunately, that sort of behaviour was disapproved of in a public place.

Polly glanced round quickly, then brushed the back of her hand across Veronica's cheek. "We can have fun later, Nika."

She snatched her hand back as someone came through a door.

"Is Mrs Martaci not here?" said Lawrence.

Veronica consulted her watch. "She is late."

"Then let me escort you, Veronica," he said. "It is probably a minor delay and we may meet her on the way." He pressed a button set in a brass, dome-shaped mount on the wall. Veronica heard a bell ring in the distance.

Then he offered his left arm, the hand of which had been stroking her quim only minutes before. That did not, however, relieve Veronica's concerns about walking through the town. "We could just go home."

"Nonsense. If you had been to Mrs Martaci's home, you would not miss the opportunity to go again, and since you have not, it is important that you should."

Veronica hesitantly put her arm through his. "Do you not have work to do?"

"Mrs Martaci is also a client, therefore this is work."

The boy appeared, summoned by the bell, and opened the door for them. Their side of the street was now in shadow, but Veronica took the parasol that Polly opened for her. It helped hide her twisted back.

The town smelled of vegetables and animal dung. They passed a bakery. The shop part was closed, though she could imagine there was a great deal of work going on in the back as they prepared the bread for the following day.

The occasional cart ground by accompanied by the clopping of hooves. Then the huffing of a steam-powered tractor pulling a massive load of barrels towards the railway station. The barrels were piled so high the trailer must have had a Faraday device built into it.

The small group of stalls that had been there earlier was gone, and fewer people walked the streets. Who could blame them? The sun's heat was oppressive.

"What does Signora Martaci do?" Veronica asked, and Lawrence's arm twitched.

"She's a painter."

"What does she paint?"

Lawrence laughed. "You'll see what she paints, though the answer would be anything and everything, but a more appropriate question might be to ask what medium she works in."

"Well, I expect she works in oils, I tried watercolours and I hated it."

"Yes, oils mostly. She does watercolour sketches though."

"Has she painted you?"

Again, the arm twitch.

"Yes."

"Was it a good likeness?"

"She is a good artist."

"I hope to see it one day."

"You—you could ask to see it."

"It's not at your home?"

"Ah, there she is," he said. "I'll leave you to her tender care."

— ◉ —

A SHORT TIME LATER they were being invited into a cottage set off from the main road which continued across a wooden bridge and into the fields beyond. The front door gave directly into a living room with leather upholstered sofas. The walls were so covered in paintings there was almost no space between them.

The subjects covered landscapes with huge mountains that Veronica assumed to be Italy. There were city scenes with Roman columns and buildings. One particularly large painting was of a wide square at night, with shops lit up, people wandering the streets in outlandish costumes carrying lanterns on poles.

"Verona," said Sofia, coming back into the room with a tray of coffee and small cakes. "Where I used to live."

"Why did you come to England?" said Veronica as she moved on to a smaller picture of a man lounging in the sun.

"My husband died," she said. "That's him."

"You didn't want to stay?"

"There was nothing left for me there," she said, standing just behind Veronica and, embarrassingly, looking over her hump. "After Alessandro died, and the war with the Ottomans, I decided it was time to come home."

"You're English?"

"Did I have you fooled?" she said with a smile, then touched the face of the man in the painting. "Yes, I was born in this house. I expect I shall die here. But there are very few people who know who I was. I kept my married name and used my Italian mother-in-law's given name."

It sounded morbid, but Mrs Martaci did not seem sad.

"Your house is wonderful," said Veronica. "All these paintings." She moved to the wall opposite the fire to another large canvas. "This is the war?"

The image depicted crowds of people fleeing along a road, and many lying dead in the fields and on the road itself. Above them was a huge triple-hulled airship broken in half, and falling from the sky. There was some sort of large bird flying from within it. "I don't understand the symbolism of the bird."

"My daughter."

"Your daughter was killed, I'm sorry."

"Oh no, as far as I know my daughter is alive and well somewhere. Probably having an adventure. She was always having adventures."

Polly stared at the painting, getting closer and closer.

"That ain't a bird, Signora Martaci, that's a flying machine." She turned and stared with wide eyes at the older woman. "That's the *Pegasus*. Harry and Sellie's *Pegasus*, the one in the books." Her voice was filled with excitement. "The Edgbaston Sisters? You're Harry's mum."

Polly realised she had spoken out of turn in front of her betters. Her face fell. "Sorry, miss, ma'am. Very sorry."

But then the light was dawning for Veronica too. "The story about how they found you by following the clues in a painting. Winifred Churchill wrote the book."

Sofia sighed. "Yes, I was married to Harriet's father, and she is my daughter. But I'm nothing to do with that slave brat she calls her sister."

Veronica went numb and realised that this was clearly not a subject to be pursued. She endeavoured to change it. "Lawrence said you painted a picture of him."

There was a long silence. "He told you that?"

Veronica nodded. The tone of the question told her that in trying to change the subject she had stumbled into something else.

"Well, if he told you he must expect me to show it to you," said Mrs Martaci. "Are you special to him?"

It was Veronica's turn to feel embarrassed. "N-no, he's just a friend, I suppose. Well, he's my solicitor." *Since an hour ago and I'm still wet where he touched me.*

Their hostess stood and Veronica followed suit. Polly started to come over.

"Your maid should remain here."

Polly stopped. Veronica shrugged, since there was little she could do under the circumstances.

"I keep my private collection in the second bedroom."

The wooden stairs creaked as they made their way up. There were two doors on the small landing; one was open and Veronica could see a neat bedroom with plain materials covering the bed and chair. Mrs Martaci did not seem to like patterns.

"Why do you pretend you're Italian and Catholic?"

The older woman paused at the door. "My daughter couldn't stay out of the newspapers with her ridiculous stunts, and those books just made it worse. They all think she's some sort of heroine. If people knew who I was, I would be plagued by excited visitors like your maid every minute of every day. I'm not interested in that, and I'm not interested in her. I prefer my life to be quiet. If I can keep people away, so much the better."

Veronica could understand that to a degree, even if the woman's dislike of her daughter and apparent hatred of her adoptive sister, was unpleasant.

However, what was also known was that Sofia had abandoned her husband and daughter to go to Italy—Winifred Churchill's books did not hide the fact, nor that Harry's mother, had adulterous relations with other men in Italy. It was not said explicitly, of course, but it was implied, and that would be a lovely scandal for the newspapers. Little wonder she did not want her real identity known.

Sofia opened the door into the second bedroom. It was even more packed with pictures than the downstairs. On the floor there were canvases three or four deep. All of the images she could see at first glance were figurative. People standing, reclining, some on their own, some in twos and threes.

And every single one of them naked.

Not only that, each one in a pose or position that was suggestive of—Veronica stared—sex. A man lying on a bed with his back to the viewer, the position of his hand clearly implying he was playing with his prick.

There were several of women in similar types of position. And one where an older woman was brazenly looking out of the picture, sitting on the edge of a bed with her legs wide apart, dark hair at her delta, and holding an artificial phallus in her hand.

"I do like that one," said Mrs Martaci. "The others are usually too shy. She was a pleasure to work with. Are you old enough to understand what these pictures depict?"

Veronica nodded. "Yes, Sofia."

Was it only this morning she had been looking at photographs of her parents having sex with one another, and other people? The photographs were precise, yet lifeless, but the paintings were filled with energy, as if the lust of the models were part of the very paint that made them.

Veronica looked around the room with different eyes and a sense of wonderment. All these pictures of people who had willingly allowed this woman to paint them in their most intimate moments of pleasure.

"Lawrence is over here."

Tearing herself away from the image in front of her, Veronica followed Mrs Martaci across the room and round a central display. He was naked, though that was no surprise, and sitting on the edge of the bed. Unlike the others, this one appeared to have been painted much closer, so that he occupied a much larger proportion of the canvas.

"He didn't want to perform."

He wasn't touching himself, and there was something unaccountably sad about the way he leaned forwards with his elbows on his knees, his chin in his hands looking out at the viewer. His prick was quite large—and Veronica felt she was becoming a good judge of this after the photographs and the paintings, and the fact she had touched it earlier.

"Why did he want it like this; didn't he know what you expected?"

"Oh yes, he knew, but if you want to know why, you'll have to ask him."

"Thank you for showing me."

"As I said, young lady, if he hadn't wanted you to see it, he wouldn't have mentioned it."

———◆———

THEY RETURNED TO THE parlour. It was clear Polly was desperate to know what Veronica had seen, but she would have to wait.

"I'm getting married," said Veronica. She still had trouble with the idea; saying it out loud didn't make it any more real.

"I know, to Edwin Jameson."

"I wondered if I might commission a painting."

"What sort?"

"In my wedding dress."

Mrs Martaci did not look impressed. "Why not just have some photographs done?"

"There will be photographs, of course, Sofia," said Veronica, "but the dress is special, designed by Mademoiselle Vionnet, and your paintings are so alive."

The older woman eyed her for a long moment. "I will need several hours."

"All at one time?"

"Over a week."

"The dress is being brought on Friday and I'm not really doing anything next week. Could you do it while practising Italian in the mornings?"

"Perhaps." Mrs Martaci looked thoughtful. "Is this a painting for your betrothed, or for my gallery upstairs?"

"It's not a gift, it's for me, but—could there be two? One that anyone can see, one for the gallery?"

The woman nodded. "Would you want me to hide your deformity?"

Veronica hesitated. To see herself as she might have been? She already knew what that looked like in the photographs of her mother. She shook her head. "No, I want you to paint me as I am."

"Good. If you had said anything else, I would have refused to paint you. *Ti farò una bellissima sposa.*"

⸺●⸺

VERONICA DID NOT REALISE how tired she had become until the ride home. She yawned incessantly as they made their way along the sunny, tree-lined lanes. With the driver within earshot she still couldn't tell Polly about the paintings.

She half-expected to receive a rebuke from Mrs Jenkins when they arrived back at Versyns at nearly five o'clock, but the housekeeper was not at the door, so Veronica gratefully made her way to her parents' room. *My room.*

Veronica lay on the bed with the Faraday adjusted to provide a slight lessening of pressure, and managed not to fall asleep this time. Polly ran her bath and helped her into it. Then was suitably astonished then shocked when she learnt about the special gallery and its contents.

"But why does she hate her daughter?" said Polly. "Harry stopped a war and saved the Empire more than once. And why does she so dislike Harriet's half-sister?"

"I can answer your second question: because she's a black African slave."

"But Harry's dad rescued her."

"My parents despise me, Polly, because I am not perfect like them. You might as well ask why they don't love me as ask why Sofia Martaci dislikes her own child." *Although in my case the answer could be that I am not my father's daughter.*

They went down to eat in the ballroom, although there hardly seemed any point since its furniture remained covered to protect it. However, it seemed during the afternoon it had been equipped with electric lighting.

Progress was being made, even though it felt as if she would be living with these workmen for the rest of her life.

XV

Thursday was, thankfully, an uncomplicated day. She and Polly made love in the morning, bathed, and went down to breakfast. The post had a single letter for her, from Lawrence, confirming a meeting at his office with her and Edwin at ten in the morning.

"I need an appointments diary," said Veronica as she read it.

"I believe Mr Laughton has a supply, miss," said Mr Jones. "I will arrange for one."

"Who needs to know my comings and goings?"

"Both the housekeeper and the steward, miss, so that they can inform and arrange the rest of the household."

"Do they know Mademoiselle Vionnet will be arriving tomorrow with her staff?"

"I did inform them, miss."

"That's good," she said. "What have I forgotten?"

"Painting, miss," said Polly.

"Oh yes. Each morning next week, at least until Wednesday, Mrs Sofia Martaci will be here painting me in my wedding dress. That's instead of Mr Plumley's tutoring."

"And which room will you be using as a studio, miss?"

"I suppose that depends on what Signora Martaci needs—" *and the privacy needed for something more salacious,* "—but she'll be here later, so we can sort that out then."

"Of course, miss."

Although not ideal, Sofia declared the library as the best choice when she arrived. Partly for the same reason as Edwin had said he liked it, it was north-facing so never had direct sunlight, but also because it could be locked.

While Sofia was examining the room to decide on how she might like to frame her picture, Veronica spoke quietly to Mr Plumley.

"I am so sorry we have not had the opportunity to indulge your pleasure, Mr Plumley. After all, I did promise."

He glanced quickly over to Sofia then back. "P-please, M-mistress Nika, do not b-be concerned. I understand this is a v-very difficult time for you. The house has b-been in uproar. You are to b-be m-married. I have no claim on you."

As they spoke, Sofia had gone to her bag and pulled out a small camera, and took photographs of the room from different angles.

"Have you known her very long?"

"Since our nannies pushed prams together through the town," he said.

"You know who she really is then."

"I recognised her when I first saw her on her return."

Veronica took a chance, hoping that she would not betray Sofia's confidence, but if Mr Plumley had really known her that long...

"And you know about her..."

Mr Plumley waited for her to finish the sentence, but when she did not, "Second b-bedroom?"

"Yes."

"I m-must say, m-Mistress Nika, you do w-work very quickly."

"Do I?"

"You have b-barely known Sofia a w-week and yet you are already p-p-privy to her secrets."

Veronica thought it would be best not to mention Lawrence at this point. Mr Plumley might know about the room, but that did not mean he knew everyone who was depicted on canvas there.

"I have asked Sofia to do a second picture."

"One suitable for her special collection?"

"Quite so."

"You are asking me to stay away."

"Oh no, Mr Plumley, quite the contrary. I want you to be here."

"Are you sure? You will m-most certainly b-be in a state of *dishabille*. P-possibly entirely naked."

"It will draw less attention if you are here. After all, you are the person my parents appointed to be my tutor, not Sofia."

He considered the point. "You are correct. Then I will sit and read with my b-back turned so that you are not embarrassed."

Veronica put her hand on his arm and smiled, though he could not see it in her down-turned face. "I said before that you are a gentleman, sir, and you prove it to be true once more. But I do not deserve your grace, since I am less than a lady." She fully expected him to protest, so kept going before he had the chance. "Did I not encourage you to reveal your desire? And I was not disgusted when you did so. On the contrary, I offered my feet to you. Worse, I sold that part of my body to you in return for favours. No, sir, I am not a lady, perhaps little better than a well-bred whore, and for that reason I want you to see me. If you can bear exposure to my deformity."

"You m-may have p-prostituted your b-body in part, m-Mistress Nika, but m-make no m-mistake: in a world where a w-woman has so little p-power, and you less than m-most, you simply used w-what you had to gain some f-fraction of control in your life. You and p-Polly are a delightful couple, why should you not have p-privacy."

"You know?"

"Sapphic love is hardly uncommon, m-Mistress Nika. And I w-would have to b-be as b-blind as Tiresias not to see the way you two are w-with one another."

"I thought we hid it well." Except Mr Jones knew, and probably several others of the staff. And Seth, of course.

"The two of you spend more time in my p-presence than perhaps any other single p-person."

⸺◆⸺

THE REST OF THE DAY was a happy return to normality. Sofia helped them with their Italian before and after luncheon, while Mr Plumley either listened or read. After the teachers left at four o'clock, Veronica and Polly took a turn around the gardens. They did not see Seth, but took a moment to inspect the progress on the cold conservatory and the photographic room.

"We don't have a studio," said Veronica.

Polly laughed. "We have the world in which to take our photographs, and—" she glanced round and dropped her voice to a whisper, "—our bedroom."

"I know, but Sofia has given me ideas."

"When?"

"When I was in her special gallery."

"This is another thing that could get us into serious trouble, isn't it?"

"I was just thinking that if people want to have sexual paintings made, I could do sexual photographs."

"Your parents have already done that, and you have the fruits of their work in your album."

"I know, but that's just personal."

Polly laughed. "I think having photographs taken diddling yourself, sticking things up your quim, or getting fucked, are very personal."

"I was just thinking people might pay to own pictures like that. People pay Sofia, after all."

"Who would let themselves be photographed to make money?"

"Seth."

Polly paused. "He might."

"Me," said Veronica.

Polly said nothing.

Veronica frowned. "You think nobody would want a picture of a hunch-back."

"I didn't say that."

"You didn't have to, but—" she looked around, there were no workmen in sight but you couldn't be too careful, "—we can't have this conversation here."

Veronica retired to her room with Polly. She decided she didn't want any further revelations from her parents' album tonight. So, after they had eaten, she sat at the table in the bedroom and said, "Carrots."

"Oh no."

"Carrots, and a couple of paring knives."

———◆———

VERONICA'S HAND WAS aching by the time she had stripped off the outside of her carrot, then cut off the ends and whittled the shape into some-thing resembling a prick—she had chosen one about the size of Seth's, but by the time she had finished cutting, it was rather smaller. She shook her hands to relieve the ache.

Polly's effort was more accurate in shape, but considerably smaller—given her experiences Veronica didn't blame her. She had already decided not to push the point if Polly didn't want to do it at all.

On the positive side, the carrots were still quite moist even after being in the dressing room for a couple of days.

"I don't think I'm in the mood after all that," said Veronica, now massaging one hand with the other.

"If you think I'm going to have spent time hacking up a carrot for nothing, you are quite mistaken, Nika." She stood and came up behind Veronica.

"Don't hit me."

"Hit you? Why would I hit you?"

"You did when we were playing with Seth."

"Yes, well, that was a special occasion. I have something else in mind."

Veronica felt Polly's head beside hers on the left, and then teeth nibbling at her neck. A tingle ran across her face and down her arm. Then a hand slipped under her arm and cupped her breast through her dress.

"That's not fair."

"Of course it isn't."

Polly gently squeezed as she licked her mistress from collarbone to ear. Veronica made a little noise. Polly's tongue licked around the folds of her ear.

"Lift up your dress, Nika."

She obeyed, pulling fold after fold into her lap until the lower part of her thighs were exposed to the air. She could feel something going on at her back while Polly's hand continued to manipulate her breast through the inconvenient layers of material. Warmth spread through her in the anticipation of pleasure.

"Spread your legs."

They had been pulling apart of their own volition anyway. Veronica opened them as wide as she could, pushing the folds of her dress further up her thighs.

"Stay there."

Polly moved away, leaving Veronica adrift. She stared down at the carrots on the table, and imagined one in her pussy. Then in her rear. The lust continued to rise, but she did as Polly instructed and simply waited. Anticipation increased pleasure.

"Move forward on the chair."

She slid awkwardly until her bum was right on the edge, and felt pillows being tucked in behind her.

"Lean back."

Veronica smiled and did so. "Thank you."

Polly's lips pressed against hers and they kissed for a long moment, until Veronica jumped as something cold and damp touched her thigh.

"You wanted this," said Polly into Veronica's mouth.

"Cold."

"Not my concern."

The cold thing slid up the inside of Veronica's thigh until it pressed against her pussy. It was warming a little now, but it was still an almost unpleasant shock. Polly rubbed it up and down Veronica's lips. The surface had not seemed rough when she shaped it, but now it seemed to be nothing but edges and bumps—and it made the lust within her increase a thousandfold. She moaned.

Then whined as Polly removed it, and pulled away.

"Open your mouth wide."

Veronica did as she was told and moments later the irregular phallus slipped between her lips. Her own scent and taste was familiar to her, but mixed with the moist carrot it seemed strange. Polly slipped it a short distance in, then pulled it out again. Then in, as if it was fucking Veronica's mouth. Each time a little deeper, until it touched the back of her throat.

Closing her eyes, Veronica remembered what it was like to have Seth's member in her mouth, and imagined the carrot was flesh. As it moved in and out, she sucked and licked it. The heat between her legs simmered and she growled in animalistic pleasure. Finally, Polly withdrew it completely and brought it back between Veronica's legs. She slid it once more down her crack, turned it, and found her pussy hole. She held it at the opening.

"You really want this in you?"

"Yes." Veronica's intense reply was like the hissing of a snake.

"Yes what?"

"Yes *please*."

Veronica held her breath as the phallus slid into her. The roughness pulled at her, causing sparks of lust. It came to a halt. Polly pushed harder, but it barely moved.

"Wrong angle," hissed Veronica.

Polly did something and the uncomfortable pressure went away.

"Yes, in!"

Veronica gasped as Polly slammed it the rest of the way, then grunted as it came to a stop. The feeling was astonishing. She felt full and it just seemed right, as if there should always be something inside her.

Polly threw her leg over Veronica's thigh and sat.

"Now I can see what I'm doing, and I get to have some pleasure myself," she said and promptly started rubbing her pussy back and forth on Veronica's knee. At the same time, she moved the carrot in and out.

"Oh god," said Veronica breathlessly. She reached down to rub her nubbin. The world shrank and all she knew was the sensation going in and out of her hole, and the building tension as she stimulated herself. She grunted in time to the penetrations. Polly was moving her own hips faster and making her own little noises through clenched teeth.

Veronica had enough consideration to slide her hand under Polly's dress until she found a pair of bloomers, and added stimulation there as well.

The fire inside drove out all remaining rational thought. Veronica could barely rock her thighs with Polly bringing herself to paroxysm on her knee, so she grabbed Polly's wrist between her legs and slammed the carrot harder and faster into her body. Polly got the idea and did not hold back.

Veronica screamed as the paroxysm took her, then clamped her mouth shut. Her body spasmed a dozen times, then Polly too squealed and Veronica could feel her pussy muscles clenching again and again.

Moments later the energy went out of her and she relaxed.

Polly leaned forward and rested her head on Veronica's shoulder. It took a minute for their breathing to settle. The carrot, which had seemed wedged inside, slid out and thumped onto the floor.

Polly giggled. "That's going to be all dirty now."

"I need to lie down," said Veronica.

"Can't move."

"My back…"

"Sorry." Polly stood, taking the pressure off Veronica's leg, and managed to disentangle herself. She helped her mistress to her feet so that she could make her way to the bed. Veronica turned the Faraday to maximum and fell forwards into its cloud-like embrace.

Sexual games were very enjoyable, but exhausting.

Polly clambered on the bed with her and stripped her. With the Faraday operating at maximum, Polly was able to lift Veronica and turn her as if she were nothing more than a doll.

They went to sleep in each other's arms.

xvi

The next morning Veronica lay in bed while Polly cleaned the room, tidied away all evidence of carrots, and hid the photographic album.

"Have we got that appointments diary?" said Veronica.

Polly came out of the dressing room and found it before she went through the adjoining door into 'her' room. Veronica found today's page.

"When did my last monthly start?"

"Last Saturday," Polly called from the other room.

"And what's my cycle?"

"Three-and-a-half weeks."

"About twenty-four days then?"

There was no response.

The diary was one page per day, so Veronica counted on the number and made a shape like a water droplet by the printed date of Tuesday, 16th August.

Then she went back to the eighth, wrote 'Wedding', and promptly realised she had not been given a time. "Men are useless," she muttered.

"What?"

"Men are useless!"

"Better stick to carrots then."

"What are you doing in there?"

"Making it look like I actually sleep in this room."

"Damnation," said Veronica, then looked round to make sure no one had heard, and laughed at herself.

"What's wrong?" came the disconnected voice of Polly.

"My next courses are the second week of the holiday."

"I'll pack your pads then."

Veronica set about filling in all the dates she knew. The meeting with Edwin on the Friday before the wedding; three days of being painted Monday to Wednesday; being fitted for her wedding dress over the weekend.

"We should have a bath," said Veronica as Polly returned—still naked.

"Any particular reason?"

"In case Mademoiselle wants to start the fitting immediately."

Polly went into the bathroom and moments later came the sound of water thundering from the taps, and the roar as the heater caught.

Veronica's mind went from the arrival of Madeleine Vionnet, to the fitting (perhaps), to the evening meal where there would be herself, Vionnet, her staff, and Polly. But surely Polly and the staff would not eat with them. Of course, technically, even Mademoiselle was a servant, because she was being employed to make a dress, but there was no way that Veronica could possibly treat a *couturier* like one of the staff.

Usually, in the evening, she and Polly simply came up to the bedroom to play and then went to bed. But if there were guests?

"Oh no."

Veronica launched herself lightly through the Faraday field, flying above the bedclothes until she passed over the edge of the bed and came down hard on the wooden floor.

She rushed into the bathroom where Polly was emptying bath salts into the tumbling water.

"I have to *entertain!*"

⎯⎯⎯●⎯⎯⎯

VERONICA WAS STILL in shock at breakfast.

"Are you all right, miss?" said the butler.

She looked at his waist. "Did my parents ever entertain?"

"In the house, yes, miss, it was not uncommon." There was a curious quality to his voice that changed his soft Welsh tones.

Yes, of course they did, and I have seen the photographs.

"Yes, I remember your comment about seeing things you did not wish to see, Jones," she said carefully, "and I believe I may even have some idea what you are referring to."

"You are concerned about the arrival of Mademoiselle Vionnet and her *entourage?*" He said the last word with a distinctly French twist.

"Can you help?"

"Well, miss, there are, of course, certain protocols to be obeyed..."

"The men smoking cigars and the ladies withdrawing."

"Quite so."

"What if there aren't any men?"

"Miss?"

"What if I invite Signora Martaci?"

"You are perfectly entitled to do so, miss."

"And what if she knows someone she could bring, a woman?"

"That would be acceptable."

Veronica had a sudden idea. "Does Edwin—I mean the *Honourable* Edwin*—have any sisters at home?"

"Lady Katherine has had ten children, the youngest two are Ruth and Esther and they are still at home."

"I could invite them too," she said. "If I'm to have sisters-in-law, I should get to know them." *Though they might not want to get to know the beast of Versyns House.*

"If I may, miss, it would be inappropriate to invite the youngest daughters alone. You could, however, invite Lady Katherine *and* her daughters."

Veronica was suddenly excited; she had been presented with a household problem and had solved it, *except*, "Can Cook cope?"

"You will need to speak to Mrs Jenkins on the matter."

Veronica nodded and thought quickly. "Let me write the letter to Lady Katherine first. Then I will speak to Sofia when she arrives for the lesson, and then I will see Mrs Jenkins as soon as the reply arrives."

"Very good, miss. I will fetch the writing slope."

He left and Veronica turned to Polly. "What do you think?"

"I think that will work very well..."

There was a *but* hanging in the air between them.

"What's wrong?"

"Nothing."

"I may be damaged in body, my love, but not in mind. Tell me."

There was a pause. "I can't be part of this life with you."

"You can be there."

"Only to serve, not to take part."

Veronica's excitement dissolved.

VERONICA WAS UNSURPRISED when Signora Martaci agreed to attend the hastily arranged party.

"I will bring Mrs Tiffany Cooper."

"Who is she?"

"Her husband is the master of Inglethorpe Manor. He was a wool merchant, and now owns several large textile companies. He's away from home a great deal and she would enjoy a pleasant, ladies-only evening."

"But she's not common?"

Mrs Martaci put her head on one side. "I did not think you were concerned with such things, Miss Clifford-Hughes."

"I'm not, but Lady Katherine, my future mother-in-law, is also invited."

"I am of very common birth, Veronica, even if my life has been less than pedestrian, and you did not even think to ask it of me. Rest assured Tiff was born of good merchant stock. It was her money her husband used to expand his business, though her investment has been repaid a dozen times over. She is quite used to moving in more exalted circles. Lady Katherine has purchased my paintings, and I know she has met Tiff before. You need have no worries on that score."

"They just have to agree to come."

THE LETTER TO LADY Katherine had been sent by messenger rather than through the post, to expedite its timely arrival and answer. The short response, arriving shortly after eleven, indicated that Lady Katherine would attend with her two youngest daughters.

With mounting trepidation, Veronica rang for Mr Jones and asked him if he could fetch Mrs Jenkins to the ballroom.

She sat, then realised if she did that and Mrs Jenkins remained standing, all Veronica would see would be the woman's legs at best. So she stood, and arranged a chair for Mrs Jenkins to sit in. That reversed the authority roles, but at least Veronica would be able to see the woman's face.

She rehearsed half a dozen different ways to open the conversation, but each of them ended up being an apology, and Mrs Beeton said that the lady of the house was like a general leading her troops. She must not apologise, but also not be rude. Firm, but not forceful.

It was all very well a woman in a book fifty years old saying that, but how were you supposed to manage it? Especially with the habit of eighteen years as a victim.

I must not be Veronica, I must be Mistress Nika. Easy to say—

Mrs Jenkins entered, but before she had a chance to speak Veronica said, "Please sit down, Mrs Jenkins. I would like to be able to see you properly, so I must stand."

Whether it was from surprise, or from the experience of being discovered by Veronica in Mr Laughton's office, the woman did not protest, but did as she was instructed.

"Since we have Mademoiselle Vionnet staying until Sunday, we must provide an evening's entertainment tonight. I have invited Lady Katherine, and she will be coming with her youngest daughters."

"Lady Katherine?"

"Well, she is going to be my mother-in-law," said Veronica. "And also Signora Martaci."

Mrs Jenkins did not look happy.

"Is there a problem with that, Mrs Jenkins?"

"Since you ask, Miss Clifford-Hughes, that woman is an artist and a *foreigner*."

"I am well aware, and she is bringing Mrs Cooper of Inglewood Manor."

"I suppose that's better."

Veronica frowned. "I do not require your approval, Mrs Jenkins, my only concern is that the meal will be appropriate for my guests. Can Cook deal with this on such short notice?"

The housekeeper shifted in her chair. "We'll need to buy additional provisions, and change the selection for today."

"But you can do it?"

"It can be done."

"And the dessert? What would you suggest?"

Mrs Jenkins thought for a moment. "We have fresh gooseberries, so we can have baked gooseberry pudding with a thin, rich custard."

"Oh yes, that's delicious."

Mrs Jenkins *smiled*. "Thank you, Miss Clifford-Hughes."

"You make it?"

"Cook's not the best on puddings and desserts. I usually make them when there's fresh fruits available."

"I didn't know."

"No reason you should, miss."

"I suppose not, but I do now. Thank you."

"I better be getting about the tasks, miss, there's a lot to do with your Frenchie and her people coming as well."

With that she stood and left. Veronica leaned back against the table. That had gone much better than she expected. And that Mrs Jenkins made the puddings she loved was even more of a surprise.

It had been an interesting day, and it was less than halfway through.

She made her way back to the library where Polly was practising her Italian with Mrs Martaci.

"What on earth do we do after the meal?" she said as she walked into the room.

xvii

At twenty-two minutes after three that afternoon a carriage drew up at front door and Mademoiselle Vionnet stepped down.

Veronica stood at the top of the steps that led up to the main door; she leaned on her walking stick. She realised her free hand was compulsively clutching at her dress, and forced herself to hold still. She was painfully aware how unprepared she was to become a hostess and wished, a little, for the days when she had no responsibilities like this.

Polly had given her hand a squeeze before they had come out into daylight, and now stood a little back behind her. Mr Jones loomed at her side, and some of the other staff waited in the shadows, ready to fetch the luggage. Mrs Jenkins was not present, but busy making sure everything was running smoothly below stairs.

"Do not be concerned, miss—" the butler's voice was pitched so only she might hear him, "—remember that this is your home and you are happy to see them."

"I'm terrified."

"Place a smile upon your face and the rest will follow."

"Should I go down to greet her?"

"Not at all, miss. Mademoiselle Vionnet may be an important person in her own world, but she is working for you. An employee, as it were. You can if you wish, but you are not required to do so. Even if she were someone of quality, it would not be required as you are not able-bodied."

Not able-bodied? She knew he had not meant any harm by it, but there were only ten steps and she was not an invalid. Veronica forced the mask of good humour on to her face and set off down the steps.

"Mademoiselle Vionnet, I am so pleased to see you," she said as she reached the bottom. "I hope your journey was not tiresome."

Vionnet's dress was an off-the-shoulder creation of flowing lines in reds and purples, brought up tight below her bust and criss-crossed in a Grecian-style pattern. She wore a wide-brimmed hat echoing the colours, but adding to them with a blue scarf.

She did not reply, but stepped up to Veronica and kissed her on both cheeks. "*Ma cherie*, I am so glad to be here. The heat in your railway tubes was stifling. I did not believe I would ever breathe the fresh air again."

Two more women descended from the carriage, both dressed *a la mode*, but less ostentatiously than Mademoiselle Vionnet. They were of a height, but one had long and straight auburn hair to her shoulders, and a beauty spot, while the other seemed chiselled from alabaster, with short, black curls. At that moment, an engine started up somewhere round the side of the building, along with a regular metallic banging.

"And what is this? Has London come with me?"

"I'm afraid the house is being remodelled, mademoiselle. There are a great number of workers in and around the house, and will be into next week I'm afraid."

"We must have a private place to do the fittings."

"Your rooms are finished, mademoiselle." She thought that was a good moment to turn towards the steps and hope that Mr Jones took that as a signal for the staff to come and collect the bags. "And my bedroom might be suitable if nowhere else can be found.

"*Ça fera*, Miss Veronica, that will do. These are my staff, Miss Josephine Massingham—" that was the redhead, "and Miss Clio Mayhew." The two women nodded their heads in acknowledgement, but turned to the rear of the carriage as housemaids arrived.

"I'm sure you would like to refresh yourselves after the journey," said Veronica. "Dinner will be at seven. We will have some other guests, Lady Katherine, her daughters, and some interesting people from the town."

Veronica could not help but notice the pursing of Mademoiselle Vionnet's lips—as if she expected "interesting people" to be not that at all.

"The person paying the bill will be here then," said Vionnet. "I will not show her your dress."

"I don't think she's expecting you to," said Veronica. *I hope not.*

The next few minutes was a whirl of coordinated activity which Veronica had little part in, as the guests' luggage was taken inside. Then, after walking back up the stairs and into the building with the new arrivals, they too were escorted to their rooms.

It was not even four o'clock and Veronica stood with Polly in the hall, listening to workmen calling, whistling, and making loud bangs.

"This is a nightmare," said Veronica.

"Signora Martaci said she would prepare some ideas for the evening."

"I should be doing that."

"If someone else offers to do something when you don't even have the first idea of what's right, that's a good thing."

"I'm not ungrateful, I just..." Her voice trailed off because she did not even know what she wanted to say.

"Come on," said Polly. She took Veronica's hand and led her into the ballroom and then through to the garden. "Let's sit in the arbour. You can calm down in the quiet and I'll fetch you a drink."

"I don't even know if the correct etiquette is for mademoiselle's staff to eat with us or with the servants."

"They aren't servants, so they eat with you. It's easy."

They reached the sheltered spot where they could see the garden but were hidden from the house, and most of its noise.

"But what will Lady Katherine think?" said Veronica, perching on the edge of the bench.

"Does it matter?"

"Of course it does."

"Why? She's not even coming to the wedding. Nobody is invited, just you, Edwin, Mrs Jenkins, and Mr Laughton. I only get to be there because you wanted a bridesmaid."

"This must be the worst wedding that has ever been."

"And you will be in a dress designed by Mademoiselle Vionnet. You will look beautiful."

"That's impossible."

"Nika!" said Polly sharply. "No self-pity. Or I may be forced to beat you."

"Nika is just a game, Polly."

"Well, I prefer her."

A voice floated through the leaves: "I, too, will prefer this Nika to a whining girl."

Veronica jumped to her feet and wished that she had not, as pain went through her back. Mademoiselle Vionnet appeared around the bush.

"This is a very pleasing and private place," she said. "But your voices, they are not so private."

Vionnet had changed into another dress already. This was powder blue and in the modern style which showed off her S-shape without corsetry, or unnecessary fabric.

"I'm sorry, mademoiselle," said Veronica, "I fear I will not do justice to your dress, and no one will see it."

Mademoiselle Vionnet brushed the bench next to Veronica with her handkerchief, and sat.

"Have you forgotten already, Miss Veronica, all women are beautiful. And my creation, it will show your beauty to the world. Besides, the one you love will be there." Vionnet nodded at Polly. "And Vionnet will be there also."

"You're coming?"

"*Mais bien sûr*, do you think I would allow you to dress yourself?"

"I will dress her," said Polly with a hint of annoyance.

"You will be dressed by Vionnet also. You will not have time to dress your mistress. My girls will also attend, since I will. Your faces will be like the doll, and your hair will be a work of art—all to complement the genius of Vionnet."

"But what is the point, mademoiselle? Why waste your time and money?"

"If you do not listen, what is the point of explaining it once more," said Vionnet. "I hope the workmen are gone by next week."

Veronica took a deep breath to calm her nerves. "My future husband was insistent the house be ready by the wedding." Then something occurred to her. "May I ask you something, Miss Vionnet?"

"Will you listen to what I say?"

She thought about protesting, but decided to ignore the comment. "It's about my husband."

"You wish to know about what happens on the wedding night?"

"No, mademoiselle, I know what happens."

"I am glad to hear it. You English are such prudes, and so many girls *agneau à l'abattoir*."

"I'm sorry?"

"Like the lambs to be killed."

"Lambs to the slaughter?"

"*Oui*, they are told nothing of men, or worse, they are lied to. I have seen so many."

"No, mademoiselle, I am familiar with men's nature and desires."

Vionnet shifted her position to face Veronica. "You are a surprising young woman, Miss Veronique, or perhaps I should call you Nika?"

Veronica hesitated. "I do not mind you calling me that, but it must be in private only."

"*Bien sûr*, I understand. What is your question, if it is not about what a man desires on the wedding night?"

"That's the thing, mademoiselle, my future husband is very strange, and he says he will not be sleeping with me, but in a downstairs room so he can be near nature. I don't even know if that means he will want to consummate the marriage even on the first night."

Vionnet was quiet for a moment. "Does he prefer the company of men? You know what I mean?"

"Yes, I do know." Veronica recalled the images of her father and the man, but her father was also pictured with women. It seemed he did not mind either. "But I don't know if that is Edwin's preference. He's only marrying me out of duty to his family, as far as I know. He's not really interested in me, but from what I know of him, and it's little enough, I'm not sure he's interested in men either."

"Les animaux?"

This time Veronica *was* shocked. "Animals?"

"*Oui*, it happens."

"It does," said Polly.

"Oh," said Veronica, trying to absorb that piece of information. "Well, I don't know."

Vionnet shrugged. "It is not usual."

"Oh, good." Her curiosity had been piqued, but she knew, with an absolute certainty, she did not want any details.

"Perhaps," said Polly, "his pleasure is a bit simpler, Nika. You know, like Mr P. Perhaps you just need to find out what Edwin likes."

"Yes, well, that would be all right, but how am I supposed to find out if he doesn't even want to spend the night with me."

"Now is not the wedding night, Nika," said Vionnet. "Perhaps you should wait until then to decide what you will do."

"Anyway," said Polly, "Mr Slack said that if Edwin doesn't do you like he's supposed to, you can divorce him."

"I don't think we should be talking about divorce when I haven't even married him," said Veronica. "What should I do if he decides not to bed me the first night?"

Vionnet laughed. "You have two choices, Nika: you can spend the night with your pretty bridesmaid lover, or—" she growled her next words, "—*le forcer à te baiser.*"

Though she knew she had a good command of French, Veronica looked blank.

Vionnet put her hand on Veronica's arm and leaned in. "Make him fuck you, Nika."

Polly laughed and Veronica managed to force a smile onto her face. She wasn't feeling much like Nika at that moment.

Vionnet turned back and faced the garden. "It is pleasant here, but I would miss the traffic of London in less than a week. Now, Veronique, did you order the clothes?"

"I did, and they arrived today. Thank you so much for your help."

"And what will you be wearing this evening for your first *soiree*?"

Veronica hesitated. "This?"

The Frenchwoman made a sound of disgust. "You have so much to learn and I have so little time to instruct you. Show me these clothes that have arrived, and Vionnet will see what must be done to make them wearable."

xviii

Among the dresses that had been supplied was a modern crimson design that Vionnet rapidly unpicked and re-stitched to shape it around Veronica's back. The fit was quite perfect, so much better than any other dress she had ever had. And Vionnet had even explained everything she did to Polly.

The Frenchwoman might be tremendously arrogant, but her skill was without question, and she was happy to share her knowledge.

"Why are you doing all this?" Veronica asked as Vionnet threaded a very fine needle.

The woman had not even paused as she said, "I have decided you are my sister."

Veronica had to retreat to the bathroom and dab away her tears until she was fit for company again.

Then Veronica's hair and make-up had been done by Miss Massingham, and Miss Mayhew respectively.

Once they had returned downstairs, Mr Jones had politely explained, apologetically, that it was impossible for Polly to attend—which sent Veronica into a panic. Even if Polly had simply been in the room sitting to one side, it would give Veronica the strength she needed, but without her she would be like a ship in a storm that had lost its anchor.

"Your Polly will have a pleasant evening," said Vionnet putting her arm through Veronica's. "She and my girls will eat and drink and laugh together. And did I not say you were my sister now? I will stand for your *cherie* and make sure you do not fall."

At fifteen minutes to seven, Veronica stood in the main lounge; she might have been glad for Vionnet's support, but she was still paralysed with fear.

She was grateful when the first guests to arrive were Mrs Martaci and Mrs Cooper, the latter of whom looked to be perhaps fifty, but still energetic.

"Just call me Tiff, my dear, and that is such a beautiful dress."

"And your hair," said Sofia, "did your Polly do that?"

Try to be Nika, try to be Nika.

"No, it wasn't Polly, Sofia, but please let me introduce Mademoiselle Vionnet. My hair was arranged by Vionnet's hairdresser. They're here to fit my wedding dress."

"I hope I may steal her, Miss Vionnet."

"I do not think there is much chance of that, Mrs Cooper, but I may be willing to lend her out."

The conversation flowed comfortably and Veronica relaxed a little bit as she found she did not need to say a great deal, just smile and look interested.

The door opened and a maid entered carrying a tray of drinks—it was Ursula, tall and willowy. Veronica felt embarrassed now that she was face to face with the girl from whom she had stolen Polly.

But Ursula smiled as the drinks were taken, and then she was gone. To be replaced by Mr Jones.

"Lady Katherine, Viscountess Launceston, Miss Ruth Jameson, and Miss Esther Jameson."

A woman, perhaps only a little younger than Mrs Cooper, swept into the room in a midnight blue, modern-style dress of the highest quality—no doubt a Paquin design. Followed by the two girls who were younger than Veronica, wearing pink and purple that complemented their mother's colours. While the mother was clearly confident, the girls were less so. Their gaze landed on Veronica, slid to her right shoulder, and their eyes widened.

Everyone else had managed to be polite and avoid looking, at least when Veronica could see them.

Be Nika.

Veronica pushed a pleasant smile on to her face, stood as straight as she could, despite the strain, and walked across the carpet.

"Lady Katherine, how kind of you to—" then it hit her, she knew her face, "—come."

Veronica went cold. Lady Katherine was the woman in the picture. The one sitting on her father's face while she sucked him—being taken from behind by Veronica's mother.

"Miss Clifford-Hughes, delighted to make your acquaintance at last."

Veronica realised she had been holding the woman's hand too long—a hand that had gripped her father's prick, made him come—and released it.

"Thank you, Lady Katherine, the pleasure is mine. Did you know my mother?" The words rushed out though they seemed premature.

"Of course, Madge and I were very close at one time."

So close she fucked you with an artificial phallus. "Sadly, I haven't seen her or my father for a long time."

Lady Katherine did not respond to that. The air around them grew cold.

"Please, I would like you to meet my other guests. I think you know Mrs Cooper."

"Hello, Tiff, Sofia."

"And this is Vionnet."

"Madame Paquin's *protégée*. I don't think we've met."

"Quite so, Lady Katherine. Sadly, Madame was too busy to make the dress for your son's future bride. Vionnet has taken the task."

Veronica looked round to find the daughters. She held out her hand, almost in spite since they were rude enough to notice her deformity.

"Hello, I'm Veronica."

━━━━●━━━━

TO VERONICA'S RELIEF the conversation did not dry up, although there was far too much standing up for her liking. They sipped sherry, and talked about how hot the weather had been and if it would last until the wedding. Everybody said they hoped it would.

Lady Katherine discussed, when asked, her daughter's achievements, and it seemed both girls were very accomplished at the piano, and Ruth had a good singing voice. Both were students at Roedean School and Ruth would be off to finishing school next year. The older sister had already had her season, and it would be Esther's turn next year.

Sofia enquired whether they had considered going to university, but they both laughed at such a silly idea.

Nobody asked Veronica about her accomplishments, or whether she wanted to go to university—but then a hunchback was not expected to have any accomplishments, and she was marrying Edwin, so the idea of university was simply a nonsense. Why bother even mentioning it?

She kept smiling, but Veronica was getting angry. Mr Jones announcing dinner broke the spell and they headed into the dining room.

There was plenty of wine, and Veronica made the most of it. It helped to ease the strain in her back. If Polly had been there, she would have arranged cushions to help support her spine.

The meal courses came and went. Conversation went on around her; sometimes everyone spoke about the same thing, sometimes it would break up and multiple discussions happened at one time. Veronica found it confusing; she had never been in a situation like this. The only thing she could rely on was that, across the table from her, sat Vionnet, and the *couturier* would smile or nod at her to tell her that everything was all right.

"Sofia has agreed to paint me in my wedding dress," Veronica said out of the blue. She felt light-headed and knew she had been silent for a long time. As the hostess, she should speak.

"Oh, Sofia is so good," said Tiff. Veronica did not fail to notice the glance that passed between them and the slight smile on Tiff's face. "My husband bought one of her paintings and has it in Inglethorpe Hall."

"Could she do me, Mama?" said Esther.

"I'd love to," said Sofia. "And Ruth too, of course."

"Together, perhaps," said Lady Katherine.

"It was *my* idea," whined Esther, "why does she have to be in my picture."

Sofia laughed. "There does not need to be just one painting."

"Wouldn't I have to pose for hours and days?" said the younger daughter. "I could be like Ophelia."

"Go mad and die?" said Veronica.

"Why would that happen?"

Veronica placed her knife on the plate in front of her. "Ophelia by Millais is about her death in Shakespeare's play, but it's said the model, Lizzie Siddall, became ill because she was forced to lie in a cold bath for hours for the painting. And later she, too, died."

"That's horrible."

"Or," said Sofia, "she just got ill because sometimes people do."

The plates from the main course were cleared away and Mrs Jenkins appeared at the door. She stood to one side as two trays of desserts were brought in.

"Shall I switch on the electric lights, miss?" said Mr Jones.

Veronica looked around and realised the room had been getting dim with the twilight. She nodded and moments later she was blinking against the flood of light. And suddenly she could see everything clearly again—including the dessert on the trays.

"Baked gooseberry pudding," said Veronica. "Made by Mrs Jenkins."

"Gooseberries?" said Mademoiselle Vionnet. "I do not know them."

"I don't know what they are in French," said Veronica.

"*Uva spina* in Italian," said Sofia, but Vionnet shook her head.

"*Groseilles à maquereau*," said Lady Katherine as the plates were laid in front of the guests.

"*C'est vrai?*" Vionnet stared at the slightly red pie in her dish, edged with puff pastry. "Are they not green?"

Veronica looked at Mrs Jenkins, hoping she might offer an explanation.

"It happens in the cooking, Mademoiselle Vionnet. Even gooseberry jam can come out red."

"Cream or custard, Vionnet?" said Veronica, indicating the two jugs. She went for the cream.

Esther giggled. "You called her by her surname. It's like being at school."

The Frenchwoman looked up and smiled. "But I *am* Vionnet, there is only one and I am she. As you would call Bonaparte, or Wellington."

"At school they call Ruth 'Jameson Maxima', and I'm 'Jameson Minima.'"

Veronica poured the thin custard across her baked gooseberry pudding, cut into it with the spoon and took a mouthful. It was so light in texture you might think it was under the influence of the Faraday, but sharp to the tongue while the custard made a perfect sweet accompaniment.

"That is lovely, Mrs Jenkins, thank you."

The housekeeper blushed and retired. Her reaction pleased Veronica and she hoped that her plan for Mrs Jenkins worked out. Perhaps they might be able to tolerate one another, and the house would not need to be upset by the addition of a new housekeeper.

Finally, all the eating was done and they sat at the table for a little while to digest the meal. The conversation lagged.

"This would be the moment," said Lady Katherine, "that the gentlemen would light their cigars, pipes, and cigarettes, sip their brandies, while we ladies would withdraw."

"But there are no gentlemen here," said Veronica.

"I have cigars," said Sofia and pulled a silver holder from a pocket in her dress. Without even asking she offered one to Tiff, who accepted it. They accepted a light from the butler.

"Drinks are in the cabinet, miss, if your guests require something of that nature." He nodded toward the far wall where the tantalus had been unlocked. "As I am the only one of the male sex here, I will withdraw," he said with a smile. "Ring if you require anything, but I'll send some girls to move the table."

"Thank you, Mr Jones."

The fire had been lit. These sunny August days cooled quickly in the evening and it took the edge off the cold. Sofia and Tiff went to stand next to it as they smoked.

There were several sofas. Ruth and Esther fought over an armchair until their mother called them to order and they shared it, whispering and laughing. Veronica couldn't help but feel they were talking about her, but she tried to push the thought into the background.

She, Lady Katherine, and Vionnet stood to one side as the dinner table was pulled apart and moved to the side of the room.

Veronica took a deep breath. "I would offer a drink, Lady Katherine, but I am afraid I wouldn't know how much, or which glass. In fact, I would not even know which bottle."

"As we are all girls together, my dear, you may call me Kat, or even Aunt Kat, if you prefer."

Veronica's heart turned to ice as the woman's words reminded Veronica how close her parents had been to the mother of her future husband. And the truly terrifying thought that perhaps Lord Jameson had been the one taking the pictures, and that he joined in as well.

There was no doubt as to Veronica's matrilineage. *But what if Edwin really is my half-brother?*

Either because Lord Jameson was her natural father, or that her actual father had sired Edwin. Or both.

Yet they had both agreed to the marriage, desired it; were they confident she and Edwin were not related? Or, given that they apparently enjoyed sexual games in any combination, perhaps did they not care?

"Veronique? Are you well?"

Veronica forced herself back to the present. She was not sure she did feel well, but whether that was because of the strange possibilities going through her mind, or because she had eaten an unaccustomed amount of food, and drunk more alcohol in a couple of hours than perhaps her entire life before, she really didn't know.

"Are we ready for some games?" said Sofia to the room.

"Games?" said Veronica.

"We must have games. We have an evening ahead of us, and while we could spend it eating, drinking, smoking, and singing bawdy songs like a company of men—" Esther and Ruth giggled "—we are not men, and some of our party are too young for bawdy songs." There was subdued laughter from Tiff and Lady Katherine.

But I don't know any games. "I did not think, and have not prepared anything, I'm afraid."

"Fear not, Veronica," said Sofia, throwing the end of her cigar into the fire. "I have everything in hand and came prepared with a list."

"Magic music!" said Esther.

"They don't have a piano in here," said Ruth.

"It is on my list, and we shall begin with that," said Sofia.

"But they don't have a piano," insisted Ruth.

Sofia flicked her hand dismissively. "Vionnet, you are nearest to the drinks cabinet, a brandy glass and a swizzle stick if you please. And, since you did protest too much, Ruth, you will be *it.*"

Ruth huffed and left the room, pulling the door shut behind her. Veronica had no idea what was going on. Sofia reached into her pockets once more and pulled out a dark green velvet bag. She counted the number of people in the group, then pulled something from the bag and placed it back in her pocket.

"Everyone draw a stone. They are all black except for one which is white. I will take the last one so I cannot cheat."

They gathered round her and one by one plunged their hand into the bag. Vionnet drew the white stone.

"Spread out a little," said Sofia. "But not too far apart, we shall make it hard for the pianist."

"She only likes this game if she's the one at the keys," said Lady Katherine. "Likes to be in charge, doesn't like to be the one being laughed at."

Who does?

"Come in now!" shouted Sofia.

Ruth came back in and stood at the door. "If you choose the wrong person there'll be a forfeit."

"But there's no piano!"

Sofia lifted the glass and struck it lightly with the stick. A gentle ringing tone filled the room.

Ruth stared at her and frowned. She walked directly towards her sister. Sofia made the glass chime again a little louder. But when Ruth came up to her sister, Sofia just made the glass ring once, and no louder.

Choosing her mother next, and walking slowly, she was pleased when the chiming got more frequent and louder. Behind her back, Esther was making faces at her sister.

Ruth put out her hand and then hesitated. "I haven't played it like this before, what would it sound like if I was close to the right person?"

"No other clues," said Sofia.

It was obvious to Veronica that Ruth should just go to everyone and see what it sounded like, but she was embarrassed because she didn't know everyone and had made a fool of herself over the piano. Veronica felt sorry for her; games were supposed to be fun, but for Ruth this was more like punishment.

But it seemed she had worked it out. Veronica was close to Lady Katherine, and Ruth closed the gap, avoiding her mother. The chimes became less frequent, and softer. Ruth turned. She had already chosen her sister, so she aimed for Sofia, to be rewarded by a faster rate, but it did not reach fever pitch when she was close.

That left Vionnet. Now confident in her choice, she walked across while Sofia clanged on the brandy glass so hard and fast Veronica thought she would smash it. Ruth placed her hand on Vionnet's arm and everyone cheered.

Ruth was grinning. "I got it without your help."

Vionnet took a turn and successfully found Veronica, who then found herself outside the door and standing in the cold hall. But she was smiling. It might be a little late, but she felt like this was her eighteenth birthday, with her favourite dessert, she was wearing one of her presents, and there were guests playing party games.

xix

The games went on, all of them completely new to Veronica: Thus says the Grand Signior, The Courtiers, Speaking Bluff, although, for that one, everyone knew when it was Vionnet or Mrs Martaci. And the young girls were not good at disguising their voices.

Veronica was surprised how Lady Katherine joined in with as much enthusiasm as her daughters; she had expected the woman to be more aloof

Sofia kept a little book containing the forfeits each of them accumulated. Veronica was fairly sure everyone had at least one. She knew she had three.

There came a time, much later, when they all sat tired and happy, drinking more wine or spirits as the fancy took them—with no need to worry what a man might think. And Sofia declared she had no more games. There was some cheering.

"If we were in mixed company," said Sofia, "we would have much fun with ladies being required to kiss a gentleman as a forfeit. In fact, most forfeits—and I have researched this most diligently—involve that activity."

"I don't have a problem with that," said Tiff so quickly that Veronica had an idea they had it planned from the start.

"Nor I," said Lady Katherine.

While there had been no photograph of her kissing Veronica's mother (that she had yet seen), Veronica had no doubt it had occurred.

"I am happy to do it," said Veronica.

Vionnet gave a French shrug and suggested only the English cared about such things. Lady Katherine's daughters said they often kissed their friends at school. They had spoken in complete innocence, but the adults—which Veronica considered herself, at least in comparison to the girls—smiled and exchanged looks.

"*Eccellente,*" said Sofia. "Our lovely hostess has three, Esther has only one, everyone else has two. This could take some time, so here's what I propose—Vionnet, Kat, Tiff, and I will each stand in a corner."

Veronica furrowed her brow in confusion as they went into the corners of the room.

"The first forfeit is that Veronica must kiss each corner of the room."

She suppressed a smile and pretended to be shocked instead. Ruth and Esther giggled.

The nearest corner was occupied by Tiff, so Veronica went to her. "I'm afraid either I have to stand on something or you need to lower yourself. I cannot lift my head high enough."

The woman bent her legs until she was just below Veronica's level. She had brown eyes and her hair had silver strands.

"Thank you for coming to my party, Tiff, it is the best I have ever had." Then she leaned forwards, closed her eyes, and pressed her lips against Tiff's. They were softer and more full than Polly's. Veronica had to consciously prevent herself opening her lips and sticking her tongue in the older woman's mouth, but even so she felt Tiff's lips part slightly, and tasted her breath. Veronica's heartbeat quickened, but she pulled back.

Next was Vionnet, who had already lowered herself. "Thank you, Vionnet, for all my wonderful clothes, they are the gifts I have never had." Before she had a chance to move, Vionnet kissed her quickly on each cheek, but then pressed their lips together. Just as it had been with Tiff, Vionnet's mouth opened, and it was only the presence of the younger girls that prevented Veronica from spearing her tongue between them.

They separated and, moments later, Veronica found herself face-to-face with Sofia. "Thank you for making my party so much fun. I have never had party games, and I am very glad I had this forfeit." They kissed. Sofia's lips were thin and her tongue immediately darted into Veronica's mouth, so she touched the tip with her own and sucked it a little. Before breaking their embrace.

"You are full of surprises, Veronica," Sofia said quietly.

She just smiled in reply and moved on to her final forfeit. The woman her mother had fucked at least once, and the mouth she was about to kiss had been around her father's prick. "Thank you, Kat, for agreeing to come to my party. It has been an evening I will never forget." The woman's skin was soft, and her lips wide. Lady Katherine kept her lips chaste until Veronica let hers open. This time she did not hold back, the girls could not see, so Veronica pressed her tongue into Kat's mouth. The woman jumped, then sighed and seemed to relax. The other tongue pressed back and Veronica sucked it as she pulled away. *Do I kiss as well as my mother?*

The next set of forfeits did not involve kissing. There was blowing out a candle blindfolded, which was amusing, and a couple of puzzles like putting "an elephant" through a keyhole, which Veronica had no idea how to do until Sofia handed her a piece of paper from her notebook and a pencil. Imitating animals ended in laughter.

Then they were all down to one forfeit each.

"Everyone choose a song," said Sofia.

"I don't know many songs, which one?" said Veronica.

"Doesn't matter. Choose one you know and don't tell anyone what it is."

There was a pause. All she could think of was *What Shall we Do with the Drunken Sailor*. She hoped no one would laugh for her choosing something too simple.

"On the count of four, everyone sing their song. One ... two ... three ..."

"Together?"

"Four."

The room was filled with a riotous cacophony as everyone sang a different song at the same time, which rapidly decayed into hilarity.

———◉———

VERONICA WAVED OFF the guests who were going home in their carriages. Then said goodnight to Vionnet, who hugged her gently.

"You were very good, *ma cherie*."

"I didn't think I was."

"You are not a person who is able to judge," said Vionnet, and gave Veronica a final kiss. "We will begin the fittings in the morning."

"I have lessons. Mrs Martaci is helping me with my Italian for my honeymoon."

"You have a fitting with Vionnet."

"Can Sofia join us?"

"*Non*," said the *couturier*. "I do not expect an audience."

"Of course. I'm sorry."

Vionnet gave her hand a squeeze, then headed upstairs.

Polly emerged from the shadows beneath the stairs and handed Veronica her walking stick.

Together, and in silence, they headed slowly to the bedroom.

———◆———

THE SUNLIGHT MADE SQUARES on the inside of the curtains. Dust motes danced in the air. Birdsong filtered in along with the occasional bleating of sheep.

Veronica missed her assignations with Seth. She wanted to stand on a chair by the window and display herself to him, but the windows here gave out onto rooftops and not the garden. She could prance around naked as much as she liked, but there would be no one but Polly to see her.

In the lightness of the Faraday, she sat up easily. She hoped she would never become so familiar with it that she failed to appreciate how much good it did her.

Polly lay facing away on the other side of the bed. She hadn't taken the time to tie her hair before coming to bed and it lay like a golden, tangled mat around her head. The unblemished skin of her shoulders and back glowed in the morning light.

Veronica needed to finish looking at the pictures in the album, though unfortunately there was nothing they could do to confirm or deny her worry that she might be marrying her half-brother. But even so, she had to know who else was in the pictures.

She slid from the bed and managed the transfer to normal gravity with ease.

The clock said it was a quarter past six. She would have to send a message to Mr Plumley and Sofia to say the lessons were cancelled. She marvelled at the simplicity of that thought—and yet the profound difference to her former life.

Two months ago, it would not even have occurred to her that she could tell Mr Plumley she could not have lessons because she was doing something else.

Now it was a routine thought, and yesterday she had arranged a *soiree* that at least Vionnet had said went well, although if Sofia had not been prepared with the games it could have been rather less enjoyable.

And she had kissed four new women. Veronica smiled. She had enjoyed that part very much—well, Nika had enjoyed it. And she had given Lady Katherine a very thorough kiss, the woman who had enjoyed an orgy of carnal activities with her parents. And also the person who should know with reasonable certainty whether Veronica and Edwin were related.

She searched the dressing room and located the photographic album under a pile of shoes. Most of them were new ones delivered yesterday. Veronica was able to wear ordinary shoes, her feet were not deformed, but she tended to wear them out on one side because she could not walk normally.

But it did not matter. When she wore out this lovely pair of white leather pumps with the polished clip, she could just buy another.

Once more she sat at the table with the large album supported at an angle. She did not rush through the images, but started from the beginning and studied each one in turn again. That they stirred her lust could not be denied, so she let her left hand play with her breasts, squeezing gently to add a little fire while she used the album as an instructional manual as to what could be done between adults.

She had become used to seeing her mother—the perfect version of herself—and her father performing these carnal acts. It no longer shocked her. And then there were the pictures of Lady Katherine. They would have called her Kat when taking these photographs, and her mother would have been Madge. That's what both Lord Jameson and Lady Katherine had called her.

Unable to help herself, Veronica imagined she was the one performing the acts in place of her mother. Sucking and fucking. She reached the page showing Kat being fucked by her parents, one at each end.

There were only three or four more pages to go. She should be able to get through them quickly. The next spread had more variations of Kat with her parents, but now with Kat wearing the phallus. It seemed clear enough that there was an equality in the way they behaved together.

While she was trying to be objective in her viewing of the images, Veronica found herself being pulled into them. The image where her mother was sitting on Kat, penetrated by her, but also with her husband's prick in her rear was particularly exciting. Veronica liked the idea of that one, and tried to imagine what it might be like to have both her holes filled at the same time.

She turned the page.

She stopped playing with herself and stared at the picture she had been both expecting, and hoping would not appear. The picture that neither proved nor denied her possible relationship to Edwin.

Lord Jameson, the Viscount Launceston, penetrating Veronica's mother, while she simultaneously sucked her husband.

There it was.

The rest of the images were more variations of what could be done with several people, inserting body parts into holes.

Veronica was tired of it. She shut the book. She didn't care what was on the other pages any more.

Across the room, Polly sat up revealing her small but delightful breasts, her hair floating wildly in all directions. She stretched sweetly and brushed her hair back over her head.

Veronica smiled at her. "Good morning, wife."

"We ain't married, Nika."

"We will be."

"Oh yes, when's that then?"

"Monday week, of course."

"You going soft in the head? That's Edwin."

Veronica went over and climbed on to the bed, feeling the Faraday effect pass from her hands and head along her arms and torso through to her legs and feet.

"When I say my vows to him, Polly, I will be saying them to you."

"I don't get to say them back though, do I?"

Veronica sat back on her heels. "I'm trying to be romantic and you're just spoiling it."

Polly looked serious. "I love you, Nika, you know I do. But last night, that's what we have to remember. That's what our life is going to be. You have a night with your posh friends and I can't be there. It's like what you said before, everything outside that door is a lie. The only place we can be ourselves is here, alone."

"I wish we could go back to the way we were."

"No, you don't. That was a hundred times worse for you, and we still couldn't be ourselves."

Veronica let herself topple sideways. Under the reduced gravity, the fall took long moments until she landed with the gentlest thump on a pillow. Polly leaned over and took one of Veronica's nipples in her mouth, sucking and licking. Veronica closed her eyes as the muscles between her legs tightened convulsively, and let herself succumb to the wave of pleasure that shot through her. One of Polly's hands wormed between Veronica's thighs, rubbing back and forth.

Polly's wild hair tickled Veronica's skin, but the pressure between her legs became more insistent and she let her legs slide apart. Her breathing became quicker and shallower. Two fingers slipped inside her, while the thumb slid back and forth across her nubbin.

Polly ground Veronica's nipple between her teeth. The pain was ecstasy. Veronica's paroxysm exploded in her and her cry was almost a whimper. The sucking and licking continued. The lust did not diminish, and Veronica thrust her hips into the hand between her legs. She wanted something more solid there, that she could push against hard.

Swinging her leg over, Polly sat on Veronica's face and applied both hands between her legs. Veronica took a moment to focus and orient herself on the silken skin that pressed against her lips. Her tongue slipped out and into the channel between the lips. She licked up and down, tasting Polly. Her nose was just at her lover's hole; she wished she might be Pinocchio, so her nose could extend. She giggled at the outrageous thought, and applied herself to bringing Polly to the climax of lust.

Polly lay forwards until her head was between Veronica's legs, while her hands were clamped round her thighs. This put the top of her pussy in Veronica's mouth and gave easy access to her pussy hole. Veronica freed her right arm and pushed her thumb into Polly's wet hole. Her other hand reached along Polly's body and found her breast.

Under the three-pronged assault, Polly panted and writhed. She rubbed her pussy against Veronica's chin and began to grunt rhythmically. It took only a few moments more before her body went rigid and Veronica felt her muscles spasm once, twice, and again.

As Polly slowly relaxed, Veronica continued to lick her lightly and gently pulled her thumb out. Under the Faraday Polly wasn't heavy, but Veronica gently turned so she rolled off, then moved around to kiss her lover.

Polly opened her eyes. "Thank you, that was nice."

"Thank you too, but only time for a quick one this morning," said Veronica. "We must both bathe and wear clean underthings, so Vionnet has nothing to complain about when she's doing the fitting."

"She's French," said Polly, "she'll complain anyway."

XX

Vionnet did complain, but mostly about the inadequacies of the facilities.

They had decided Veronica's bedroom was the best place to use for the fitting, since it had a bathroom and the adjoining room. It provided both privacy and space.

However, there was no raised platform for Veronica to stand on, or Polly when it was her turn. Mr Jones was sent to find something suitable and it took nearly half an hour for him to return with a couple of other staff carrying four footstools of the same height, and a round tabletop which apparently had legs that unscrewed. The footstools were arranged between the bed and the window—the usual table was removed to one side—and the tabletop placed in position.

The men were sent on their way, leaving Veronica and Polly with Vionnet and her two staff, plus three large trunks.

"Please remove all of your clothing," said Vionnet in a tone that did not brook disobedience.

Polly helped Veronica out of her dress and underthings, then, under the glare of Vionnet, removed her own clothes. Veronica did not care who saw her, while Miss Josephine and Miss Clio had the decency not to stare. But Polly hated it. Veronica could see the tensions in her muscles as she tried not to cover herself.

"Put these on." Mademoiselle Vionnet had two sets of pale cream, silk undergarments, one in each hand, but as Veronica and Polly reached for them, she pulled her hands back. "You have bathed?" They nodded. Vionnet let them take the clothes, and pulled more packages from the trunks.

Polly quickly pulled on the silk bloomers. "Where's the rest, mademoiselle?"

Vionnet gave her a long look. "There is no 'rest'."

"But—"

"Whatever Margaine-Lacroix can do, Vionnet can do better."

155

Veronica had no time to ask who that was before Polly cried out.

"We're going to be naked!"

"You will be dressed by Vionnet!"

Polly looked pleadingly at her mistress. Veronica still *was* naked; she just shook her head. "Help me into these Polly, we will do as we are told."

"Veronique, if you please?" She gestured at the makeshift podium and produced a tape measure from somewhere. "Polly, go in the other room, my ladies will find the best arrangement for your make-up and hair. You may wear a dressing gown if you prefer at this time."

Once Veronica had climbed up the measuring started again, but this time Vionnet seemed to be just checking that nothing had changed.

"You are not with child then."

"I said I wasn't the first time."

"People say many things, usually what they want others to hear."

Vionnet left Veronica standing on the podium to set about unwrapping parcels and packages. She smoothed out a white dress on the bed, then glanced up at Veronica. "Please to get down."

"It won't fit?"

"You accuse Vionnet of making a dress that will not fit?"

"No, I—"

"The dress will fit perfectly, Miss Clifford-Hughes, but there are some minor adjustments I must make before we try it on. Please go away."

Veronica stepped away as Vionnet carried the dress and a needlework box to the table. There was nothing to do. She was in a state of undress, so could not go for a walk—though the workmen might find it entertaining. Instead, she went to the door of Polly's room and leaned against the frame.

Polly was seated with the two attendants working on her. One in front with the make-up, and one behind building her hair up. The dressing gown had been pushed down to expose Polly's shoulders.

Veronica gasped at the transformation that had already occurred, even though it was not even close to complete. Polly looked like a princess—no, a Greek goddess. The make-up was heavy around the eyes, and her face had been made to look even narrower than it already was, with prominent cheek-bones. Her hair was up, making her neck seem longer and aristocratic.

"Is it that bad?"

Veronica did not understand. "Bad?"

"You're staring."

"You look wonderful."

Josephine smiled and reached into her bag. She extracted what looked like a gold necklace with pale green and amber stones. She laid the strands of it across Polly's hair; the gems stood out and complemented Polly's hazel eyes.

Veronica's hand went to her mouth. "Where's the camera?"

"You're not taking a picture of me like this."

"I must, just tell me where you put it."

"Bottom drawer."

Veronica found it in a moment and checked the film. There were another ten images available and they had one spare film. The Kodak Box Brownie was easy to operate, you just had to point it in the right direction, check the viewfinder, and click. Then wind on the film. That was why they were so popular.

Veronica brought it up to her eye and got Polly in the viewfinder. "Smile!" *Click.*

"You wait, Nika." Realising what she had said, Polly froze, but if the two women noticed the lack of proper respect between a maid and her mistress, they said nothing. They must have been in enough households, seen so many brides, bridesmaids, and mothers that nothing would surprise them. Or, if it did, they would make no sign of it.

"Keep still and do not talk, Miss Noakes," said Clio.

Veronica moved round to the side and took a profile.

"I did not know you could make hair do that," she said as Josephine pinned and built it up, adding lots of curls.

"We'll do better than this on the day," said Clio. "This is just practice so we know what's possible."

"I wish we could keep it like this."

"It wouldn't last a single night."

"And your pillow would be covered in make-up."

"I'm having someone paint me in the wedding dress next week. It won't look right without your work. I wish there was something we could do..."

"If you don't mind me saying so," said Clio, pausing with the brush she was using to apply rouge to Polly's cheeks, "you're already doing something." She pointed at the camera with the brush's handle.

Veronica stared down at the box in her hands for a moment, then smiled. "We could give the pictures to Mrs Martaci."

"We can't," said Polly bluntly.

"We just have to get them developed," said Veronica.

"No. We can't."

"What are you talking about, of course..." Veronica trailed off when the reason for Polly's obstinacy dawned on her. "Perhaps I should change the film."

Josephine laughed. "Got some naughty pictures, have you?"

"Yes," said Veronica without thinking. Polly's face contorted with the pain of embarrassment.

"Don't blame you. My young man loves taking pictures of me with nothing on."

"You or him?" said Clio with a laugh.

"Both, of course." They both laughed so much that Veronica smiled, although Polly remained mortified on the one hand, and horrified by the conversation she was listening to.

"You do it?" said Veronica.

"'Course we do, luv," said Josephine. "There's no harm in it, is there?"

Veronica thought about the album of photographs in the dressing room; somehow they did not seem harmless.

"How do you get the pictures developed?"

"Her Brian does it himself," said Clio. "It's not hard, though it makes a right stink in the kitchen."

"You have your own place together?"

"And another couple of girls," said Josephine.

"Not supposed to have gentlemen friends that visit," said Clio.

"But we're on the ground floor, so he can get in through the window easy as pie."

Vionnet's voice penetrated the babble of voices.

"Veronique, please return."

She got up and went to the door, before turning back. "We're having a dark room here. It's just been built, if there's any way we could get the pictures developed—"

"Veronique!"

"Yes, mademoiselle."

Vionnet was standing near the window, with the white dress draped over one arm so Veronica couldn't make out any of the details. It reflected the sunlight as if it was itself glowing. The *couturier* lifted the dress and let it down to the ground in such a way that it was a circle on the floor.

"Step into the middle please."

As soon as Veronica had done so, Vionnet knelt down and took hold of two parts and lifted them. There was a slight squeeze as a band of thicker material went over her waist, then one part came to a stop under her right arm, and Vionnet stepped to Veronica's left side.

The material caught up round her bust and lifted them; she could feel the band in the middle clinching her waist, while the weight from there down seemed to rest on her hips. The material was all pleats, but not heavy. Vionnet was doing something at Veronica's left shoulder and, after a moment, there was a click. Cold metal rested against her skin there.

Vionnet stepped back and eyed the dress. Then she stepped forward and adjusted the middle section, turning it and—without warning—lifted Veronica's breasts in turn, adjusting their position in the dress.

She moved back once more, then prowled round Veronica like a tiger.

"What have you done?" said Veronica.

"What do you mean?" replied the woman, in a voice so distracted it was almost as if she had not been listening.

Veronica could not believe it. The dress only went over her left shoulder. Her entire right side was bare. Not a single inch of material covered her hump.

The stupid, stupid woman. Veronica burst into tears. "You said you would make me beautiful. But they'll all see it. They'll laugh. They'll jeer at me. They'll see me for the monster I am!"

Polly was suddenly arguing in the other room. Veronica looked up as the goddess burst in and came to a halt.

"Oh god, Polly, look what she's done!"

Polly's headlong rush came to a faltering halt.

Veronica watched Polly's eyes as they darted back and forth, taking in every aspect of the dress. Her eyes widened and she looked straight into Veronica's face. "You look like a queen."

"What?"

"I want to go down on one knee, Nika. I want to offer my life to you."

Veronica sniffed. "But...the dress." She gestured at her bare right shoulder.

Vionnet thrust a handkerchief at Veronica. "Do not cry on the dress."

Polly came forward. She reached out and traced the curve of Veronica's neck down her shoulder to her upper arm, then took her hand. "I know. I understand but...but Mademoiselle Vionnet is right. You shouldn't hide it. You shouldn't be ashamed."

"Also, it is practical," said Vionnet. "This arrangement means I do not have to work the cloth to compensate for the shape."

Polly took the kerchief from Vionnet and gently wiped Veronica's eyes.

"She has done what she promised, Nika. You are beautiful, and everyone will see it."

"Also, for those without the wit to see beauty when it is presented to them, the veil will make the deformity less prominent."

Polly smiled at Veronica. "It is good."

Veronica nodded, took the kerchief, and blew her nose.

"Glad you're doing the make-up and not me," said Josephine.

⬤

AFTER VERONICA HAD recovered from her upset, things went more smoothly. They got her in front of the full-length mirror and she had to admit the dress was beautiful; it clung to her shape in a way she had never seen before. There was a wide section in the middle that looked like a belt and pulled her waist in, while at the same time providing support for her breasts. Having her hump exposed was disconcerting since she always tried to hide it, even though that was impossible.

"I will arrange for your flowers also," said Vionnet.

"You don't have to."

"It is not a matter of 'have to', Veronique, I must. Even the flowers must complement the dress, the entire design."

With Veronica back on the podium Vionnet made adjustments and notes. Then they tried the veil, which seemed to go on forever. There were several layers around the head, but these disappeared until the fine tulle veil stretched across the ground.

"You are my *pièce de résistance*," said Vionnet. "You will make me famous. For you, I have made a *voile de cathédrale*, a cathedral veil."

"How long is it?"

"Not quite three metres."

"The church is not that big."

"With this dress Vionnet is saying that she has arrived in the world, and for the bride it says 'I am the most valuable thing the groom can possess.'"

"I somehow doubt it will have that effect on Edwin Jameson. He doesn't care about those things."

"It is not his thoughts that matter, *cherie*, it is the thing that everyone else will think."

Veronica sighed. Every time she thought that Vionnet was doing this for her, it turned out that the designer was only thinking of herself.

Polly was finally deemed complete and allowed out. She was clearly impressed, and took a couple of pictures—for Mrs Martaci.

Veronica was stripped back to the silk bloomers, and went into the side room while Vionnet took charge of Polly.

"Don't you want something to cover you up?" said Clio.

"I don't mind people looking at me."

"Except the hump," said Josephine as she attacked Veronica's brown hair with the comb.

"Except that," said Veronica, aware that her words were contrary to what she was doing at that very moment, though right now she felt safe.

Clio held up her palette of colours beside Veronica's face. "Does it hurt?"

Veronica sighed. "It doesn't hurt in itself, but everything aches because of it. Sometimes it can be very bad."

"So, we're here with mademoiselle until tomorrow," said Josephine. "If your dark room is properly equipped, I could do your pictures for you."

"She just wants to see those other ones you've got," said Clio.

"Obviously," said Josephine with a laugh, "but if we can sort out what you need as well."

"Perhaps we can look at it later and you can tell me if it has what you need."

"Can you lift your chin a bit more?" said Clio as she started to work cosmetics into Veronica's face.

"I can't lift my head higher very easily, and I certainly can't hold it."

"Oh."

"Usually I slip down further in the chair and have cushions to support me."

Josephine grabbed the pillows from the bed. Veronica edged forwards, which pulled the silk bloomers tight against her crotch. Then, with the pillows tucked in tight behind her, she leaned back, and the two women set to work in earnest.

⸺◉⸺

VERONICA HAD NEVER had this kind of attention before, and fell into a kind of reverie as the two manipulated her hair and head, dabbing brushes and rubbing colour into her face. She wasn't even sure how much time had passed before something white moved across her vision and there was the snap of the camera.

Someone stood there, a woman wearing the purest white dress and looking like a marble Greek statue. She smiled at Veronica.

"What do you think?"

Think? The voice was familiar. Veronica woke up.

"Polly?"

"I don't know how I can bear to show up in church wearing it, but isn't it beautiful?"

She turned slowly and Veronica's eyes widened.

It bore similarities to her own dress, but there was a brooch at each shoulder and it revealed less *décolletage*. Polly had a smaller bust, but the band around the waist was the same, except with a simpler pattern that echoed the design of Veronica's. It had fewer pleats, and exposed her bare feet. The effect when combined with the hair and make-up was breathtaking—at least, Veronica found herself speechless.

"Hang on," said Josephine and rummaged in her bag. "Here we go, try this on." She hurried over and handed Polly a bracelet, relieving her of the camera. "It goes on your upper arm, luv," she added when Polly found it was too big for her wrist.

It completed the effect. Veronica would have believed Polly had stepped out of the past riding Mr Wells's fictional time machine.

"Well, Nika?" said Polly, and Veronica realised she hadn't said anything.

"People will think you're the bride."

"The veil will make sure they don't make that mistake."

Vionnet appeared behind Polly and looked at Veronica. "The hair is not finished."

"A few minutes more, mademoiselle," said Josephine and hurried back.

"You want me to take some more pictures?" said Clio. "I'm done." She took the camera from Josephine and stood up.

"Have you used enough *rimmel* on the bride?" said Vionnet.

Clio looked back and put her head on one side. "I think so. Too much mascara would look whorish."

Vionnet nodded. "Very well. When Josephine has finished, we will get her back in the dress and examine the whole look."

Veronica was used to being treated as an object, it had been much the same when the doctors and quacks had been trying to straighten her back, but it had been so much harder when she had been so young. At least now she understood Vionnet was attempting to achieve a particular image.

Clio took Polly back into the main bedroom for some additional photographs. And Josephine completed her hair with a net of gold entwined with plants and ripening corn. Finally, she was declared as done and allowed to look in the mirror. She stared unbelievingly at the goddess in the glass.

"Theros," said Josephine.

"I'm sorry?"

"Vionnet said you're to be Theros, goddess of summer. That's why we put the wheat in your hair."

"She was one of the four Horae."

"If you say so."

"I was thoroughly schooled in the Greek myths," said Veronica, turning her head slightly left and right trying to see her hair better. "What's Polly?"

"No idea, a nymph?"

Veronica smiled. "Yes, I think nymph would be a good description."

"If Veronique is complete, let us have her back," called Vionnet from the main room.

A few minutes later, Veronica was staring at herself in the long mirror once more. The transformation was complete. No longer Veronica, not even Nika, but Theros, minor goddess, to be married to her Zephyros, god of the west wind.

If only. Unfortunately, there was nothing about Edwin that reminded her of a Greek god.

Vionnet added the veil and Josephine pinned it in place. Clio ran out of film and it took a couple of minutes to get the new one in. Then they took the entire reel's worth, and Veronica insisted pictures were taken of the others as well.

"It's a shame there's no timing device," she said, "then we could all be in the same picture."

They were stripped once more, the make-up removed and their hair taken down. Veronica didn't want to get dressed in her normal clothes, because then she would just be herself again. But her stomach growled and, checking the time, she found that it was almost two. She could not believe so much time had passed. It had seemed so quick.

She rang for Mr Jones, informed him they were ready to eat, and that luncheon should be served in the same room as they had eaten last night.

Then she sagged and sat on the bed. She lay down as everyone bustled around her. She heard the click of the Faraday and felt the lightness come upon her.

xxi

The next thing Veronica knew was Polly kissing her lightly on the lips. "Wake up, Sleeping Beauty."

"Is that you, my prince?"

"Just the maid, the prince is off shooting pheasant."

Veronica pushed herself into a sitting position with her feet off the bed and out of the Faraday field; it made her skin tingle. The sun was still shining and looked to be high in the sky.

"What's the time?"

"About half past three."

"I fell asleep."

"Is that what it was?"

Veronica chose to ignore that remark. "Where are the others?"

"They got tired of waiting for you to wake up and went to get something to eat. And I let you sleep for a while and then brought yours."

"Do I have to entertain tonight?"

"No idea," said Polly. "Mademoiselle has disappeared into her bedroom to make adjustments. The other two spent the meal making notes on what they would do differently next time, and then went for a walk. They said they'd find the dark room and see if it had everything needed to develop the films."

"I'm surplus to requirements then."

"Yes, but if you'd like to come to the table there's some of that baked gooseberry pudding left over from yesterday."

Veronica pushed herself off the bed and walked across to the table. The plates on the tray were piled with sandwiches; there was a teapot with cup and saucer, milk jug, plus the bowl with the pudding.

"Do you want some tea, Polly?"

"Miss Clifford-Hughes will note that Mrs Jenkins did not supply an additional cup and saucer since it would be highly inappropriate for the lady's maid to eat with her mistress."

"It's against the rules for her to sleep with her mistress, but we manage that every night."

Polly gave her a kiss on the cheek. "As explained before, that's not the same thing at all. You can have your way with me as much as you want. I just can't be treated as an equal."

Veronica was frowning as she took a bite out of an egg sandwich. It took her a couple of swallows before she could speak again.

"What's wrong?"

Polly sighed and sat down on the other side of the table, leaning her chin on her hands. "It's not you, Nika. Just what we've been talking about. I can't be part of your world."

"That's why we have our own one here."

Polly shook her head. "It doesn't work."

Veronica put down the sandwich. "Don't you want to get married?"

"Nika, stop it. We're not getting married, and I can't pretend we are. You're marrying Edwin. Yes, you can pretend you're saying the vows to me, but I can't say them to you, and even if we can still spend our nights together here, we can't be together out there." Her eyes filled with tears. "We can *never* be together out there."

Veronica didn't know what to say.

Presently, Polly got up and bustled about the room cleaning and tidying. She turned down the bed, then went into her own room and shut the door.

For a long time Veronica stared at the closed door, numb and confused. Finally, she got to her feet, ignoring the rest of the meal, and left the room.

It seemed strange going out without Polly, but she descended the stairs, went through the ballroom, and out on to the patio. The sun was descending in the west, but it would be a while before it was dark.

The air smelled sweet from the ranks of flowers, and there was a gentle breeze bringing the earthy smell of the Downs. The occasional bleating of sheep punctuated the constant birdsong.

She was not wearing outdoor shoes, she had no parasol, and she had no one to accompany her.

"If I am the lady of the house, there is no one to tell me what I should or should not do."

"Except your British propriety," said Vionnet behind her. "A rule for every occasion, and no occasion without its rules."

Vionnet sat on a lounge chair with her dress pulled up to her knees, in exactly the way that Veronica would never have dared to do—before. The *couturier's* eyes were hidden behind some form of spectacles that had dark lenses.

But, despite my British propriety, I am going to walk semi-naked down the aisle of the church. What if the vicar refuses to wed me to Edwin because of it? Or he refuses to marry a whore ... or Horae?

"I'm sorry, mademoiselle, I did not see you there."

"And if you had seen me you would not have revealed your true thoughts, of course."

"It is not the done thing."

"No, you British will never do something if it is not the 'done thing.'"

"I am going to wear your dress in church even though it is outrageous and an insult to all proper-thinking people."

"I do not think you truly care for the thoughts of proper people, Veronique—" her lips smiled, but Veronica could not see if it was reflected in her eyes, "—or is it Nika who does not care?"

"The goddess Theros does not care," said Veronica. "After all, what interest does a deity have in the opinions of mere mortals."

"Yet you are not the goddess, only a facsimile."

"No, I cannot change society."

Vionnet got to her feet and stood beside Veronica, looking out on to the garden.

"The Faraday device is an interesting thing, *n'est ce pas?*"

Veronica frowned at the change in subject. "In many ways, yes."

"It makes things light, but they are just as hard to move."

"Inertia."

"*Oui.* A difficult thing to understand, is it not?"

"Weight is not mass."

"That is how they say it, yes. The Faraday device, it removes the weight, but it does not take away the mass."

Veronica was surprised to be having such a technical conversation with a dress designer, but it was not that hard to understand, as long as you understood that weight and mass were different things. Contrary to certain opinions, a woman was perfectly capable of understanding such things.

"Shall we walk?" said Vionnet. "There will be less chance our conversation will be overheard."

They walked down the steps together. Vionnet gave Veronica her arm to lean on. They crunched across the gravel, walking away from the house.

"Why are we talking about the Faraday effect, mademoiselle?"

"You and your servant are in love."

Veronica hesitated.

"Do not be foolish with me, Veronique. It was obvious when you first came to the shop, and she calls you by a private name when you are alone. You are lovers, do not deny it."

"Yes."

"But you talk of changing society. You wish that you could be open in your love as if you were a man and a woman together."

"If I could marry her, I would."

"*Bien entendu*, you are both young and passionate, but the world is against you."

They walked on, their steps in rhythm.

"Do you have any advice, mademoiselle?"

"Society. It is like the matter of the world. I can make a dress that challenges all the propriety of the British, that is shocking and will cause much comment, but it is like the Faraday: it can take away the weight for a moment, but the inertia of society cannot be taken away. It can only be ... *poussé du coude*. I do not know your words."

"Pushed?"

"Less than pushed."

"Nudged?"

"*Oui*, it can only be nudged." Vionnet sighed. "And one week or two when nobody is talking about your dress any more, a woman will come to ask that Vionnet makes a dress like yours again. Perhaps less revealing, less shocking, but it will be made and it will be seen and the world will become a little more accustomed to it."

"So I am nothing more than an advertisement for Vionnet?"

"In the world, Veronique, there are only two types of people. Those who command the world, and those who let the world command them. If you let the world command you, your life may be simple and easy, but you will achieve nothing of value." She stopped there, and gave Veronica time to fill in the rest.

"Is it worth being someone who commands the world when there is so much pain?"

"I think, Veronique, you already know the answer. Does your body not try to command you?"

Every hour of every day—but now I command the night and it cannot hurt me.

"So, if I am your mannequin, does that make me one who commands, or who is commanded?"

"Only a man would think that if he is in command, no other can be," said Vionnet. "We are not men, we can command together. Me for my reasons, and you for yours."

"But I cannot simply kiss my lover in church and make vows with her." *They would lock me away in Bedlam.*

"You could," said Vionnet, but then smiled and held up her hand to stop Veronica's protest before it started. "But the inertia of society is very great, and you must choose your moments."

"Give me a lever long enough, a fulcrum on which to put it with a place to stand, and I could move the world," said Veronica. "Archimedes said it."

They had walked almost the entire way round the flower garden, but Veronica gestured for Vionnet to take the path that led towards the outer buildings where the furnace and generator lay—and the dark room.

They crossed the vegetable garden, which reminded Veronica of the meeting she would be having with Edwin. That was a battle she must fight, and that she must win if the house was to continue running successfully.

As Vionnet said, she must choose those things she could achieve, but that did not get her any further with Polly.

"Did you wish to speak of any other matter?" said Vionnet, coming to a halt.

Veronica shook her head. "You have given me good advice, mademoiselle, and I am grateful for that. But there are some things I think I must resolve for myself."

"Be brave, *ma cherie*." Vionnet gave her a kiss and headed back towards the garden.

———◆———

VERONICA TAPPED ON the connecting door to Polly's room as the last of the sun's rays were angling in through the bathroom window and playing across the bedroom floor.

"Polly."

There was no reply.

She knocked harder.

"Polly."

When there was still no response she became worried and tried the handle. The door opened easily. Two dressmaker's dummies stood by the window attired in the bride and bridesmaid's dresses.

Polly lay on the counterpane of her bed, still fully clothed. Her eyes were open and looking at Veronica.

Veronica remained at the entrance.

"I can't change the world overnight."

"Of course you can't." Polly's voice cracked as she spoke and, as Veronica's eyes adjusted to the light, she could see the maid's eyes and cheeks were red with crying.

"I am as trapped as you are. If I had a choice, I would marry you and not Edwin."

"There's no point talking about the impossible."

"Which is why that's what's going to happen."

Polly pushed herself up on to her elbow, her hair stuck to her cheek. "You're not making any sense."

"Can I come in?"

"What? Of course."

"No, Polly, it's not 'of course'. This is your room and I will never presume to enter it without your permission."

"You own it. You own me."

"I remember that someone very wise for her years told me that self-pity is a very ugly thing, and I was not allowed to indulge in it."

Polly got all the way up and sat on the edge of the bed.

"Do I look that bad when I've been crying?" said Veronica.

"Yes, probably. What were you talking about?"

"First rule: no self-pity. Agreed?"

Polly nodded.

"Promise?"

The maid sighed. "Yes, I promise."

"Good. Now, can I come into *your* room, Polly?"

"Yes, Nika, you have my permission to come into *my* room."

"Thank you." Veronica walked over and sat beside Polly, allowing a hand-breadth of space between them.

"Now will you tell me?"

"Of course, I shall need to do some reading in the library, but make no mistake Miss Polly Noakes, you and I will be married on Monday week next."

"What if I don't want to?"

Veronica's heart sank. "You don't want to? But I thought—"

Polly laughed and touched her fingertips to Veronica's cheek. "You haven't asked me, Nika. You have to ask if I am willing first."

"Am I the man then?"

"No, Nika, you are much softer than a man, but you are the one insisting we be married."

"Very well then, will you marry me?"

Polly shook her head and stood up. "That's not doing it properly."

Veronica frowned. "I have a deformed spine, Polly." She hesitated, and then also stood up. "No, you're right, if this is important then it should be done properly."

She faced Polly and, using the bed for support, got down on one knee. In this position she couldn't raise her head at all, and only Polly's skirts were visible. But she managed to lift her left hand enough to take Polly's right hand in her own.

"Miss Polly Noakes, will you do me the honour of becoming my wife?"

"Miss Veronica Clifford-Hughes, my answer is yes."

"Even if the marriage is not recognised in British Law?"

"Even though it is not."

She helped Veronica back to her feet, and they kissed.

"Have you got me a ring?"

Veronica looked shocked. "No—I—it was all spur of the moment."

Polly laughed.

"You're teasing me."

"I am."

"Good. Well, the evening is setting in, so let's go to bed," said Veronica.

"I think we should sleep in separate beds until we're married," said Polly with a straight face.

Veronica suppressed the protest in her heart. "Yes, of course, you're right. I'll say goodnight."

Polly laughed again. "Oh Nika, it's just so easy when you're being serious. I couldn't stand to be apart from you for that long, especially not when you're in the next room."

"You were joking?"

"I was joking."

"Again."

"Yes, again."

"That's a relief."

xxii

Sunday morning, only eight days to the wedding. Another day of sunshine, though the weather worried Veronica a little. She wanted next Monday to be as perfect as it could be; she would be upset if it decided to rain, but there was nothing to be done about it.

She lay in bed, with the Faraday on, and Polly lying in the crook of her arm. It was as perfect as it could be.

Except she had to get up and go to church. And so did Polly, even if they could not go together. Veronica would accompany Mrs Jenkins as usual, and Polly would go with Ursula.

An idea sparked in Veronica's mind and she smiled to herself. She hoped Polly would not be silly about it. Oh, and there was another idea. *Of course.* She managed to squeeze out from under her lover without waking her—a task made a lot simpler with the Faraday. Mass may not be weight, but it was a lot easier to move people around without waking them in a Faraday, since they did not fall as quickly.

She found her diary and titled a new page for today, then wrote two cryptic clues that she would understand and Polly would not, if she happened to see them: *Use the bear* and *Thank you gift.*

***

AFTER THE EVENTS OF the previous day, the walk to church did not feel as onerous as it usually did. In fact, Veronica strode ahead, swinging her walking stick, and left Mrs Jenkins to catch her.

The morning was bright and warm. A good night's sleep in the Faraday field had eased her aches, and given Veronica a great deal of energy. Polly had put out one of the lovely new dresses which, at some point, she had adjusted following the pattern suggested by Mademoiselle Vionnet.

In Mrs Beeton's book it said that a lady's maid had to do everything for her mistress—but a gentleman's valet could get other people to do the work. The idea was completely outrageous, and utterly biased in favour of the man.

"We'll see about that," said Veronica to a beech tree whose roots had tripped her more than once in the past. Veronica tapped the big exposed root that crossed the path with her stick. "Not today, Mr Beech."

She stepped over the root and waited for Mrs Jenkins.

"I do realise, Mrs Jenkins, that it is quite unprecedented that I have a servant as a bridesmaid."

The woman blinked at the sudden pronouncement but recovered quickly. "You've decided otherwise? Good."

"Oh no, unfortunately my hands are completely tied on the matter. Mademoiselle Vionnet is in the employ of Jeanne Paquin, who is the dressmaker of Lady Katherine. It was at Lady Katherine's request I should be dressed by House Paquin, but Vionnet will not permit me to wear her dress unless she also makes a dress for the bridesmaid." Veronica smiled as they walked along. "At the time of choosing I had no options and if I were to refuse to allow Polly to be my bridesmaid now, then I would not have a House Paquin dress, and that would be an insult to Lady Katherine since she has paid for it."

Mrs Jenkins was silent for a few moments. "In that case, why did you bring it up?"

"Because, this week, we have Signora Martaci over each morning. She is going to be painting me, and Polly, in our wedding attire. And we will require another maid to help us dress."

"I do not see how that can be arranged."

"Oh, well I'm sure Polly will be able to dress me, but who is going to dress her?" Veronica allowed a pause of three heartbeats. "You don't expect me to do it, do you?"

"How long?"

"Perhaps an hour before and an hour after."

"I'll find someone."

"Ursula."

"Sorry?"

"Miss Clifford-Hughes."

"What?"

"I think you're supposed to say, 'Sorry, Miss Clifford-Hughes?'"

There was silence from Mrs Jenkins.

"I suggest Ursula," said Veronica as if nothing had happened. "I understand the girls shared a room, so there won't be any awkwardness between them."

"She's just a housemaid."

"Do we have anyone who would be any better?"

Veronica knew that Mrs Jenkins herself would probably be a better choice than Ursula, in terms of knowing what to do, but there was no chance she would suggest herself.

"I'll take your silence as a no. Starting tomorrow from nine until ten, and then twelve-thirty until one o'clock. And it's just from Monday to Wednesday; it shouldn't interfere with your schedules too much."

"As you say," said the housekeeper. "Miss Clifford-Hughes."

———◉———

IT WAS A VERY SMUG Veronica who crossed off the first of her cryptic clues. The second would be very much harder to deal with.

Vionnet visited their rooms one more time and did some work on the dresses, then gave strict instructions for them to be kept covered while on the tailor's dummies when not in use. And that the prospect of Hell would be a kindness in comparison to her wrath if they were damaged during the week. Then she and her girls went off to pack.

Luncheon passed pleasantly with Vionnet and her staff, although it pained Veronica that Polly was forced to stand to one side and not join in.

"Polly adjusted this dress, mademoiselle," she said.

Vionnet looked up and then stood. "Let me examine it."

Veronica gestured for Polly to come over as she allowed the *couturier* to examine the work.

"This is not terrible," said Vionnet.

Veronica shivered as fingers brushed against her hump. She said nothing, but wished the woman could be more positive in her way of speaking.

There followed a detailed analysis of what Polly had done, which Veronica understood barely half of, and then information about what Polly ought to have done.

"Come," said Vionnet, "sit by me."

"Miss?" said Polly, because she shouldn't sit with them.

"If Mademoiselle commands, Polly, we must do as she says."

Vionnet smiled and pulled a sewing kit from her bag as Polly pulled up a chair. "Let me show you some things."

And from that moment Veronica was surplus to that conversation.

"Miss Clifford-Hughes?" Josephine was sitting across the table from Veronica and Clio. "We have something for you." She grinned and winked. "We're off after lunch, but we thought we'd better give these to you personally."

"Something for me?" said Veronica with a frown.

"Let's go to the window," she said. "It's more private."

The three of them walked across the tarpaulins that still covered the floor of the ballroom.

Josephine extracted a thick envelope from her skirts. "We developed your pictures this morning." She emptied the photographs into her hand.

"The dark room had everything?"

"Very well stocked, that future husband of yours certainly knows how to spend his money. I'd hang on to him if you can."

"Did they come out all right?"

"Oh yes, very good."

She started to go through the stack showing the group shots they had done when Veronica and Polly were dressed. Veronica could only stare at how she looked—it didn't even feel like her, and she really did look like some of the statues of Greek goddesses in the house.

Then they came to the ones of the hair and make-up. "Those will be really helpful to Mrs Martaci," she said innocently as Josephine flicked to the next picture which showed Veronica lying naked on the bed. "Oh."

"Well, we saw most of you yesterday," said Clio. "You look nice."

"You've got great tits," said Josephine.

"Thank you," she said weakly. They're just like my mother's and yet all I can see is the hump.

"And your Polly's got a nice pair too."

There were a couple more of Veronica in slightly different positions and then they paused on a very embarrassed looking maid, lying on the bed looking as if she was about to cover herself up.

"She does have nice tits," said Veronica.

Josephine laughed. "You should know; bet you two have a great time."

"It's not bad," said Veronica feeling her cheeks heat.

Josephine flipped through the next few images showing either Polly or Veronica, each with more clothes than the previous image. It hadn't been planned, but it took Polly a while before she was willing to strip completely for the camera.

"Now this one's great," said Josephine. "I love it."

Veronica gasped. It was from their very first tryst with Seth. She didn't even know Polly had taken it, she was just supposed to be waiting to hit Seth if he got too frisky. It was Seth from the back showing his muscular back and posterior while naked Veronica crouched in front of him. You couldn't see what her mouth and hands were doing but it wasn't hard to work out. *Thank goodness there weren't any from our most recent evening with him—except, why not? There was no point lying, I am excited by these people seeing me engaged in sexual activities.*

"Isn't that one of your gardeners?"

"Seth."

"Oh yes, we met him. Doesn't say a lot; showed us the dark room."

"If only I'd known then," said Josephine and laughed. "You certainly have a lot of fun out here in the middle of nowhere. How the other half live, eh?"

Then there was a picture of Veronica biting Seth's nipple, to which Josephine's comment was, "I have to try that with Bob."

"Seth didn't think I should do it."

"But did he like it?" said Clio.

"Oh yes, he did very much."

Then there was a man sucking Veronica's big toe.

"Nobody's ever done that to me," said Josephine. "Looks fun."

"Who is he?" said Clio.

"I can't betray his trust."

"But those are your feet," said Clio.

"Yes."

"Do you really like that?"

"Well, yes and no," said Veronica. "I don't dislike it—" *especially when he's sucking rather than licking,* "—but it's more of a favour really."

Josephine replaced the pictures in the envelope and passed them to Veronica. "Well, Miss Clifford-Hughes, if you ever have an orgy, and we're not too low class for you, my man and me would love an invitation."

"Orgy?"

"Don't play coy."

"Hush, Jo," said Clio. "You know what an orgy is?"

Veronica shook her head.

"This stuff you do, when you have lots of people—well, at least four or five, and just do it with whoever you fancy."

"Oh, no. I haven't done it with that many, just three."

"You, Polly, and the gardener or the toe-sucking man?"

Veronica smiled. "The gardener."

She hid the photographs in a pocket of her dress. It looked like she would have to get a photographic album for her own pictures.

xxiii

Monday morning. Only seven days to the wedding.

"According to Mrs Beeton," said Veronica to the sleeping Polly, "a lady's maid is supposed to be up, dressed, and ready to serve before her mistress even wakes up."

Polly snored.

"And yet here I am every morning watching you sleep."

Polly made noises that sounded as if she was talking, but it made no sense.

"You're quite right, yesterday did not go entirely according to plan," she said as she slipped off the side of the bed. "I had really wanted Josephine and Clio to show us how to develop the pictures, and instead we got nothing but a *fait accompli.*"

The pictures were on the table. Veronica flicked through them, separating the wedding ones—suitable for Mrs Martaci—from the others. Then she paused, holding the one of her naked on the bed. Sofia was no stranger to painting nudes.

Veronica thought it strange the way people let Sofia keep the paintings. On the one hand, yes, it might be difficult having a painting at home—you wouldn't put it on the wall. But if someone were to discover that trove of less-than-appropriate imagery all together, it could turn the whole town upside down. Perhaps more than that; Sofia seemed to have a lot of connections. And if the person who discovered it were of a criminal inclination, they might use it for blackmail.

She imagined poor Lawrence being forced to pay out to prevent his body parts being put on display. He would certainly lose his job at the very least. There might be some that would be arrested.

Once more she considered the fact that Lawrence had intentionally told her about Sofia and the painting.

What did that mean?

She smiled at the thought of him and glanced across at the bed imagining him lying cosily between her and Polly. A very pleasant thought indeed. She added the nudes of herself to the pictures for Sofia. Polly probably wouldn't want a painting, and Veronica certainly wouldn't presume to hand over the pictures without asking.

It was another bright and sunny day which lit up the bedroom.

Veronica padded into the bathroom and, after utilising the water-closet, set the taps running. Vionnet would not be pleased if either of the dresses were soiled.

And now I'm drawing a bath for my maid, but no, this is for my lover, for my betrothed.

Her plan was that, once they were dressed for the wedding, with Vionnet, Josephine, and Clio as witnesses, she would marry Polly here. The problem was that she didn't know whether she ought to warn her; Polly could be a bit funny about surprises. Perhaps a white lie, or even the truth but not with all the detail. She really must arrange for a ring.

And then someone knocked on the door.

Veronica stood stock still. The knock had been quite firm, but Polly had not even stirred. There was a long pause and then the knock came again. Veronica went back into the bedroom and grabbed her dressing gown. It was reasonably thick and was long enough to hide her feet and ankles.

"Just a minute."

Veronica had her hand on the key.

"Who is it?"

"Ursula, miss."

"Aren't you supposed to be here at nine?"

"It's eight-thirty, miss, and I have your breakfast."

Veronica stared at the clock. It was eight-thirty-three, they had overslept. Polly had told her that Ursula had brought her to paroxysm many times, so the maid was familiar with Polly's naked body. Veronica made a decision. She unlocked the door and opened it sufficiently for the maid to enter, carrying a wide tray.

"Just put that on the table." Where the nude photographs of me and Polly are...

Ursula was taller than Polly, and swept in with the slightest hint of jasmine that was rapidly overwhelmed by toast, bacon and tea. She took three long steps into the room and froze as Veronica shut and locked the door.

Turning her head and using a sidelong glance made it easier for Veronica to look up, though she did not tend to do it because she had to be facing away from the person to make it work. But she could see the maid, with her red hair bound up tightly under her bonnet, staring at Polly lying naked in the bed.

"Just put the tray on the table," said Veronica again. Ursula seemed to recover her wits. The large tray covered most of the table's surface, and the things on it, including the photographs. The supplied breakfast was enormous, not just the teapot, milk jug, covered plate of toast, there was another of the bacon, mushrooms, tomatoes, and pots for butter and marmalade.

"Can you check the bath, and then you might want to wake the sleeping princess?"

"You want me to do that, miss?" Ursula's voice, quite refined with no clear regional accent, was very different to Polly's London tones.

"I think so, it'll be amusing to see her reaction."

"As you wish, miss." She strode into the bathroom.

Veronica sat at the table watching the maid as she checked the water temperature and spent a few moments with her sleeve pulled up and her arm in the water, swirling it around. Then she checked the temperature of the water coming out of the taps, examined the pipework—pausing to study the heater—then, after a moment's hesitation, adjusted the flows.

She disappeared out of view. Veronica got some toast and buttered it, then helped herself to two slices of bacon and some mushrooms. She savoured a mouthful of bacon—which unfortunately then reminded her of Edwin's edict that she must somehow overturn—she thrust the thought aside.

Ursula reappeared and approached the side of the bed. She reached out, then pulled her hand back as if it had been burned. "Oh!"

Polly stirred and moved her arm, which pulled the sheet down and exposed her breasts.

Veronica swallowed her mouthful. "There's a Faraday under the bed, that's what you felt. It's harmless."

Ursula's eyes flicked up at Veronica and she nodded. Breakfast was temporarily forgotten as Veronica tried to see what Ursula's response was to Polly and her nakedness. At first Ursula simply tested the Faraday effect, letting her fingers go in and out, getting used to it. Once confident there was no danger, she stretched out and shook Polly by the shoulder.

"Wake up, Pol, Mrs Jenkins is on the rampage!"

Polly sat bolt upright, dishevelled and confused. She flung the sheet off and it floated through the air over the bed, while the force of Polly's movement lifted her off the bed and made her drift back towards the bedhead. The look on Ursula's face was almost as confused as Polly as she gyrated in the air, reached the apex of her climb, and fell back.

Veronica burst out laughing which attracted Polly's wild stare. Then she realised where she was and looked round to see Ursula, who was also wearing a grin.

"Good morning, sleepy-head." Ursula glanced up at Veronica as if she was uncertain how her using familiar terms would be received, but Veronica was still chuckling and buttering more toast.

"What are you doing here, little bear?" said Polly

"Miss wanted me to help you into your bridesmaid dress today."

This again seemed to confuse Polly. "I haven't missed a week?"

Veronica waved the toast in her direction. "I told Mrs Jenkins we'd need more help. Having the painting done is a good chance to practice. I thought you'd like that help to be Ursula."

"You did?" said Polly. "I mean, yes, I would. Thank you."

"Why don't you take a bath first while I eat breakfast, then I can bathe while you have yours. Ursula can help." She almost said *scrub my back*, but Veronica felt awkward again. Silly though, her hump had been plainly visible to three women this weekend, and they barely noticed. Even on Friday night everyone had been really good about not staring—except Ruth and Esther, but they were young. *Only a little younger though.*

Clearly not in the least embarrassed about being naked in front of Ursula, Polly crawled to the nearer side of the bed and turned down the Faraday—sinking deeper into the springs of the bed as she did so—until it was at its minimum and she switched it off. Then she headed into the bathroom with her arm through Ursula's.

A twinge of jealousy leaked into Veronica's heart, but she knew it was completely unjustified. Why shouldn't Polly have her own friends, and lovers? After all, Veronica had Seth, and perhaps Lawrence—even if the result of that was yet to be seen—as well as a future husband who remained, for now, an enigma. She had taken Polly away from Ursula, and could not be jealous since she was the one who had arranged the reunion.

But the green monster refused to go away, she could only suppress it and pretend it wasn't there.

BY TEN O'CLOCK THEY had eaten and were dressed. Ursula had departed, taking the tray with her. Veronica had Polly hide their nude photographs along with the ones of Mr Plumley.

"We could just give him these ones," said Veronica.

"Don't we need to keep them?"

"We can make more from the negatives." Her hand went to her mouth. "All the negatives must still be in the dark room."

A horrified look went across Polly's face. "What if someone finds them?"

"No one would think to look," said Veronica, although she didn't even sound convincing to herself. "We'll fetch them this afternoon." She needed to change the subject. "How do we look?"

"So close to naked as makes no difference," said Polly. "We can't go down like this."

"Dressing gowns. Besides, nobody should see us in our dresses, it will spoil the effect on the day."

"No one's going to see us outside the house and the church anyway." Polly helped Veronica into her dressing gown which covered up most of the dress. Then she put on her own.

"Well, we can take some nice photographs and send copies to your family."

"Gawd no, Nika. They'd bloody disown me if they saw me in this. And bridesmaid to the mistress of the house? Nobody does that."

"But aren't I the one whose dignity is damaged by having a servant as bridesmaid?"

"Don't matter to my lot, it's the wrong thing so it would look bad on them."

"That's ridiculous."

"That's people, Nika."

Veronica couldn't deny it.

They made their way downstairs, and did not meet any workmen or other staff. In fact she noticed the amount of noise from workmen seemed quite reduced. She could still hear them, whistling or talking loudly to one another, but there was no sound of heavy machinery, or even hammers. Perhaps it would all be done on schedule after all.

They found Mr Plumley and Mrs Martaci already in the library. She had set up her easel with a canvas, but was sketching parts of the library in a book, using a small set of watercolours. She also had a large camera sitting on its tripod. Mr Plumley rose as they entered.

"There you are," she said. "Very good. Is everything well?"

"We are ready, Sofia," said Veronica as Polly turned the key in the lock.

"Well, just take off your wraps and stand over there near Mr Plumley. We'll see the best way to arrange you."

Veronica smiled at her tutor, undid the half-bow at her waist, and shrugged off the dressing gown.

"Oh m-my," said Mr Plumley. "That's a w-w-wedding dress?"

"Remarkable," said Sofia. "But it exposes your deformity, was that intentional?"

"I doubt Vionnet is capable of doing something with a dress that is not intentional, Sofia, do you?" said Veronica. "It works because of the design of the dress."

"The veil and train covers it," said Polly as she unrolled the package she was carrying. "It's a shame we can't do this with the hair and cosmetics. They make a lot of difference."

"We have some photographs, though," said Veronica. Polly passed the stack to her and she divided them between the ones for Mrs Martaci and those for Mr Plumley—taking care not to get them mixed up. She handed the one set to Mrs Martaci, and while she was going through them went over to Mr Plumley and gave him his.

He took one look at the exposed image and shoved them directly into his pocket. Then looked over at Sofia, but she was still occupied looking through the ones she had. And nodding to herself.

Polly still had not removed her dressing gown. Veronica went over and undid the knot herself, then, as the two sides opened, she pushed it back. Polly's shoulders and arms were completely uncovered; the dress was loose around the low neckline but clung to her shape down to the belt at the waist, then hung in folds to the floor. She had put the bracelet on her upper arm.

Then Veronica kissed her firmly but briefly on her lips. It had required a definite stretch to do it, and pain shot through her back. There was a gasp from Mr Plumley, and Polly blushed in embarrassment.

"You are beautiful," Veronica said in a whisper only Polly could hear.

"When you two have quite finished, we need to make a start," said Sofia. "Where do you want us?"

THERE HAD BEEN CONSIDERABLE discussion over the position they should be in, now that Sofia had seen their dresses. Since Veronica could not stand upright, they had to choose a position that catered for her deformity, while still making a picture that was worth something.

They had toyed briefly with the idea of her lying on a *chaise longue* with Polly behind, but Sofia had rejected it as giving quite the wrong impression. She decided that Polly crouched at Veronica's feet adjusting the dress—and lifting it slightly so her feet were visible—was right. It meant the tilt of Veronica's head became a natural part of the picture. Meanwhile, Polly had been given a footstool to sit on.

Sofia had taken several photographs to make sure the positioning remained correct in the following days.

By the end of the morning, Veronica ached all over as if she had run miles instead of merely standing still, but Polly could not even stand without help and was forced to sit.

"Can I see?" said Veronica, indicating the painting which Sofia had covered once she declared the sitting over.

"There's nothing to see yet," said Sofia abruptly. She glanced at Mr Plumley, who was massaging Polly's feet and calves, then back at Veronica. "I noticed that you have provided me with more pictures than I need."

"For another painting?" said Veronica.

"More appropriate to my special collection?"

"Yes, but I want it."

"You want it? Where will you put it?"

"On the wall."

"You would dare?"

Veronica smiled. "Yes. My house is filled with nude Greek statues. I will be adding to the collection."

Sofia nodded. "You want me to create something in an old style, featuring goddesses partially disrobed, that would not seem out of place among the art here."

"Yes, can you do it?"

"There will be a fee."

"Of course."

Veronica noticed that Mr Plumley was still working on Polly's feet, and a thought crossed her mind. "My tutor does like feet."

"Does he?"

"Oh yes."

Sofia hesitated. "In what way?"

"He worships them."

"Really?"

"I probably shouldn't say more," said Veronica. "But I'm afraid his wife does not indulge his appreciation. And what with the wedding and then being away for weeks..." She left her sentence unfinished, certain that if Sofia were interested she would pick it up.

There was a long pause. "Why would your wedding be a problem for him?"

"I have given him access to my feet," she said as if it had no importance, "but there just has not been time recently and, when I am away, there will be no opportunity at all, of course."

"What do you get from it?"

"You mean apart from the thrill of having a man worshipping literally at my feet, and the delight of having him clean them with his tongue? He has managed an important favour for me."

"Why are you telling me?"

"Because I know you can keep a secret, because he's your friend and I thought, perhaps, you might be able to help him."

"I see." Sofia stared at the man kneeling in front of Polly, his thumbs massaging the sole of her foot. "He doesn't want anything else?"

"Nothing."

There was a knock at the library door. Mr Plumley almost dropped Polly's feet, stood, and hurried to the other side of the room. Polly got to her feet and stumbled stiffly to the door.

"It's Ursula," she said after a moment.

"Let her in," said Veronica.

Polly unlocked the door.

"So, Miss Clifford-Hughes, the same time tomorrow?"

"That would be most agreeable. I look forward to it."

Sofia smiled. "A very smooth lie, Veronica. I know how unpleasant it can be."

"Well, I might not enjoy it, but I am looking forward to it."

With Ursula's help she and Polly got wrapped up then headed back to the bedroom.

xxiv

Back in the bedroom, Veronica was quiet as Ursula helped Polly out of her dress and they put it on the dummy.

Polly's words about not being able to join her world kept coming back to her. She was right, of course. Even if, for some reason, Polly gained an independent income and did not have to be a maid, what would she do? Open a flower shop? She still couldn't become Veronica's companion because she did not have the social rank, and would *still* be unable to be in the same world.

In the short term, the honeymoon—or business trip, she was still angry about that—would be as bad. They would get no chance to be together and there was unlikely to be any arrangement where they could spend the night together.

Once Polly was dressed in her maid's uniform, they came through to dress Veronica.

"I've been thinking," said Veronica.

"That's a bad sign, Nika," said Polly giving Ursula a wink.

Veronica chose to ignore the implied slur. "Ursula, you are quite strong I think?"

There was no way Veronica could see beyond the girl's waist, but the lack of response and the way she froze suggested perhaps it hadn't been a good thing to say.

"She is," said Polly. "Strong as a horse."

"Well, how would you like to go to Switzerland?"

"Me?" It was almost a squeak.

"Yes. For one thing there will be lots of heavy bags to carry, and it doesn't seem fair on Polly that she has to do it all."

"There will be porters, Nika."

"Even so, many hands and all that. More importantly, I don't know how much time we'll have together, Polly, and it might be terribly boring for you, so I thought if Ursula was there you two could talk, or do … whatever."

"Whatever, Nika?"

"Yes, Polly, *whatever*."

"And you won't be jealous."

Veronica was standing completely naked in the middle of the bedroom with Polly next to her, holding a pair of bloomers.

"I am jealous, Polly—" Veronica sighed, "—but I have no right to be. So yes, *whatever*. I might end up doing *whatever* with Lawrence if my husband is otherwise engaged or chooses not to sleep in the same room."

"Am I permitted to say no, miss?" said Ursula.

There it was again. The girl's language was not something you would expect from a housemaid. It was probably better even than Mr Jones.

"If you don't want to go, I won't make you."

"Thank you," said Ursula, "I would like to go. If that would meet with your approval, Miss Clifford-Hughes?"

"That's settled then. I'll write to Mr Slack to make sure there's a ticket, and arrange things with Mrs Jenkins."

"Thank you, miss."

Veronica looked at Polly. "Is that all right?"

"Thank you, Nika."

⸻ ● ⸻

THE DAY WAS OVERCAST now and the wind had picked up. The sunshine of the last week had been very pleasant, but this was not. The temperature had not dropped and the atmosphere now seemed stifling.

"We could be in for a thunderstorm," said Polly as they left the garden and headed for the dark room.

The clouds broke just before they reached the outer buildings. They made a dash for the door but were drenched in seconds. Then they had to stand in the deluge as Veronica got the key in the lock and managed to get the door open.

They stumbled inside, with water sluicing off them and making pools between the worn flagstones. The room was dark and only the grey light from the open door lit the benches and stools. The place was mostly in shadow.

Lightning filled the room with white brilliance that immediately vanished again, leaving them half-blinded. Moments later a thunderous roar crashed over their heads and Polly screamed.

Veronica slammed the door shut and Polly squealed again.

"Sorry."

Thunder rumbled across the buildings. Veronica got the impression the floor was shaking because of it.

She expected her eyes to adjust to the dark, but if any adjustment occurred it did not bring any sight.

"I'll find the light," said Polly.

"No!"

"What?"

"You're soaking wet, you might get a shock."

There was a long pause, then Polly said, "They made it very dark."

"It's a dark room."

"I'm cold."

Veronica was feeling the chill as well. "We need to get these wet things off."

"I'm wet all through."

"So take it all off."

"Here?"

"Why not?" Veronica hadn't moved and her hand was still on the door. She found a bolt and threw it. It had been oiled and made a satisfying thunk. "No one knows we're here, and no one can get in."

She could hear movement as Polly was—presumably—removing her clothes. Veronica, however, was stuck. There was very little she could do to remove her own clothes, the buttons were in out of the way places she just couldn't reach. Instead, she went down on one knee and started with her shoe buckles. Her shoes were soaked, and when she got to them, so were her stockings, but she managed to peel them off.

Then she pulled up her skirt and petticoats to remove her bloomers.

"I'm done," said Polly. "Feels strange."

"What?"

"Being naked outside."

"Except we're not."

"But we're not in a house, not in a bedroom, we're in a shed," said Polly. "It's a bit scary."

Veronica was trying to reach the buttons that ran down the back of her dress with the one hand that could reach, but it was very awkward and a strain.

"I can't get my dress off."

"Hang on." There was some shuffling, a quiet curse, and then Polly slammed into her from the side. Veronica grabbed at her and found cool, damp skin. Her left hand quickly located Polly's bum and gave it a squeeze. "Sorry, tripped on something."

Veronica leaned forwards and her lips landed on Polly's shoulder. She gave it a nip.

"Ow, look, we can play if you like but I thought you wanted your clothes off."

"I've done my shoes, stockings, and bloomers."

"Sounds like you, easy access to your feet, legs, and pussy."

"Just get my dress off will you, it feels horrible on my skin."

"Not sure this is the best idea, Nika," said Polly as she got behind Veronica and started to undo the buttons. "These aren't going to dry here, and we'll never be able to get them on again."

"Then we'll walk back to the house naked."

"That's not funny."

"Wasn't meant to be."

"You're impossible."

"Doesn't it stir up your lust and desire, though?" said Veronica. "Knowing someone might see you, taking the risk?"

"No, Nika, that's just you."

"I don't think it is." The dress was loosened and, with difficulty, Polly managed to pull the material from Veronica's shoulders and then extract her arms. "That room Sofia has, it's full of paintings of people with no clothes on, sometimes doing lustful things. Not only did they do it in front of her so she could paint them, the paintings might be seen by anyone."

"Yes, well, I wouldn't want a painting like that."

The moist dress was finally round Veronica's ankles along with her petticoats. The dampness evaporated from her skin now it was exposed to the air, and she felt better.

"I'm going to try for the light," she said. "The switch is bound to be somewhere near the door."

It took a couple of minutes of running her hand up and down the wall next to the door, but eventually she located the metal conduit for the wires and then, at its end, the switch itself.

She closed her eyes to protect them from the expected blaze of electric light, and flicked it on.

Much to her surprise, the room filled with a dim red light.

"Oh."

"You didn't warn me," said Polly.

"It didn't matter."

"You didn't know that."

Veronica took in the eerie image of Polly—completely naked except for her hair still tucked up inside the bonnet. She was red highlights and black shadows. Like a German expressionist painting. Clothes were scattered around them.

Veronica wanted to get between Polly's legs for the thrill of doing the forbidden away from the bedroom, but Polly was right, they needed to deal with the clothes first.

Another crack of thunder burst overhead. Polly jumped, then threw herself at Veronica, squeezing their naked bodies together. Once more Veronica allowed her hand to descend to Polly's behind, and she manipulated it rhythmically, pushing her fingers deeper into the crack. Polly gave a little sigh and relaxed, then lifted her leg to give Veronica easier access.

By sheer will, Veronica stopped moving her fingers and gave Polly a gentle pat on the bum.

"Let's see if we can't hang the clothes up so at least they can dry a little. Then find the negatives so we don't forget them when we leave."

Polly made a disapproving noise. "You can't just leave me hanging like that."

Veronica kissed her way down Polly's neck to the apex of her breast; she sucked the nipple into her mouth and licked across it.

Then blew a raspberry on it.

Polly gasped and pulled herself away, her arms covering her tits. "You bitch, I hate you."

Veronica burst out laughing.

"I'll get you for that, you see if I don't."

"My sweet love, I look forward to your revenge."

Veronica gave her back a stretch and took in the dark room properly for the first time since it had been completed. There were a lot of shelves, with glass bottles holding chemicals, all of which were labelled in such a way they could be read even in this light.

From her own reading Veronica knew that the red light was used because it had the least effect on undeveloped negatives and photographic paper.

There was a wooden box marked 'Kodak Film Tank' and two cylinders already out on the workbench, and another set on the shelf above. Veronica opened the box to reveal a complicated-looking winding mechanism. "This gets the film from the camera reel on to..." She opened the larger of the two metal cylinders which had a big cylindrical holder inside. "This. Then we pour the chemicals in through the hole in the top, which fixes the image on the negative."

There was a device that resembled a huge microscope, although it was too big to peer in through the top. It had a power cable with a switch. She flicked it and a blinding white light shone out. She turned it off in a hurry.

The shelf above had racks of envelopes. "That's the photographic paper, and we shine a light through the developed negative so the image goes on the paper for a certain amount of time." She found a clock-like device. "The timer." She flicked a switch on the side and it started ticking as a single hand moved round the dial. She switched it off and moved on a little further to a place where there were several odd-looking trays with ribbed bottoms.

"And these hold the chemicals that fix the photographic image on the paper." The end of the bench had a sink. "Then we wash the chemicals off, and it's all done. Easy."

"Easy?"

"Well, we'll have to practice to get the times right, and the concentrations of chemicals, but it's not hard. Oh, it's got a hot water tap. Look."

"That's nice." Polly sounded singularly unimpressed.

"If it's got hot water, we're really close to the furnace here, so there might be a heater." She peered into the shadows. "There! I suppose I should thank Mr McCloud. He's been very thorough."

They had to move a table and some chairs to expose the large cast-iron radiator set against a wall, similar to the ones in the house. A quick examination showed that it was plumbed in. Crouching beside it, Veronica managed to turn the valve and could feel the hot water flowing up through its body.

Meanwhile Polly had collected the clothes and, between the two of them, they placed the dresses directly on the radiator while they hung stockings and underthings on chairs which they placed close to it.

"Now," said Veronica, "we just have to wait for them to dry out enough to put back on." She brushed off one of the other chairs—they were hoop-backed and had no padding on the seat which was cold to her naked behind, but it was better than standing.

Polly did the same but Veronica caught her by the hand and pulled her closer. Then patted her lap—or rather, her naked thigh. Polly sat facing away. "Turn around."

The maid giggled, and did as she was instructed, sitting with her legs wide on either side of the chair. She shuffled in closer until Veronica's head was nestled against her breasts, and her arms were around Veronica's neck.

Veronica slipped one arm around, so she was cupping Polly's bum again, and wriggled the other down between their bodies. She once more squeezed and manipulated Polly's behind rhythmically while gently rubbing her knuckles from the base of Polly's quim to the top, letting it roll from side to side to stimulate the spread lips. Polly groaned and arched her back.

Stretching her right arm a little further, Veronica ran the tip of her finger gently around the ridges of Polly's bum hole.

"Oh god, I hate you doing that to me," said Polly, her voice more breath than words, as she lifted her legs in an effort to get more pressure front and back.

"Want me to stop?"

"No."

"I thought not." Veronica reduced the pressure even more until she was barely touching. The back of her left hand was getting very wet. It was a strain, but she reached under Polly until she could dip her fingers into Polly's pussy and then bring the moistened tips back to Polly's anus. She spread the lubrication around and then gently, rhythmically, applied pressure directly into Polly's hole.

The girl's breathing became faster; she wriggled and pushed harder with her bum, but as she did so Veronica retreated and applied more pressure at the front instead. Moments later Polly tried to push harder there, and Veronica changed back to her rear.

"Stop it," Polly whined.

"Beg me," said Veronica as she reduced the pressure until she was barely brushing Polly's skin.

"Please make me come, Nika!" She thrust her bum out and managed to get a solid push against Veronica's finger. "Please!"

"How should I do it, Polly?"

The girl growled and pushed back again, but Veronica was ready and just let her finger move away. She rubbed hard against Polly's nubbin. Polly screamed in frustration.

"How, Polly?"

"Don't make me say it..."

Veronica opened her mouth and licked then bit Polly's tit. "How, Polly? Tell me!"

"I really hate you."

Veronica's finger circled Polly's anus.

"Shove it in."

"Shove what where?"

"My bum, shove your finger up my bum."

Veronica toyed with the idea of stretching it out a bit longer, but decided against it. Polly might get violent. She rubbed her knuckles hard against Polly's quim and pushed her finger against the circle of her rear.

Polly hissed and thrust hard against the finger, again and again, as if she were being fucked. Her breathing became ragged and she lost the rhythm. Veronica kept pushing hard although her finger muscles were aching. She added the middle finger just to spread the load.

Polly gave an extra hard thrust and both fingers slipped in deep. The girl screamed and shuddered. The muscles of her bum spasmed again and again, crushing Veronica's fingers. Her legs pulled in hard enough that they might both end up with bruises. Polly went limp and leaned on Veronica, panting into her neck and hair.

As Polly's breathing slowed, Veronica extracted her fingers gently.

"Ow."

"Sorry."

"You're not."

"I'm not sorry I did it, I'm sorry if I hurt you."

They sat for a while longer but Veronica's back started to ache and her legs were growing numb.

"Sorry, Polly, but you have to get off."

Polly managed to get one foot on the floor by leaning to the side, then lifted her weight from Veronica.

"Pity there isn't a bed in here."

Polly looked around. "If we put the chairs in a line, you could lie down on them."

"What about you?"

"I'll stand for now; if I need to I could use the workbench."

"Make sure there's nothing spilt on it, I'm sure some of those chemicals can burn."

They arranged the chairs and Polly helped Veronica lay herself out. It wasn't comfortable, but it did relieve some of the pressure on her back. The radiator was working well and the air was noticeably warm, though also very damp. Outside, the thunder had growled off into the distance and was gone.

"I need to get Mrs Jenkins on our side," said Veronica once she was settled, while Polly was checking and rearranging the dresses to dry better.

"Good luck with that."

"I have an idea, but I don't know how to make it happen."

Polly had found a stool which she set against the wall next to the radiator; she sat so that her back was supported.

"What's your idea?"

"Mr Laughton is a horrible lover."

"How do you know?" said Polly in sudden horror. "Did you let him do you? When?"

"Oh no, I saw him fucking Mrs Jenkins ages ago. Then I had my chat with her after he did her last week."

"You didn't tell me."

"Which one?"

"Either of them."

"Well, she willingly lets him poke her, but it's like you told me, he just does it for his own satisfaction. He gets her worked up and leaves her without coming."

"He's a man, Nika, what do you expect?"

"I know, he's a nasty fellow. Anyway, you know we taught Seth how to pleasure a woman properly."

"I taught Seth."

"What?"

Polly stood up and stretched, displaying the lithe beauty of her body in shades of red and black. "I taught him, Nika, and you were my plaything."

"Yes."

Taking long strides that made her legs scissor through the light and shadow, Polly leaned on the chair back by Veronica's head.

"You want Seth to make Mrs Jenkins come properly, so that she'll be happy to stay at Versyns?"

"I just can't think how to get them together."

"Send a message that the steward wants her, but send Seth instead, and he can start when she's not looking."

Veronica frowned. "That doesn't seem right."

"As long as she comes it doesn't matter."

"No," said Veronica. "That would make what we do as bad as what my father did to you."

"Why would I care? Jugsy has never been nice to me; she isn't nice to anyone."

"Jugsy?" laughed Veronica.

"It's what the below-stairs maids call her. She's so thin but has those huge tits."

"They are big," said Veronica, "but I expect they just seem bigger in comparison to her size."

"You make it sound like you care about her."

"I do."

"Why?"

"She cried."

"Crocodile tears."

Veronica tried to move, but found she was effectively trapped by chair backs and her inability to push down without causing herself pain. Polly must have seen what she was trying to do, and helped her into a sitting position.

"She's still a woman, Polly. Her husband was killed in South Africa, and she was genuinely grateful when I said I would give her good references."

Polly sat in the chair next to Veronica. It was facing the opposite way and it was almost as if they were in a love seat.

"Whatever the plan," said Veronica, "it has to be her decision."

"What about Seth's decision?" said Polly.

Veronica gave a short laugh. "Oh well, he's a man, he won't need much encouragement if a woman is giving herself to him."

Polly reached up and stroked Veronica's cheek. "You have learnt your lessons well."

"Have you changed your mind about men?" said Veronica. "After all, you were happy to sit on his face and let him make you come with his tongue."

"It wasn't his dick, and everybody has a tongue," said Polly, and then she pulled a face. "Besides, he was prickly, made my thighs itch for hours after."

"How would you know, you were asleep?"

"Well they were itchy up to when I went to sleep."

Polly's hand dropped to Veronica's right breast and she scratched along it from her collarbone to the nipple, which hardened. Polly rolled it between her thumb and forefinger. Veronica felt herself unfocus and groaned as the lust bubbled between her legs.

Leaning back, Polly got her other hand on Veronica's other breast. She stroked and twisted, dug her fingers in hard, then scratched.

Veronica made little noises in the back of her throat. She grabbed the back of the chair at her side and put her other hand on Polly's thigh for support. As Polly scratched and squeezed, stroked and then licked, the intense carnal lust grew and throbbed from her quim to the top of her head; she felt as if she was going to explode.

Then Polly's frantic manipulations slowed. She drew Veronica's nipple into her mouth, sucking like a baby, and squeezed the other in a gentle rhythm.

The lust within Veronica simmered, but it was as if her whole body was drawn into the fire. Her muscles strained, and her knuckles went white as she gripped the chair and Polly's leg tighter.

"I. Hate. You." The words broke apart as she fought for breath.

"Beg."

"Please, Polly. Please. Make me come."

"What else?"

"Please. Hurt me."

Polly scraped her teeth across Veronica's trapped nipple, and she scratched her other breast. Veronica squealed.

"More. Do it." Then a belated, "I beg you."

Sucking Veronica's tit hard Polly bit down and rolled the nipple between her molars, while she dug her fingers into the other one and twisted her hand as if she was going to rip it off. The ecstatic pain ripped through Veronica and the lust couldn't be contained. Her body shook, the muscles in her legs spasmed, and the pent-up tension exploded through her. For a moment she could not draw breath, then she screamed as if it was the only thing in the world. The world disappeared and there was only white light in her mind.

Then it was gone.

XXV

Polly limped slightly as they made their way back through the mists gathering in the woods and across the lawns. The damp in the air chilled them after the heat in the dark room.

Their clothes were mostly dry. Before they left, Veronica remembered why they had gone there in the first place, and picked up the negatives. They turned off the radiator and locked the door.

"You've done something to me leg," said Polly.

"And I'm going to be bruised again."

"You asked for it."

"I know. Trouble is, we never think about consequences at the time," she said. "Like having men with scratchy bristles between our legs."

They managed to get to the bedroom without encountering any other staff, and were able to change before dinner. Veronica put the negatives with her parents' album. Then stared at the place where the workmen had pulled up the floorboards. It had been a good hiding place; unfortunately it was now nailed firmly in place.

<hr>

THE FOLLOWING DAY THEY were up before Ursula arrived with breakfast. At which point, Veronica realised she had completely forgotten to speak to Mrs Jenkins, or send a letter to Mr Slack. So, while Polly had her bath, she sat down and wrote two letters. She popped them in envelopes and addressed them.

"Just give them both to Mr Jones and he'll make sure they get to where they need to go," she said as she submitted to the two of them dressing her.

"If you were expecting to have carnal relations," she said casually as they arranged her clothes, "you would be quite disappointed if they didn't happen, wouldn't you?"

Ursula said nothing.

"Is this about you?" said Polly.

"It's a serious question. Yes, I mean, if I'm expecting to do it with you, or even Seth, there's the anticipation. You start to get warmed up, and if it doesn't happen you'd feel bad."

Polly and Ursula dropped the dress over Veronica's head and she wriggled it down on to her body. She had not ceased to be surprised by the way it stretched and clung. Polly slipped her hand inside the dress and adjusted Veronica's boobs.

"Wouldn't you feel that way?" insisted Veronica.

"I suppose," said Polly.

"Suppose?"

"Yes, all right. If I'm expecting to have fun and come, I would be disappointed if it didn't happen."

"What about you, Ursula?"

Silence.

I wish I could see her face.

"What do you think?"

"Miss, I..." Ursula's words fell into an awkward silence.

Veronica realised she had made a bad mistake. Poor girl must be completely embarrassed, even though Polly had said Ursula had brought Polly to paroxysm lots of times. *But not herself.*

"I'm sorry, please don't think you have to answer. I shouldn't have asked. It's none of my business." She took a deep breath. "I'm done, why don't you sort Polly out?"

She sat in the chair and let the other two go off into Polly's bedroom while she berated herself for being so insensitive. Everybody had their demons. For Polly it was being raped by Veronica's father, for her it was ... well, visible to everyone who cared to look. Mrs Jenkins had her loss which perhaps she was trying to hide by letting Mr Laughton treat her so badly. There was no reason why Ursula should be any different.

And I'm making these plans without even consulting Seth. Perhaps he would hate the idea of fucking Mrs Jenkins.

She thought through the ideas of how she might get Seth and Mrs Jenkins in the same room together. The idea of Mrs Jenkins bent over a desk and Seth penetrating her was stimulating in its own way. There had to be some trickery to get them together, but there must not be any coercion, it would make Veronica as bad as her father, even if she wasn't doing the fucking herself.

Which reminded her of the artificial phallus her mother had been wearing in the photographs. She stared at the floor of the bedroom. Was it hidden in another location under the boards? She shook her head. That would be silly—also, not relevant.

She must somehow get Mrs Jenkins to think she was going to have carnal relations with Mr Laughton, and have Seth turn up naked instead. And then Mrs Jenkins would be horrified, declare there was no way she was going to be fucked by the under-gardener, and that would confirm her decision to leave. The complete opposite of what Veronica needed.

Oh, wait... Veronica smiled. Perhaps it could be done.

———◦———

THE FIRST SITTING FOR the painting had been interesting. The second sitting was plain boring. It also did not involve any sitting, which meant the aching settled in early and she spent the entire time barely able to think of anything except how she might relieve the stress without changing position: a fundamental impossibility.

Polly wasn't in a much better state. Having to sit in such an awkward position for such a long time was a terrible strain on her joints.

Sofia spent the time speaking in Italian, trying to help Veronica and Polly practice. Unfortunately she was so focused on the painting that her words tended to come out slowly and disjointed.

Mr Plumley sat in an armchair off to one side. Veronica often caught him staring at Veronica's feet. When he saw she had seen him he could immediately bury his nose back in his book.

"Now, Miss Clifford-Hughes," said Sofia quite suddenly, shocking all three of the room's occupants from their individual reverie.

"What now, signora?"

"I have done sufficient work on your bride picture. It is time for the other picture." She then pointedly stared at Mr Plumley.

"Oh good," said Veronica, and relaxed from her position. Polly creaked into a standing position as if she were an old woman. "Can you help Polly get me out of the dress?"

"Perhaps Mr Plumley should leave?"

"Oh no, he remains."

Mrs Martaci stared at Veronica. "Are you sure?"

"Quite sure, Sofia. We have already discussed the matter."

It took a few moments for Sofia to adjust, but then she shrugged, wiped her hands clean, and went to help.

A warm sense of pleasure went through Veronica as the two women helped her out of the dress. Veronica herself slipped her bloomers down and stepped out of them. She looked directly at Mr Plumley, who stared at her. She could see his eyes moving as he looked up and down her nakedness. Only the second man ever to see her like this.

"Do you have any idea of the sort of picture you want?" asked Sofia.

"I need to lie down on the *chaise*, and I want both Polly and Mr Plumley."

Polly's exclamation of "I ain't taking my clothes off!" was mixed with Mr Plumley's less strident protest, "I couldn't possibly..."

Up until that moment Veronica had not intended to include her tutor, but she had another idea that might work out if she did it right.

"Yes," she said. "I will lie on the *chaise*, Mr Plumley will be at my feet, while Polly and I kiss."

"You do not expect m-me to remove m-my clothes, m-Mistress Nika?"

"No, of course not, and your face will be hidden."

"But I will be touching your feet?"

"Of course."

"I see."

"I'm not taking me clothes off," said Polly again. "Just you."

"Just me."

Sofia once more accepted Veronica's decisions and they quickly arranged the *chaise longue* where they had been standing before. Polly arranged the cushions so Veronica could lie back comfortably, with her right foot on the floor, and the left one up on the *chaise*.

As a single concession, Mr Plumley removed his jacket, and knelt on one foot. "I'm sorry, Nika, I will not be able to maintain a position so low down for the time needed." He indicated her foot on the floor. She could see he was desperately trying not to look at her breasts, and definitely not between her open legs.

"I want you to lick the other one."

"But—" He seemed almost helpless, knowing in that position his focus could only be her nether regions.

"I want you to," she said gently. "Nika wants you to."

Veronica looked at Sofia and found she was unable to decipher the expression on the woman's face. Somewhere between humour, surprise, and professional detachment.

Polly moved behind the chair and leaned over it. Sinking into the cushions, Veronica was able to put her head back; their lips touched just as Mr Plumley lifted her foot and his tongue licked around her toes.

"Don't get carried away," said Sofia. "This is a painting, not a moving picture. You need to remain still."

Veronica didn't care as Polly's tongue slipped between her lips and Mr Plumley sucked her big toe. She lifted her hand and cupped her breast. She could feel her quim becoming damp.

There was a camera click. Her lovers jumped and retreated.

"I still have to take pictures," said Sofia. "The same as for the other picture. Polly and Mr Plumley's faces are obscured."

They all relaxed and went back to what they had been doing.

After half an hour, any incipient lust from the attention being given her, including her self-stimulation, had drained away. Veronica was still comfortable, but she could feel the tension in Polly and Mr Plumley.

The remaining half hour was torture, but they made it to the end. This time, while Sofia packed up her oils and equipment, Mr Plumley helped Polly dress Veronica, but he did not touch any part of her inappropriately.

Once they were in their dressing gowns, he went back to sit down.

Veronica went over to Sofia.

She spoke quietly. "About Mr Plumley's preferences."

Mrs Martaci nodded her head. "You have mentioned them."

"His wife will not let him indulge with her." Veronica said again.

"You're expecting me to let him do that to me?"

"It's your choice, of course," said Veronica. "I thought it was very strange at first, but I got used to it, and it's nice having someone worshipping your feet."

"Why did he call you Mistress Nika?"

"Because sometimes I am not Veronica."

"And do you punish him too?"

It was Veronica's turn to frown. "Why would I do that?"

"There are some who take pleasure in it," said Sofia as she clicked the latches on her painting box. "The terms mistress and master are common, as if the person being punished is a servant or slave. He called you Mistress Nika."

"Oh, no, he doesn't want that, or to do, you know, anything else," said Veronica. "He just likes to clean smelly feet, with his mouth."

⸺◉⸺

WITH URSULA'S ASSISTANCE, back in the bedroom, Veronica and Polly changed into their usual clothes. Polly had managed to adjust another day dress the way Mademoiselle Vionnet had shown her. This one had a flower pattern and the hem hung daringly above the ankle, but only at the back because of Veronica's stoop. Polly grabbed her pins to make the bottom of the dress even.

"As long as you don't do anything silly in it, that will hold," she said. "I'll sew it properly this evening."

"Perhaps you could teach me how to sew."

Polly looked at her askance. "Why?"

"Because it doesn't seem fair that you have to wait on me hand and foot. I don't do anything."

"It's my job."

Veronica held up her hand. "Yes, I'm sorry." There was no point arguing; their life was just too confusing.

⸺◉⸺

AFTER LUNCHEON THEY went out into the garden. The weather remained mixed and uncertain, but no storm threatened. Broken clouds streaked across the sky as if driven by some great wind. The sun shone between the clouds and, out on the fields beyond the garden, patches of sunlight moved across the undulating surface, highlighting the sheep.

Veronica led them straight to the arbour and then turned to Polly. "Can you go and find Seth? I need to talk to him."

"Now?"

"Yes, now," she said, "and if anyone questions it, say I want to discuss plants for my hothouse."

"You're up to something."

"Of course I am, Polly, I can't achieve anything without plans and conniving. I need to make sure Mrs Jenkins stays."

Polly frowned at her and went off at a slow pace, as if reluctant.

Veronica sat down. As Polly's footsteps crunching on the gravel diminished, the sounds of birds and humming insects came to the fore. Hoverflies flitted back and forth, then hung in the shade. Behind it all she could hear the low thump of the steam generator, but it was the kind of sound that was so constant it was lost to the senses.

It's Tuesday afternoon. This time next week I will be married, and on my way to Switzerland.

She shook her head, it did not seem real. Nor did all the things she needed to get done between now and next Monday.

I could stop. I could decide that it doesn't matter whether Mrs Jenkins leaves. I could simply do as my husband instructs and declare that the household must become vegetarian.

She pursed her lips and tried to imagine what that would be like. After all, two months ago she never did anything that was not arranged. She did her lessons and she went to church. Nothing else. The only original thoughts she had were to do with the books she read, and her imagination.

Until she exposed her body to Seth.

If she had continued to be her previous self, the marriage would have happened and the household would have fallen apart. It still could, but now she was trying to make everything work out for the best.

She had hosted a party! She had kissed a woman who had carnal relations with both her mother and father. She was having a picture painted of herself naked and being adored by a man and a woman.

Everything had changed.

No. She could not simply let the household fall apart because her husband-to-be was making an impractical and foolish choice. Perhaps she would indulge him and become vegetarian. That would be appropriate and dutiful—if unappealing—but there were no conditions under which she would be willing to enforce it on the staff.

Polly and Seth appeared on the other side of the garden. She smiled; he had shaved his face, which was curious since she was sure she had not mentioned that it was less than pleasant to have such an irritant between one's legs. Perhaps Polly had told him. As they approached she took the time to admire his physique.

"Afternoon, miss."

"Good afternoon, Seth. Are you well?"

"Very well, miss," he said. "And theyself?"

"As well as one might expect considering all the matters I have to deal with."

Polly sat down beside her, leaned back and crossed her legs, which revealed her ankles. Veronica was surprised; Polly had never indicated any particular attraction to Seth, after all, he was a man, but Veronica was aware of how effective his tongue could be, and so was Polly. Perhaps she wanted to play that game again.

Unfortunately, now that he was close up she couldn't see much above his knees. She sighed heavily and stood. "Sit down, Seth."

"That ain't proper, miss."

"Yes, I am perfectly well aware *it ain't proper*," she said, "but I am your mistress and I have told you to do it—so that I can see your face when I'm talking to you."

Her tone must have made an impression since he sat next to Polly immediately, ramrod straight and perched on the edge. His cap pulled off and in his hands.

Where to start? "Do you like fucking, Seth?"

"Miss?"

"I didn't think it was a hard question."

Polly giggled.

Veronica sighed and glared at her. "Not a *difficult* question."

"I bain't sure how to answer, miss."

"You've fucked someone before? A girl or woman?"

"Not you."

"No, not me, and not Polly. Someone else."

He hesitated. "I mebbee have, miss."

"Don't you know?"

"Not sure I should say, miss."

"I don't care who it was, I just want an answer." *Although I'd be quite interested to know who.*

"I 'ave done it, yes miss."

"You liked it?"

"'Course I did, miss, what you take me for?"

"Good. Now, do you get it often?"

"Not often, no."

"Recently?"

"No, miss. Not since I saw thee in the window."

Veronica smiled, then lost it again. "Have you been saving yourself for me?"

"I thought you'd like that."

Oh dear. Veronica looked up the garden to the house and stared at the window that used to be hers. A single event had changed everything.

"Did I do wrong, miss?"

"No, Seth," she said, "I think that was very sweet of you."

"You don't want me to fuck you, miss?"

"I did, Seth, and in some ways I still do," she said carefully, "but things changed."

"Saving yourself for your husband."

"Yes." At least it seemed he understood that, so he wasn't going to be upset about it.

"And I don't want to be fucked," said Polly, "just in case you were thinking you might."

"Orright, Pol."

"You call her Pol?" said Veronica.

"We be cousins," said Seth and grinned at Polly.

"Second cousins," said Polly, "once removed. Barely related at all."

"Brought up by the same aunt."

"Your mother, and not really my aunt."

Veronica thought that explained a few things: Polly's initial reluctance about Seth, and then the way he easily obeyed her instructions, but this was getting off the subject.

"Yes, that's interesting, but Seth—" He turned his attention back to her, "—last week, when you came to my room and Polly showed you how to pleasure me, in fact pleasure any woman."

"I liked that, but I hurt your titties."

"Yes, you did, but Polly was right, I like that sort of thing in moderation." *And talking about it is making my thighs slick.* "It was the best come I ever had, and you did it—" Polly frowned. "—with Polly's help, obviously."

The folds in Seth's trousers could not hide the fact that he too was stimulated by the discussion. *Good, it should make him more amenable to my suggestion.*

"You know how Mr Laughton fucks Mrs Jenkins?"

Seth grinned, clearly remembering the day he lifted her up to spy on the housekeeper and steward through the window.

"Well, he never leaves her satisfied. He just does it for his own pleasure and when he's spurted he leaves her there."

The expression on Seth's face now was a little confused. The staff did not, on the whole, like Mrs Jenkins, and why should he feel sorry for her?

Veronica sighed. It seemed there was no point in trying to be clever about this.

"Look, Seth, I need you to make Mrs Jenkins come. Not just come, I need you to do to her what you did to me. Do all the things you've been taught, and fuck her too. Give her the best time she has ever had with a man, because if you don't she's going to leave, and I don't want her to."

He stared at her.

"Fuck Mrs Jenkins."

"Yes."

"Make her come."

"Yes."

"If thee say so, miss."

"What?"

"If that's what thee want, Miss Veronica, I'll do as thee command."

Veronica frowned. She wanted to say that she didn't want him to do it just because she commanded it; she wanted him to do it because *he* wanted to. But why would he want that? And, after all, she *did* want him to do it because she commanded it.

"All right, yes. Good."

Polly shifted in her seat. "You think getting screwed is going to make her stay?"

"It might," said Veronica, "at the very least it'll make staying more attractive. And once I've fixed the vegetarian issue, we won't have a revolt among the staff."

"Beg pardon, miss, vegetarian? Those folks that don't eat red meat?"

"Yes. My future husband is one of them and he wants all the staff to be as well."

"Staff won't stand for that."

"Yes, I know, Seth. I will be speaking to him about it. It won't happen."

"But my gaffer's got his instructions from your man, miss."

"What instructions?"

"Putting the whole garden and as much land as possible to vegetables and fruits."

"Well, perhaps that won't happen after all."

"No, miss, you're not understanding. The amount of land. It's like the new master wants to feed an army."

xxvi

"You received my note about Ursula coming on the trip to Switzerland."

"If you don't mind me saying so, Miss Clifford-Hughes," said Mrs Jenkins, "there's something strange about that girl."

It was Wednesday afternoon, and they were sitting in Mrs Jenkins' office. Veronica was nervous, but tried to remember that she was Nika, who was capable of anything.

The morning's painting session had gone off the same way as Tuesday, and she could not deny she was grateful that they were not required to sit for it any more—if only what they had been doing was mere sitting.

"How do you mean 'strange'? Has she been any trouble?"

"No, she works hard and does her tasks well."

"Trouble with the other staff?"

"Nothing I've heard about."

"I assume her references were satisfactory?"

"She came very well recommended by the previous family."

"So why do you say she's strange?"

"Frankly, Mrs Clifford-Hughes, she's not common."

"I'm sorry...?"

"She talks like a toff, begging your pardon."

Veronica couldn't deny the truth that she had noticed herself, but she wasn't going to give Mrs Jenkins' prejudice any encouragement. "And why is that a problem?"

"Because servants shouldn't talk like their masters, it upsets the natural balance of things."

"I see, well, thank you for your thoughts on the matter. I will be taking Ursula, and we'll see how it goes, won't we?"

"Is that all, Miss Clifford-Hughes?" She looked as if she was about to stand, but Veronica remained resolutely in her seat. Mrs Jenkins was forced to relax back into her chair.

"No, there are one or two more things I wish to discuss," said Veronica. "First, I don't think I had the opportunity to thank you for the pie last Friday. It was as delicious as I remember."

Mrs Jenkins blushed. "Just my job, miss."

"Oh no, Mrs Jenkins, please do not undervalue your contribution. All the guests commented on how delicious it was." There. That was one of the white lies, but while they might not have said anything, her guests did eat the pie with gusto.

"I...thank you, Miss Clifford-Hughes. Was there a second matter?"

Veronica took a deep breath. "Yes. It is an awkward and embarrassing subject which I hope we can negotiate with the minimum of difficulty. Plain speaking, I think, should be the order of the day."

Now the housekeeper looked worried and spoke with some hesitation. "Is this about your wedding night?"

Veronica pursed her lips. "Why does every woman think I'm going to ask about the wedding night? No, Mrs Jenkins. I can assure you I know precisely what to expect. You need not be concerned on that account." The housekeeper did not disguise her look of relief. Veronica pressed on before the woman started wondering how Veronica knew. "However, it is, in some ways, related, and as this is a personal matter, perhaps we might dispense with formalities. You can call me Nika and I will use your given name, if you could tell me what it is?"

"That's highly improper, Miss Clifford-Hughes."

"Yes, I know, but what we are going to discuss is also highly improper but woman to woman, not mistress to servant. What's your given name?" Veronica allowed the part of her that was Nika to take control, and her voice was quite stern.

"Esme."

"That's lovely, and I am Nika."

"As you say, miss."

"Nika."

Mrs Jenkins almost coughed on the word, as if it were trying to choke her. "Nika."

Veronica smiled. "When I caught you last week, you had been having carnal relations with the steward."

The woman's face took on a pained expression, but Veronica pressed on. "He is using you as a receptacle for his seed, Esme, a convenient plaything for his pleasure. He does not care whether you receive any enjoyment. He might as well be using his own hand to make himself spend."

Mrs Jenkins went pale. Her hands had the arms of her chair in a grip that would have crushed the neck of a lion.

Veronica looked at her expectantly then, when there was no response, she said, "Tell me, do you ever come when he fucks you?"

"You are the devil's spawn. I always knew it and now you prove it with your disgusting words."

"Perhaps I am," said Veronica, "or perhaps I have been so mistreated by those who see my deformity as a sign of evil, they could not imagine I could be anything else. Who's worse, the one who is beaten, or the one who takes delight in it?"

"I never took pleasure in it."

"John Laughton did, though, didn't he?" said Veronica, suddenly angry. "He loved to see you with the cane, bringing it down on my hand, or my legs, or my bare behind. Lie before the Lord if you don't want to admit he took lascivious pleasure from it."

"I'm not sure."

"Remember that conversation about lying I had with the vicar?"

Mrs Jenkins sighed. "Yes."

"And the servants, do you punish them on his behalf too?"

"Yes."

Veronica's anger had reduced to a simmering rage directed at the steward, but that was for another time. "As I said, Esme, I have no desire for you to leave. The household runs well with you at the helm, and I have no experience in doing it myself, or knowing who I could possibly employ."

"I've said I'll stay a three month, miss."

"Nika."

"Miss Nika."

"Just Nika," said Veronica. "I understand you want to leave, there is no real reason you should remain, and I will keep my promise about giving you good references, but..."

She stopped. Was the opportunity to have one's carnal lusts satisfied really enough to make someone want to stay?

"You must be so frustrated, Esme. To be promised bodily satisfaction only to be betrayed every single time."

"Women are subservient to men; we are there to fill their needs."

"Utter nonsense, and he's not even your husband—you don't owe John Laughton *anything*. He owes *you*. How many times has he fucked you, Esme?"

"You must stop using that word, miss."

"Nika."

"Nika."

"Fuck. Tits. Quim. Piss. Shit."

"Stop it."

"They're just words, Esme, calling it carnal relations doesn't stop it from being what it is. You're just wrapping it up in a pretty bow. You think the toffs don't call it fucking? You know they do. You're not aspiring to be like them, you're making yourself stand out as a snob." She paused for a breath. "Even the King shits every day. Just like you, me, and Mr Laughton."

Mrs Jenkins wiped her hand angrily across her cheeks, leaving damp streaks. "What do you want from me?"

"I want you to accept a gift, Esme."

"What?"

"I want to give you something."

"Give me?" Mrs Jenkins seemed to be looking to see if Veronica was carrying something.

"Yes, but if you're being a snob, I don't think you'll want it."

"I'm sorry, mi—Nika, I don't understand."

"I am offering sexual fulfilment."

A range of expressions played across Mrs Jenkins' face, from fear and disgust to, perhaps, a flicker of interest.

Veronica waited until:

"How?"

"A man who will put your pleasure before his, and who knows how to provide it."

"No."

"How long since you enjoyed sexual relations with a man, Esme?"

The woman bit her lip and said nothing for a long while. Then, "My husband."

Veronica had not expected her to answer, but was happy that she seemed to be making progress. They were silent for perhaps a minute, and the sound of nature crept in from the outside.

"Do you remember what it was like?" said Veronica.

Esme nodded.

"You can have it again."

"In exchange for me staying? Is that it? You want to buy my loyalty with—" she hesitated, "—a *male whore*?"

Veronica laughed. "I don't think Seth would like to be called that."

"The under-gardener?"

Veronica pushed herself to her feet and went to the window overlooking the garden. Mrs Jenkins had not followed, so Veronica gestured to her. "Come and look."

As instructed, Seth was tending a flower bed quite close to the house; he must have noticed a movement because he glanced up and then quickly away. He had shaved, and put on a clean shirt. She had not even asked him to.

Veronica leaned against the window frame as she felt Mrs Jenkins come up beside her.

"Does he not look fine?"

Almost as if he had heard a cue, Seth stood straight, pulled off his shirt, threw it over the arm of his wheelbarrow, and then stretched. His musculature was clearly delineated, then he went back to working at planting.

"I can't."

"Why not? You do it with Laughton."

"He's not a gardener."

"As I said, you cannot accept the gift if you are being a snob. What was your husband before he went to war?"

"A confectioner."

"I wish I could have tasted his sweets," said Veronica, belatedly realising the words could be misunderstood, but apparently Mrs Jenkins had not noticed. "But what was his station before he went into confectionery?"

"His father was a labourer."

Veronica said nothing.

Mrs Jenkins had not taken her eyes off Seth's body, but even as she stared, she said, "How can you give him to me?"

"I asked him first."

Mrs Jenkins turned away from the window and faced Veronica. "And how do you know what he is capable of, mi—Nika?"

"I will tell you, Esme, but can we sit down again, so that I can see your face and you can see mine."

Once seated, Veronica took a deep breath. "I won't tell you the full story, you would be very shocked. Suffice to say, I am not the innocent child that I was on my eighteenth birthday, but I can assure you I am still a virgin. And, to my knowledge, Seth has never fucked anyone in this household." She took another deep breath. "However, I do know, since I was present when it occurred, that Seth has been taught the details of a woman's secrets, and what can be done to bring her the most pleasure. I know we are all different in our desires, but I am confident he will perform the task well, and you can instruct him in your personal needs."

"It just seems...so sordid."

"And letting Laughton have his way with you for his personal pleasure isn't sordid?"

Mrs Jenkins stared at the desktop in front of her. "I will think on it."

"Don't think, Esme. Call him in now."

Almost like an automaton, and without questioning, Mrs Jenkins went to the window, and gestured. There was a pause.

"No! Use the door, and put your shirt on first."

Esme returned to her seat. Her face was red. "He was going to climb the wall."

Veronica smiled. "He can be very direct."

Seth must have run because it was only moments later when there was a knock.

Mrs Jenkins said nothing, just stared at the door.

"Come in!" called Veronica.

Seth entered and shut the door behind him.

"Did thee want I, Mrs Jenkins?"

In a very small voice, Esme said: "I do."

Veronica stood up and headed for the door, but paused beside Seth, taking his hand in hers for a moment.

"Be gentle, Seth."

xxvii

Thursday morning. Only four days to the wedding. Veronica lay on her back, courtesy of the Faraday device, and stared at the ceiling. As usual, Polly was snoring gently beside her. Only a sheet covered them because it had been a warm night and they had thrown off the blankets and counterpane.

Veronica wondered how it had gone between Seth and Mrs Jenkins. She would have liked to have stayed and watched, of course, but she imagined most people did not like an audience. She let her hand slip between her thighs and gently rubbed herself as she imagined Mrs Jenkins with her legs up on the arms of her chair, with Seth between them applying his tongue to her nubbin. *Clitoris* was the proper name, she had looked it up in her father's library. Her clit.

Her wandering thoughts took her to the pictures of her father and mother and the other people, including Lord and Lady Jameson. What if Lord Jameson was her father? What if Edwin had come from the union of her father and Lady Katherine?

What did it matter? Nobody knew the truth—even she didn't know the truth. It was easy to see the influence of her mother in Veronica's body, especially how their tits were just the same, but she couldn't see her father in her, nor Lord Jameson.

Which meant nobody could.

She was still playing with herself, but there was not the slightest stirring of lust. It had been the same last night. She went through the motions with Polly, but she was distracted. It had been an effort to focus enough to come.

By way of experiment she dragged her nails lightly across her tits. She shivered and felt the pleasure, but it ebbed as fast as it had emerged.

She dropped off the bed into normal gravity and sat at the table with her diary. Carefully, she thought about all the things she needed to do today.

Nothing.

There were no meetings with people, no relationships to arrange, and even the house was quiet. The workmen had all but gone. Just the final touches of decoration to the house, now transformed.

Mr Plumley would arrive and they would have their last lesson until after the wedding and honeymoon.

Veronica wiped away a tear. It was the end of her old life and somehow, though that life had been tedious and uninteresting, losing it was tearing away a part of her heart.

"He'll still be here when I come back," she told herself. Yet it would be a completely new life, as if she were being reborn, like Athena from the head of Zeus.

She looked down at her bare feet. She had bathed every day this week and they were perfectly clean, with nails perfectly shaped—thanks to Polly. Veronica made a decision.

She turned down the Faraday—watching Polly sink into the mattress as she did so—and switched it off.

"Get up sleepy head, we have things to do."

The shape in the bed muttered something.

"Up. I want my toenails polished, then I need to walk round the garden a dozen times with socks and my heaviest shoes on."

"What about clothes?"

Veronica leaned over the bed and kissed Polly's cheek. "If I could get away with wearing nothing in the garden except socks and boots, then I would do so. If I could wear nothing all day and every day, my life would be perfect. But they would lock me up in the mad house for such a thing. So, no. I will also require clothes."

Polly stretched and groaned then sat up. "Did you have to turn the Faraday off?"

"It's for me. I wasn't in bed any more."

"You can be a cow, Nika."

"And you're a virago."

"Is that a good thing?"

Veronica grinned. "A violent and bad-tempered woman."

"When have I ever been bad-tempered? Even when you wake me up like this?"

"And it can be a lady warrior."

"I like that better."

"But that's the archaic definition, nobody uses it any more."

Polly got off the bed. "Like I said, a cow. What day is it?"

"Thursday."

Polly frowned. "You got some special plans then? I can't think we have to do anything special today."

"Exactly."

"You're not making any sense."

"Trust me."

"I'll run your bath."

"No. No bath. Socks and heaviest shoes, then I'm in the garden until ten o'clock."

Polly stared at her for a long moment, then smiled.

"Let me get dressed. I'll sort you out."

⸺◉⸺

VERONICA SPENT HALF an hour walking around the garden, to the point she became quite fed up with all its bright colours, and was sure she knew every paving slab and lump in the gravel. Her feet were already tired and it felt as if she had not just spent the entire night in the Faraday.

Mr Jones emerged from the ballroom, he was so tall he ducked to avoid banging his head, then walked along the paths to where she stood.

"Breakfast is served in the dining room, Miss Clifford-Hughes."

"Thank you, Mr Jones."

She started back with the butler at her side. Attempting as innocent a voice as she could manage, she asked, "Have you spoken to Mrs Jenkins this morning?"

"I have, miss."

"How was she?"

"She seemed well."

Veronica hesitated, she wasn't entirely sure how she could elicit the information she wanted without asking bluntly. "That's good. But, um, did she seem any...different?"

"Not specifically, miss," he said. "However, the house staff did seem rather nervous."

Oh no. "Nervous?"

"Yes, apparently they were concerned because Mrs Jenkins had not shouted at them."

Veronica sighed with relief. "That's all right then."

"Yes, miss."

———◦———

AFTER BREAKFAST, VERONICA went back out into the garden to pace again; she could fit in half an hour before her tutor arrived. There was no reason for her to stop letting Mr Plumley lick her feet once she returned, but because this felt like an ending she wanted to make it the very best she could for him.

Rather than just walk around the garden, she detoured through the gate and headed towards the furnace room. And met Seth coming the other way with his barrow and spade.

"How was it?" she said.

"Good."

"You made her come?"

"I did, miss. Three or four times, if I was countin' aright."

"She must have been desperate."

He nodded. "I treated her as you wanted, miss, she was content by the end."

"And you?"

"Content too, miss."

"Mr Jones told me she didn't shout at the maids this morning."

"That's well, miss."

"Thank you."

"Bain't no hardship, miss."

She smiled. "No, I suppose it isn't, but I wasn't sure how she would be with you."

"She did cry some after the second time."

Veronica placed her hand on his forearm and squeezed. "I hope you were considerate."

"Like my younger sister, miss; when she's sad I just holds her."

"That's good—do you want to have some fun tonight? I'm sure we could get you into the bedroom, and I have a Faraday under the bed just like you suggested. It really does help with sleeping, and games."

He looked suddenly awkward. "I be pleased you got the Faraday, miss, but I can't be playing tonight. Mrs Jenkins already asked."

"Oh."

Veronica felt awkward and quite cold all of a sudden.

"I best be getting on, miss." He touched his finger to his cap and lifted the arms of the wheelbarrow.

"Seth?"

"Miss?"

"Thank you."

"Glad to oblige, miss."

"No, I mean, thank you for everything you've done for me."

"I?"

"You didn't look away in disgust when you first saw me naked in the window."

"I liked what I saw, miss."

"You're the first person who did, Seth."

Veronica felt the tears welling up and rubbed both her eyes. "If it hadn't been for you, I don't know what would have happened, but I wouldn't have been strong enough. It would have been bad."

He put the wheelbarrow down again and held out his hand. She went willingly as he pulled her gently behind a large hydrangea with pink flowers. Knowing that she couldn't look up at him, he bent his legs to lower himself to her level.

Then kissed her on the cheek.

"Stop, you'll make me cry again."

"Bain't nothin' bad about tears, miss." His arms went around her and she sobbed into his shoulder. "You be a good person, miss, don't let any say ought."

"That's not what they would say in church, Seth." *And I'll never look any different to what I do now.*

"Those that love thee that matter, none else."

And she cried again.

Then there was the sound of shoes crunching on gravel in the garden. Seth let her go and they both extracted themselves from between the wall and hydrangea.

"It's getting on for ten, Nika," said Polly, staring hard at the both of them. Then she frowned. "You've been crying. Seth, what did you do, you great lummox?" She hurried over pulling out a kerchief.

"He didn't do anything. He was just holding me while I cried."

"Why were you crying, then?"

Veronica shook her head. "Nothing and everything."

"I best be getting on, miss, Pol."

He picked up his barrow once more and trundled it off into the garden.

"Come on, Nika, let's get you inside and tidy you up." Then she gave a little shriek and hit Veronica's head with her hand.

Veronica jumped back. "What did you do that for?"

"Spider in your hair. A big one."

Veronica suddenly wished for a mirror and flicked her hair a few times where Polly had hit her. "Is it gone?"

"That'll teach you to hide in bushes."

"Is it gone?"

Polly peered, then extracted a couple of leaves. "Gone."

Veronica now felt itchy under her clothes, as if things might have got inside. She pushed the thought away and followed Polly back to the house. They went into the library where Polly did her best to make Veronica more presentable.

"You can't go around throwing yourself into the nearest bush with whoever you please."

"He said he loved me."

Polly shook her head. "Men say things like that to take advantage."

Veronica gave a laugh. "Surely they're more in danger from me?"

"Perhaps, but that's not the point. You can't trust them."

"You weren't there."

They were silent for a short while.

"He brought Mrs Jenkins to paroxysm four times."

"Four?"

"He wasn't sure, three or four anyway."

"You think that will make her stay? Not that I know why you want her."

"I hope it will, and she's good at her job—better the devil you know."

"That's as maybe, but she's a tyrant to the staff."

"Mr Jones said she didn't shout at the maids this morning. And now they're terrified."

"Little wonder." Polly laughed.

The door opened and Mr Plumley came in with his books and briefcase. He must have been deep in thought because he jumped when he saw them waiting.

"Oh m-m-my, m-m-Miss Clifford-Hughes. P-Polly."

"Good morning, Mr Plumley. Polly, help him with his things, won't you?"

"Yes, miss."

Within a few minutes they were sitting at the table. Polly pulled the curtains, then went to the door and locked it.

Veronica looked into Mr Plumley's eyes and smiled. After a moment he looked away.

"Did you like sucking my toes when I was naked?"

His face flushed with embarrassment. "It was m-most uncomfortable to b-be in that p-position for so long, Mistress Nika."

Veronica stood up. "You, sir, are avoiding the question. You saw me completely naked. Did you enjoy that?"

"M-m-m-m-my p-p-p-pleasure is in cleaning f-feet," he said, his speech even more hesitant than usual. She took that for an admission that he had liked it.

She turned her back on him. "Oh dear me, Polly, I am so hot. I cannot bear to have these clothes close to my skin. Help me undress."

"Oh dearie me, Mistress Nika, it is so very hot today."

Veronica stood still while Polly undid the buttons and slid the dress from her body. There was a mirror above the mantel. Veronica could see Mr Plumley staring at her. She smiled, she wanted to make this as special as she could for him. She knew he would not want to touch her anywhere except her feet, but that somehow made it even more exciting. The warm lust filled her.

Her chemise and bloomers went as well, leaving only her shoes and the woollen stockings. Polly arranged the cushions and Veronica lay on the *chaise longue* in just the same position as she had when Sofia was painting her.

"Polly, why have you not removed my shoes and stockings?"

"Oh no, Mistress Nika. I ain't doing that. Your feet do stink to high heaven. It would make me faint dead away, or just dead, if I was to smell them."

"Then who will be my knight and save me from this heat?"

Mr Plumley stood up and cleared his throat.

Veronica feigned surprise. "You, sir, will you remove these shackles and free my poor feet?"

He tried to speak but no sound emerged. He cleared his throat. "I can save you, though I am not worthy."

"Kind sir, please approach and do so."

As she expected he went down on his hands and knees. He might not like being stuck in a single position for hours, but he was willing to bend for flavoursome feet.

He did not rush but crawled across the carpet to the *chaise*. He unbuckled the first shoe and slipped it off. He breathed in deep through his nose, savouring the atrocious smell that emanated from her foot. Even Veronica was impressed at how successful her efforts had been.

The other shoe came off and from his position at her feet his eyes scanned upwards, following her stocking-covered calves and knees, thighs, the dark gap between her legs—she hoped her pink inner lips were visible, his eyes did linger there. Then he continued further up. Almost without thinking she took a breast in each hand and gently squeezed them—which triggered waves of desire. She closed her eyes and breathed deep as she crushed and pulled at them.

She felt his hand on her upper leg and shivered with delight, but he was removing the garter. Then he rolled the stocking down slowly. She opened her eyes and watched it finally come off her foot. He brought the rank sock to his nose and breathed in, long and deep.

He did the same for the other one.

"Thank you, kind sir," she said. "But my poor feet are so sweaty and odorous, can you not help?"

He said nothing, but his hand went under the heel of her left foot, lifted it, and his mouth closed over her big toe. Much to her own surprise, Veronica groaned with pleasure. She had never been in such a heightened state of lust before when he had licked her feet. But this time, every sensuous touch simply added to her passion.

She closed her eyes again and gently played with her breasts. She did not want to embarrass Mr Plumley with her paroxysm. She jumped when she felt someone looming over her. Opening her eyes she found Polly's face above hers and their lips touching, then opening. Their tongues moved smoothly and delightfully against one another.

Veronica closed her eyes again and wallowed in the pleasure of Polly's kiss, Mr Plumley's mouth, and her own touch. Polly had made the painting Sofia was creating into an actuality.

Then Polly's hand came down on Veronica's stomach and slid towards her quim. Gently, to avoid upset, Veronica intercepted the roving hand and brought it instead up to her breast. Then with the other hand she found Polly's tits, though there was not much to be done through the heavy fabric of her uniform.

When Mr Plumley was done, he withdrew while Veronica brought herself back to reality. She gave Polly a kiss on the nose and got dressed with her help, though they left off the stockings.

"Would you like them?" said Veronica to Mr Plumley.

"A kind gesture, M-m-miss Clifford-Hughes, b-but difficult to explain should Mrs Plumley ever discover them."

Veronica smiled, though they were too close for him to see it, and laid her hand on his arm. "Thank you for everything."

"I have m-m-merely been your tutor, m-miss." He hesitated. "B-but, you sound as if this is the very last time we shall m-m-meet."

"That's because I just don't know what will happen when I return from Switzerland."

"I understood it was your intention to continue your studies."

"It is," she said, "but just in case, I wanted to make today special."

"You have done that, and I am grateful for the little scene you p-p-played out for me."

"Like the first time."

"I recall it with p-p-pleasure. And this one surpassed it."

"You were not offended by my lewd behaviour?"

"I was honoured you trusted m-me."

Polly appeared to her side. "If you'll excuse me, miss, there's things to be done." Her voice contained a definite element of annoyance.

Veronica was about to confront her on it, but Mr Plumley turned and spoke first. "And m-may I say, p-p-Polly, that I appreciated your p-p-part in the little p-play as well. It would not have w-worked without you."

"Just doing my job."

"I do not think disrobing your m-mistress in front of her tutor is usually considered a duty of the Lady's m-maid. Nor kissing her w-without b-being asked," he said. "You are a delightful companion, and may I say your Italian has come on very well since you started from nothing."

"Yes, well, thank you, Mr Plumley, I'm sure." She bobbed a curtsy.

"Thank you, p-Polly. And I haven't forgotten how kind you w-were to allow me to smell your feet."

"Not sure I was being kind, following orders more like."

"Even so, it was a great kindness to me."

There was an awkward silence until Veronica said, "What do you need to do?"

"Packing's not going to happen on its own, miss, and there's your other new dresses to be altered. Tomorrow afternoon you're going to Mr Slack, and on Saturday Vionnet's coming back. And who knows what else must be done."

"Oh yes, of course. I'll be fine with Mr Plumley."

Two months ago, there would have been no thought of her being left alone with him.

For the rest of the morning, until luncheon, they continued to practice her Italian. Working with Sofia for a couple of weeks had completely changed the way she pronounced the words. With Mr Plumley she had been an Englishwoman speaking a foreign language, but now she thought she could feel its rhythms—almost as if she *was* Italian.

Not that she had the ability to express every thought, since she simply did not have the vocabulary, but speaking the words she did know felt so much better.

The same thing probably applied to her French and German, perhaps she would meet people from those countries and would be able to practice with them.

She was excited about travelling abroad and seeing new places, but that could have been achieved simply by going to Aberystwyth, or Edinburgh, or Dublin. In fact anywhere in the United Kingdom that wasn't Mayfield.

But they would still speak English, or at least a version of it. That was what made this trip so special, and so terrifying—the people might not understand her. Assuming they did not shun her because of her deformity—she suspected that would be commonplace everywhere.

Mr Plumley had always previously taken his luncheon in a room off to the side of the kitchen set aside for servants to eat.

Veronica decided this was not appropriate since he was not technically a servant, even if he was providing a service. As they were finishing the morning's session she rang the bell and Mr Jones arrived promptly.

"You rang, miss?"

"Mr Plumley will have his luncheon in the dining room with me."

"As you wish."

"Oh no, m-m-Miss Clifford-Hughes, that w-would not be right."

"I am mistress now—" *or will be soon enough,* "—and I have decided that it is how things will be. If this is to be our last day, I will treat you with the respect you deserve."

Mr Plumley acquiesced.

xxviii

Thursday afternoon passed without further incident. Mr Plumley simply went over the words and phrases she already knew and had her practise them. Polly did not return.

At four o'clock, Veronica shook Mr Plumley's hand for perhaps the last time. He departed and she stood alone in the library.

Of all the rooms in the house this one had, perhaps, the fewest changes. An electrical conduit had been attached to the wall by the door, with a light switch at its end. By lying on the *chaise* again, she was able to look up and see where they had managed to feed the cabling for the main light through the ceiling without damaging the delicate plasterwork.

She was aware that ceiling decorations could be quite elaborate, but her unfortunate spine meant she seldom looked at ceilings—*although she had spent much time in bed looking up recently, though she had usually been distracted*—so she examined the shapes above her. Bunches of grapes, leaf patterns, pineapples, cherubs, animals, women and men in sexual congress.

She stared unbelieving for a moment, but the more she looked, the more it was entirely plain that the shapes in the ceiling were sexual. Continuing to catalogue them, she exclaimed when she saw what was clearly a woman being mounted by a horse. And next to it a man in a similar position.

These were representations, of course, the event need not have happened for the sculptor to have created the image, and yet it was somehow more erotic than the photographs of her parents with their...other partners.

In the sculpted ceiling art, the imagination could run free. There were indeed a great number of images of men and women with animals in a variety of positions. She scanned further from the central circle. The next collection involved humans and devils—and they all had exaggerated body parts. The female ones with outrageously large breasts and behinds, the male devils had pricks as big as themselves. It was almost comical.

One section was quite macabre, with body parts being cut off; she passed over that quickly because it killed the simmering lust the others were generating. It was not that she wanted to do what was shown—well, not most of it—but that did not mean she was not stimulated. She found it interesting.

———— ◈ ————

"THERE YOU ARE!"

Veronica woke with a start. The light from the window was dimmed and the entire ceiling was in shadow. The voice was Polly's.

"What are you doing in here?"

Light flooded the room, blinding her, and she cried out, "Off! Off!"

It must have taken Polly a few moments to grasp her meaning. Veronica threw her arm across her eyes to hide from the dazzling light until it went dark again with a click.

"Sorry."

Veronica rolled over on her side and sat up on the edge of the *chaise*. There were spots in her eyes.

"I fell asleep," she said and then yawned. "What time is it?"

"Just after eight. We started to get worried when you didn't come for dinner."

"We?"

"The staff."

"Why would they care, they don't like me."

Polly shut the door. "Can I put the light on now, Nika?"

"I suppose."

The room flooded with light again, but Veronica was prepared and had her eyes shut.

"What were you doing in here, anyway?"

"Looking at the ceiling."

"Oh," said Polly. "That."

"You knew?"

"Everybody knows."

"I didn't." Again. Why does everybody know except her? Because nobody had spoken to me as a human being in eighteen years.

Veronica's eyes had adjusted and she leaned back so she could see Polly properly.

"Does Mr Plumley know about the ceiling?"

"I have no idea. I'm not sure it has anyone licking feet."

"It has people with animals."

"I know."

"That's..." She couldn't think of an appropriate word.

"I know."

"It's in the Greek stories, but those are all legends and myths about gods and heroes," said Veronica. It had never been stated explicitly, but now she thought about it she could see where it had been implied: Leda and the Swan, the siring of the Minotaur and of Pegasus, and many more. "It's hard to believe people really do that."

Polly craned her neck and looked up. "It happens."

"Really?"

"Well, I haven't done it!"

"I didn't mean that, I meant, what do you know?"

Polly sighed and sat down on one of the hard-back chairs by the desk and looked across the room at Veronica. "Shepherds with their sheep."

"There's a lot of sheep around here."

"Yes."

"What else?"

"Horses."

"Isn't that dangerous? I mean, horses are very big."

"I think the size is the point."

Veronica stared blankly for a moment. "I didn't mean...oh. I suppose they build a contraption like Queen Pasiphaë."

"Who?"

"She did it with a bull, and gave birth to the Minotaur. Her engineer was Daedalus and he made a cow body she could get inside, so she could do it without getting crushed. I was just thinking you'd have to do that with a horse."

"I don't know. I suppose if you have money." Polly got up. "Your dinner's cold, but it's waiting for you."

Veronica got to her feet and followed her maid.

⎯⎯⎯⎯●⎯⎯⎯⎯

RAIN BATTERED THE WINDOW, but Veronica felt warm and safe in bed, cuddled up with Polly. It was morning and Polly still slept. Perhaps she was making up for all the years she had been forced to wake early to tend to her maid duties as well as looking after Veronica.

Only three days to go. Everything was in hand so far, but her greatest test was going to come this afternoon when she met with Edwin. She thought of Lawrence Slack, he was a fine-looking gentleman, and unmarried. She would be very happy to let him "plough her furrow". She laughed to herself. Kissed Polly gently on the nose and detached herself—so much easier in low gravity.

If she and Polly lived together in a small house, just the two of them, Veronica would get up in the morning and make breakfast for her lover. Like a wife would. Which reminded her about her idea.

Rings were out of the question, people would notice. But perhaps they would not notice a bracelet, which had the additional advantage that it did not have to be carefully measured. There was not a great deal of time left; the Army & Navy catalogue would be no help for jewellery. She did not think Lawrence was really the right sort of person to carry out the task; she thought for a moment of Sofia Martaci, but felt somehow she was not right either.

Then she realised the one person who would be exactly right. She sorted out her writing slope, paper, and pen.

Dear Mademoiselle Vionnet,

I hope you are keeping well and that all your preparations are running smoothly.

I must humbly request a favour of you. I understand you may be too busy and if it is not possible then I will completely understand.

Veronica hesitated. She was about to commit to paper the fact of her relationship with Polly. No crime had been committed, but the scandal, if it were discovered, might affect everything. And it was not just her own life, it was Polly's too. She must be discreet while also being clear in her intentions.

Prior to my marriage, I wish to exchange gifts with a person who is of great value to me—who you have met. It occurred to me that matching bracelets, perhaps in the Greek style, would be appropriate since they could be worn during the ceremony.

If you are able to purchase such items, I would be able to arrange prompt recompense through my solicitor.

She read and re-read her words. It was true that anyone who knew her would be able to discern who the valued person was, but it did not really imply more. Vionnet knew what Polly meant to Veronica; she would be able to work it out.

She finished the letter, blotted it carefully, and placed it in the envelope which she addressed to the studio in London. If they caught the early post, it would arrive before five o'clock and Vionnet would stand a chance of being able to purchase the bracelets.

Veronica glanced across at Polly who was still fast asleep.

She gathered up the clothes Polly had put out for the day and took them into the bathroom, closing the door.

The rain from outside drummed on the skylight, and grey light filtered in.

She had never even tried to dress herself before. Polly had been there to do it, and before her there was Mrs Winstanley. Veronica felt guilty; she had been no more than an automaton, a doll to be dressed and undressed.

In truth, she had barely even been alive. She breathed, ate, and used her piss-pot as needed, but she had no real thoughts of her own, and her only escape had been the books. Mr Plumley had been right when he described her as a caged bird—except the cage had not even been real.

Mere chance had shown her the door.

She sighed. It was not right that someone should dress her, she should be able to do it herself.

Carefully, to ensure she did not strain her back, she set about with the stockings. It took her much longer to do than it would have taken Polly, but that was because she did not know the best way, and could barely remember how Polly did it.

Then the bloomers. At least they were easy. The chemise was the first real test; she could lift her left arm but not her right, but managed to work it up her body and get her arms through that way. She dispensed with all but one of the petticoats and, doing that, could get the dress on from her feet upwards. Getting it over her hump was awkward, but accomplished without too much delay.

Then the shoes and she was done—she saw herself in the mirror. Her hair looked as if she had been dragged through a hedge backwards.

She returned to the bedroom. Polly slept on. The rain seemed to have lifted a little.

Veronica found the hairbrush—it was one of the new easy-clean American ones with the artificial bristles. She spent five minutes in front of the mirror taming her hair into a semblance of neatness. The fact she couldn't raise her left hand high enough, and that her hair needed more than five minutes, meant the result was not particularly good. Then she remembered that Vionnet had recommended she buy several *bandeaux*. The question was: where had Polly put them?

She investigated the chest of drawers and discovered more underthings and stockings, but one level down were scarves and the headbands. She pulled out the pure white one on the basis that it should go with anything.

It needed tying round her neck first—but she could use both hands for that—then turning so the knot was at the back, and then pushing up on to her head so it held her hair. The first two attempts failed because she had made the loop too small, but it was right on the third attempt and, with the help of the mirror, she managed to get it looking right.

Veronica looked accusingly at Polly still fast asleep, offended that her lover had slept through all her trials in getting dressed. But then that had been the point.

She unlocked the door, took the key and locked the door behind so that nobody accidentally walked in on Polly. If she woke, she would be able to go into her own room and leave that way.

It was half past seven and the house was still quiet. The maids would be at their respective stations, cleaning. The men would be doing whatever it was the men did. She needed to find Mr Jones, or Mrs Jenkins—she did not trust Mr Laughton to make sure the letter was sent.

She tried to remember what Mrs Beeton's book said about where the housekeeper would be at this time of day. Probably in the kitchen supervising breakfast.

Taking a deep breath, Veronica set off along the corridor, her shoes making no sound on the carpet. She reached the main staircase which led down into the hall and followed its curve to the chequerboard-patterned floor.

The route took her into the smaller passages for staff, and thence to the kitchen. She heard and smelled it before she reached it. The buzz of voices and the delicious scent of fresh baked bread.

The activity in the room was efficiently chaotic. Some of the maids glanced in her direction, but returned to their work immediately. Veronica could see Cook, but Mrs Jenkins was not there.

She turned away and found a very tall person in the way.

"Are you looking for someone, miss?"

"Mr Jones, yes, I was looking for Mrs Jenkins, or you."

"You have found me."

"Yes."

A maid hurried past them.

Veronica pulled the envelope from a pocket in her dress. "I need this to go to Mademoiselle Vionnet in London with all speed."

"When would you like it to arrive?"

"Lunchtime if at all possible."

"Of course, miss. I will arrange for one of the lads to hop on his bike and get it to the post office in Mayfield by nine. The post from there will be on the train and in London before midday. I'm sure it will be delivered before two, if that is satisfactory." He took it gently from her hand. "Is anything wrong, miss?"

"No, not really, just a last-minute thought."

Another maid pushed past them, busy doing something.

"Shouldn't Mrs Jenkins be in the kitchen at this time?"

"She often is, miss, but not always, and not this morning."

"Do you know where she is?"

"I am afraid I haven't seen her today. Have you tried her office?"

"No, it's not important, I only needed to get the letter sent."

"Very good, miss. I shall deal with it forthwith."

He turned and walked away swiftly with his long, giant stride.

Veronica went to the ballroom. The rain had stopped for now, but the clouds were still hanging heavy in the sky. Grey and ominous.

She had a pretty good idea of why Mrs Jenkins was not at her usual station: Seth had happened.

And now she felt jealous. Again.

Jealous of Polly with Ursula, now jealous of Seth and Mrs Jenkins. Yet she had arranged both those situations.

"My apologies, Miss Clifford-Hughes, I'll come back."

The devil.

Veronica did not turn from the French window, but she could see the reflection of the maid standing in the doorway. "No, Ursula, please come in."

"We're directed not to clean when someone's here."

"I want to talk to you." *Although I don't know what to say.*

"As you wish, Miss Clifford-Hughes."

The figure in the reflection moved away from the door and approached. Veronica turned round. "Please sit down."

"I could not possibly, miss."

"I am ordering you to sit down, so I can see your face."

The girl pulled out one of the chairs from the table, its feet scraped on the tiles, and sat. Veronica turned to face her. Her red hair was tied tight around her head, partly hidden by her maid's cap, but nothing could hide the freckles that filled her face.

"What's your full name?"

"My full name?"

"Yes."

"Have I done something wrong, miss?"

"Why are you avoiding telling me your name?"

"Skipworth."

"Ursula Skipworth?"

"Yes, miss."

"That sounds like a northern name."

"Lincolnshire, miss."

Veronica walked slowly towards the girl. "But you don't sound northern." Which was a guess because Veronica really didn't know much about the more subtle English accents, but, as it was, Ursula's erudition and diction was not rural, so it was a reasonable assumption.

"I was brought up in Horsham, miss. My family comes from the north originally."

There was something about the name Skipworth that struck a chord with Veronica, but she couldn't put her finger on it.

"How old are you?"

"Nineteen."

Veronica hesitated. "What is your relationship with Polly?"

"I'm not entirely sure I understand what you mean, miss."

"She has told me."

Ursula remained silent.

"She told me you used to touch her."

"If you wish me to leave your employment, I understand."

Veronica's face flushed with a sudden anger she did not expect. "What do you mean, you understand?"

"You don't want a rival."

"Are you a rival?"

"No, Miss Clifford-Hughes," said Ursula in an unhurried way. "I am not a rival."

"You don't love her."

"No, miss, you would be incorrect, I do love her." But before Veronica could say anything, Ursula raised her hand. "But please, allow me to finish. I do love her, but not in the manner that I understand you do. I care about her, as if she were my sister."

"I believe I would be right in thinking sisters do not normally touch as you have."

Ursula smiled. "No, miss, that would be true, but then she is *not* my sister. I gave her what she needed. Now she needs you, and that is satisfactory."

Veronica's thoughts were in conflict. On the one hand, she still wanted to be angry, but the girl was completely calm and reasonable—and so damnably well-spoken. More so than Veronica was herself, if she were any judge.

"Where do you come from?"

"Horsham, miss, as I said."

"Where in Horsham?"

"Do you know the town?"

Of course I don't. "You're avoiding the question again. Who are your family? You are not a servant; at the very least you were born the highest of the middle classes, if not into the aristocracy."

The delay before Ursula's response was far too long for Veronica and she was about to demand an answer again.

"My family were well-off, miss, but misfortune ambushed us and we were made destitute. I am the eldest and I was forced to go into service simply so I could have employment and send money home to my parents. They have no trade and do their best to survive."

"I'm sorry."

"Is that all, miss?"

"Yes. I'm sorry."

Ursula stood, curtsied, and headed for the door. She stopped and turned.

"Do you still want me on your trip to Switzerland?"

Veronica felt as if she had had a spear pierce her chest. "I...yes. Yes."

"As you wish, miss."

And she was gone.

xxix

Veronica let herself back into her bedroom, feeling worse than she had ever done.

Polly looked up from the sewing she was doing at the table. "I don't know whether to shout or cry. I woke up and you were gone. Your clothes were gone. Everything was out of place. I didn't know what had happened."

"You can shout at me," said Veronica. "I deserve it."

She sat on the bed. Her skin tingled as she went through the edge of the Faraday field. On another day she might have chastised Polly for not turning it off. Instead, she let herself fall back into the gentle cradle of the effect, and curled up with her head on the pillow.

"What's wrong?"

"Nothing."

"Why are you lying to me?"

Veronica sighed and wished she could just disappear.

"Tell me what's wrong, Nika."

"I wanted to know why Ursula talks the way she does."

"Her family had money and they lost it."

"Yes, she said."

"You're upset because her family lost everything?"

Veronica wished she could lie and say *yes*. "No, I thought she was hiding something, and I treated her like a criminal."

"You're jealous."

"I'm not!"

"That's just what you are." And then Polly laughed, although it wasn't one of happiness or joy; to Veronica's ears it felt like knives.

She cried.

The bed barely moved as Polly climbed up, lay down, and hugged her. They lay together for what seemed a very long time.

"I don't deserve this." Her voice muffled by the pillow

"We've talked about self-pity, Nika," said Polly in her ear. "What did you say to Ursula?"

Veronica told her, although it took a while as she dragged out each painful word.

"You were really rude."

"I know."

"And you went out just to say that to Ursula?"

Veronica pulled back. "No, it wasn't planned. It was...an accident."

"So why did you get up?"

"I...needed to do something."

"What?"

"I can't tell you."

"You were meeting Seth."

"No! I can't tell you because it's a surprise." Veronica sighed. "And I didn't want to tell you about it at all because now you know there's a surprise so you'll be expecting it. So it won't be a surprise."

"Are you going to tell me what it is?"

"No."

"Are you going to tell me when it's going to happen?"

"No."

"So, it's still a surprise."

"I suppose."

"And you got dressed—by yourself."

"I tried."

"It looked all right, what I saw of it. Come on, up you get and I'll sort you out."

"Stop treating me like a child."

"Stop behaving like one." Polly backed off the bed and on to the floor. "Look, you made a mistake. Everybody does. You owned up to it, you said you apologised to Ursula."

"I did."

"So, let it go."

Veronica pushed herself up in one smooth motion and landed in front of Polly.

"That's easy to say, Polly," she said. "It'll haunt me for the rest of my life."

"Well, don't dwell on it." Polly lifted Veronica's hem and tutted. "Not straight. Let's get you sorted."

While Polly re-organised the clothes then properly brushed and arranged her hair, Veronica thought over her talk with Ursula.

It was all very well saying she should let go of the fact she had made a mistake, the trouble was that despite everything, Veronica was still not convinced there was anything to let go of.

THERE WAS POST TO DEAL with after breakfast. Veronica was pleased but very surprised. It was not that she hadn't received any letters before—not many, and only recently, but it had happened—but they had been in response to communications she had sent. These were not expected.

So, while Polly continued with the dress adjustments and packing in preparation for Tuesday, Veronica took the letters into the library.

The first was postmarked for Mayfield and was from Lawrence Slack the Younger. It was more or less a form letter reminding her of the meeting that afternoon with her future husband. She sighed. This had already been a difficult day and it looked as if it was not going to get any better. She could only hope she could be sufficiently persuasive—she had to make Edwin see that his plans would be catastrophic for the household.

She put it to one side.

The next letter appeared to have been addressed by an inexperienced hand, and the letters were formed much the way she did them, small and restrained.

Dear Miss Clifford-Hughes,

We hope you are keeping well.

Veronica looked to the bottom of the letter: it was signed by both Ruth and Esther Jameson—the two younger sisters of her betrothed. She certainly was not expecting any form of communication from them.

We would like to thank you again for the delightful evening last Friday. It was most enjoyable and the dessert a particular favourite.

If you would not consider it an imposition on your privacy, both my sister and I would like to attend your wedding to our brother on Monday.

Veronica stared at that paragraph. *An imposition on my privacy?* Was that the excuse Lord Jameson had been putting about to explain why he, his wife, and other members of the family were not attending? Because she didn't want them there? If so, they would probably have made some allusion to her deformity and that she did not want to be seen.

What were they really embarrassed about? That she was to become joined with their family, or that their somewhat peculiar son was being married at all?

Perhaps it was both. She still had no idea why they considered it such an advantageous arrangement. Of course, for her parents, it aligned them with the aristocracy and that was very valuable, but she could not fathom why it might be of benefit to Lord Jameson. Perhaps there was money involved, that was often the case in the stories she read: the wife's family had money which the aristocrat's family needed.

But she knew from the newspapers that Lord Jameson's munitions business interests were doing well, especially with the constantly bubbling threat of war with Germany.

She sighed. It was unlikely to be something she ever discovered unless someone decided to tell her. And even if she seduced Lawrence, not an unpleasant prospect if the picture in Sofia's private gallery was accurate, she suspected he would still keep silent on the matter. He was honourable.

The final paragraphs of the letter, once she returned to it from her fruitless musings, were simple courtesies.

Veronica smiled. The two girls wanted to come to the wedding even though it had been suggested they should not. If they were effectively disobeying their parents, Veronica felt that was something to be encouraged.

She wrote replies to both letters, in the first instance acknowledging that she would be attending the meeting, and the second to Ruth and Esther saying—not too enthusiastically—that she would be honoured if they were willing to attend. She paused. There was something else about weddings that she had not considered.

She rang for Mrs Jenkins, who arrived a short time later.

Veronica stared at her. It was not as if she looked any different on the surface: she was in her uniform, as thin as she had always been, with her large breasts jutting prominently from her chest, looking curiously as if they might belong to someone else.

But something *had* changed. Before, Mrs Jenkins had always seemed wound as tight as a watch spring—yet now she was relaxed. Her movements before were almost mechanical in their abruptness, and now she moved almost like water.

"You rang, Miss Clifford-Hughes."

And her voice had lost its jagged edge.

"Yes. I should have enquired before, Mrs Jenkins, but are there any plans for a wedding breakfast after the ceremony?"

"We received no such instructions, miss."

"You mean there isn't a wedding breakfast of any sort?"

"Not of any sort, no, miss."

"We probably should."

"It is a little late in the day to organise such a thing."

Veronica thought quickly. "It is very soon, however—please correct me if I am in error—but since there is no arrangement at present, the only additional workload for Cook would be catering for Mademoiselle Vionnet and her girls?"

"That's about right."

"Would you mind sitting down?"

"That would be most inappropriate if you remain standing, Miss Clifford-Hughes."

Veronica sighed. How many more times did she need to explain this? "Yes, I know, but I find it quite hard to converse when I can only see you from the waist down. Please sit!"

Mrs Jenkins sat.

"Thank you," said Veronica. "I have decided we will be having a wedding breakfast. The guests will be my husband and I, my bridesmaid—" the look on Mrs Jenkins' face showed that, while she might have mellowed, she was still concerned about proprieties, and having a maid sitting at the top table with the aristocracy was most certainly not *proper*, "—you, and Mr Laughton."

"Who will take the place of the father of the bride?"

Veronica stopped as if she had walked into a wall. "Who's giving me away?"

Mrs Jenkins also looked nonplussed. "Mr Laughton?"

"I suppose that makes sense," said Veronica, though it was not a prospect that appealed. Still, she could put up with it for the short time it would be necessary.

"Anyone else?"

"My future husband's younger sisters, Ruth and Esther Jameson. Signora Martaci, Mr Plumley and possibly his wife, Mademoiselle Vionnet with Miss Massingham and Miss Mayhew. Also Lawrence Slack, the son, not the father."

"Is that all?"

"Probably, though I imagine my intended will have at least a best man. I don't suppose we want it to go on too long, after all we are going off the following day, so perhaps a few simple courses and one of your lovely desserts?"

To Veronica's astonishment, Mrs Jenkins smiled. "I will see what I can do, Miss Clifford-Hughes. Is there anything more?"

Veronica was desperate to ask her about how things were with Seth, but doubted Mrs Jenkins would want to discuss such things.

"No, I think that is all. Though perhaps you could confirm with Mr Laughton that he will stand up for me at the wedding."

"I will do that, miss." She made to stand up and then sat back. "There was one thing I wished to say, if I may?"

"Of course."

It was almost as if the woman had shrunk in the chair, as if she had become a child, as she did not seem to know which direction to look. And did not look at Veronica.

"I...thank you."

"I'm sorry?"

Mrs Jenkins took a deep breath and raised her head to look at Veronica full in the face. "Thank you, Miss Clifford-Hughes, for arranging my liaison with Seth Otley."

"It has been satisfactory?"

"It has been very...satisfying."

"I'm glad," said Veronica. "And I apologise for the embarrassment I caused you earlier."

The older woman raised her hand. "Please do not apologise, you have demonstrated that my behaviour with Mr Laughton was not acceptable."

Veronica frowned. "Oh no, there was nothing wrong with you wishing to satisfy your needs with him, that was not my concern. You must understand, it was his behaviour towards you that was not acceptable. If he had satisfied you as well as himself, then I would not have minded at all. It was his disregard for your needs that could not be tolerated."

"I see."

The silence was very awkward.

"Do you think," said Veronica, "you will continue to meet with the steward?"

"On the whole, miss, I think that would be the best course of action."

There was a curious tone to her voice, a kind of reluctance, but as if it was something she felt compelled to do.

"I see. Well, it is your decision, of course."

It looked as if the housekeeper had a dozen things she wanted to say, but, after a long pause, she simply stood up. "I have said what I need to say. If there is nothing more?"

"I will have some letters to be sent in about half an hour."

"That will be no trouble."

She left and Veronica turned back to her pen. She finished inviting the Jameson sisters to the wedding and the meal afterwards. Then wrote to the others she had mentioned to Mrs Jenkins to ensure they would attend. Not that she doubted Sofia or Mr Plumley were likely to miss the event.

Once the letters were properly addressed, she rang for a maid and handed them over.

She went to the window and looked out. The sky had cleared, but clouds still moved rapidly past. It was eleven. An hour and a half to lunch, then off to Mayfield at two.

She had no idea what she was going to say to Edwin. She addressed the shadowy image of herself reflected in the glass. "Edwin, I am afraid it is quite impossible for you to insist that the staff become vegetarians, or else."

Or else what?

Or nothing. "I have no leverage."

It was hopeless, but she must try.

"Miss Clifford-Hughes?"

She turned to the speaker with a smile on her face. Polly shut the door to the library and locked it. Veronica had not realised how much she had missed her lover, and almost ran across the carpeted floor. Enveloping Polly in her arms she snuggled her face into the girl's neck and kissed—wishing that the uniform was not in the way.

"What's wrong?"

"Missed you."

"It's been two hours."

"It felt like years. Come to the *chaise*, kiss me."

Polly helped Veronica with the cushions then sat beside her. They spent minutes enjoying each other's lips.

Polly's right hand moved down Veronica's body and pressed against her breast. "Lower, Polly, I can barely feel you through the dress. Make me come."

Polly giggled, shifted her hand to Veronica's belly, and dragged the folds of her dress and petticoats higher. Veronica felt the air on her thighs and spread them. Polly shifted her position so their lips could remain together, reducing the amount she had to stretch.

Her hand slid across Veronica's nethers making her shiver with pleasure. A finger dipped into her hole and a thumb pressed against her clit.

"Hard, please."

Polly moved her hand up and down faster, pressing as she did so.

"Harder."

"I'll hurt you."

"Just do it."

Veronica could tell Polly was trying as hard as she could.

"Stop."

Polly stopped. "What's wrong?"

"It's not working."

Polly's hand still rested between her legs, pressing gently against her. "Do you want me to use my mouth? I could stick my finger up your bum as well."

"You don't like doing that when it could get dirty."

Unable to deny it, Polly changed the subject. "Are you unwell?"

"No, I don't think so. My mind is just too busy. There's too much happening."

Polly removed her fingers from Veronica's quim and absently sucked her fingers. "You could have a lie down until lunch, stay here and read, or we could go for a walk." She glanced out of the window. "It's not raining."

"Let's walk."

<hr>

THEY TOURED THE GARDEN, then the outer buildings—the door to the furnace room was open as usual and they watched the stoker and his mate for a short time—and finally they circumnavigated the entire building. Veronica noted the place where a conduit had been dug to carry the electricity cables under the path and into the house. The wind had dropped and the clouds were moving more sedately, with the sun breaking through much of the time.

They went in for luncheon, although Veronica found she was not very hungry, and then went to her room to change into clothes more appropriate for a visit to the town.

There were piles of clothes everywhere.

"I've finished adjusting all your clothes and started on the packing," said Polly as she helped Veronica undress. "I know Switzerland is supposed to be warm in summer like it is here, but it is mountains after all, so I'm packing everything I can think of that you might need."

"What about you?"

"That won't take long."

"But you did get some new clothes for the trip?"

"I did, and some for Ursula should arrive tomorrow."

Once Veronica was dressed, in demure grey, they returned to the library and watched the clock for half an hour. Once it had arrived, Polly helped Veronica into the carriage and climbed up beside her, handing her a matching grey parasol.

"It'll help to hide your problem," she said.

It was only Veronica's third trip into the town and she had not lost the excitement of travelling along the roads and seeing the deep green of the trees, bushes, and the great hedges that bordered the fields. They surprised a squirrel in the road and it vanished into the undergrowth in a flash of red-brown.

A magpie flew over.

"One for sorrow," said Polly, then, "Two for joy," as another chased after it.

They rounded another corner and overtook a man carrying a huge bundle of willow withies across his back. There was a tremendous explosion of *ca-ca-ca* noises from behind the hedge and four more magpies took flight.

"Five for silver, six for gold," Polly said, reciting it like a prayer.

"Gold is not what I need," said Veronica. "Another three and I'd have a kiss."

"Unless two of those were the ones we saw before."

"A secret then."

They laughed and Veronica felt better. It was good to be outside, why had she never known this?

But her mood became more sombre as they reached the buildings at the outskirts of the town.

XXX

The scene today was rather different to their last journey into Mayfield. It was market day and the streets thronged with people threading their way between stalls selling everything imaginable: vegetables, fruit, meat, pots and pans, fabric in bolts, linen and lace. The cries of the stallholders were like a cacophonous sing-song, where each vied with another to exceed them in volume.

The speed of the carriage slowed to a walking pace, as those on foot disregarded the wheeled traffic, whether horse-drawn or mechanical. If Veronica had been worried about people looking at her, it could not be justified, today the carriage was nothing more than an inconvenient barrier, and its passenger of no concern whatsoever.

They finally reached the far end of Market Street and drew up outside the solicitor's office. Moments later they were let inside by the boy, and the noise outside muted by the closed door.

Veronica checked her watch. They were five minutes early.

"Shall I take that, miss?" said Polly. She indicated the parasol that Veronica still had open and over her head. She brought it down and furled it.

"I'll hang on to it."

It served as a walking stick, and perhaps a weapon if she grew angry with Edwin. She took a deep breath and tried to calm her thoughts. She needed to stand when she was talking to him, so she could see him, but if she stood, they, being gentlemen, would stand as well.

"I don't think I can do this," she said quietly.

Despite the obvious risk, Polly took Veronica's hand in hers and gave her a quick kiss on the cheek. "You can. I love you."

Polly's hand dropped away as an inner door opened and the boy emerged once more.

"Mr Slack is ready to see you now, Miss Clifford-Hughes."

They followed him through the sombre surroundings, once more passing a room with the odd clattering sound, and finally to the door. The boy knocked twice and Lawrence Slack's voice invited them in.

There was a clang from the front door and the boy rushed away.

The room was the same, with the sun filtering through the window, illuminating the dust motes that filled the air.

Lawrence emerged from behind his desk and held out his hand. Her gloved fingers gently squeezed his, then she pulled him in and stretched awkwardly up to plant a kiss on his lips.

He did not protest, and returned it.

Polly cleared her throat. "He's coming."

They separated. "Good afternoon, Miss Clifford-Hughes."

"Mr Slack."

Polly stepped aside as the pale thin ghost of a man that was her husband-to-be came through in a relaxed swagger, pulling off his gloves. The boy stood at the door.

"Veronica. Nice to see you."

"Edwin. The same, of course."

They shook hands.

"Slack."

"Mr Jameson. Shall we sit? Miss Clifford-Hughes, if you would care to take this chair by the window."

She would have flashed him a smile, but he wouldn't have seen it. The memory of what had occurred on her previous visit—which stirred a warmth between her thighs—was most pleasing. However, while it had been set against the light, it was not the same chair. This one was considerably taller, with a footstool in front of it for her to step on. Polly was there in a moment and took her hand as she stepped up and sat on the pile of cushions.

Thus enthroned, she was taller than either of the gentlemen in their chairs. She could see them clearly, and they could only squint up at her. She vowed she would give Lawrence the most delightful time of lust-filled pleasure he had ever experienced. Certainly more than any woman he had previously had. He deserved it for his thoughtfulness.

"Refreshments?"

"Tea please," said Veronica, "and chocolate biscuits if you have any."

"I will take tea as well," said Edwin. "No biscuits."

Lawrence nodded at the boy, who disappeared.

There was a silence which lengthened into awkwardness.

"Have your parents gone away yet?" Veronica asked casually.

Edwin cleared his throat. "They have indeed departed."

"It's a shame they could not attend the wedding."

"Yes."

"I should probably inform you, Edwin, that I have arranged for a wedding breakfast after the ceremony with a few select guests."

"Is that entirely necessary?"

"It is *fait accompli*. I should have spoken to you first on the matter, but when your sisters said they were coming to the wedding, I felt it was important."

"Why are my sisters coming to the wedding?"

Veronica could only look at him. Did he not want his sisters there? She understood why her parents didn't want to attend, and similarly Lord and Lady Launceston, but...

Thankfully, Lawrence intervened. "Mr Jameson, do you have any specific objection to a wedding breakfast?"

There was a long pause. "I have no specific objection, no, but I should have been consulted."

"I do apologise, Edwin, of course. This is all very new to me and I was only doing what I thought best."

"Of course."

"That's good, because I am very much looking forward to our trip to Switzerland."

Once again, a curious guarded expression came over Edwin's face. "Yes, the scenery is very engaging."

"Perhaps if you could tell me who would be in your party? I can inform my housekeeper of the numbers."

"Four."

Veronica exchanged glances with Lawrence as the conversation lapsed once more. She took a deep breath, looked over to where Polly stood by the door. Her lover nodded in encouragement.

"Edwin."

He turned to look at her but said nothing.

"There is an important matter that we must discuss in regard to the strictures you plan to impose upon Versyns House."

He frowned. "Strictures?"

"Yes, I will say this plainly so there can be no misunderstanding—" She broke off, trying to find the right words.

"What is it you want to say?"

"You cannot force the staff to embrace vegetarianism. To do so would result in almost all of them leaving our service. We will be without housekeeper, cook, gardeners, butler, indeed all the staff are likely to leave." She knew Polly wouldn't, but there was no point in providing exceptions.

"Then we will employ new staff who will accept the rules. This is my house, Veronica, they will do as they are told."

Suddenly she was angry. "They will *not*, Edwin. This is the twentieth century, not the Middle Ages. You do not own them body and soul. They are employees and they may go where they wish. If you insist, we will be completely without staff within a week—in fact, when we return from Switzerland it will be to an empty house. No cleaning. No food. Do you expect me to do it all on my own?" She chose not to highlight her deformity, he could see it plain enough. "We can attempt to find new staff, but how long will it take to find any that will willingly accept vegetarianism?"

"I cannot permit this state of affairs. I will not have *blood lappers* in the house. If we must make do while we find new servants, so be it."

"But you will not be the one to suffer, will you, Edwin? You can go to your club, or wherever you go. You can stay away from the house as long as it does not meet your requirements. Instead I will suffer, is that your intention?"

"It will not take long to find staff. Vegetarianism is spreading even to the uncultured classes."

Cold anger took an icy grip of her heart. This was something she had never felt before, such contempt for a fellow human so filled with arrogance he was unable to see the world around him for what it was. There was only one card she could play.

"Then, Edwin," she said in a voice that cut the atmosphere between them, "our wedding is cancelled."

There was a very long silence. Then: "You can't."

"You think so, Edwin? Because you cannot force me."

"Your father made an arrangement."

"But *I* did not, and while I may not have my full majority, I am of age. And we have witnesses here who have heard my declaration, and that message will be passed on. How do you think it will look for your father if the newspapers are full of how *you* caused the collapse of his business?"

That was pushing far beyond the barriers of what she knew to be truth, but she suspected that Edwin would not know the true details of the pact between their respective fathers. (Or shared father, perhaps.)

Edwin went quiet. The threat of his father's wrath seemed a good motivator.

The tea arrived and was distributed. She had a plate of those new chocolate biscuits. The boy left.

"Mr Jameson," said Lawrence in a conciliatory tone. "Since I was made aware of your intentions, I have consulted experts on the matter and, I'm afraid, attempting to enforce vegetarianism on the staff at Versyns is of questionable legality."

"I see."

"However, I am sure we can reach a compromise which, while not perfect, may go some way to satisfying both sides."

Edwin was closed in on himself like a sullen child. "What do you suggest?"

"That vegetarian meals should be made available for the staff if they require it and, through the natural wastage of staff, your future wife will be able to engage staff who are more willing to accept a vegetarian life."

"And I will become a vegetarian," said Veronica suddenly. "I would not want to discomfort you by eating anything you disapprove of in front of you."

"I am not happy about this," said Edwin.

"But you accept?" said Lawrence.

"It seems I have no choice."

Veronica found it hard to keep her face sombre when, inside, she was so relieved and happy at the outcome. *I won!*

Lawrence stood as Edwin got up. Veronica stayed where she was; she was not entirely sure she could get off all the cushions safely without help.

"Until Monday, Veronica."

"I will be there, Edwin."

The boy was summoned and he escorted Edwin from the room. Polly closed the door after them.

Veronica held it in as long as she could, but her mouth curled into a smile and she began to laugh. The sheer relief after all the concern and worry made her feel as light as if she were in a Faraday field. Lawrence joined in, and then Polly.

She stretched out her arm to her lover. Polly must have thought she wanted to stand, but Veronica pulled her closer and kissed her full on the lips. For a moment Polly tried to pull away, but if she was concerned about what Lawrence might think, it was too late. Veronica opened her mouth and touched Polly's tongue with the tip of her own.

She felt Lawrence take her other hand and kiss her fingers. She turned away from Polly, though still held her arm around the girl's waist, and she pulled Lawrence closer and kissed him too. His breath smelled, but she didn't care and she closed her eyes.

"Can the door be locked?" said Polly.

Lawrence's hand had sneaked below Veronica's hem and slid up her thigh.

"Nobody's going to come in," breathed Lawrence, pulling away for a moment so he could speak. "I'm not seeing anyone else today." His lips dragged across her cheek. His teeth gripped Veronica's ear. She grabbed his arm and pulled his hand up to her quim.

Polly's hand landed on Veronica's left breast and she squeezed hard. "Your boy might."

"Just be quick," hissed Veronica. Two of Lawrence's fingers were already in her and his thumb was pressed hard against her nubbin. His tongue traced the contours of her ear. She groaned as the pleasure took control of her.

Polly forced her head round and kissed her to smother her noises.

"Lift your dress," said Veronica into her mouth. Polly grabbed her dress, and pulled it up until Veronica could get her hand between Polly's thighs. Veronica found Polly's nubbin and rubbed it awkwardly, while she stretched out her other hand to find the bulge in Lawrence's trousers. She grabbed it through the material and with the same rhythm she was using on Polly, tried to stroke him. She was rewarded by him grunting in her ear.

The threat of being discovered heightened her pleasure; her body thrust hard against Lawrence's hand as Polly squeezed her tits through the material. She came in a shuddering rush that, for a moment, consumed her thoughts and froze her as the muscles between her legs spasmed.

With his unoccupied hand Lawrence freed his prick from its confinement. Veronica focused, leaned over, and took him in her mouth. He was larger than Seth, but she could accommodate him. She stroked him rapidly as he made little thrusting motions into her mouth—she appreciated his restraint as she played her tongue on the underside of his member.

Polly had moved more to the front so Veronica was still able to frig her while simultaneously dealing with Lawrence's needs. He must have been ready because he tensed, then his muscles contracted, launching his come into her mouth. She sucked and swallowed, keeping everything clean as she had learnt with Seth.

She realised that Lawrence and Polly were leaning over her; she could only imagine they were kissing—which was surprising since Polly did not seem to like men. Veronica's hand was still on Polly's quim so, maintaining a gentle hold of Lawrence, she reached further in and pushed a finger into Polly's hole. She was rewarded by a muffled sigh, so she pumped her fingers awkwardly while trying to rub the heel of her hand against her nubbin at the same time.

Polly's breathing quickened and then she clamped her thighs closed over Veronica's hand, crushing it, as Veronica tried to keep the movement going. She felt the muscles of Polly's pussy spasm then all the tension seemed to go out of her, and the crushing pressure on Veronica's fingers relaxed.

There was a double knock on the door.

Lawrence stepped away and organised his trousers. Veronica pulled her hand from between Polly's legs and her dress simply fell back into position. Meanwhile Polly grabbed Veronica's dress and arranged it.

It had taken barely a count of three.

"Enter," said Lawrence as he sat behind his desk. The door was opened by the boy in his neat uniform.

Polly stared at Veronica for a moment. Then pulled out her kerchief and wiped her mistress's chin.

"The carriage is here for Miss Clifford-Hughes, sir."

"Tell them to wait, Clive, we're not quite finished."

"Sir."

He left.

They looked one to the other and then the air was filled with their laughter.

"Gawd," said Polly, "we'd've been in so much trouble."

"Well, we weren't discovered," said Veronica, "so, Lawrence, I would like to thank you for your delightful hospitality. Earlier today I was so bothered by everything that I was quite incapable."

"Incapable?"

"Of enjoying—" she grinned, "—hospitality."

He smiled. "I am pleased you were able to appreciate my hospitality, Veronica, and Polly."

"Nika," said Polly. "Or Mistress Nika, depending."

Lawrence stood and bowed. "My apologies, Mistress Nika. I won't forget again."

They drank the tea and Veronica ate her chocolate biscuits enveloped by a comfortable silence.

"Yes, well, we need to go, I suppose," said Veronica.

"Allow me to escort you to your carriage."

"I hope to see you on Monday."

"I will be there. My father requires me to be a witness."

"Can you attend the wedding breakfast afterwards?"

"It would be my pleasure, Mistress Nika."

xxxi

The journey back to the house was without incident, though both Veronica and Polly giggled a great deal without commenting on their reason for doing so.

Polly helped Veronica change into something more appropriate for indoor wear. There had been an afternoon postal delivery which contained an acknowledgement from the Jameson sisters. Clearly Edwin had not been expecting them to attend, which made her even happier that they would do so.

It was not that she felt the need to antagonise her future husband, it was more that she wanted to see them disobey their parents.

Sofia Martaci had also accepted, as did Mr Plumley and his wife.

She looked out of the window of the library. The clouds had gathered once more and were threatening a shower. She sat at the desk and wondered what on earth she and Polly could do until dinner, still a couple of hours away.

She rang for Mr Jones and ordered afternoon tea.

It was strangely easy to fall into the habits of the mistress of a house, things she had read about in books and never imagined she would do.

"Polly? Were you kissing Lawrence when I was sucking him?" she asked out of the blue.

"Do you mind, Nika?"

"No, of course not."

"Not even a bit jealous?"

"I just thought you didn't like men."

"I wouldn't want one up me, no. But kissing's all right. Everybody's got lips."

"Lawrence is nice."

"I like him."

The door opened suddenly and Veronica turned, expecting tea and cakes. But it was Mr Laughton entering in a rush, his eyes sweeping the room.

"Miss Clifford-Hughes, what are you doing?"

"Waiting for afternoon tea."

"The vicar's here."

Veronica stood up as the Reverend Peacock entered behind the steward.

"Ah, Miss Clifford-Hughes, I'm so pleased to find you at home."

"Reverend Peacock, I wasn't expecting you." She didn't know what to say, Mr Laughton storming in made her feel self-conscious, and she was certain she must have been discovered and that there would now be terrible trouble. Had someone observed her with Lawrence? With Seth? Had they made too much noise? What if the pictures had been found?

Her wild thoughts were interrupted when she saw Polly miming drinking from a cup.

"Yes, I'm so sorry—"

"Do you want some tea, Vicar?"

"—what? Oh, yes. Tea, excellent."

"Please ring, Polly."

Mr Laughton sat down on the sofa by the empty grate. Veronica stared at him, but he was oblivious as he pulled out his pipe and tapped it against the firedog. She dragged her attention back to the vicar.

"I'm sorry, I interrupted you; what were you saying?"

"Well, Miss Clifford-Hughes—"

"Shall we sit down?"

Polly took the hint and as the vicar sat down beside Mr Laughton, she came up with the hard-backed chair.

"Surely you would like a gentler seat?" said Reverend Peacock.

"Oh, no, if I'm higher up it's easier for me to see you."

"Oh yes," he said as she sat carefully. "How clever."

"The vicar wants to go through the ceremony," said Mr Laughton.

"Do you have daughters, sir?" asked the vicar.

"I've had sons. Good strapping boys. Grown men. Army, Navy."

"Oh well, then you've never had to give a woman away in church."

"Never." Mr Laughton pulled a pouch from an inner pocket and deftly crammed tobacco from it into the bowl of the pipe one-handed. "Can we keep this brief?"

"Well, yes, of course."

The maid came in with tea for two and placed it on the table.

"Did you also want tea, Mr Laughton?" asked Veronica.

"No time for that."

The maid left and Polly poured, handing a cup to the vicar and then to Veronica.

Mr Laughton pulled out his pocket watch, flipped it open, and stared at it.

"Yes, well, the bride's party should arrive at two o'clock and will wait in the office at the side of the entrance."

The pocket watch snapped shut. "Wedding's at two-thirty, why so early?"

"Well, Mr Laughton, you see there are always delays, especially for weddings, so aiming for that time allows for any problems."

"So I don't need to be there right then."

"I suppose not—"

"Good."

"At the appointed time, the music will be begin and you will escort the bride, along with her bridesmaid, down the aisle to where the groom will be waiting."

"I know how it works."

Veronica had a good idea of how it worked in general, but not the real details. It had become very real and she wished she could hold Polly's hand.

"I will welcome everyone and we will sing a hymn. If you or your future husband have any particular preferences, Miss Clifford-Hughes, do let us know."

She smiled. "I do not think Edwin is the kind to have such preferences, and I think we would be happy with any choice you make."

"Of course, my dear. There is so much to think about, I shouldn't be giving you more problems. After the hymn we ask whether anyone thinks you should not be married—"

Veronica's blood ran cold—what if Edwin really was her half-brother? What if someone knew?

"—but that never happens. That's why we read the banns in church, so everyone knows and if they have any objections, they can mention it earlier."

"What if someone does?" said Veronica.

"Well, they never do."

"If they did?"

"It would depend on the claim. If a gentleman claimed that you had promised to marry him first, then we would take no notice, but if it were a more serious claim, such as the groom already being married..." He took a deep and serious breath. "Then I would have to stop the ceremony until the claim could be examined."

Veronica nodded. A claim that Edwin and she were too closely related would stop the ceremony. She understood. But then it was something she did not know as a certainty, and even if it was true, there was no way she could have known. The photographs could never be made public, and they really didn't prove anything on their own.

And what would happen? The respective parents would be questioned, they would answer, 'No, it's nonsense', and that would be an end of it. In fact, since Edwin's father was a lord, they would just dismiss it anyway.

Probably.

"Are you all right, my dear?"

The steward tutted. "Just get on, Vicar, I haven't got all day."

"You make your commitment to one another, a relevant bible reading, then I give a short sermon on marriage."

"God help us."

"Well, yes, Mr Laughton, that is, of course, the entire point."

Veronica allowed herself a secret smile; Reverend Peacock had allowed a certain edge into his voice. Mr Laughton adjusted his position and struck a match against the grate to light his pipe. He had noticed the rebuke and it had hit home. Her opinion of the vicar went up considerably.

"After that comes the vows. He puts the ring on your finger, and I bless your union in the Lord's name."

"I haven't been measured for a ring."

"Oh, that is interesting and a slight concern; perhaps you may wish to communicate with Mr Jameson on the matter, can't have a ring that doesn't fit."

Veronica gave her head a little shake, she could not imagine a wedding so poorly conceived and executed. It was as if the parties who arranged it really did not care how it went, as long as it happened.

But the vicar was continuing. "More readings from the Bible, then we withdraw with the witnesses for the signing of the register. The congregation have another longer hymn at this point. You have witnesses, I hope? You need two."

"Yes," said Veronica. "Mr Slack says he's been instructed to be a witness. And Mrs Jenkins, I suppose. I could ask her."

"Very good." The vicar glanced at Mr Laughton. He was now puffing his pipe in silence and apparently ignoring all that was said. "Once that's done, we have prayers, and the newly-wed couple follow me down the aisle. Everyone follows, and that is that."

Mr Laughton got to his feet. "Good. Shouldn't take long then. Half an hour?"

"I would expect an hour would be a closer approximation," said Reverend Peacock. "It rather depends on how long I decide to make the sermon."

That seemed to cause a little discomfort in the steward, and he did not see the wink the vicar gave Veronica.

"I'll show you out, Vicar," said Mr Laughton.

"Oh, that's all right, you go on. I believe I have one or two things to discuss with Miss Clifford-Hughes."

"What sort of things?"

The vicar stood. "I am afraid, sir, these are private matters between me, my parishioner, and the Lord."

If Mr Laughton wanted to argue, he must have thought better of it, and simply walked out without even a goodbye. The door slammed behind him. He failed to notice that Polly was still in the room.

The vicar smiled for moment, but then became serious. "Are you all right, my dear?"

"All right?"

"Are you being forced into this marriage?"

She thought about lying for only a moment. "Yes."

"You don't have to go through with it. It is against the law to coerce anyone into marriage."

"It was rather sprung on me," she said. The vicar frowned as she continued. "And it does involve some sort of financial deal between my father and Lord Jameson. But I do want to go through with it. It's my decision." *I think.*

Reverend Peacock tutted. "This is not right."

"No, I know, but you have to understand that Edwin was given *carte blanche* and has transformed the house. We have electricity. I have a Faraday device under my bed so I can sleep comfortably at night. Polly is properly my maid and is being paid appropriately. I have a dark room for developing photographs. I've been to London and I'm going to Switzerland. I'll be mistress of the house, when before I might as well have been a ghost."

"But is it worth the price?"

"Yes!"

"I see. If you're sure."

"I am sure, Vicar."

"Do you love him?"

"No, and I doubt I ever will, but I believe he has just as much interest in me. He cares about the house, and being its master. There is some plan he has in mind, I think, though I am not privy to it," she said. "I suspect it has something to do with the trip to Switzerland."

"And when you give your vows? To love, honour, and obey? Is it your intention to lie before God?"

She sighed. "I'm sorry, Vicar, I cannot say that I will do all those things. But God knows in my heart that I have no ill will to my future husband, and I expect I will give Edwin more regard than he will give me."

"I do not want you bound into a loveless marriage."

"I will not be without love, Vicar, I can promise you that. I'm sure I will be happy, and if I am not then I will deal with it as I may."

He gave a humourless smile. "I could refuse to marry the two of you, but there is little point in that. You would not be the first to perjure themselves at the altar, and someone else will perform the ceremony if I do not, or it could be carried out in a civil court."

"I would rather you did it."

He nodded and got to his feet. He held out his hand to help her stand.

"Thank you for coming, Vicar."

"I hope I was of some assistance."

"Well, at least we know what hasn't been sorted out. Will you come to the wedding breakfast too?"

"Of course, I would be delighted."

Once he was gone Veronica stared out the window once more. The clouds had thinned and the sun was warming the grass and the flowers once more.

"You'll have to stop inviting people to the wedding breakfast," said Polly. "Cook needs to know the numbers."

"I know," she said. "Am I doing the right thing?"

"Not for me to say."

"Of course it is, Polly, it's your life too."

"If things work out the way you said, with Edwin staying in his own room downstairs while we keep the main bedroom, I can't see there being any problem at all."

"Let's hope that's what happens then."

xxxii

Saturday. Two days to the wedding.

Polly had been up early for a change, without even a pause for a cuddle and fumble. Just a kiss and she was away. Once dressed, she set about checking through all the clothes she was planning to take, and seeing what needed a needle taking to it. The pile was not insignificant.

Leaving Veronica with nothing to do.

She lay in bed not wanting to interrupt Polly, but the prospect of dressing herself again did not appeal. Even if she did need more practice. Instead, she dozed for another hour and wished she had a book to read.

Later, Polly stopped sewing, helped Veronica dress, and they went down to breakfast. After which Polly excused herself and went back to the bedroom to carry on with the sewing.

Moving to the library, Veronica sat at the desk and wrote a letter to Edwin, pointing out that he did not know the correct ring size. There was a ball of string and scissors in the desk which she used to make a length that wrapped her finger. She attached it to the paper by making a small incision and sliding it through.

She summoned Mr Jones, who delivered the morning mail and went off with the communication for Edwin.

A letter from Vionnet confirmed that she had received Veronica's message from the previous day and would be able to supply her need. And that she would be arriving at half past three with the Misses Massingham and Mayhew, and a certain Miss Winifred Churchill.

Veronica rocked back on the chair and stared at the name. She knew of Winifred Churchill—who didn't? And there was no doubt in Veronica's mind that this was the investigating journalist who had reported on the plight of women in the South African concentration camps during the Boer War—and her articles had been instrumental in drumming up public support that forced the government to change its policies. The woman who had exposed the truth behind the crashing of the Albatross—the first Royal Navy vessel to go into space. Who had been at, and reported on, the Great Catterick Air Disaster of 1892.

The woman had written those wonderful books about the adventures of the Edgbaston Sisters in their flying machine—Veronica had read every single one of them; she glanced up to where the volumes stood side by side on the bookshelf.

The great Winifred Churchill was coming to her house. She could ask her to sign the books. A realisation swept through her. Veronica's hand went to her mouth and trembled against her lips.

Oh no. What has Vionnet done?

But she knew precisely what the *couturier* had done: she had taken the steps necessary to ensure that Veronica's wedding dress reached the biggest possible audience. She had invited Miss Churchill to write about it in whatever magazine or newspaper wanted the story. And if she wrote it, they would buy it.

Veronica's name and picture would be all over news, spread across the world; she would become famous as "The Cripple Bride". And her parents would see it.

Then something else occurred to her and her heart froze.

This is God's punishment, it must be.

Miss Churchill was a great friend of Harriet and Khuwelsa Edgbaston. If she realised Sofia Martaci was Harry's mother, Marianne Edgbaston? And wrote about it? It did not bear thinking about. She had not been kind in her description of Harry's mother; anyone who read that book would come away with a dislike for the woman. Veronica had experienced it herself, when Sofia mentioned Khuwelsa. The woman disliked her own daughter and hated her adopted daughter.

She felt as if everything was becoming unstuck, and there was nothing she could do about it. It was not that anyone had intentionally conspired against her, or even that she had done anything wrong, it was coincidence—perhaps spiced with a little self-interest.

Veronica had wanted a wedding dress. She had been given to Vionnet, the only *couturier* who would make her one. As Vionnet had said the first time they met, she was opening her own house in Paris, so she wanted her work to be in the news. And what better way than to dress a deformed cripple, which would be guaranteed to get into the newspaper. But she also happens to know Winifred Churchill, so that's who she asks. And the journalist could not possibly turn down a story like this.

But Veronica just happens to be friends with Sofia Martaci, who just happens to be the estranged mother of Harriet Edgbaston, who just happens to be a good friend of the same Winifred Churchill.

The furnaces were at full heat and the engine of her wedding was flying down the tube.

Towards a dead end.

She walked unsteadily to the fire mantel and pulled the rope to summon Mr Jones once more.

"Miss?"

"I think I need something alcoholic, Mr Jones."

"At this hour, miss?"

She slumped on to the *chaise*, and sighed.

"Is there something wrong, miss? Shall I fetch your maid?"

"Polly's got too much to do."

"Is there anything I can do, miss?"

"Alcoholic drink?"

"I wouldn't advise it, miss."

"I think I need it."

"Quite so, miss, but as my mother always used to say, drink when you fancy it, not when you need it."

"She sounds like a sober and sensible person."

"Drank herself to an early grave, miss, not that I like to speak ill of the dead."

"Lemonade?"

"Yes, miss." He left the room, and returned a few minutes later.

"I have taken the liberty of adding a splash of rum, miss, for medicinal purposes."

The sweetness of the rum complemented the bitterness of the lemonade. And she could feel herself relaxing.

"It's nice. Does this mixture have a name?"

"If it were stronger you might call it rum punch, miss," he said. "However there is barely any rum in it."

"Perhaps it's a rum kiss?"

Mr Jones smiled. "Indeed, miss. I believe it now has a name."

She sipped it as he stood there.

"If I may make so bold, miss, I understand that the coming wedding is causing you considerable concern."

"It's out of control, Mr Jones."

"Perhaps it's best not to try."

"But I'm going to be in the newspapers, and people are coming who have cause to dislike each other intensely, and they are all invited to the wedding breakfast—at least this new person cannot be refused, and I wouldn't want to."

"New person?"

"Winifred Churchill."

He raised an eyebrow. "The investigating journalist?"

"The same."

"And she is a problem, miss?"

Veronica took another drink. That Mrs Martaci was really Marianne Edgbaston was not generally known. "Signora Martaci has reason to dislike her. And *vice versa*."

"I see." He hesitated. "Do you think either woman would be so rude as to upset your wedding day?"

"I don't know."

"I believe there is little point in concerning yourself with something that may not happen, when you have no control over it."

"You're probably right."

"I would concern myself only with those things within my power."

Veronica sighed again. The rum, what little there was of it, seemed to be relaxing her, physically if not mentally.

"Will that be all, miss?"

"Perhaps you would inform Mrs Jenkins about the additional guests? Edwin's party is four additional, and now Miss Churchill."

"Of course, miss."

"Thank you, Mr Jones."

He departed and shut the door with barely a click.

The house was silent now. The last of the workmen had gone. The staff would be about the house performing their tasks quietly.

And the kitchen would be in uproar as they prepared for Monday while ensuring the usual meals were delivered as expected. At which point she got to her feet, rummaged around in the bureau for a sheaf of papers, and headed down towards the kitchens.

It was a bit late in the day, but it had to be done.

⸻⊙⸻

"MRS JENKINS? COULD I have a quick word?"

Veronica smiled at the changes in herself. Not so long ago she would not have gone into the kitchen, and certainly not summoned the housekeeper. She had come almost all the way down the stairs, but stopped on the fourth step. It meant she could see anyone on the ground easily.

The woman hurried up, wiping her hands on a cloth. Her dress was protected by a white pinafore with a floral design picked out in red.

"I don't have long, miss. The desserts need attention."

"I won't keep you. Two things. First, you will be delighted to learn that my future husband has agreed not to attempt to enforce vegetarianism on the staff."

"I see, miss."

"However, I have had to compromise with my own diet, and I will become a vegetarian, if somewhat reluctantly. It did not seem proper that his own wife should ignore his strictures and beliefs."

"Very good, miss."

Veronica held out the sheets. "These are my husband's—future husband's—notes on vegetarian meals. We will have to have something at the wedding breakfast, even if everyone else is eating meat."

Mrs Jennings wiped her hands again and took the papers, then glanced at Cook who was, at the moment, wielding a meat cleaver on a haunch of beef. "Cook's not going to like it."

"I understand, but it's the best that could be achieved."

"Is that all?"

Veronica wanted to ask how her evening with Seth had gone, but she had a good idea that it must have been successful, since Mrs Jennings' temperament had calmed considerably. But that was not on her list of questions.

"What does Mr Laughton do?"

The housekeeper looked astonished at the question. "He's the steward."

"Yes, I know, but his duties?"

"I'm sure you'd have to discuss that with him."

"Well, thank you, Mrs Jennings, and please get back to your desserts. I'm looking forward to them—if they are vegetarian."

"Fruit pies and puddings, miss."

"Sounds lovely."

VERONICA WENT BACK to the library and pulled out Mrs Beeton's guide and studied it. There was almost nothing on the duties of the House Steward, except to say that one is appointed in larger households and was responsible for the accounts; where one was not present, the housekeeper was second-in-command (to the mistress), and did the accounts.

Why so little information? Perhaps because a steward would take orders from the master of the house? One wouldn't expect him to take orders from the mistress. Clearly Mrs Beeton did not consider a steward to be within the scope of her book on household management.

She mulled it over waiting for the gong to chime for luncheon.

POLLY SAID SHE HAD completed most of the repairs and adjustments, so put away her sewing kit to help Veronica get changed for greeting her guests in the afternoon. The process took a little longer than it probably should have, since they spent some time kissing on the bed, with the Faraday on.

But, all too soon, the clock indicated half past two, and Veronica's hair needed repair. Polly even applied a little rouge and lip colour, quite a modern thing to do in the middle of the day.

At three o'clock, Veronica went down to the drawing room and waited, staring from the window at the rain. "Rain on your wedding day means it will last," she said to no one in particular. She found she could not decide whether she wanted it to rain on Monday.

Polly came in. "They're here."

Veronica got to her feet. She was not concerned about Vionnet or her staff, but the prospect of meeting Winifred Churchill made her heart pound.

"You'll be fine."

"Is it that obvious?"

"I know you."

They went through the hall to stand beneath the portico as a steam-powered carriage, with the name *Lewiston's of Hyde Park, Faraday Carriages* on the door, drew up at the bottom of the stairs. It seemed Vionnet's party hadn't taken the train after all, and must have been driven down. After a pause, the whole body sank on its suspension as the Faraday device was disengaged.

The driver's door opened and Veronica was astonished to see a woman's foot, in a brown leather shoe, emerge and crunch on the gravel. The woman, perhaps in her forties, climbed out. She wore a plain beige day dress, and stood staring first at the whole building in front of her as if she were memorising it, and then focused on Veronica, seemingly oblivious to the rain. There was little question this was Winifred Churchill, who, it seemed, had chosen to pilot the vehicle from London.

Thankfully, the woman looked away and assisted Vionnet to emerge like a butterfly from a cocoon. Her dress was pink and blue; it clung to her shape above the waist, but flared out beneath. The ginger hair of Josephine Massingham appeared on the other side of the carriage, followed by the dark hair of Clio Mayhew.

Veronica remembered what Mr Jones had said about protocol and decided, on this occasion to remain where she was. Three maids brushed past her and headed down the steps unfurling umbrellas. Miss Churchill took one and held it over herself as the second maid protected Vionnet, and the third hurried round the vehicle to the other two.

Miss Churchill offered Vionnet her arm, as if she were a man. They climbed the stairs until Veronica could no longer see their faces, but she did see Miss Churchill's gloved hand thrust out.

"Miss Clifford-Hughes, this is Winifred Churchill."

Veronica shook the outstretched hand—the woman's grasp was firm, but not domineering.

"Welcome to my home, Miss Churchill." The hissing of the rain intensified. "Shall we go in?"

The guests were shown their rooms so they could refresh themselves after the journey while Veronica paced the lounge, and Polly stood by the door.

It did not surprise Veronica when Miss Churchill was the first to come down, after barely ten minutes. They shook hands again.

"I do apologise, Miss Clifford-Hughes, I'm afraid Vionnet has very little in the way of scruples when it comes to promoting her undoubted skills." And then she sat down without waiting for Veronica, placing herself so that Veronica was able to see her.

"But you came anyway, Miss Churchill," said Veronica. That had not been what she intended to say and she surprised herself.

The woman smiled. "Yes. If I had refused she would have found someone else, and I could not allow that."

"Am I such an important story then?"

"There are aspects of the story that are important, I think, but you personally? Since we are clearly being frank, let me say that you are an interesting story, but not an important one."

"I see."

"I doubt that you do. In the newspaper world, the women who write, even now, are restricted to the society pages, and fashion. Do you read them?"

"Yes."

Miss Churchill rummaged about in her bag and brought out a cigarette holder. She inserted a cigarette and extracted a match from a silver Vesta case. She lit the end and took in a deep breath of smoke, then let it out slowly. The smell of it drifted across Veronica and tickled the back of her throat.

"Given that you read them, how do you think they might cover your wedding?"

Veronica did not have to think about it. She had seen it plain enough on more than one occasion when they felt the bride or groom were less than perfect. "They would not be sympathetic."

"They would cut your husband to ribbons as a vegetarian, and as a pale imitation of a man, married to a deformed witch because they could do nothing else with him. Vionnet herself would receive praise, of course, doing her best in such a trying situation, and perhaps mooting the idea she had been blackmailed into doing it." She took another long draw at her cigarette. "How do you rate my assessment of the likely outcome?"

"You don't need me to tell you."

"Ha! I like you Miss Veronica Clifford-Hughes."

Veronica remembered her manners and asked Polly to have afternoon tea served. Then she lay down on a *chaise longue* at an angle that meant she could still see the unexpected guest. She wanted to mention Sofia Martaci, but it was impossible. The fact that Sofia was really Marianne Edgbaston was not common knowledge; if Veronica mentioned it, she would be handing the woman another story—and one which could end up being very unpleasant.

"You're very thoughtful—can I call you Veronica? You may call me Winifred, but not Winnie, I dislike that."

Veronica swallowed. It was almost as if the woman could read her mind. "Yes, I was wondering, Winifred, if I might ask you a question."

"Fire away. I can always refuse to respond."

"Yes, of course. You come from a large household, I think?"

"Blenheim Palace. Huge."

"Does the house have a steward?"

The woman barked a laugh. "Of all the questions I might imagine you would ask, that was not among them. Well, Veronica, I never really lived there. Ancestral seat, to be sure, but not my father's. His older brother's. But yes, it had a House Steward and an Estate Steward."

"What are the responsibilities of a steward?"

Winifred Churchill frowned and pursed her lips. "To the best of my knowledge, and this is not something I know a great deal about, they manage the day-to-day running of the household staff, and look after the accounts."

"Isn't that the housekeeper's job?"

The woman did not respond, but a slight smile appeared on her face. "You have a steward? Here? You can't have a staff of more than fifteen, surely?"

"Not if you don't count the gardeners."

"How curious."

At that moment the door opened and Vionnet arrived, followed by her staff. And the discussion was replaced by social niceties.

xxxiii

Sunday morning. Veronica stared through the window at the clouds that crossed the sky like an army on the march. The wind was up and shook the trees constantly. If this kept up until Tuesday, they would not be flying anywhere, but this was Britain and the weather changed on a whim.

She heard Polly slide out of bed and her bare feet slap across the floor of the bathroom to the indoor water-closet. Civilisation had its quiet pleasures. A short time later Polly came back and then went through into her own bedroom.

Veronica turned from the window and followed her lover into the adjoining bedroom.

Polly had just slipped out of her nightdress and was naked. She stopped, as if waiting for Veronica to speak, but Veronica sat on the end of the bed and stared at her wedding dress. Unlike Polly's dress beside it, Veronica's did not sit quite properly on the dummy. *Because my shape is not normal.*

"Penny for your thoughts."

"I can't tell you."

"Why?"

"Because you would accuse me of self-pity."

"I could help you relax." Polly's hand came to rest on Veronica's shoulder; she took her lover's hand, turned her head, and kissed her fingers.

"I think even that would fail."

"It'll be all right."

"I don't even know if it's what I really want any more."

"Then don't do it."

"But everything is in motion. We have dresses, the church is booked, the meals are planned, and people are invited and arriving."

Polly moved round in front of Veronica and knelt. "But it isn't for them, or about the church, and it's not about the dresses."

Veronica smiled, but it held no emotion. She pushed back a lock of Polly's hair and ran her fingers down her cheek. "And what would happen to me?

Things could not go back to the way they were. The house has been remodelled, and there is an agreement between the parents. I know Edwin does not care for me, and who would expect him to. Ow—"

Polly had slapped her leg.

"What was that for?"

"Self-pity."

"It wasn't. It wouldn't matter if I was the same shape as everyone else, I still don't think he would care. My future husband has loftier plans in mind, I am quite sure. For him, a wife would be either a means to an end, or a minor inconvenience."

"And you are?"

"I have provided him with an estate he can use."

Polly straightened up and kissed Veronica on the nose. "I can't choose for you, so you had better decide. Honestly, if I don't have to walk semi-naked down the aisle of the church, I'll be a lot happier."

Veronica kissed Polly on the lips to avoid repeating the train of thought that led from cancelling the wedding to her being thrown out of the house, or worse, ending up in an asylum.

Mr Plumley had been right when he said a woman had to play whatever cards she was dealt in order to succeed. And at this moment the strongest hand meant she must go through with the wedding despite any misgivings she might have. It would ensure her position in the household while Edwin would execute whatever it was he planned.

Besides, without the wedding she would not be able to show Polly how much she loved her.

"I'm sorry, Polly, I'm afraid we must go through with it. It will be a single hour from our entire life. Let's get dressed."

<hr>

BREAKFAST WAS DOUBLY strange for Veronica. In the first instance, it was Sunday and they usually went to church before eating—but there was to be no church this morning. And the second unusual aspect was to have so many there, even if it was only the addition of Miss Churchill compared to when Vionnet had stayed before.

Cook had arranged for the food to be served buffet-style, as they did in the larger houses when there were many guests all arriving at different times. The fare was the usual though, kedgeree being the mainstay, with plenty of buttered toast to follow with marmalade or honey. Two maids were on hand to supply coffee or tea.

"I will require a fitting once more today," said Vionnet, "and my girls will practice the hair and make-up once more. All must be perfection for tomorrow."

All five were seated around a single table. Miss Churchill was the most senior, since she was at once the oldest and of the most aristocratic birth, even if she did not have a title. If it had been anyone other than her, they might have objected to a mere seamstress and her assistants sitting with them, but Winifred Churchill was not that woman.

"Do you mind if I attend the fitting? It would be good to get some pictures and background material for the article."

Veronica instantly thought of her parents' photographic album, that would certainly provide a colourful story. "What sort of background?"

"The house, the bedroom, the preparations, and so forth."

"I see."

"And, if I may, I'd like to talk to the staff."

The panicked look on Veronica's face must have been obvious. Winifred laughed. "Don't worry, I'm just after some simple quotes. I could probably make them up and still get it right. People tend to lack imagination when it comes to weddings."

Veronica forced herself to smile, but she suspected the answers would not be quite what Miss Churchill expected. This was not a normal household. She tried to change the subject.

"You've never been married, Miss Churchill?"

Vionnet made a sound through her mouthful of toast—she had turned her nose up at the kedgeree—that might have been a dismissive laugh.

"My choice of life is not conducive to marriage. Who knows what part of the world I might be popping off to, at a moment's notice."

"And you have not met a man you've liked well enough," said Vionnet in a tone that lacked even the slightest attempt at subtlety. "But Miss Clifford-Hughes understands that."

Veronica felt her face flush, and at the same time focused her attention on her kedgeree.

"Nor a woman, Madeleine, as you well know. All I ask for is a little fun along the way."

"Like your mother, *n'est-ce pas*?

"Quite so, though she has the pick of Society, even at her age."

Veronica tried to change the subject again. "Your mother has a title even though she's American, I don't really understand why you don't, Winifred."

The woman gave her a sideways glance, and smiled. "Easy enough to explain. If titles were always passed on, the whole country would be awash with lords and ladies. My father was the third son, he had a title, but his children—including me, despite being first-born—get none. Built-in limitations." She smiled, and her voice suddenly changed to a strange accent. "Not only that, but my father had no dough, that's why he married little Jennie Jerome from Brooklyn. He had the aristocracy, and her father had the money."

"I didn't know," said Veronica.

"It's no secret. My mother and I get on well enough now; it was not always that way, but she is very far from virtuous. She had an affair with Edward, God rest his soul, and Alexandra knew but didn't mind. This is England, so nobody cares."

"I didn't recognise the accent you used, was that Irish?"

"New York. I'm not very good at it, but I picked it up from Mother."

Veronica ate the rest of her breakfast in silence, although she knew she ought to be stimulating conversation in her guests. Vionnet's comments, as well as Winifred's admissions, suggested the woman was as relaxed in her bed partners as Veronica was, or would like to be.

She felt as if there were lessons she could learn from Miss Churchill, but how in the world would you ask someone to teach you about relations with both men and women? And what if you had misunderstood?

———●———

AFTER BREAKFAST THEY spent some time simply digesting. Mr Jones had brought the Sunday newspaper, and Veronica let Winifred read it. She hadn't followed the news in detail since her life changed. It was probably something she should return to, but not until after the honeymoon.

But after half an hour Mademoiselle Vionnet was getting restless, so the entire group headed back to the master bedroom. Josephine and Clio took a short detour to pick up their equipment, and Winifred fetched her notepad and camera.

Once more Polly and Veronica allowed themselves to be little more than dolls to be dressed. They stripped to silk bloomers and light dressing gowns, then submitted themselves to the artistry of cosmetics and hairdressing. Winifred took a lot of pictures, but kept up a commentary as she did so, sometimes praising the artists, and sometimes the art. Other times she told risqué stories about things she had done, or seen.

Veronica was impressed at how she kept it up for nearly an hour without stopping. Polly laughed louder than all of them at the humorous and rude anecdotes. But at no time did Winifred reveal enough information for anyone to know precisely who she was talking about, although Veronica was sure that, with a little research, she would be able to identify the Russian prince.

Then they were done. Their hair once more beautiful Grecian sculptures, and their make-up mirroring the style but with a more modern look.

Polly's dress went on first, and she was once more embarrassed at revealing her bare breasts to a group of women she barely knew.

Winifred immediately launched into a story of how she and a dozen other women, including her mother, had stripped naked to create a Roman *tableau vivant* at some great house near Manchester, for charity, with only the thinnest of materials covering them. Unfortunately, one particular lady had swooned and brought the whole group of them crashing to the ground, exposing a tangle of limbs for all to see.

Polly was horrified—though no longer concerned about her own exposure—until the story was rounded off with the fact that the gentlemen attending had increased their charitable donations almost tenfold.

Once Polly was decent, Mademoiselle Vionnet checked the dress thoroughly to ensure it still lay as it had been designed. The curious elasticity the *couturier* managed to bring to her fabrics ensured it still clung to Polly's frame, displaying her shape almost as if the cloth were transparent, at least to her waist.

Veronica's concerns about her body had nothing in common with Polly's and she was terribly aware of her back as Miss Churchill continued to take her photographs. She was dressed, stockinged, and the shoes added. Then Vionnet and her assistants brought the train behind her and attached it to the cords that wound around her bodice.

"Your newspaper will not print those," said Veronica, her words half question, half statement.

"No, nor would I wish them to embarrass you, Veronica."

"From the front and below, I look almost normal."

Vionnet was placing the veil on Veronica's head and brought it down to cover her face and shoulders

"Quite honestly, my dear, you look wonderful. It's Vionnet's skill, she can always bring out the beauty in a woman."

She took more pictures.

Vionnet checked everything and declared the dress to be ready.

Winifred peered into the bathroom. "Let's do a couple of pictures in here, with both of you together."

Veronica was not impressed. "In the bathroom?"

"It will be fine. I don't want the bath or the WC, but the dark wall tiles will contrast well with the dress. And I've been doing this a long time. Trust me."

They stepped through into the bathroom.

"Stand together." Winifred lined up the camera, then put it down again. "I see the problem."

Veronica knew what the problem was. She couldn't straighten up, so with Polly standing next to her, it just looked wrong. *She* looked wrong.

"It only works if I'm sitting, or lying down," said Veronica. "We were having a painting done last week by Sofia Martaci and…" Her voice trailed off.

"Sofia Martaci?" said Winifred Churchill. "The painter, Sofia Martaci?"

Oh no.

"How do you know Sofia Martaci, Veronica?"

"She lives in the town, Miss Churchill."

The woman gave a short humourless laugh. "Mayfield, it hadn't occurred to me. Of course, she does. And I can see from your desperate expression, you know who she really is."

Veronica nodded. "I beg you, Miss Churchill, please don't spoil it."

"What do you mean?"

"I have had very little in my life that you might consider special. You had been all over the world by the time you were eighteen. I have been to London just once, for a day. You have dined with the most important people in the world. You're the most important person I have ever met." She took a deep breath. "But tomorrow is my wedding day, Miss Churchill. It may not be perfect, I may not love my husband, but it is the most significant day in my life so far. So I beg of you, please do not spoil it."

"There are two reasons I have never married, Veronica. One is that I have never found someone who I felt I would enjoy spending the rest of my life with, to the exclusion of others; the second is that I could not forgo my profession in favour of providing children of such a union with a stable life." She fiddled with the camera for a moment and wound-on the film. "To bring a child into the world and to then abandon it, is not the act of good person."

"Such were my parents," said Veronica. She could feel the tears welling up and fought desperately to hold them back, she must not ruin her make-up.

"Indeed, and so with Marianne Edgbaston."

"I read your book."

"I was much harsher. Harry refused to let it be printed as I first wrote it."

"And I am asking you not to cause trouble. Please."

Winifred shook her head. "Of course not. I would never do such a thing. I like you, Veronica, and I hope we can be friends. I have eaten meals with people a thousand times worse than a selfish woman guilty of abandoning her child, and being a horrible bigot into the bargain. At least she's a decent painter."

Something had happened to Veronica's eyelashes. She blinked and her right eye refused to open.

"Ow, no! My eye!" It was stinging as if filled with tiny biting ants.

"Keep it closed," said Winifred. "Here, Polly, take my kerchief and dab it to remove moisture and the mascara. Miss Mayhew! Your make-up is in the bride's eye."

Veronica was guided back into the bedroom where Vionnet covered her dress, to avoid getting any make-up on the cloth as it was cleaned off.

THE REST OF THE DAY dragged, while at the same time it flew past.

During the afternoon, Vionnet drew her to one side and produced two grey boxes with the name "Tiffany & Co" embossed in gold on the top. Veronica took one and gently lifted the lid. Inside was an armlet looping three times, with a snake design. The hallmarks were clearly marked on the surface.

"It's beautiful," said Veronica. "But I can't—"

"They are my wedding present to you and your lover," said Vionnet. "And they will complement my dresses perfectly."

"I can't—"

"A gift," said mademoiselle firmly.

"Thank you, *merci*."

LATER, SHE SPOKE TO Mrs Jenkins, who said that everything was in order, including the vegetarian food for Edwin and Veronica.

"Thank you, could there be bacon for breakfast please? And ham? If it is to be my last meal with meat, I would like it to be a good one."

"Of course, miss." She made as if to leave, then stopped. "And I will not be giving my notice, miss, not yet anyway."

Veronica sighed with relief, feeling as if a great weight had been lifted from her. "Thank you, Mrs Jenkins." Then daringly she added, "I take it the new *arrangements* are to your liking?"

To Veronica's astonishment, Mrs Jenkins blushed. "They are very much to my taste, miss."

"I'm pleased. There is one more thing, though."

"I am at your disposal."

"You do the accounts, I believe?"

"I do. Is there a problem?"

"No, of course not, no problem at all. And, in my admittedly limited experience, you are in control of the staff."

"I am. For the most part, though, Mr Laughton prefers to be consulted in regard to the hiring of any male servants."

Veronica nodded. "Thank you."

———•———

IT WAS TEN O'CLOCK in the evening and Veronica sat on the side of the bed in her nightgown. She reached out and turned the knob to increase the strength of the Faraday field. With each click, more of the stress went from her back. Her legs tingled where they left the field.

Polly was humming as she removed her uniform. She preferred to be naked in bed and Veronica smiled as more of her flesh came into view.

"What?" said Polly when she realised Veronica was watching.

"You remember the first time you made me come?"

"You and your boobs. I still don't understand that. You could rub mine raw and nothing like that would happen."

"I wouldn't want to rub them raw, but I was thinking you might like to rub mine."

Polly stripped off her stockings and padded across the carpet to stand in front of Veronica. She cupped her palm beneath Veronica's left breast and lifted it as if weighing it. Then she flicked her thumb across the nipple.

Veronica took a sharp breath as the sensation echoed between her legs and her muscles clenched involuntarily. Polly shook her head, but was smiling. "Shall I get a bowl and a washcloth?"

"Yes."

Polly returned and sat next to Veronica. The water in the bowl moved slowly in the reduced gravity, like a jelly that was not quite set, but a wet cloth was still a wet cloth as Polly gently stroked it from Veronica's collarbone down across her breasts, as if she were cleaning them.

The sensation of rising lust that had been so new when they had performed this ritual the first time was now something Veronica understood and welcomed. Her nipples were hard and Polly gripped each one firmly, almost to the point of pain, as she continued to stroke above and below.

Veronica closed her eyes, focusing only on the pleasure building within. She knew she was making the bed damp—a thing she had not comprehended that first time. Her breathing deepened. She almost growled with the pleasure. Polly was there, naked beside her, all she had to do was reach out—but that would spoil that first moment of intimacy they were reliving.

Polly's warm mouth closed on her nipple and sucked hard as she took a handful of the other breast and squeezed. This had not been what happened before, but Veronica was past caring. Teeth bit down on her nipple and sent her into a sudden paroxysm. She shuddered as the built-up energy washed through her.

Then Polly stood up, took the bowl, and left her. Just as she had that first time.

Veronica rolled over onto the bed and let the Faraday cradle her. Moments later, Polly landed beside her. They kissed gently, and Veronica's hand found its way between her lover's thighs and gently rubbed her. She got the heel of her hand against Polly's clit as her fingers pressed at the entrance to her hole.

Polly clung tighter as the tension built within her, then her thighs clamped hard, crushing Veronica's fingers, and the girl cried out in delightful agony as the passion exploded in her.

They fell asleep clinging to one another.

xxxiv

Monday 8th August. Clouds filled the sky, but they were high and there seemed no immediate threat of rain. It did not seem right getting dressed in normal clothes on her wedding day, but Vionnet had said they should not start the main preparations before noon.

They rose as if it were a normal day, save for the fact neither Veronica nor Polly were interested in anything other than kisses and hugs. The coming ordeal weighed heavily on Veronica; perhaps it did on Polly as well, if for different reasons.

They performed all their morning activities in almost complete silence.

Polly had arranged luggage for the honeymoon and it lay on the bed in her room. She set about the packing. "For something to do," she said.

They went down to breakfast for nine-thirty.

Mrs Jenkins was as good as her word. Apart from the buttered toast with marmalade and honey—which her future husband would no doubt approve of—she was presented with a plate piled with bacon, scrambled eggs, even some cold roast ham.

Veronica insisted that Polly ate with her, though it made the girl uncomfortable. "Today you are my bridesmaid, and you are my friend. You eat with me."

The guests appeared as time wore on and they too were given the full breakfast—though Vionnet declined and consumed only the toast with honey.

"I do not promise your dress will fit after consuming so much, Miss Clifford-Hughes."

But she did not forbid the meal.

Mr Jones brought the post. There was a card from Lady Katherine wishing her well which was a surprise. Then came a letter. Veronica dropped both letter and opener as if they burned her fingers. The knife clattered on the plate before falling to the floor. Veronica left the table and went to the window. Her fingers were trembling.

Polly was at her side in a moment. "What is it?"

"My mother."

"Oh."

"I don't want to read it. I don't care what she thinks she has to say to me."

The sound of the envelope being opened split the quiet of the room. Veronica turned to see Miss Churchill extracting the letter itself.

"What are you doing? That's mine."

"I was going to read it and then tell you what it says."

"No."

Miss Churchill held the letter out to her. "Then read it yourself. It's only one side and I imagine there's about enough space for her to explain why she can't come to the wedding, even though the envelope is postmarked—" she checked, "—from Kensington. They'll be some sort of placatory words about it being the best for you, and that Edwin is probably a fine fellow. In the end, it will simply be a justification for her treating you badly."

Vionnet, Josephine, and Clio focused only on their breakfast.

"It might not say that."

"I'm willing to wager a guinea, are you confident enough to take it?"

"I will not bet on the contents."

Winifred shrugged. "Very well, I see you still believe everything will turn out all right with your parents in the end."

I don't.

"You've known nothing but books all your life and you think it will turn out like a fairy story and you'll live happily ever after."

I don't.

"So, decide, Miss Clifford-Hughes, who will read this letter? You or I?"

Veronica stared at the sheet of paper Winifred dangled between her thumb and forefinger. "Give it to me."

Winifred stood, but Polly was across the room and had taken it from her in a trice. She brought it back and handed it to Veronica. In a voice barely above a whisper she said, "I can just burn it, Nika."

Veronica unfolded the letter and stared at it unseeing, until she forced herself to read the words.

When she was done she crumpled it into a ball and handed it back to Polly.

"Burn it."

"Do you owe me a guinea, Veronica?"

"I do not," she said, holding the tears back and emptying her voice of all emotion. "She did not provide any justification for not attending. Clearly that was a given."

"I am sorry, Veronica."

"It doesn't matter. I have survived this long without them. I can manage for the rest of my life."

Vionnet had plans. Once breakfast was complete, she gave her orders.

"You will bathe, Miss Clifford-Hughes, I have oils and scents for your bath. Then Clio will trim, colour, and polish your toenails and your fingernails." She glanced at her bracelet watch. "It is now thirty past ten. You have until fifteen past eleven. The decoration of your nails will bring us to the time to prepare."

⸻ ◉ ⸻

VERONICA LAY IN THE warm and scented bath.

It's happening.

The prospect of marriage had never even entered her mind—at least after she had realised that princesses in stories never looked like her. They were always beautiful and perfect.

It had not stopped her from reading the books, but from that time she had never seen herself as the princess to be rescued. Sometimes she thought she might be the evil witch, after all they were always hunched over with warts on their faces.

But she could not fool even herself. This was not a fairy-tale marriage. She was the princess forced to marry according to her father's wishes, and there was no hero riding to her rescue at the last moment.

The vicar had given her a way out and she had chosen not to take it. She did not mind. What she was doing now was the best choice she had.

Seth and Polly had given her some confidence in herself, and the marriage gave her a little power to wield.

And if she was going through with it, then she wanted it to be as good as possible.

But there is one more thing that I must do, if I dare.

Polly washed her then helped her dry before she went to see Josephine in Polly's bedroom. Meanwhile Polly, under Vionnet's insistence, emptied the bath and used fresh water for herself, with Ursula assisting. Veronica was surprised to see her, she must have been so deep in her own thoughts she had not even noticed the girl arrive.

From now on, at least for today, Polly was no longer a maid, she was just Veronica's bridesmaid—best friend and one true love.

Josephine jabbered while she trimmed Veronica's nails, but Veronica barely listened. It was not that she was thinking about anything in particular, just that she was in an almost dreamlike state as she was tended on—literally hand and foot.

Then her nails were painted purple, and polished.

"They have to look their best," said Josephine. "Everybody will see them."

Veronica wondered just how cold the stones of the church were going to be.

Then the work on her face and hair began in earnest as Clio took over. They had been through it twice before, so now it was almost routine. Time passed and the goddess Theros took shape. Polly came in attended by Ursula. She sat, and the creation of the woodland nymph started.

Finally, Veronica moved into the main bedroom where Vionnet waited. The *couturier* had already changed into a powder-blue dress for the wedding. Veronica was surprised that, although it had the trademark elasticity and cling of Vionnet, it had the appearance of being quite plain.

Ursula helped as Veronica was placed in the two pieces of clothing she was to wear. The silk bloomers and the dress that clung to her body in the way that Vionnet's clothes always seemed to.

And she was ready.

"It has been said to me, Veronique, that the weather here is not as pleasant as that in *la belle* France. And it cannot be denied this is a dull and wet country."

Veronica couldn't think how she was supposed to respond to this, but Vionnet was delving into one of her bags. She withdrew a pair of very simple sandals.

"Also there may be stones and dirt upon the floor. You may wear these."

There was barely anything to them. The sole, a loop for the big toe, and a leather cord to loop around the ankle and tie off. Ursula did the honours. It was strange how much better it made Veronica feel to have them, though they did not provide the support she really needed.

"Thank you, mademoiselle."

"You have a rhyme, do you not? 'Something old, something new.'"

"Something borrowed, something blue."

"The sandals, they are new, and I see Miss Massingham has already put a blue ribbon in your hair."

Veronica raised her hand to the structure on her head, but dared not touch it.

"These," said Vionnet, touching the box containing the armlets she had bought, "they are quite old."

"But what can be borrowed?"

"You will return to me the silk bloomers."

Veronica laughed. "Very well, Mademoiselle Vionnet. Thank you for letting me borrow the underthings."

"Nika."

Veronica turned to see the vision of Polly entering. Ursula took a sudden breath. And Polly was smiling, which made such a difference.

"Let's get on with it, mademoiselle," said Polly. "If I am to expose myself to the world let us do it quickly before I have a chance to change my mind."

Veronica went to the bed, switched on the Faraday, and sat. She was not sure if a dress by Vionnet would crease easily, but in partial gravity she was barely pressing down on it, creasing should be minimal.

While Polly was being dressed, Josephine and Clio were changing into their dresses. There was much hilarity in the process.

And then they were ready.

For the first time Veronica allowed herself to look at the clock. Twenty-three minutes past one. Just sixty-seven minutes to go. It would take ten minutes to drive to the church—she realised she did not know whether they were using the old carriage, or if something had been ordered. Something else she had failed to organise. Hopeless.

"I can't…"

"Nika?"

Veronica stared at Polly. "I can't do it."

Mademoiselle Vionnet made a very French sound of derision.

"It's all going to go wrong. I haven't arranged transport. Perhaps we can walk? I just don't want to get the dress dirty."

"What are you talking about, Nika?"

"The food won't be edible."

Polly turned away from Veronica. "I am sorry, but I must ask you all to leave."

"Every bride I have ever known," said Vionnet. "They all do this. It is nothing."

"Please leave the room, Mademoiselle Vionnet. Take everything you will need."

It took a couple of minutes for the room to be vacated. Ursula still hung back.

"You too."

She left. And Polly sat down beside Veronica.

"Can't we just go back to the way it was, Polly? We could go to bed right now and I'll make you come like never before."

"Shut up, Nika."

Veronica hesitated. "You can't talk to me like that."

"Why? Because I'm just your servant? Fine, if that's the way you want it. No more Polly and Veronica. I'll stay in the other room and you can sleep alone for the rest of your life."

"No—"

"You can't have it both ways. Either I'm your servant, or I'm your lover and equal. Which is it?"

"Lover, always."

"Then you can't tell me how to talk to you, Nika."

"I'm sorry."

"Good. Now, tell me. What is this nonsense?"

"I can't do it."

"You're scared."

"No...yes," she said. "You know me. This isn't me."

Polly took her hand. "You're not in the cage no more, Nika. Cages keep you in, but they keep everything else out too. Do you want to go back in the cage?"

"If I could."

"That don't sound very likely."

Veronica sighed. "No."

"You decided to go through with this."

"I know."

Polly glanced at the clock. "We need to get moving."

"All right," said Veronica. She let herself slide off the bed and land on her sandaled feet outside the Faraday field. She took a deep breath. "I would kiss you, but Vionnet would not be pleased if we damaged our make-up."

"We've got all the time in the world, Nika."

XXXV

The others were waiting just along the corridor from the bedroom. Vionnet stared fixedly out of the window while Josephine and Clio watched them emerge. Ursula was not in sight.

Vionnet turned. "We are ready, *n'est-ce pas*?"

"We are ready, Mademoiselle Vionnet," said Veronica.

"*Allons-y alors.*"

Veronica took Polly's arm and they walked steadily along the corridor. At the top of the stairs, they stopped. Several of the staff, including Mr Jones, waited at the bottom of the stairs. Murmurs of astonishment reached Veronica's ears. Whether they were in appreciation of the art of Vionnet, or the extravagant and revealing nature of the clothes, Veronica was not sure.

Whatever it was did not matter, as Mr Laughton appeared, dressed in tweeds.

"About time."

Tweeds?

It did not matter. It simply strengthened her resolve, although she could hear a flow of French invective from behind her—she could not be completely certain Vionnet was swearing, but it seemed very likely. Though her concern would no doubt be more for how her clothes would look set against such inappropriate clothing.

Veronica descended the steps, but stopped five from the bottom so that she could still see everyone properly.

"What are you waiting for? The vicar said to be there by two. Times a-wasting."

Veronica gripped Polly's arm tightly; everyone was looking at her.

"All in good time, Mr Laughton. There is a matter to be dealt with."

"What?"

He stormed across the chequerboard floor and stood directly in front of her. The recollections of the regular beatings came flooding back to her. His leering face as Mrs Jenkins applied the strap.

"Your services are no longer required at Versyns House, Mr Laughton."

Veronica had always thought the phrase about things being so quiet you could hear a pin drop to be literary rhetoric with no basis in fact. Yet here it was. Utter silence. Then—

"You can't fire me!" The man's face was reddening and he almost choked with the anger that boiled out of him.

Veronica pretended to look at a non-existent watch on her wrist.

"No, sir, not for perhaps another hour. Then, when I point out to my husband that your position in this household is not only costly, but completely superfluous, you will find yourself without a job." She took a deep breath, saw he was about to speak, so interrupted him. "This is *my* wedding. I will not permit a brute such as you, who does not care for me, to be the one who gives me away."

The man looked about to explode.

"If you, Mr Laughton, utter a single word of attack against me, anyone I hold dear, or any member of this household, I will ensure you receive the worst possible reference. If you go now, quietly, I will see to it you receive something that does not condemn you."

He moved towards her, which prompted Mr Jones and three others of the male staff, including an old gardener who resembled Seth, to follow with the clear intent of intercepting him.

"I know things," muttered Laughton. "I can bring you and your family down."

"Feel free to attack my parents, Mr Laughton. You should realise that I have no love for them. Though I think you'll find them untouchable. As for me? I will be married into the aristocracy, do you think unprovable slurs from a disaffected servant would have any effect on me?" She gripped Polly harder to stop herself from trembling. "No, sir, you will be gone by the time I return with my husband. And be sure that you only take that which is yours."

"You dare imply I am a thief?"

"I am being clear where we stand."

The front door was flung open and Miss Churchill breezed in. She opened her mouth to speak, then stopped. She focused her attention on the steward, then on Veronica.

"This looks interesting," she said.

Veronica pulled her eyes from Mr Laughton. "I was relieving this gentleman of the responsibilities of his post."

"This ain't over," said Laughton.

Miss Churchill laughed, and it dripped acid. "Spoken like a villain in a melodrama." She turned her attention to Veronica. "We'd best be off, can't keep the groom waiting."

"In your machine?"

"Absolutely. It's fast, roomy, and has an excellent Faraday device. I shall be happy to drive you."

As she spoke, the male staff gathered round Mr Laughton and ushered him out of the way. Veronica breathed again, descended the remainder of the steps, and headed across the floor. A smattering of applause came from the staff.

I mustn't cry, it'll spoil the cosmetics.

Two maids held the doors open for them, and they descended the outside steps to the waiting vehicle. Polly climbed in first, then helped Veronica in and got her sitting down without difficulty. Then the other three piled in, and Ursula sat up front with Winifred Churchill.

The diesel engine roared into life and moments later the Faraday engaged. Veronica sat facing the front. She could see the road ahead—she wished she couldn't as Winifred powered the car along the gravel drive then out on to the road, only slowing a little for the turn.

She was driving like a mad woman along the narrow lanes, but there was scarcely a bump inside, and although Veronica panicked at every turn, expecting to see a cart or a herd of cows blocking the way, they saw nothing until the roads widened. As they approached Seven Ashes, she slowed and pulled through the gate into the church of St Agnes—patron saint of virgins and gardeners. The vicar was standing outside with two girls. Ruth and Esther Jameson, Edwin's younger sisters. They looked lovely in their matching pink dresses, and hats.

Veronica smiled.

"Remain here," said Josephine. "Better make sure the groom's inside before you get out."

So everyone left the vehicle except Veronica and Polly.

"You got rid of Mr Laughton." She sounded awed.

"Mrs Beeton says you only need a steward for a big house which Miss Churchill confirmed to me, and besides, he doesn't do anything."

"Yes, everybody knows that, but you *fired* him."

The vicar came over and poked his head in. There was a moment as he took in the bare feet with painted toenails, the barely concealing dresses, the sheer quantity of female skin on display, the hair arranged in such complex forms, and finally the painted faces.

He said nothing as he took it all in. Veronica did not fail to notice his eyes flicking to her chest, and then Polly's.

"My dears, you both look...quite exceptional."

"I hope Mademoiselle has not stepped too far over the line, Vicar," said Veronica. *Would it all fail at this moment, if he refused to perform the ceremony?*

"I suspect there are members of the congregation, those who lack a grounding in the Classics in particular, who would be outraged, Miss Clifford-Hughes. They might have the vapours seeing you like this."

"I'm so sorry."

"However, they are not here, and I see a work of great artistry and beauty."

"It's Mademoiselle Vionnet that did it."

"I do not think she could have been so successful without such a foundation to work on."

Veronica had no idea how to respond to his words. She had never received such a compliment in her entire life.

"Be that as it may, and I will be sure to congratulate the artist," he said, "I understand that you have no longer have anyone to give you away."

"Do I need someone?"

"It's not essential, but it is traditional."

Veronica already knew her answer; it was as she had planned when she decided to remove Mr Laughton. "Is Mr Plumley inside?"

"With his wife, yes," said the vicar.

"Can I talk to him?"

The vicar left, and entered the church while the women standing outside talked, casting occasional looks inside. Veronica realised she was looking at a woman she did not recognise, with long red hair—*Ursula?* The dress she wore was not the sort of thing you could afford on servants' wages. She was already tall, but her shoes added at least three more inches. Not only that, but she was talking with the Jameson sisters—did they not recognise her as being one of the maids from last Friday?

Apparently not.

Presently Mr Plumley appeared, wearing a proper suit, and looking flustered. He focused on the vehicle and came over, putting his head in just as the vicar had done.

"Come in and sit, Mr Plumley."

He did so.

"What is the p-p-problem?"

"I appear to have broken my cage."

"And this is a p-problem b-b-because?"

"I terminated Mr Laughton's employment."

There was a short pause. "W-well done, m-Miss Clifford-Hughes. He was an odious m-m-man."

"And I would like you to be the person who gives me away."

"I?"

"If you would not mind. I would rather you than anyone else."

His face went red. "Why, Miss Clifford-Hughes, I accept this honour, but I must inform my wife of the situation."

"Of course, and thank you."

He climbed out and headed back into the church. Then Vionnet came over and they finally stepped out on to the gravel. The air was cool, the sun was not shining but there was no hint of rain in the air. Perhaps the best compromise in weather that anyone could hope for.

Polly offered her arm again. The Jameson girls had disappeared into the church. Josephine and Clio checked their hair and make-up and, when satisfied, they went inside too.

"Nearly ready?" said the vicar.

"I must attach and prepare the veil and train," said Vionnet.

Together they went inside to the vestibule. Mr Plumley reappeared and Vionnet laid out the train and placed the veil on Veronica's head; she was about to let it down when Veronica interrupted.

"Vicar, can I beg an indulgence?"

"That would be the Catholics, Miss Clifford-Hughes." But he smiled as he said it. "What is it you need?"

"I don't know if you can do this..." She hesitated, was she going too far? "Can you bless a friendship, or a symbol of friendship?"

"I can do both." He glanced at Polly as if he already understood.

Vionnet was rummaging in her bag once more, pulled out the two boxes, and held them out to Veronica.

She took one and removed the lid, removed the silver snake armlet, while Vionnet did the same with the other.

Veronica almost cried because she couldn't straighten enough to see Polly's face, but she took her left hand and slipped the armlet on to it, and pushed it up until it came to rest around her bicep.

"You really want this, Nika?"

"Of course I do."

"I forbid any crying," said Vionnet.

Vionnet must have given the other one to Polly because she pushed the armlet up Veronica's left arm.

They held hands and faced the vicar. He made the sign of the cross over their hands. "O Lord, our God, we ask your blessing upon these ... bracelets ... that they may be constant symbols of the love and devotion between these two people. Amen."

Veronica and Polly repeated the amen.

"Thank you," said Veronica while she wondered what the vicar would think if he knew what he had just done. But she sighed and felt herself relax, even her heartbeat seemed to slow, as if it were recovering from exercise.

"How long is the train?" asked the vicar, eyeing the large quantity of material.

"Cathedral," replied Vionnet.

"In that case, I would suggest the bridesmaid walks in front. Do you have bouquets?"

To Veronica's astonishment, Vionnet went blank, then stared around. "*Où sont-ils?*"

"*Pardonez-moi, mademoiselle, je les ai laissés dans le véhicule. Un moment.*"

It wasn't until Ursula hurried past that Veronica realised who had spoken. Her French accent was impeccable.

She opened the front door, where she had been sitting, and brought out two bouquets, although they didn't appear to have much colour. As she drew closer, one looked yellow and brown while other was just green.

Veronica's bouquet matched her hair, with entwined stalks of hay and grass, some green leaves, and some berries for colour. Polly's was comprised of twigs and leaves from trees. The goddess of summer and her nymph.

"Are we ready?" asked the vicar. He had a wristwatch, which he checked, but he didn't say what the time was. No one said no. "Very good, I will go through and take my place. Then I will signal the organist to begin. Then you should enter."

He disappeared through the doors. Vionnet fiddled with the train, spreading it out backwards. Mr Plumley hesitated, then came to stand at her left side.

Ursula took up position by one of the double doors, Vionnet took the other, then gave them all a critical look.

"It is good enough."

Polly took her place in front, then turned.

"I love you, Nika."

"And I love you, my beautiful Polly."

xxxvi

The music started, uncertain and awkward, but Veronica did not care. Vionnet and Ursula pulled open the doors.

Veronica strained to raise her head as high as she could. She wanted to see the church, she wanted to see the people. There were bouquets of flowers tied to the end of each pew.

Polly had not started moving.

"Pol," said Ursula, which seemed to start her from whatever mental hole she had bolted down.

She stepped forwards, and after three more she entered the church proper. Veronica was not sure what she was expecting, but the pews, not as full as they were on a Sunday, were not as empty as she expected. And, it seemed, most of the congregation were on her side of the church. The sound of people standing echoed from the stone walls.

As she followed, she felt the train pulling as it stretched out behind her. She could not keep her head up and had to return to her usual view of the ground. Though, at least for now, what she saw was the hem of Polly's dress and the ankles she had caressed more than once.

The organ was very loud, but she could hear murmurs. Astonishment, or was it simply disgust? There were those who thought she was no more than a demon. Did they think she would burn up in the sight of the Lord? Not that she had in all the years she had been attending.

One step after another she walked slowly behind Polly, covering the distance between them. She could have sneaked looks to the side to see who was in the pews, but in some ways she didn't even want to know.

Polly suddenly stepped off to the side and Veronica saw the robes of the vicar. She turned her head to the right, and saw Edwin. And, peeking round him, a man she did not recognise, though he seemed of similar age if far more rotund. Edwin's best man? It had to be.

The music died away. And the vicar began.

WHEN SHE TRIED TO RECALL the wedding ceremony, there were specific points which she could picture with complete clarity, while the remainder—the prayers, the hymns, the sermon—were like an out-of-focus photograph.

The vicar asking if anyone knew of just impediment stood out because she held her breath. At any moment she expected the voice of Mr Laughton to shout out that he knew something. That he knew Edwin was her half-brother.

But could anyone know that as a certainty? Even if both her father and his had left their seed in her mother, how could they know which had taken?

Then there was the exchanging of vows. She was glad she had not been able to see the vicar's face as she said, "I do", knowing it was a lie. But then Edwin committed the same crime, so they were perhaps well-suited.

Then there was the signing of the registry with their witnesses: Lawrence Slack, Esme Jenkins, and Ursula Skipworth. Veronica noticed Ursula used her left hand, which was very unusual. Was it really her name? Veronica doubted it, and, if it was not, did that mean the wedding was void?

And then it was over.

Edwin failed to lift the veil properly the first time and it caught on something in her hair. He let it drop back and tried a second time, successfully. There was no way he could kiss her properly without one of them contorting themselves, so all she received were his thin cold lips pressed against her temple.

They turned and he offered her his arm. Polly gave her back her strange bouquet and they walked slowly back down the aisle. Ursula and Vionnet once more dealt with the doors and they walked out on to the gravel.

Veronica had not exchanged a single word with the man who was now her husband.

There was a sudden noise of feet running on gravel, and the clicking of a camera interspersed with the sound of the film being wound on.

"Look up, love," shouted someone. "Give 'er a kiss, your lordship."

"Get lost, Ray."

"'Orright, Winnie, should've known you'd be tight with a bunch of toffs."

"You got a picture. Now get lost."

They had reached the car and Edwin opened the door for her. She climbed in and was grateful to be able to sit on something comfortable. Her husband landed next to her while Polly moved to the other side of the vehicle and on her other side. Their hands found each other. Veronica sighed and closed her eyes.

"Oi, you can't do that! I'm press."

There was the sound of a scuffle, and Ray swore. Polly twisted round to see through the back window. She gasped and then there was the sound of something hitting the gravel hard.

"Gerrof, you fucking cow!"

Someone slammed the door of the car. And it went quiet inside.

Polly turned back. Winifred Churchill climbed into the driver's seat while Ursula, her skin flushed even more scarlet than usual, slipped into the seat on the other side.

"What happened?"

Ursula was doing something in the front, Veronica couldn't see what exactly until she wound down the window and threw out a large camera, and then a film flying like a ribbon, its brown and grey surface exposed to the daylight.

"I'm not exactly sure," said Polly. "Ursula grabbed his camera, then the Ray person hit her."

"Oh goodness me. Is she all right?"

"That's where I'm not sure what happened, because the punch missed, then Ursula moved and this Ray person ended up on the ground. I couldn't see, it was too quick."

"Bartitsu. Must be," said Edwin as if his words should be the end of any discussion.

"Do you think so, Edwin? I have heard of it, of course, but Ursula is a maid," said Veronica.

The Faraday engaged, which gave Veronica even more relief, and Winifred guided the vehicle from the church. There was a crowd standing at the side of the road. People from the village perhaps, or even Mayfield. To see the demon marry the son of the local lord.

"Who is that driving?" said Edwin.

"Winifred Churchill."

"Do I know that name?"

"I don't know whether you do, Edwin, but she's the eldest daughter of Lord Randolph Spencer-Churchill."

"I am familiar with Lady Spencer-Churchill."

"Her mother?"

"Of course. But why is she being our *chauffeur*?"

"She hired the vehicle, apparently she likes to drive." Veronica clutched Polly's hand tighter as the car's speed increased until it was flying between the hedges that bordered the road like a bullet along a rifle's barrel.

"She seems competent—for a woman."

———⬥———

A FEW MINUTES LATER they pulled on to the gravel drive that led to Versyns house. Someone must have been on the lookout for them because, as they approached, the entire staff (that had not been in the church) emerged and stood in ranks on the stairs in welcome.

Veronica bit her lip.

"Edwin?"

"Veronica."

"I should probably mention, before you wonder where he is, that I dismissed Mr Laughton from the household."

"You dismissed Laughton?"

Do you have to repeat what I say? "Yes. It was not on a whim, I can assure you. It seems that his position had become redundant. Mrs Jenkins, the housekeeper, does the accounts and deals with staff concerns. Obviously this is not a large house and a steward is not required. He was an unnecessary expense." *And I disliked him intensely.*

"That was a little presumptuous."

"I completely understand, but I thought it better to get it out of the way, so that you can start with a clean slate, as it were. I'm sure you don't want to be bothered with that sort of thing."

There was a long pause. The car came to a stop.

"I think, Veronica, that our pairing—as much as it was a surprise to all parties—may turn out to be quite effective."

"Thank you, Edwin."

"Though I expect you to consult with me on such matters in future."

"I'm sure I will," said Veronica.

Polly pinched her arm.

The door was opened by Ursula, who seemed to have returned to her usual colour.

Edwin stepped out and straightened his jacket, then offered his bony hand to Veronica to assist her to step out into the world of which she was now the official mistress.

⸻ ◉ ⸻

"CONGRATULATIONS, MRS Jameson," said the butler.

"Thank you, Jones. Is everything ready for the guests?"

"It is all in order, madam." His transition from 'miss' to 'madam' seemed effortless.

"I don't think I'm ever going to get used to that," she said quietly as they crossed the hall. "What are these for?" She indicated a table that had been arranged at an angle across the back of the hall.

"Your receiving line, madam. So that you and your husband can greet your guests after they have been relieved of any coats; you can accept presents if any are offered." He pointed further along. "They will move along, take a drink if required, and pass through to the ballroom."

"We don't have that many guests."

"The proprieties must be adhered to, madam. In addition, I have taken the liberty of arranging for a chair to be brought out for you, and there is a small platform for it."

Veronica laughed. "I'll be like the old queen."

"I believe you will be a Greek goddess enthroned, madam."

She saw Edwin's shoes approaching. "The staff have things well organised," he said.

"Could you help me sit down, Edwin?"

"Sit?"

"The chair, there. So I can see my guests without further strain on my back."

He offered her his arm again and led her to the platform, and then stood beside her as Ursula appeared, already changed into her uniform, and helped her into the chair.

"What do I do?" said Polly. "I feel like I should be getting people drinks and such."

"You're my maid, you can just attend me," said Veronica, then quietly, "I want my wife with me."

She touched her snake armband and squeezed Polly's hand.

———— ◈ ————

THE STAFF THAT HAD been hurrying back and forth as they prepared by adding more tables and seating, seemed to evaporate just as Vionnet, Josephine, and Clio appeared at the entrance—along with the gentleman who had stood with Edwin, and three more men and two women, all in their twenties as far as Veronica was able to judge. Mr Jones stood at the end and announced the guests as they approached Edwin and Veronica.

Edwin greeted Vionnet pleasantly, but was perfunctory with Josephine and Clio. He was, however, effusive with the group of young people. Veronica was introduced, but the names went in one ear and out the other. The best man, however, was George, Earl of Lundy. Veronica recognised his name from the papers, he had inherited when his father had died in the Great Catterick Air Disaster in 1892—which meant the fellow must be close to thirty.

He kissed Veronica's hand.

"May I say, Mrs Jameson, you look utterly ravishing."

"Thank you, Lord Lundy."

"And who is this delight for the eyes?" He took Polly's hand.

"My friend, Polly Noakes."

"Miss Noakes, on any day your beauty must shine as bright as the bride herself."

"Thank you, your lordship."

His lordship was not fooling Veronica. He was staring at Polly's figure, so clearly outlined in the dress—but at least he had the decency not to stare at Veronica's deformity. After he moved on she and Polly exchanged glances.

The other guests were less successful. And if they did not stare, they avoided looking completely and moved along quickly. Marriage did not change the way she was viewed. They probably pitied Edwin.

Veronica realised that Winifred Churchill must be heading back and forth to the church ferrying people—though perhaps not Edwin's friends. The next group to arrive was Mr Plumley and his wife, along with Sofia Martaci, and the Misses Jameson. Veronica was not sure of the propriety of leaving the Jameson girls to last, but they were young and Winifred almost certainly outranked them, so if she chose to leave them, that was her choice.

Nobody seemed upset.

But it was noteworthy, she thought, that there seemed very little affection between brother and sisters. Perhaps that was just because he was older, and a little strange, while they were typical young women. *As if I know what a typical young woman is like.*

They were pleasant to Veronica, if a little reserved towards Polly, but then they knew her real station.

Miss Churchill herself finally appeared escorted by Lawrence Slack, the younger. Considering all the rushing about she had done, Winifred seemed completely cool and composed, and not a lock of her hair was out of place. Lawrence was as handsome as ever.

Winifred gripped Veronica's hand and gave her a firm kiss on the cheek. "There, you see, my dear. I even transported Sofia Martaci, and neither of us has murdered the other yet. Today we have a truce in your honour."

"Thank you."

Winifred moved on to Polly. "The two of you looked absolutely gorgeous. I know this was embarrassing for you, Vionnet can be a terrible taskmaster, but Society is like the frozen polar caps. And while Vionnet may have been the designer, you two are the ships that have split the ice. Your pictures will go down in history."

"That ain't comforting, Miss Churchill. I'd rather be forgotten."

"Nonsense. One day you'll appreciate it—or laugh about it."

Lawrence shook Edwin's hand firmly and congratulated him, then moved on to Veronica. He kissed her hand, but she felt his tongue dab her skin; the risk of it thrilled her, but he did not linger. He also kissed Polly's hand.

⎯⎯●⎯⎯

THE SMELL OF ROASTED meats—beef, lamb, and ham—wafting from the kitchen was delicious and Veronica's mouth watered. It made the fact that she would not be eating it even more painful. No wonder Edwin did not want anyone in the house eating meat, the smell was so tempting it could easily make one break their vow.

They entered the ballroom, Veronica on Edwin's arm, and Polly beside her.

She had never known so many people in the house, although the ballroom was big enough that even their numbers did not truly fill the space. The sky outside remained cloudy, but the French windows had all been thrown open so fresh air, filled with the scents of the garden, filled the room.

And everyone was talking. Edwin's friends were particularly loud, but the clumps of people had drinks in their hands and seemed happy.

This is a strange thing. My life has not seen much happiness, but here they are. Laughing and drinking.

Edwin was heading towards his friends, which was understandable, but she wanted to talk with hers.

"Can I have a drink, Edwin?"

"Sherry?"

"That would be lovely."

He waved his hand and the butler appeared. "My wife would like a sherry, I will take the same."

"Of course, sir."

Mr Jones moved away as smoothly as he had arrived, and Edwin brought her to the group of his friends.

And she stood there, bent over, unable to see their faces, unable to truly take part in the conversation. Unless you were deprived of the ability to see another's face, you would not realise how important it is. She was cut off despite being the centre of attention.

At first she listened to them. Only the men spoke, and apart from discussing the cricket, and then how easily Britain could defeat Germany if there was a war—because our navy was so much better than theirs, and our army the most disciplined and well equipped—they exchanged joking personal slights that each tried to top.

She felt Edwin really did not do well in that game. Lord Lundy, however, was excellent at putting others down.

Eventually she gave up listening to what was said. No conversation was being addressed to her. She might as well be the feeble-minded fool that Edwin's father had taken her for the first time they met—the *only* time they met.

"Your chair has been prepared, Mrs Jameson," said the butler.

At first she didn't even realise he was talking to her.

"Madam? If you would care to accompany me."

"Veronica," said Polly quietly. "Take my arm."

She suddenly realised what they were saying.

"Edwin, I do apologise for interrupting."

"Yes, my dear? What is it?"

"I'm going to sit down, my back is strained with all this standing."

"Oh, of course, do go ahead." He loosed his arm from hers and it was replaced by Polly's, who guided her across the room—the guests parted as she moved—to the *chaise longue* from the library that had been placed against the wall.

Polly arranged the cushions and Veronica, with a sigh of relief, lay back with her head supported. And suddenly she could see the room and all the people there.

And she smiled.

Sofia Martaci was the first to approach, after a sidelong glance at where Winifred Churchill was standing, in conversation with Clio and Josephine.

"Congratulations, Mrs Jameson."

"Please, just Veronica."

"You need to get used to it."

"I don't think I ever will."

"I have a present for you."

"The painting?"

"The public painting, yes."

"Where is it?"

"Ready to be unveiled in the dining room."

Veronica looked astonished. "But how?"

Polly leaned down by her ear. "You're not the only one who has secrets, Nika."

"This morning, when you were preparing for the wedding," said Sofia. She stood straight and glanced over to where Edwin was still talking to his friends. "I hope the benefits outweigh being married to that person."

"Well, I've already fired the steward."

Sofia laughed. "The power is going to your head."

———— ◦ ————

AFTER AN HOUR, WHEN most of the guests came over and spent some time talking to her—even the women in Edwin's group, though not the men—the wedding breakfast was announced.

Veronica had been perfectly comfortable, though perhaps a little hungry. Edwin appreciated his duty and immediately came over to help her up. They led the guests through into the dining room.

So much had been organised without her having to do anything. Even though she had disposed of Laughton only a couple of hours before, the seats next to her on the top table had name tags for Mr Plumley and his wife in his place, with Polly beside them.

Edwin and his best man were on the other side with Winifred Churchill—Veronica was not entirely sure why she was there, but imagined it might be due to the woman's rank and, perhaps, to keep Lord Lundy under control. He was already quite loud.

Her chair had once again been raised and there was enough room for her to slump so she could see everyone clearly. The thoughtfulness of Mr Jones, because it had to be him, was a blessing.

There were at least three serving staff that Veronica did not recognise, but she had no time to dwell on it as the first course was served. Everyone had soup. Hers and Edwin's was a very green pea soup, which was exactly the same as everyone else except, and she studied Mr Plumley's dish carefully, there were very definitely pieces of ham included. She was eating pea and ham soup, without the ham.

"This is very good," said her brand-new husband.

"Yes, it is."

It wasn't that it wasn't good, just that she would have liked the ham as well. Then she told herself off; there was no point coveting the meat. She had made her decision.

While cook had managed to make the first courses similar, there was no such luck for the second. The guests had roast beef and Yorkshire puddings with plenty of cabbage and boiled beetroot. They had the same, but with some sort of lentil patty instead of the beef. It tasted very pleasant. She tried not to look at Mr Plumley's plate.

"I can't see why the staff wouldn't want this," said Edwin. "The cook clearly has a good grasp of what's needed."

"Yes, Edwin, but as Lawrence said, we can't force them."

"No, no, I understand. But one day, Veronica, one day it will be very different here."

And that comment, more than anything else, worried her. He had plans for her home that he was not sharing with her.

The dessert was the same for everyone, fruit salad, which included pineapple—not especially rare nowadays with fast air transport, but still a treat when fresh like this.

She looked along the faces. People were eating and talking. Some were serious and others smiling. She had never been at a table like this before, with so many people, and more than half were people with whom she was acquainted. Now they were sitting still, and in ordered rows, it was no longer overwhelming, and she could appreciate them.

"My lords, ladies, and gentlemen. Pray silence for Mr Plumley."

The butler's voice quieted the room in a matter of moments, and her tutor got to his feet. She wondered that he had been willing to speak in front of everyone with his speech impediment, even more so since he would not have had any opportunity to plan what he was going to say.

"I have known m-Miss Clifford-Hughes—now m-m-Mrs Jameson—for m-many years as her tutor. She is intelligent, knowledgeable, and scholarly.

W-while I know she did not always want to learn, she w-was always studious. She has grown into a delightful young w-woman, and I w-was happy to take the p-place of her father today, to p-perform the duty that any p-person who truly knew her w-would be *honoured* to do." He paused to take a sip of red from his wine glass. "Veronica has taken these new challenges in her life in her stride, and has done very w-well in acquiring young Edwin Jameson as her husband.

"At this p-point I would like unveil the painting of the bride by Mayfield's own Sofia Martaci."

He directed his attention to the wall on the right. There were mostly appreciative murmurs from the guests though Lord Lundy said something she didn't hear, but it sounded unpleasant.

Veronica suddenly panicked. What if it were the wrong picture?

But the two Jameson sisters were already at the wall and pulling off a red cloth.

Veronica closed her eyes and held her breath.

There were no exclamations of horror, only "That's lovely." "She's really captured the dress." "Is that her bridesmaid?"

She opened her eyes and found it was not the wrong painting. And it looked exquisite.

"So," said Mr Plumley to regain their attention, "I p-p-propose a toast—" he lifted his glass, "—the b-bride and groom."

Each person stood, save for Veronica and Edwin, and echoed the toast like a broken chorus. Glasses were sipped, or drained. And they sat again.

"The best man, Lord Lundy."

Veronica couldn't see him easily, but she watched the eyes of the others at the table as he stood.

"Ladies and gentlemen, and Lord *Me*." He laughed at his own joke. Veronica was sure he was inebriated, though he managed to keep his voice steady. "Eddie here, and I, have been best pals since he cleaned my boots at Eton. I knew from the way he did that he was born for greatness. Funny how wrong you can be."

There were a few titters from the guests, mostly from his group of hangers-on. Veronica had no idea how Edwin was taking it. His hand gripped the armrest of the chair; she placed her hand on his.

"Only joking. Eddie's come on by leaps and bounds, even if he had to compete with all his older siblings. He found his own way. While his old *pater* has been flying to the planets, Eddie's been consolidating his hold on the vegetable garden. But, look at the little girl he's managed to capture. I haven't known Veronica long, but I'm certain—hey! What!"

"Oh, I am so sorry, George, I'm so clumsy."

Veronica twisted in her seat and peered past her newly acquired husband. Winifred was using a napkin on Lord Lundy's trousers. Two glasses on the table were on their sides.

Winifred's gaze caught Veronica's eye and a smile flitted across her face, before she went back to dabbing at George's groin. Though it seemed to be less dabbing and more, hitting.

"Get off, woman."

Lord Lundy left the table and hurried out, followed by the butler.

There were no further speeches and the entire party withdrew to the ballroom. A *chaise longue* had already been brought in, but she chose not to use it for now. Hot drinks were available as well as more alcohol, though Veronica was of the opinion the guests had probably had quite enough already.

Edwin's sister, Ruth, sat at the piano and started in on some music hall tunes, which Esther gave voice to. Veronica listened with Edwin beside her. Perhaps he had been affected by her concern at the table, but he continued to hold her hand, though it was not the most elegant of positions when she was stooped over.

The atmosphere in the room relaxed; the gentlemen smoked—though not Edwin—as did several of the ladies.

And it was still daylight because it was barely five o'clock in the afternoon. It was strange, the day had been so filled with activity it felt as if it should be much later.

I am married. My name is Mrs Edwin Jameson. She gave her head a slight shake. *No, I will never think of myself as a female extension of my husband. I am Veronica Jameson. I am my own person. And the person I love is standing beside me.* She took Polly's hand and gave it a gentle squeeze.

And received one in return.

xxxvii

The party had broken up at eight. Veronica was grateful because she was exhausted. Edwin's friends had departed for London. Those who lived nearby had taken their leave; she kissed each of them as befitted her degree of familiarity. To Lawrence she gave a particularly warm kiss.

"Until tomorrow," he said.

Edwin declared that since they would be leaving first thing in the morning they should get an early night. Veronica and Polly were escorted to the main bedroom by Vionnet, Clio, and Josephine. There were plenty of off-colour remarks made by the latter two while the bride and bridesmaid were stripped of their costumes, the cosmetics removed, and their hair returned to normality.

"Are you certain you have no questions about the wedding night, and men?" asked Vionnet, and Veronica was touched by her continued concern.

"As I said, I am fully aware of the nature of men."

Vionnet raised an eyebrow. "You have *l'expérience*?"

"Really, is that a question to ask?"

"In France, it is."

"Then, mademoiselle, I will say that while I do have experience, I am still a virgin."

"Then I hope your Edwin, he is a good lover for your first time."

And they left. Leaving Veronica in sudden quiet, sitting on the side of the bed, wearing only her nightdress. Polly came through from her room.

"I'm sorry, Polly."

"What for?"

"We can't sleep together."

"There'll be plenty of time for that in future." Polly switched on the Faraday and turned it up to full power.

Veronica allowed herself to fall back and sank into the counterpane with the weight of a feather. She closed her eyes and felt herself swimming in the place between awake and sleep.

"You should get under the covers, miss. Can't have you exposing your legs like a common girl."

Veronica crawled to the top of the bed and Polly managed to get the sheet and single blanket out from under her. Veronica slipped back and pulled the covers up to her neck as she lay on her side.

━━━━◉━━━━

"VERONICA."

"What?" she said through layers of sleep that clung and threatened to take her under again. *That wasn't Polly.*

"It's Edwin."

She pulled herself up in the bed. There was a candle on the table, and no light filtered through the window. She couldn't see the clock.

"What time is it?"

"Just past ten." His voice was coming from the side of the bed nearest the bathroom. She turned to look at him. He was in a padded dressing gown. She wondered if he had come here dressed like that from his room downstairs, or changed in the room.

She didn't know what to say. She realised she was nervous, and didn't understand why. She had known two men and touched them intimately. How could she be nervous?

Veronica glanced at the door that led to Polly's room. Was she on the other side asleep? Or was she listening? Did she have a poker to hand?

She took a deep breath. He was waiting for something, and she could guess what it was. She took hold of the covers on that side of the bed—where Polly usually lay—and pulled them back, inviting him in.

He undid the belt and slipped the dressing gown from his shoulders. He was naked and his prick was highlighted in the candlelight. It was still small, and hung there, angled slightly to one side. Edwin folded his dressing gown, she noticed how thin he was, and placed it on the chair beside him then climbed into the bed.

His movements slowed as he entered the Faraday field, as if he were taking care.

She was about to reach out to take his prick in her hand when it occurred to her: she should not act too bold and experienced. He might guess the truth. The clinging scent of cigarette and cigar smoke rose from his skin.

What does one say at a time like this?

She knew what he was expecting, but how should she act? Even if he had been with women before, they would not have been shaped as she was.

His hand landed on her thigh, through the material of her nightdress; he was cold and she shivered.

"There is no need to be afraid."

"What do you want me to do?"

He pushed himself up on his elbow, but overdid it and his entire body lifted for a few moments.

"The Faraday makes this awkward," he said.

"We can turn it down, or off."

"Let us see if we can manage."

He pulled the covers down and exposed her down to her knees. Veronica rolled on to her back, with her head supported by the pillows—the reduced weight meant her back was not under too much stress. She pulled her night-dress up, exposing her skin to her waist. He took in the dark vee of hair between her legs as she raised her knees and spread them apart.

I'm not ready. It was what Polly had said to her, it was what they had taught Seth. No one had told her husband, as he crawled down the bed and between her thighs. He moved up, avoiding any contact with her body until his hips brushed her legs. She could see that he was ready now, all too ready.

She needed to take control, but had to be careful to neither alarm him nor make him suspicious. "Wait, Edwin, please."

"Why?"

"This is my first time."

"Of course, it is."

"Can I touch it?"

"Why?" He sounded like a petulant child—she should know, she had done it herself enough times.

She forced a smile on to her face, hoping he could see in the candlelight. "I'm curious, and I think—I've heard—gentlemen like it..."

He said nothing, but inched forward on his knees until his prick was standing out a few inches above her stomach. It wasn't that she had touched many, but she was confident. She focused her attention on it, putting the person to whom it belonged out of her mind. This one was thinner than either Seth's or Lawrence's, but otherwise a similar length. Moving slowly, she touched the end where clear liquid was forming, then spread the liquid over the top, then ran her finger underneath and along the ridge below.

Edwin breathed in sharply. His hands gripped her thighs near the knee.

"Was that nice, Edwin?"

"It was curious." His voice held a strained quality and she knew she had him.

She did the same again. With the same result. She brought her other hand up and gripped the shaft while her finger played back and forth along the ridge. His hips thrust forward, pushing his prick through her clenched hand. Drops of the clear liquid landed on her belly.

"Sorry."

"Nature does not need apology, Edwin. And this feature of nature is very interesting." She could feel the warmth of lust growing between her legs, and she moistened. Edwin thrust through her fingers again and she imagined taking him in her mouth. She wrapped her other hand around him and pumped backwards and forwards. He moved to the same rhythm. He grunted on each thrust. His grip tightened on her knees.

Then she released him. His eyes flew open and he stared wildly at her.

"Put it in, Edwin."

There was a flurry of activity as he pushed himself back and almost fell off the bed, but she caught his hand before he went too far. He focused on the dark space and held his prick as he desperately tried to find the right location.

"Lower, Edwin ... too far."

Then he was there and she felt him at the entrance, but there was no time to savour the unique sensation before he pushed in.

She had the presence of mind to fake a look of pain and cry "Oh!" as he slammed hard inside her—so much better than Polly's fingers!

"Wait," she said and gripped his arm, digging her fingers into his skin.

"What's wrong?" She admired his self-control in managing to bring his body to a halt.

"I want to get used to it." She closed her eyes and let the feelings wash through her; her lust was ready to overtake her and she desperately wanted to squeeze her own tits, but she feared how he might react to that.

"I cannot wait—"

He withdrew a short distance and the delightful sensation of his skin rubbing against her insides pulsed through her. Her pulse raced. He pushed in—and pulled—and thrust with increasing rapidity until he was pounding against her hips. She grunted on each thrust. She could feel a paroxysm rising like a wave inside her, so unlike anything she had felt before.

He stopped thrusting and held himself hard inside her. She felt each contraction as he spent. Then he pulled out and sat back on his heels.

She stared at him, her eyes wide. "You stopped!"

"I finished."

She could not help but say it. "But what about me?"

His prick was already lying limp and damp against his legs. His come was dripping from her, just as it had from Mrs Jenkins when Mr Laughton left her unsatisfied.

"I don't understand?"

She shut her mouth to prevent herself from saying anything she might regret. He had consummated the marriage, she would be unable to divorce him on that count—if she ever wanted to.

Never mind.

She forced a smile on to her face and drew her legs together, then rolled over on her side. "Don't mind me, Edwin."

He didn't say another word. She felt him leave the bed; he must have picked up his dressing gown. The door opened and closed.

She felt empty. Abandoned. He had used her.

Turning her face to the pillow, she screamed into it and then sobbed. Her throat catching on every breath until it was sore. Another door opened.

"Nika!"

"He left me, Polly. He just got up and left."

The strength went from her and she collapsed slowly into the rumpled bedclothes. Her eyes blinded by stinging tears. She sobbed, and every wracking breath was torn from the air as if she were being strangled.

Then Polly was on the bed and her arms wrapped Veronica in warmth.

"I hate him." Her voice raw with pain. "I'll never let him touch me again."

"Do you want his child?"

"No."

"Better wash yourself out then, no guarantees but it will help."

Veronica needed no further prompting and felt her anger slightly assuaged as she washed his semen from her body.

Good riddance.

xxxviii

Breakfast had been a hurried affair. Veronica and Edwin had eaten at the same table, mostly buttered toast with marmalade and honey. Veronica did not speak to him and he read an early edition—her lack of communication did not seem to concern him.

A wife should be seen and not heard.

Polly was supervising the luggage, and wore a dark woollen dress with a wide belt. It was not her uniform, but somehow communicated the fact that she was still only a servant. Ursula kept to her uniform.

Veronica was in one of her new dresses, but after the previous night she was in no mood to appreciate it.

Shortly before eight o'clock, she, Polly, Ursula, and Edwin stepped out into the cloudy day; it was still summer so was not cold, but they wore light coats against the possibility of rain. There had been a downpour in the night and a haze hung in the air as the day warmed.

Their transport was similar to the car Winifred Churchill had used, but even larger. Their luggage was already loaded and all four of them climbed into the passenger compartment which was divided into two seating sections. The servants took the front, with Veronica and Edwin in the rear.

Polly gave Veronica her book: *The Tenant of Wildfell Hall* again. It somehow felt appropriate. Anne Brontë may have died too early to be a suffragist, but this book showed that was where her heart lay. And Veronica fully embraced that now.

They stopped in Mayfield to collect Lawrence. Thankfully, he sat in the back with Edwin and Veronica, but her husband insisted in engaging him in conversations about business. It was not that Veronica found it dull, it was that her opinions would clearly not be welcome. It seemed Edwin was of the old guard when it came to opinions on women.

Though it did not seem to make sense since he was so forward thinking in his vegetarianism. She could only conclude that men could be as complicated as anyone else. Even Edwin.

THE TRIP TO BRIGHTON airfield took a little over an hour. The vehicle turned off the main coast road before they reached Brighton, and into a large fenced area. There were collections of curiously shaped buildings. And flyers.

She stared through the window. Most of them followed the Brunel rotor system, whereby propellers could lift the vehicle from the ground, then be turned from vertical to horizontal to drive the vehicle forward. She did note two fixed-wing designs. These were preferred for faster travel.

There were no ornithopters, of course; the bird-wing machines had been obsolete even when Harry and Sellie Edgbaston flew the Iron Pegasus. But there was something magical about them, perhaps they would have their day again.

The vehicle drew up in front of a building with the name Jordan Airways on a big sign above it. The name sounded familiar, but she couldn't place it. Perhaps she had read about them in the newspapers. A large four-rotor flyer stood in an open area nearby; it might be steam-powered, but it lacked a funnel, so she guessed it was diesel. Several people were queueing by some steps to get aboard.

"Lawrence, you have the tickets?" said Edwin.

He tapped his coat pocket. "I'll get us checked in, sir."

They waited in silence as he left the car and went into the office. It seemed a long time before he came out again, spoke to the driver, and then climbed back in.

The car followed the paved area along the side of the buildings and then out to where the flyer waited. Finally, they all climbed into dreary light. Polly, Lawrence, and Ursula went to the back of the vehicle to deal with the luggage while Edwin and Veronica crossed the flagstones to the silent waiting flyer—the queue had already been dealt with by the man with a clipboard. He had a uniform that looked slightly naval.

"Mr and Mrs Edwin Jameson, and staff," said Edwin and waved in the direction of the car. The pile of luggage was building up.

If the man looked askance at Veronica she wouldn't have known, she couldn't see his face. She assumed he wouldn't insult a paying customer. So that was something, although she could not shake the idea that the other passengers were staring at her from their windows.

"Yes, sir, please go aboard. The first-class compartment is to the front."

Edwin went up first. Veronica followed him. The interior of the flyer smelled of cleaning materials and perfume. Edwin went to the right. The vehicle had wooden panelling, but Veronica guessed it was fake. She knew from reading the adventures of the Edgbaston sisters that, even with the Faraday effect, they would want to keep the weight to a minimum.

A short passage, with a door at either end, and yet another one marked W.C., led through into the first-class cabin. The seats were more like armchairs, though they were all fixed in one direction. There were two rows with an aisle through the middle and five seats on each side. There were no other passengers at present.

"Would you like a window seat?" said Edwin.

"Thank you, yes," she said. She was never going to forgive him for the way he had treated her, but she found it hard to maintain her anger. It had settled into a constant simmering annoyance.

The seat supported her back well and she could see, not only to the side, but there was a big window to the front. The space for the pilot was accessible through a door, and the window afforded her a view of the—what would it be called? The bridge?

She stared out at the gloomy world beyond the glass. Tiny drops of rain speckled the surface and obscured the view. Somewhere to the left lay the sea, but everything in the distance was simply grey.

To her right was one of the four stubby wings with the engine at the end of it, standing vertical with its rotor horizontal to the ground—ready for launch.

Lawrence came through to say the luggage was loaded, and the three of them had taken their seats in the back.

Veronica missed Polly. She imagined she could still feel Edwin soiling her insides, even though she had bathed thoroughly this morning. Polly was sympathetic. While Edwin's entry into Veronica had not been the violent affair Polly had suffered, they now shared the same feeling of violation.

It wasn't even that Edwin had done it; she had been expecting it, of course. She had taken control. But he had destroyed it all by his casual disregard for her, as if her own desires had no value. No, she would never forgive him for that.

There was a clock above the door to the bridge. The flyer was supposed to lift by nine-thirty and there were only eleven minutes to go. The sound quality changed as the outer door slammed shut. There was some discussion she could not make out, and then two men, one who had the clipboard and another older but dressed similarly, walked through. The older man used a key to let them into the bridge area.

The time ticked through another three minutes.

An engine coughed, whined, and then roared into life. Veronica glanced at the one beside her, but it was quite still; she looked round Edwin and saw the one on the other side was not moving either. The sound of the engine reduced, but she could feel the deck shaking with the rhythm of its rotations.

The interior lights came on.

The engine on the wing beside her came alive with its own, quieter roar, then the one on the other side. She could not see, but heard the other two start up. The vessel shook and the noise was deafening.

The clock ticked the final minutes as the engines warmed up and grew quieter; their speed was reduced until it became an intense hum that seemed to go right through her.

"Have you flown before?" said Edwin.

"Never."

"If you become nervous you may hold my hand."

If I did become nervous, you would be the last person to know it.

A klaxon sounded through the vessel and, moments later, the ship's Faraday came alive and the strain on her back faded away. Together the four rotors increased velocity once more. She felt the flyer sway and realised they were already a few feet above the ground.

The power increased again. The flyer turned slowly. The buildings appeared below them. Veronica gasped, they were like toys. The turn continued. The town of Hove came into view—the roads, vehicles moving along them, horses in a field. There were fleeting impressions as she tried to see everything, but already the grey weather made the ground indistinct. And then there was nothing to see as they came full circle.

A new whine faded in briefly and she saw the rotor beside her tilt forward. There was no sense of movement in the greyness that surrounded them, but she knew they were on their way. They might already be over the sea, but there was no way to tell.

The rotor angled more sharply. The rain on the window directly ahead was being driven up and sideways by their speed, and horizontal lines of water formed on the one to her side. How high were they now?

The engines made their final turn and were now fully horizontal. The flyer would be careening across the sky at a hundred miles per hour, perhaps more.

It took twenty minutes for her to become bored with nothing beyond the windows but varying shades of grey. A woman in uniform came through and offered them drinks. Edwin suggested they have lemonade, and Veronica didn't argue. Alcohol had its place, but it was too early in the morning, though she could imagine that on long flights it would be easy to simply keep drinking to quench the monotony. He also asked for a copy of *The Times*.

A few minutes later Polly arrived. She was walking carefully in the reduced gravity—clinging to every handhold she could find as if it was a lifeline, and she looked a little pale. She moved up behind Veronica along the empty second row.

"Are you all right?"

"I'll be glad when we get down."

Veronica almost made a joke about her being fine with the Faraday in bed, but managed to stop herself in time. "How are the others?"

"Fine."

"I could do with my book, do you know where it is?"

"I'll get it. Is there anything else you need, miss...madam?"

"I think I'm hungry."

"They will not have vegetarian food," said Edwin.

"I'll see what they have that's acceptable," said Polly and made her way out slowly.

Then something occurred to Veronica; she wondered why she hadn't noticed before. "You don't have a valet, Edwin."

He let the newspaper drop. "I do not."

"Why not?"

"My needs are simple."

"Who—I mean, if you do not mind me asking—who dressed you for the wedding? Who unpacked your clothes?"

"I unpacked at Versyns and packed by myself for the trip. I admit I allowed the staff at my *former* home to prepare me for the wedding." He said 'former' as if it were some sly joke between the two of them. She gave him a humourless smile in acknowledgement.

It was clear to her that her husband lived in a world of his own, but she did not question it; if that was his desire, then why not?

After a while Polly returned with a plate containing a cheese and cucumber sandwich on thick crusty bread, with some pickled onions on the side. She also had the book—as a result she had been forced to walk without holding on.

"There's a tabletop what lifts up from the wall, miss...madam."

Veronica found the mechanism, and when it lifted a spring mechanism pushed the support into place. Polly reached over and put the plate down, then handed Veronica the book.

The cabin was suddenly flooded with sunlight.

Veronica blinked and stared out. Below them the sea was green, but sparkling in the light. Fishing boats dotted the surface, and she could see the men working on them. She could even see their upturned faces as the flyer roared overhead.

And ahead, the coast of France. In less than a minute they had crossed it. The entire countryside was a haphazard patchwork of irregular fields, with tracks, roads, and streams running between them. There were farms and tiny villages everywhere, and it took only a few seconds to pass over a large town. Across the landscape were shadows of clouds, a small river to the left, and to the right the meander of a very large river.

The stewardess came through and stood by the door to the bridge.

"The river you can see forward and to starboard is the Seine. We will shortly be passing over Rouen and, in about an hour, Paris."

Veronica stood up and leaned forward as they raced towards the ancient city. It covered a wide area and she could see much of it was new, but there was the ancient cathedral, and the bridges across the river. And then it was past and gone as if it had never been. And they were back to fields, farms, and villages, but now the winding River Seine was always in view.

Time passed. She read a few pages and then looked out the window again. It got to the stage that she barely noticed what she was seeing, and spent more time in her book. She had just looked out and back when she realised she had seen a geometric pattern of paths. She looked again. A huge garden with perfectly tended hedges surrounding a cross-shaped lake, and beyond those a huge building shining white in the sunlight, with great wings leading away from it. It was massive—and unmistakable.

"Versailles!" She had seen so many pictures, but she could barely believe it. For so long she had been convinced she would never leave Versyns, yet here she was flying over the great palace. She raised her eyes towards the horizon. There lay Paris, a haze of smoke across it. The Eiffel Tower poked up from the buildings that surrounded it, pointing at the sky. And beyond it, the cathedral of Notre Dame. Being in the distance, she was able to watch them for longer, but eventually they too slipped into the haze.

She ate her sandwich, drank her lemonade, and read her book while Edwin worked his way through the newspaper. The terrain was now an unending pattern of fields. The engines' roar never changed. The sky continued blue and they had eventually left all the clouds behind.

Three hours passed and she ceased to look out of the windows at all.

"I'm going to stretch my legs," she said finally. It was not that she felt a strong need to do so, but the journey, for all its novelty, was now crushingly uninteresting.

The first-class cabin yielded nothing further of interest and she decided to investigate the W.C., noting that there was no distinction for man or woman, first or second class, master or servant. Everyone had to use this one water-closet whether pauper or king—though he had had his own flyers so that probably didn't count.

The W.C. itself was quite small, but structured normally. There was, however, a sign on the wall facing the door, visible as one entered: "Gentlemen, all functions must be performed in the sitting position."

Did that mean they normally didn't? It was not something she had considered.

She locked the door and looked at the bowl. It was clean white porcelain with a dark wooden seat and cover, but there was something odd about the waterline. It was difficult to make out, but she was fairly sure there was no exit pipe. Not only that, but she could feel a tingling that indicated a change in the Faraday effect, when her hands were over the bowl. The water rippled with the ship's vibration and movement, but appeared normal, as if it was not under the influence of reduced gravity.

When she sat, the urge to pee increased dramatically, almost as if it was being pulled from her. Her curiosity got the better of her, so she watched what happened when she pressed the button to flush—there was no chain. The water gushed into the bowl for a few moments, then the base below the waterline opened and everything fell through. She saw out of the vessel to the ground below.

Her waste products were raining down on France. The flush continued, then the base closed up and the remaining water filled it to a depth of an inch or two. Ingenious.

She washed her hands and exited, turning right into second-class.

Some of the other passengers were asleep. A woman stared at Veronica, but she refused to care. Ursula and Lawrence were playing cards. Polly looked forlorn and unhappy sitting by the window and staring out. She saw Veronica and made a move to stand, but Veronica motioned for her to stay put—which she did without any argument.

Seeing Lawrence stirred something between Veronica's thighs, a feeling of being unfulfilled and a desire for revenge. She wished desperately there was somewhere private they could go. Getting two people into the W.C. would be a real squeeze, though, now she thought on it, perhaps not impossible.

Veronica gave the cabin a sidelong glance. But what did she care what these people might suspect, or even know.

"Mr Slack?" He looked up. "I'm sorry to interrupt your game, but would you mind coming through?"

"Of course, Mrs Jameson."

She turned and headed back towards the passage. Her heart pounded. Did she really dare do this? Then she thought of how Edwin had satisfied himself and then abandoned her.

I dare.

She entered the short passage and opened the door to the W.C. "Follow me," she said quietly as Lawrence came up behind her. She went in and leaned over the porcelain. He came in, shut the door, and locked it. His body pressed against her bum and the lust flared inside her.

"Fuck me, Lawrence."

"Now?"

"Of course, now."

"You were only married yesterday."

"And my husband does not consider my pleasure to be part of the contract."

"He did not do it?"

"Oh, he did it, he spent in me and then left just as I was getting warmed up. Now, if you don't mind, lift my dress, pull down my drawers, and do it properly. I need it."

"As you command, madam."

Lawrence grabbed handfuls of her dress and pulled upwards, then two layers of petticoats followed until it was all laying across her back. She felt him crouch down behind her and her bloomers descended, leaving her bum open to the air.

"Lift your right foot," he said.

She felt the bloomers slip past her ankle when she did so, and did not need to be told to do the same with the other. She spread her legs until her feet were jammed against each side of the small compartment.

It was his breath on her left bum cheek she felt first, then his lips on her flesh. She sighed as she relaxed, confident in his knowledge of a woman's needs.

He kissed, then licked, then bit her behind. One of his hands landed on the inside of her calf and gently moved upwards. Then back down. She gave a little whimper to encourage him, then slipped her own hand inside her bodice. With an effort, she dug her fingers into her boob. The pleasure arced like electricity between breast and groin, but it was awkward, so she resigned herself to squeezing on the outside.

He adjusted his position slightly—if they had been under normal gravity she doubted he could have maintained himself in a crouched position, but the Faraday took away his weight and gave him endurance.

His left hand now stroked her other leg and moved up to her thigh. His right pushed her right cheek to the side, and a damp thumb rubbed tentatively against her anus.

"Yes!" she said and pushed back against him.

"You are a bad girl."

"Very bad, but if I'm going to hell—" He pushed his thumb in and she moaned. "If I'm going to hell, let it be for everything."

His other hand came up to her pussy. He dragged the tips of his fingers back and forth across the lips, as his thumb pumped gently into her behind. The tip of his other thumb went into her pussy hole as his fingers pressed gently against her nubbin.

Rationality left her. Only her pleasure mattered. Waves of lust battered her. She wanted to call out to Edwin and demand he watch how it should be done. Her hips pumped back against Lawrence, driving his thumbs into her on every push.

"I'm coming," she hissed, managing not to scream it. She shivered and the muscles in her groin spasmed again and again as she tried to force him as deep into her as she could.

Then she stood there convulsively gripping the pipework as she dropped away from the peak of lust into warmth.

Lawrence gave her bum another little bite, and stood up.

Her sigh of disappointment was interrupted by something poking between her legs. Her eyes widened as he slid into her. It seemed to go on forever and her lust came awake again.

He withdrew then thrust in again. She let out a little cry.

"Is it all right?" he whispered to her.

"More."

They became a machine. He thrust into her as she pushed back. The steady friction, the rhythmic impact, the slap of skin against skin.

She let her front down further until her arm rested on the toilet seat, and her forehead on her arm. Her feet were no longer on the floor, he had lifted her hips so she was the right level for him as he thumped into her.

She reached back with her free hand and tried to catch his balls. "Don't do that, Nika. Could hurt," he panted. His movements were accelerating. He pushed her forwards and her head hit the wall. She bit down on the *Ow*, she didn't want him to stop. She just had to keep both arms up.

The beginnings of another paroxysm grew in her. It was different to before, deeper, stronger. The pounding she was getting between her legs was stoking the power. Every thrust pushed her forwards and on every thrust he pulled her back on to him as if she was his toy.

The raw lust in the both of them was exhilarating. It was all she could do to suppress her screams. And Lawrence's grunts were not quiet. Suddenly he thrust hard and pulled her tight against him and she could feel his prick pulsing inside her, ejecting his come into her. She jammed a hand down between her legs and rubbed her clit hard; the pent-up energy exploded and she strangled a scream in her throat. Whether it was her own muscular contractions, or just that he had more to give, Lawrence groaned and spent again into her pussy.

They stood in that position for a little while. Then his prick slipped out of her. He grabbed handfuls of the toilet paper and pushed it between her legs as he let her down.

She lifted the toilet seat. Without a word, he gripped her waist underneath her skirts, lifted her almost to the ceiling, turned her, and brought her down on to the seat. The paper he had put between her legs fluttered down and she could feel drips of his come leaving her.

He gathered another handful of the paper and prepared to wipe himself, though Veronica did not think the paper, which did not absorb liquid like cloth, would be of much use. His prick was shrinking which was fascinating in itself, but she had a naughty thought.

"Let me."

She took his damp prick in her hand, brought her mouth to it, and licked round the end.

Lawrence made a pained sound.

"What's wrong? Did I do something wrong?"

"Too sensitive, Nika. It can happen, especially after a very good...fuck."

She thought it was sweet the way he didn't want to use the word, even though she had already done so. She looked back at his prick and giggled. "It's getting bigger again."

Ignoring his halfhearted complaints, she took him in her mouth, sucked gently while she moved her hand back and forth on the shaft. It took less than a minute for him to be filling her mouth completely. She set about the task of making him come again.

He moaned pitifully at first, but did not ask her to stop. She took him deep into her mouth and then sucked as she pulled away. All the while rubbing the shaft and playing with his balls with her other hand. But she was wary of causing him hurt; it seemed the balls were men's Achilles heel. She laughed to herself at the silliness of the comparison.

She took a moment to dampen her finger, reached between his legs, and wiggled it between his bum cheeks. It took her a moment to find his anus, then she treated him to the pleasure she had felt. From his suppressed groans it seemed he liked it.

His hips began to move, thrusting into her mouth. She let him take over and held still, maintaining the suction, and holding tight to his prick while her finger poked into his bum.

His hands gripped her shoulders and he came. Only a couple of pulses, and accompanied by a final exhausted groan. She swallowed his come down since it was the easiest way to get rid of it, and she was getting used to the taste.

She leaned back so she could look up.

"That's better," she said.

He shook his head as if in disbelief. "We probably should not have done that."

"Do you regret it?"

"Now? No, but I feel I may."

"Don't," she said. "I never will. Regret has no value."

I have had my revenge and my satisfaction, at last, though I would have liked it to be with Polly too.

He put his prick away and fastened his trousers.

"A philosopher as well as an expert in the carnal arts?"

"Expert? You flatter me."

He leaned down and kissed her on the lips. His tongue pushed into her mouth and she savoured the delight of the intrusion.

"It's not flattery, Nika."

He turned, unlocked the door, and left. She locked it again and closed her eyes.

xxxix

Edwin made no comment about the time she had been gone. She sat beside him reading her book as her bloomers soaked up the dampness between her legs. She had washed herself out again, she did not want a child by anyone, at least for now. Lawrence considered her an expert? It was an amusing thought, but it also meant that Edwin did not know what he was missing.

Long may that continue.

The stewardess took their order for lunch, which in this case meant a couple of boiled eggs, bread, salad, and cheese. They were not well-stocked on vegetarian choices.

Mountains loomed ahead, at first just blue shadows with brilliant white tops. Like a wall on the horizon. Veronica was marvelling at the sight when first the engines' tone changed as their power increased, and the terrain changed from fields to huge terraces rising ever higher. Then valleys between the ridges, farms, and fields in all of them.

Even though the flyer was increasing its height, the ground came up to meet them. There was a final ridge that stretched for miles in each direction and then they were over it. The ground fell away into a valley that held a huge lake with a city at one end. Geneva.

The flyer landed and normal gravity was restored. They disembarked and Lawrence found a porter for their baggage, then determined where their next flyer was leaving from.

Unlike Brighton, the Geneva airfield was very large and very busy. Not only that, but it seemed quite organised, with officials who could be consulted on departures. They spoke English well, and she heard the one they spoke to use French with someone else.

Their connecting flyer was long and thin like a bus, but it still had the four rotors. The name Benz was blazoned across it.

This one did not have a first-class compartment, but its Faraday was efficient and they were soon in the air. Unlike the stage from Brighton, this vessel was packed with passengers. She recognised French and Italian, and something that sounded like Italian but was not quite.

She had a window seat again, and Polly sat beside her. The window was much smaller, but the view was still astonishing. The flyer spent a lot of time gaining height before it switched to horizontal travel. And little wonder: the mountains were huge. In a day when there had been so many astonishing sights, Switzerland took her breath away. The mountains were so high, separated by deep valleys, many filled with lakes. She had read *Heidi*, of course, but it gave no real impression of what this land was truly like.

The flyer came down in a place where the sign said Martigny. Some people got off, and one or two got on. It really was like a bus, though Veronica had never been on one. Then it was Domodossola.

The deeper they got, the higher the mountains became, and they saw human habitations less often. The highest peaks and ridges were covered in snow and Veronica had to remind herself that this was the summer. During winter it would all be snow and utterly impassable.

Polly remained under the weather and disinterested.

After an hour and a half, which seemed interminable, they reached Locarno on the shores of a lake, and disembarked once more with all their baggage. Lawrence hired a horse-drawn carriage. Though not small, Locarno clearly did not have much in the way of modern conveniences. Veronica doubted they even had electricity.

When Lawrence showed the driver the address, he gave each of them a long stare and muttered something under his breath. Veronica thought he might refuse them—Lawrence looked concerned and pointed at the address again.

The man nodded and helped them load the baggage. There were only four passenger seats; Ursula rode up front with the driver.

Progress was slow as the horse plodded along. It was flat in the valley, but the houses were built up the slopes. The driver did not go that way, but continued along the side of the water and then over a bridge across a river that fed the lake.

They were mid-crossing when Edwin said, "There it is."

Awkwardly, Veronica managed to follow the line of his arm and saw a hill with nothing but trees covering it. No sign of any habitation at all.

There were a few houses on this side of the river, but they soon passed into memory as the plodding horse climbed the road leading up the hill. About halfway it became a track, but they kept going.

Eventually the track flattened out and they arrived in an open area which was cut off by a wall, and in the middle of the wall was a large gate.

Several children, Veronica could not determine their ages, were hanging on to the gate and staring inside but, as the carriage appeared, they ran off and disappeared into the trees.

Two brand new and very expensive-looking automobiles were parked off to one side. Veronica remembered what Lawrence had said about famous people coming here. She took a deep and worried breath.

The cart drew up close to the gates and the driver unloaded their baggage with Ursula and Lawrence's help. Edwin went to the gate and rang the bell, which echoed out across the grounds beyond the wall.

Veronica followed him. There was a lawn inside the wall here, and off to one side a rough but pleasant looking building.

Two people looked out and waved. "Just be a minute!"

The language may have been English, but the accent eluded Veronica.

A couple of children ran out from behind the building, one chasing the other.

"Oh," said Veronica when she realised they were both completely naked. But then they were not old, why shouldn't they be?

Two people, the first in a smock-like dress, the second hidden by the first, left the building, descended the steps, and came hurrying across the grass.

Veronica had assumed the one in the dress would be a woman, but the beard said otherwise. The person behind came into view.

"Oh my," said Veronica.

There were gasps of surprise from everyone except her husband.

The second person was unquestionably female, since she was wearing as much clothing as the two children.

They both approached, completely unconcerned, and smiled at their guests.

Unfortunately, that's all the books about Veronica's Life at the moment. To make sure you don't miss **THE TOUCH OF VERONICA** when it's released, why not join the mailing list: http://taupress.com/join-veronica[1] and get a free story from the Salacious Journal of Winifred Churchill (investigating reporter).

---

1. http://taupress.com/join-veronica?__src=BK-VL2

About the Author

The author of this book lives in a part of England that has big hills, some of which are right outside the door.

Other members of the household, apart from the humans, include an incredibly needy Russian Blue cat and a hyper-active Rhodesian Ridgeback dog. The dog likes the cat, but the cat does not like the dog. It seems the cat fails to realise his neediness could be satisfied by the dog if only he would allow it. The rest of the menagerie consists of even less pleasing creatures including lizards and snails. Very big snails. There are also children, who refuse to leave home despite having been old enough to do so for some time.

Despite all these burdens, or perhaps because of them, the author escapes into other worlds and returns with stories.

www.ingramcontent.com/pod-product-compliance
Lightning Source LLC
Chambersburg PA
CBHW061052190726
48286CB00006B/1713